OXFORD WORLD'S CLASSICS

French Decadent Tales

Translated with an Introduction and Notes by
STEPHEN ROMER

OXFORD
UNIVERSITY PRESS

OXFORD
UNIVERSITY PRESS

Great Clarendon Street, Oxford OX2 6DP
United Kingdom

Oxford University Press is a department of the University of Oxford.
It furthers the University's objective of excellence in research, scholarship,
and education by publishing worldwide. Oxford is a registered trade mark of
Oxford University Press in the UK and in certain other countries

First published as an Oxford World's Classics paperback 2013

10

British Library Cataloguing in Publication Data
Data available

ISBN 978-0-19-956927-4

Printed in Great Britain by
Clays Ltd, Elcograf S.p.A.

ACKNOWLEDGEMENTS

I am grateful to the Warden and Fellows of All Souls College, Oxford, for electing me into a Visiting Fellowship for the Trinity Term 2010, which enabled me to get this anthology underway. I should like to extend special thanks to Micky Sheringham, and to Ian Maclean for the translation tourney. My thanks go also to my colleagues in the English Department at the University of Tours, for their goodwill in granting me this period of leave. For help and encouragement of various kinds, I should like to thank Pierre-Alban Breton, Harry Eyres, Lara Feigel, Nick Goulder, Antoine Jaccottet, Patrick McGuinness, Gilles Ortlieb, Karin Romer, Sébastien Salbayre, Michael Schmidt, Will Stone, and Bridget Strevens-Marzo. Judith Luna, my editor at OUP, welcomed this project with enthusiasm, and has followed its progress with steady encouragement and much patience, for which I am most grateful. My immediate family has been, as ever, hugely supportive. My fond thanks, finally, to Eleonora Barletta, who read through hundreds of pages of Decadent material, and helped me towards finalizing the selection.

CONTENTS

INTRODUCTION

THIS volume is called *French Decadent Tales*, in that it assembles a group of writers associated in varying degrees with the so-called Decadent school that flourished in *fin-de-siècle* Paris. The first story here, by Jules Barbey d'Aurevilly, was published in 1874, and the last, by Pierre Louÿs, in the first years of the twentieth century. The term *décadence*, applied to a literary phenomenon which spread across the Channel, to include, most famously, Oscar Wilde, but also Aubrey Beardsley and Ernest Dowson, appears to have had its most direct origin in the short-lived literary journal *Le Décadent artistique et littéraire*, founded by Anatole Baju in 1886. As is frequently the case (one thinks in art of 'Impressionism' and 'Cubism'), the term was originally used as an insult by a journalist, but adopted with delight and defiance by the writers thus insulted. Verlaine had already, in the 1880s, danced an arabesque around the term:

I love this word decadence, all shimmering in purple and gold. And I refuse, obviously, any damaging connotations it may have, or any suggestion of degeneracy. On the contrary, the word suggests the most refined thoughts a civilization can produce, a profound literary culture, a soul capable of the most intense enjoyments. It suggests the subtle thoughts of ultimate civilization, a high literary culture, a soul capable of intense pleasures. It throws off bursts of fire and the sparkle of precious stones. It is a mixture of the voluptuous mind and the wearied flesh, and of all the violent splendours of the late Empire; it is redolent of the rouge of courtesans, the games of the circus, the panting of the gladiators, the spring of wild beasts, the consuming in flames of races exhausted by their capacity for sensation, as the tramp of an invading army sounds.[1]

Verlaine captures here the trappings and ornamentation of a certain Decadence, both in style and content, but the tales collected here cover a wider range, and have more satiric bite and acrid energy than the term denotes. Also, by far the majority of them are tales of 'Modern Life' in the Baudelairean sense, where however disturbing or horrible the events, they take place in a recognizable, urban setting, of boulevards and gaslight, hansom cabs and frock-coats. Some of the

---

[1] Quoted in Guy Ducrey (ed.), *Romans fin-de-siècle, 1890–1900* (Paris: Laffont 1999), p. xxvi.

stories belong to the genre defined in French as *le fantastique*, constituted by 'the abrupt intrusion of the mysterious within the framework of real life', and by 'the hesitation of a being who recognizes
only the laws of nature, confronted with an apparently supernatural
event'.[2] Hence, in one tale, the dreadful pall of apparently interminable darkness that falls upon Paris, when the protagonist is out enjoying
an evening stroll. Frequently, a predisposition to nervous excitement,
exacerbated by stress, breeds its own psychological terrors.

'La Décadence'

Verlaine is right in his graphic, late-imperial imaginings, for the
Decadent style modelled itself (or so it was given out) on the late Latin
literature which the classical scholar from the Sorbonne, Désiré
Nisard, in his voluminous study *Études de mœurs et de critique sur les
poètes latins de la décadence* (1834) had brought to light. It was Nisard,
in fact, who put the term *décadence* into circulation; but he meant it
pejoratively, as pertaining to works in which mere description, from
being an ornament, becomes an end in itself. He notes also that decadent art is extremely erudite, even recondite; it is a literature of
exhaustion, weighed down by the weight of past masterpieces, and it
therefore has to seek 'extreme' effects in the quest for originality. As
we shall see, this is highly relevant to this period, the tail-end of the
nineteenth century. It is an elaborate, descriptive, *recherché* author
like Petronius that holds the most appeal: his *Satyricon*, gleaming in
its rich, gold-tooled leather binding, has its place on the shelves of the
blue-and-orange *cabinet de lecture* lovingly decorated by the Duc Jean
de Floressas des Esseintes, the seminal creation, or rather confection,
of Joris-Karl Huysmans in his celebrated novel *A Rebours* (1884). We
shall have occasion to return to this book, the 'Bible of Decadence',
which provided, among other things, the model for Dorian Gray. In
the long disquisition on the Latin authors, Des Esseintes professes an
allergy to the poets of the Augustan Age—Virgil, 'one of the most
sinister bores the ancient world ever produced'—and Horace, with
his 'elephantine grace' and (hardly a quality for our writers) his good
sense. The richness of the style—inlaid with precious and false
stones, with silvery flights and terse barbarisms—that could carve

---

[2] The definition is by Tzvétan Todorov, quoted in Guy de Maupassant, *Le Horla*, ed.
Alain Géraudelle (Paris: Hachette, 2006), 208–9.

out a vivid slice of Roman life and present it whole, without moralizing or satiric intent, was what appealed to the dandy, and through him to Huysmans and to other major writers of the school, like Barbey d'Aurevilly or Remy de Gourmont, who translated from the poets of the Latin Decadence. It would be an error, however, to look too closely to Lucan or Tertullian, Ausonius, Rutilius or Claudian, St Ambrose or Prudentius for genuine analogies with our period. Remy de Gourmont, who emerges as the most perspicacious critical intellect of the time, hints that the whole of chapter 3 of *A Rebours* was an elaborate hoax on the part of Huysmans, to send the critics baffled by his style scuttling off to Latin poets they had never read.[3]

One definition of Decadence (the painter Braque puts it finely, when criticizing the academic work of the *pompiers*, painters like Bouguereau or Cabanel) is a complete facility of technique, that sets no limits to its material, and imposes upon itself no constraints. Huysmans's fertile neologisms and preposterously *recherché* descriptions actually earned praise from the Surrealists. A sentence like 'Shrunken by the shadow that had fallen from the hills, the plain appeared, at its middle, to be powdered with starch and glazed with the white of cold cream' (. . . *poudrée de farine d'amidon et enduite de blanc cold-cream*)[4] is a prize example of this Decadent straining for effect. The implacable Byzantine despots of Gustave Moreau, or Petronius Arbiter organizing, with dandified elegance, to tickle the taste of Nero, carnal and gustatory orgies, fuelled the imagination of Des Esseintes more than any genuine engagement with the literature of the Latin Decadence.

Symptomatology and the Dissociation of Ideas

If there is one quality that these Decadent Tales share on every level, it is that of self-consciousness. *A Rebours*, with its vertiginous intertextuality, is a case in point. But it is a self-consciousness so developed that it comes to resemble a set of symptoms. The nature of the illness is unclear, the prognosis uncertain, and there seems little hope of a cure. Is the consciousness itself diseased? Or is it infected by something rotten outside of it? What is the nature of the mysterious

[3] See Remy de Gourmont, 'Stéphane Mallarmé et l'idée de décadence', in *La Culture des idées*, ed. Hubert Juin (Paris: Éditions 10/18, 1983), 119–37.

[4] J.-K. Huysmans, *A Rebours* (Paris: Gallimard, collection Folio, 1983), 98.

mal du siècle, whose genealogy really begins with Chateaubriand's pale young aristocrat René, and descends through Byron's Manfred and Childe Harold, through the ascetic, hysteric dandyism of Baudelaire, down to the authors of the Decadent *fin de siècle?* Remy de Gourmont, whose stories were described by Marcel Schwob as small spinning-tops reaching their final, convulsive circuits, also wrote *Sixtine* (1890), with its subtitle, 'novel of the cerebral life'. The hero of this novel, Hubert d'Entragues, is the type of many of the protagonists gathered here, an intelligent, vaguely aristocratic young man, paralysed by inaction, fascinated by his own incapacity to function, and yet who experiences sufficient vestigial 'drives' to woo a woman, Sixtine, who is as much an extension of his own idealization as she is a being of flesh and blood. He loses her, of course, to a passionate, hot-blooded, and practical-minded Russian, who sweeps her off, leaving d'Entragues to his sepulchral solitude, where he 'resurrects' her in literature. One useful definition of the term Decadence may be drawn from this, and it is contained in the word 'effete', which means, liter-ally, exhaustion from childbearing. These melancholy individuals are the fruit of exhausted loins, they are sapped of vital energies. They are also, like d'Entragues, or Huysmans's hero Des Esseintes, *sated* by cerebral and sensual experience. They are effete, and they are sated. Above all, they are the victims of an inexplicable boredom or, to use the august French word, *ennui*, and its Baudelairean variant, *spleen*.

Writing of Des Esseintes and his kind, Marc Fumaroli has described the *fin-de-siècle* hero as being 'afflicted by a schizophrenia which spares nothing and which dissociates everything: his soul, his sexuality, but also his bodily health. He feels death corroding and working away at his mortal tatters.'[5] Fumaroli risks the clinical term schizophrenia (itself notoriously slippery and open to diagnostic error), but it did not exist in the vocabulary of the time. Instead we find terminology like hysteria, neurosis, neurasthenia, and madness, which may be generally subsumed today under the rubrics depres-sion and psychosis. One shorthand way of delimiting our complex period is to say that it succeeds Baudelaire who, with his usual pitiless insight, describes his own moral state on a particular day, thus: 'I have cultivated my hysteria with voluptuousness and terror. Now I feel perpetually dizzy, and on the brink, and today, 23 January 1862,

---

[5] See Marc Fumaroli's preface to J.-K. Huysmans, *A Rebours*, 26.

I have received a singular warning, I have felt upon me *a breath from the wing of imbecility.*'[6] As we shall see, in *Les Fleurs du mal* (1857), Baudelaire was the first modern poet deliberately to *dissociate ideas*, that is, he broke apart their perennial pairings: virtue–reward, vice–punishment, God–goodness, crime–remorse, effort–reward, future–progress, artifice–ugliness, nature–beauty; and it was the new configurations he found for them that made him (and makes him still) such a scandal. The 'schizophrenia' of the Decadent protagonist is in fact related to dissociation of this kind—a condition T. S. Eliot came to call, in a famous phrase, the 'dissociation of sensibility'.[7]

The period is also contemporaneous with Charcot's studies of neurotics and the symptomatology of hysteria at the Salpêtrière clinic in Paris, where in 1895 he was assisted by one Sigmund Freud, who published (with Breuer) his *Studies in Hysteria* in the same year. Given Freud's eminence, and his incalculable contribution to our notion of modernity, it is tempting, if too reductive, to describe the literature of the *fin de siècle* as a kind of raw material awaiting analysis and the talking cure. Adam Phillips has remarked, in the context of Freud's work, how 'a more-or-less secular capitalism produces its own counter-culture of symptoms',[8] and it was as true of the mid-to-late nineteenth century as it is now. Several of the stories here describe symptoms that might have come from the clinical casebook of the Salpêtrière, and indeed Maupassant, great psychologist that he was, followed the work of Charcot and carried out his own investigations (see in this collection his story 'Night' and, in particular, the fetishistic case study 'The Tresses'). Maupassant's curiosity, and his compassion (which reminds one of Freud's urge to explore motive, and to listen to the sufferer rather than dismiss him or her as 'mad' or 'degenerate') led him to explore what 'fetishism' might be, even before the term had been invented.[9]

---

[6] See Baudelaire, *Oeuvres complètes*, vol. 1, ed. Claude Pichois (Paris: Gallimard, Bibliothèque de la Pléiade, 1983), 668.

[7] Eliot uses the term in his essay 'The Metaphysicals' (1921); but he draws on Gourmont's seminal essay 'La Dissociation des idées' (1899), in *La culture des idées*, 81–116.

[8] See Adam Phillips, 'Introduction' to Sigmund Freud, *Wild Analysis* (London: Penguin, 2002), p. xxiv.

[9] See Philippe Lejeune's study 'Maupassant and Fetishism', in Asti Hustvedt (ed.), *The Decadent Reader: Fiction, Fantasy, and Perversion from fin-de-siècle France* (New York: Zone Books, 1998), 774–91.

Schopenhauer, Baudelaire, and Huysmans

The Decadent writers, and their commentators, invariably cite two
authors or rather two texts, that are indispensable to understanding
the period. The first is Baudelaire, already evoked, and his *Fleurs du
mal*; the second, which hails Baudelaire as an almost divine precursor,
is of course Huysmans's *A Rebours* (*Against Nature*) (1884). These are
the immediate sources, and behind them is the surging pessimism of
Schopenhauer's philosophy, and the blind, biological necessity of
Darwinism, and of Social Darwinism, as revealed in the tooth and
claw of High Capitalism. Schopenhauer precedes Darwin, and his
rigorous atheism, combined with his eloquent account of the automatic, necessary nature of human will, bent solely upon its own
perpetuation (by means of biological reproduction) in the context of
a meaningless universe, proved irresistible and even comforting to
the writers of the time. For *progress*—mocked as a delusion by
Schopenhauer—whether in the social, economic, scientific, or political sphere, is a term universally derided by this group of writers, who
are in shock and recoil at the homogenizing effects of what Flaubert
called *la démocrasserie*, and the banalization of the sacred mysteries
wrought by scientific positivism. For the German philosopher, it was
art, and notably music, which alone could provide some consolation,
being in itself disinterested and freed from the chain of biological
necessity and blind cosmic Will. In this feckless retinue of disabused
young men, seeking to lose themselves in art and novel experience,
the influence of Schopenhauer is all-pervasive.

Politically, our period falls within that of the Third Republic of
Thiers and the bourgeois republicans, which was one of social reform
and middle-class enrichment, following the traumas of the Franco-
Prussian War (1870) and the Commune (1871). It was a period which
saw, in no particular order, Bell's telephone, Edison's incandescent
light-bulb, Pasteur's vaccines, the Eiffel Tower, the Universal
Exhibition (1878), the first great department stores, free secular primary education for all, the legalization of divorce, the French *can-
can*, child labour laws, anarchy, and the Dreyfus Affair (1894–1906),
that *cause célèbre* which divided France into (essentially) radical anti-
militarist Left and nationalist, anti-Semitic Right. *L'Affaire*, in which
the Jewish Captain Dreyfus was accused (falsely, it turned out) of
spying for the Prussians, crystallized two opposed visions of France,

and it exercised the best minds of the period. This divided vision of France can be traced in the writers here; on the one hand there is a man like Mirbeau, who was drawn to anarchy, and on the other, craggy Catholic aristocrats, like Barbey d'Aurevilly and Villiers de l'Isle-Adam, who were the penurious scions of noble if etiolated lineage. The latter were unashamed elitists and monarchists, and in their writing they wage a ferocious rearguard action (and here they find common cause with Mirbeau) against everything that may be summed up by the word *bourgeois*: new money, complacency, positivism, optimism, and vulgarity. Léon Bloy, whose satirical flair and misanthropic rage rises to epic heights in his *Histoires désobligeantes* (1894), admitted to disposing of his bourgeois protagonists exactly as the fancy took him—he treats them like marionettes or even voodoo dolls.

The Victorian prophets, men like Matthew Arnold, William Morris, and John Ruskin, were equally on their guard against triumphalist capitalism and industrial 'progress'; but they were none of them voluptuaries of vice; and the contrast between their antidotes—touchstones of poetry, muscular Christianity, artisanship, and socialism—and the heady, decidedly *anti-social* attitudinizing of the Decadents over the Channel is instructive. Rather than the Victorian sages, it was the Oxford aesthete Walter Pater who begat Oscar Wilde. Pater's *Marius the Epicurean*, and the sensual conclusion to his *The Renaissance* (1868), which he originally refrained from publishing 'because it might possibly mislead some of those young men into whose hands it might fall', have the makings of another Decadent bible: 'While all melts under our feet, we may well grasp at any exquisite passion, or any contribution to knowledge that seems by a lifted horizon to set the spirit free for a moment, or any stirring of the senses, strange dyes, strange colours, and curious odours, or work of the artist's hands, or the face of one's friend.'[10] This can be read as a sublime contribution to the 'art for art's sake' movement, whose leaders in France were Théophile Gautier and Baudelaire; and Pater's 'Conclusion' was fated to fall into the hands of Oscar Wilde, who span out of it his witty, dangerous paradoxes. The stark symbolism of Wilde's downfall and public humiliation was only the most spectacular backlash of bourgeois respectability. In private, such torments were ubiquitous: Baudelaire, whose late notes in his private

---

[10] Walter Pater, *The Renaissance* (Chicago: Academy Chicago, 1978), 233–9.

journals, with headings like 'Hygiene. Conduct. Morale', read like a
set of spiritual memoranda to the self—to a self now terrified by the
spectres it has called up—provides the crucial 'reality check' which a
life of assiduous dandyism must incur. Huysmans, in his 1903 preface to *A Rebours*, and writing now as a Catholic convert, is similarly
eloquent, the book having come to represent for its author a staging-
post on the mysterious progress of Grace within his soul. 'Only
slowly did I start to become detached from my shell of impurity;
I began to feel disgust with myself... [. . .] I found myself praying for
the first time, and the revelation happened.'[11] Barbey's brilliant
insight, when reviewing Huysmans's book (the two did not yet know
each other), that 'after such a book, the author has no alternative but
to choose the muzzle of a pistol, or the foot of the Cross', is a reminder
that 'Decadence', understood as a congeries of attitudes, opinions,
and 'dissociations', when pushed as far as it was by the writers gathered here—in particular by Gourmont, Lorrain, Maupassant, or
Mirbeau—could be a game with deadly serious consequences.

Decadence versus Naturalism

The problem for the Decadents was to locate a space in which they
could express their contempt for the materialist culture in which they
found themselves, and where they could be free, so to speak, to culti-
vate their own hysteria. In practical terms, this involved finding a
physical location as protected as possible from the rising tide of vulgarity and what Baudelaire calls the 'tyranny of the human face'. In
A Rebours, Des Esseintes removes from Paris to Fontenay-les-Roses,
where he proceeds to do up a house with the exquisite furnishings,
paintings, and exotic flowers of his caprice. He ventures once into the
nearby village, sees a group of 'pot-bellied bourgeois with sideburns',
and recoils in horror. Similarly, in *Axël*—the play by Villiers de l'Isle-
Adam—the effete aristocrat Axël retires for good into the crypt of his
castle, with the immortal phrase: 'Living? The servants will do that
for us.' A dandified solitude characterizes several of the protagonists
in the stories gathered here, who live either in Parisian apartments,
hung with heavy drapes and well insulated from the *hoi polloi*, or in
crumbling familial chateaus, inspired by the Gothic, and in particular
by Poe's languid scion in 'The Fall of the House of Usher'. A part of

---

[11] Huysmans, *A rebours*, 69.

Decadent taste involves a hyper-sensitivity to anything too loud or flashy or vulgar, and by the same token, a horror at the overly utilitarian excrescence of modernity. For example, the functional, anonymous room in the *hôtel garni* or *meublé*, in all its 'sepulchral horror', then as now, is frequently the setting of choice for clandestine encounters, squalor and despair in all its forms. Jean Lorrain, for one, displays a keen sensitivity to atmosphere, whether of the sordid hotel room or the disreputable *bouge*—the low dive of Parisian night-life. As for the brothel, Marcel Schwob's story of that name conveys all the sealed mystery and suggestive horror of the place, viewed as it is through the eyes of a band of curious children, ignorant as to its true nature and function.

Another practical difficulty, though of a different order, that faced the writer of the *fin de siècle* was, quite simply, what exactly was there left for him to write about? By the end of the nineteenth century the literary landscape in France must have looked like the aftermath of a comprehensive scorched-earth policy, the giants Balzac, Hugo, and Flaubert having, in their different ways, shared out the *Comédie humaine* and the *moeurs provinciales*—not to mention the *Légende des siècles*—between them. And there was another contemporary force, of formidable influence and popularity, to be reckoned with: Émile Zola and the school of Naturalism. Zola embraces scientism, and he is the founding father of the 'statistically' researched, documented novel that draws on the welter of new information about the species made available in every kind of report, whether socio-political, economic, or medical. Faced with these monuments, who between them exhausted the art of realist description, it is not surprising that the Decadents, and their close relatives the Symbolists, clustered around Baudelaire, who hated the things they hated, who deliberately chose a rarefied, spiritual ambivalence, whose perceptions are essentially those of a solitary, and whose attractive melancholy stemmed in large measure precisely from an overdose of 'reality'. Poetry had nothing to do with description, or with reportage; it was not the things themselves, 'but the relations between them' that counted, as Mallarmé explained, in an influential essay in which the great Symbolist tries to carve out a space in which his own art could exist.[12] Mallarmé uses

---

[12] See Mallarmé's essay 'Crise de vers', in *Oeuvre complètes*, ed. H. Mondor et G. Jean-Aubry (Paris: Gallimard, Bibliothèque de la Pléiade, 1945), 360–8.

the word 'reportage' advisedly, for this period saw the heyday of the written press; the things themselves lay everywhere to hand, in the great plethora of journals which purveyed every kind of miscellanea and *fait divers*—a form of reportage that even gave rise to a literary form, in Félix Fénéon's '*Nouvelles en trois lignes*' ('Stories in Three Lines'), that consisted of barely rearranged dispatches from press agencies like Havas which landed on his editorial desk at *Le Matin*. 'Em. Girard received a chimney upon his head, at Saint-Maur. At Montreuil, R. Taillerot, who was emptying his septic tank, fell in and drowned', reads one of them.[13] Such fragments were the sustenance and delight of savage satirists of petty-bourgeois existence, like Mirbeau or Bloy. What the papers reported, day after day, was a drop in the birth-rate, the ravages of alcoholism, drugs, sexually transmitted disease, and tuberculosis, and every variety of sordid crime— things that seemed to announce a *fin-de-siècle* reversal of meliorism or 'evolution'. The Naturalists, especially, were avid devourers of the newspapers. But Mallarmé's witty riposte to the apparently incontrovertible 'facts' purveyed by the daily paper was to claim that a column of print might hold the key to the universe, if only the words were arranged otherwise. The task of the 'Décadent' or the 'Mystique' was to suggest the 'horror of the forest, or the mute, scattered thunder in the foliage', but to *exclude* 'the intrinsic, dense wood of the trees'.[14]

In the circumstances, which were crowded, to choose 'vice' as a subject, and the rare, perverse, and novel sensations and pleasures associated with it, was thus a deliberate ploy. It helped, of course, that such pleasures were deemed out of reach, shocking, and even incomprehensible to the bourgeois mentality. Pierre Louÿs has a story called 'Une volupté nouvelle' ('A Fresh Pleasure'), and it could stand as a title of many of these tales. Jean Lorrain's 'The Man Who Loved Consumptives', which is included here, describing the erotic tastes of a man in rude health who seeks out women dying of consumption, is a queasily effective example of the genre. Victor Hugo's remark in a letter thanking Baudelaire for his poems—'vous créez un frisson nouveau'—literally, 'you are creating a novel shudder', was an ambition that federates the writers of the period. So they sought out the *bouge* and the *maison close*, the opium den and the

---

[13] Félix Fénéon, *Nouvelles en trois lignes* (Paris: Éditions Macula, 1990), p. 114.
[14] Mallarmé, *Oeuvres complètes*, 365–6.

bordello—Jean Lorrain, who moved seamlessly from the smartest salon to the lowest dive, was to introduce his friend Huysmans to polymorphous pleasures. When Huysmans converted to Catholicism the friendship faltered—but Catholic ritual itself, blasphemously inverted, had been the target of choice for decadents and voluptuaries, at least since the Marquis de Sade, and it continued to be so throughout this period, culminating in writers of the modern era like Pierre Jean Jouve and Georges Bataille. Vice, and the fascination attendant upon it, is of course everywhere present in Proust's *A la recherche du temps perdu*. In one of his projected prefaces to *Les Fleurs du mal*, Baudelaire, envisages the attempt to extract the *beauty* that lies in evil—the smiling serpent has its hypnotic charm, after all. He remarks in passing that, in any case, many illustrious poets that went before him had dwelled much in the 'more flowery provinces of the poetic domain'.[15] Huysmans says much the same in his 1903 preface, where he explains how it came to be that Lust, *luxure*, was the one capital sin fastened upon by his contemporaries. Writing with the retrospective smugness of the convert, he suggests that Pride would have been a better one.

'La femme'

It is in this context that the misogyny which fires these writers, almost without exception, needs to be understood. Their misogyny is obvious, generalized, and virulent. It seems to infect their very style: the use of particular adjectives to describe a woman's physicality—either to praise or to blame—recurs in all of them. American feminists who have set to work on misogyny suggest it is a form of male hysteria.[16] It is perhaps the most disturbing aspect of the Decadent period, in that it is so widespread. Once again, it is the dissociation of ideas which enables, and indeed inflames, the misogyny of these writers, and frees them from the statutory requirements of Romance chivalry; and there is a sense in which, knocked from her restrictive pedestal, woman is freed too, her sexual power unleashed. The cerebral sensualist Remy de Gourmont applies his theory of dissociation to woman, and finds that her beauty is associated with happiness because of the accompanying promise of sensual fulfilment, which is how he

---

[15] Baudelaire, *Oeuvres complètes*, vol. 1, p. 181.

[16] See the introductory essays by Emily Apter, Janet Beizer, Jennifer Birkett, and others in Hustvedt (ed.), *The Decadent Reader*.

interprets Stendhal's definition of beauty as 'the promise of happiness'. Strip away the partiality of male desire, then woman, viewed aesthetically, is no more beautiful than the male, indeed, is less so. Schopenhauer had already concluded thus, in his notorious, jaundiced aphorisms on the fair sex. Baudelaire decided she was 'natural' and therefore 'abominable', Tristan Corbière had dubbed her 'la bête féroce' ('savage beast'), Jules Laforgue the 'mammifère à chignon' ('mammal with her hair in a bun'), and T. S. Eliot, a latecomer following Laforgue, called her 'the eternal enemy of the absolute'. Maupassant is violently ambivalent about women. His story 'Fou?' ('Mad?'), in which a possessive lover, derailed by his wife's apparently insatiable sensuality—in fact a projection of his own—and the 'infamy' housed in the sumptuous vessel of her body, finds she is taking satisfaction from horse-riding and wreaks his vengeance on both her and the horse, is a truly nasty case in point. Octave Mirbeau is perhaps the most energetic woman-hater of them all, his personal experience of marriage—to the sensual, and apparently faithless, *cocotte* and former actress Alice Regnault—explaining much. His male subjects suffer humiliation at the hands of women, who are often unconscious sadists, withholding sexual favours or placing them elsewhere. In recent readings of 'Decadent sexology' mentioned above, feminist psychoanalysts recuperate female agency in the form of a power-struggle or sadomasochistic bind; but it is often merely the persistence of their own desire, faced with the bland facts of sensuality and beauty which echo back at them (a form of the *femme fatale*, if you will), that seems to enrage and baffle the male protagonists. This is especially so in Maupassant and Mirbeau and in the quasi-pornographic stories by Mendès, and it leads them on occasion to murderous intent. Whatever the emphasis we choose to give, female sexual power is never more insistent than here, and the New Woman is threatening. The writings of these male authors constitute a kind of allergic reaction. The black humour of Mirbeau's cruel little tale included here, 'The Bath', speaks volumes.

Of course, below the surface the ancient instinct to idealize, even to idolize, remains intact—this tendency, common to both sexes, in Freud's refrigerated language, to overvalue the love-object at the expense of the ego, which becomes depleted: it is the recognition of this drive which makes woman not only the indispensable foil to the Decadent writer, but his match. In this at least, he is at one with

Catholic prejudice: woman calls forth sensuality in man—she is thus the formidable temptress that must be shunned. With her hysteria, her caprices, her swooning desires, her possessiveness, her sentimentality, her imperious moods, and her sensuality, in the *fin-de-siècle* period woman comes up against something more redoubtable even than religious censure: the glacial stare of the dandy. And the dandy strives to be the reverse of all these things, to live his life perpetually in front of a mirror. He must always be immaculately turned-out, never emotionally spontaneous, always self-controlled. He is, eternally, the detached observer; he is everything contained in that loaded phrase of contemporary discourse, 'the male gaze'. And it was to this gaze, indeed, that Charcot's beautiful female hysterics were overwhelmingly submitted in the theatre of his clinic. But the dandy, whether he be called Baudelaire or the fictionalized Des Esseintes, is dismayed to find that, come what may, he finds all these 'weaknesses' in himself. And woman, undivided in herself, will always win out, just as nature will always win out. In his misogyny, Schopenhauer is cold and simply derides, but cerebral voluptuaries like Louÿs, Gourmont, or Mendès are subjugated, and indeed obsessed, by women in their sensual abandon, at least as they like to picture them. The Symbolist-Decadent painters and engravers—Gustave Moreau, Fernand Khnopff, Félicien Rops—helped to feed the flames.

There are distinctions to be made: it was chiefly the 'legitimate spouse' of the complacent bourgeois marriage that fuelled the most venomous invective—woman as the perpetuator of the hated tribe. And it is when one of these virtuous wives proves to be whorish, and to cuckold her husband everywhere, from the marital bed to the cheese-shop floor, and with everyone (as in one of Bloy's stories here), that she is to be applauded. The Decadents, who revel in hyperbole and the grotesque, have little time for the subtler psychology of adultery *à la* Flaubert. Women whose 'career' is vice—the *filles* and prostitutes that are omnipresent in this literature—are frequently natural allies, for they are enemies of the 'normative'; as are polymorphs, nymphomaniacs, androgynes, hermaphrodites. For all of these appear—along with a subliminal homosexuality, frequently, if obliquely, evoked by Lorrain in particular—to incarnate new and forbidden pleasures. The one celebrated female Decadent writer, Rachilde (whose texts are too long to be included here), made inversion and comprehensive role-reversal her subject in *Monsieur*

Vénus (1884). Zola, reviling what the Decadents would flock to, spoke of the androgyne as 'the man-woman of rotted societies'. The woman is also admired for her use of artifice, in her *toilette* and in her make-up—the key text here being Baudelaire's 'Eloge du Maquillage' ('In Praise of Make-Up'); Baudelaire's dandy prefers the made-up woman to the natural one, just as Villiers fantasizes Hadaly, a perfect, mechanically operated automaton, as the coming ideal, the 'Future Eve', as he calls her in his novel of that name, a kind of robotic precursor to the Stepford Wives. Sometimes this apparently compulsive misogyny takes a comic form. It infects literary style, but it also effects furniture: there is a passage in *A Rebours* in which the arabesques and scrollwork of Louis XV furniture are said to envelope woman in an atmosphere of vice, by imitating her charms, even in her spasms and transports of pleasure. In his story 'Pft! Pft!', included here, Jean Richepin makes parodic play of stock misogyny; the dandified, erudite, and cynical protagonist falls into the fatal trap of falling in love with the object observed, and suffers all the torments of sexual jealousy. His behaviour exasperates his mistress, who finally acts to confirm his worst suspicions. Male hysteria and projection are shown up to comic, if gory, effect.

Dandies of the Unpredictable

Different types of pathology are everywhere attendant or consequent upon sexuality—and Freud's formal pronouncement on the matter, that sexuality, from the polymorphous perversity of babies onwards, was fundamental to all areas of human experience, was only a step away. 'There is nothing but syphilis', is the jaded view of Des Esseintes. In the famous eighth chapter of *A Rebours*, the Duke introduces a selection of exotic plants, including the carnivorous varieties, into his house; this is followed by a dreadful nightmare, in which a woman is metamorphosed into a particularly savage form of the Venus Flytrap, and the final image of him being drawn towards a gaping 'Nidularium' at the centre of the flower, that bristles with blades, is unmistakably a version of that ancient terror, the *vagina dentata*. But sexuality can also provide, obviously, the extremes of pleasure, the 'novel shudder' of the Decadent quest. It takes other forms as well—this quest for the essence and the rarefied. In the vision of *luxe, calme et volupté* that exists in his country of Cocagne, heightened by

the effects of opium or *hachisch*, in the prose version of 'L'Invitation au voyage', Baudelaire declares that he has found his 'black tulip' and his 'blue dahlia'. Jean Lorrain, who was addicted to ether, liked to sport such flowers in his lapel, and his own dandified hero, Monsieur de Phocas of the eponymous novel (1901), travels the world in search of a particular shade of glassy-greenish transparency to be found in the 'dead water' of certain precious stones, or in the eyes of Astarte, or in those of young prostitutes. A sado-erotic streak—something Lorrain is brilliant at isolating—fuels an ancillary passion of Monsieur de Phocas: rigid with a 'dreadful' anticipation, he watches acrobats performing without a safety net.

One could pass in review other quests for the *nouveau frisson*. In politics, at a time of 'mediocre' republican democracy, some passionately anti-establishment men, like Fénéon and Mirbeau, ardent supporters of Dreyfus, were attracted to the thrill and promise and sporadic violence of anarchism. There was the music, or rather the 'total art form', of Wagnerian opera (a deep and universal passion among this group of writers); recreational drugs for Lorrain; classical erudition and esoterica for men like Gourmont and Schwob; a brand of zealously reactionary Catholicism for Barbey and his protégé Léon Bloy. Many of them dabbled in spiritualism and table-turning, so prevalent at the time that it became little more than a parlour game. The new 'sciences' of mesmerism, magnetism, hypnotism, telepathy, and the like fired the imagination of Villiers, and Maupassant explored 'modern' pathologies like hysteria, neurosis, and fetishism. Jean Richepin anatomizes this quest for originality at all costs in his little comic satire included here, 'Deshoulières'. Whatever their chosen way, the Decadents were united in their hatred of the epoch, so favourable to the complacent, money-making bourgeois with his sideburns, his pot-belly, his vulgarity. Baudelaire recoiled from it, as intensely as any man, and his great cry, to be 'Anywhere out of the world', finds its echo in his followers.

The Stories

(In discussing the stories I have tried to avoid 'spoilers', but the reader may care to read the stories first, and then return to this section of the Introduction.)

This selection of thirty-six tales by fourteen authors aims to show

several facets of French *fin-de-siècle* writing, from the richly orches-
trated addition to the literature of Don Juan by Barbey d'Aurevilly,
through the more traditional ghost story by Villiers, and the inner psychic terrors described by Maupassant, to the savage anti-bourgeois
satire of Bloy and Mirbeau. Aspects of the French Decadent movement described above infiltrate these stories to a greater or lesser
degree; but any idea that decadence implies a lack of *stylistic* energy
should be immediately expelled. They have been chosen not only for
their sumptuous powers of description, but also for their verve and
bite, and for their fearlessness: the common sobriquet *contes cruels* is,
after all, an apt one. It is probably these aspects of the *fin-de-siècle*
tale—its energy and, often, its violence that still has the capacity to
shock—which strike the first-time reader.

These writers were in fact a close-knit group, so mutual influence,
admiration, affection—followed not infrequently by a cooling of
affections, if not execration—was common. It was also an age in
which writers used the dedication ubiquitously and pointedly.
Villiers, Richepin, Schwob, and others dedicate every single story to
a *confrère*. Many of them dedicate to Jules Barbey D'Aurevilly, with
whom this selection opens. Barbey was born in 1808, in the Premier
Empire under Napoleon, so belonged to an earlier generation entirely
than the *décadents*, and indeed he was of the same generation as Victor
Hugo, the one preceding Baudelaire. Dubbed by his peers *le
Connétable des Lettres* (the High Constable of Letters), Barbey was
a great writer and a grand *personnage*, descended from the nobility,
a monarchist and a staunch Catholic reactionary. It is his well-
documented loathing of the growing mercantilism, democratization,
and general secularization of the age that served to rally the Decadents
around him. Above all, he loathed Zola (the feeling was mutual), and
one of his final critical acts was to recognize the genius of *A Rebours*
and hail Huysmans's escape from the 'sordid toils' of Naturalism.
The story selected here is taken from his most famous collection, *Les
Diaboliques*, published when he was sixty-six, in 1874. Part of the
print-run was seized by the public prosecutor, and Barbey only
avoided a trial for assault on public morals by settling out of court,
unlike Flaubert and Baudelaire before him. 'Don Juan's Crowning
Love-Affair' prolongs the august lineage of the Don, who takes, this
time, the aristocratic form of the Comte Jules-Amédée-Hector de
Ravila de Ravilès. In a sumptuous set-piece description, the Comte is

invited by a group of female society hostesses to a very private dinner, in the peach boudoir of the Comtesse de Chiffrevas. Barbey relishes the kind of baroque description—of decor, costume, and of the sumptuous forms of mature women—in a vocabulary that becomes a stock feature of Decadent writing. There is in Barbey a genuine love of, and an almost chivalric respect for, women, even, or perhaps especially, when they are at their most perverse or capricious—a quality that fades out with the later writers. Barbey was one of the great French dandies: he sported ruffles on his shirts, and wore sleeves hemmed with lace. He wrote on Beau Brummel and Byron, and along with Baudelaire he attempted a theory of dandysim. The elegant, feline pasha of this story, Ravila, is one of its purest expressions. His charms may be 'satanic' and fatal to women, but it is worth noting the plangent, elegiac note that sounds through the story—Ravila is described as the Don Giovanni of the fifth act: he and his elegant listeners are a breed threatened with extinction, they are passing into history before our eyes.

Although of a different generation, Barbey has much in common with Villiers de l'Isle-Adam (1838–89). Villiers was also of noble extraction, from a Breton family that had fallen on hard times. Bad luck, inflexible patrician pride, and hopeless idealism in love ensured he would be lonely and penniless in an age whose scientific positivism he particularly abhorred. Neglected by the general public, he was, however, the centre of a very exclusive clique of distinguished writers, including Mallarmé, Bloy, and Gourmont, who treasured his eccentricities and between them helped to ensure his literary immortality. Villiers was cruelly rebuffed by an English heiress, whose beauty was only matched by her vulgarity. There is a legendary, tragi-comic adventure in which Villiers travels to London in astrakhan coat and new dentures—neither of which were paid for—to claim his new bride. The lady in question, perhaps understandably, took fright at the peculiar Frenchman, and fled. Coat and teeth then had to be returned. This episode probably explains the tinge of misogyny in the story 'Sentimentalism', which is in part a meditation on the 'artistic sensibility'. It involves the dandified notion of strictly controlling emotion: such is the explanation of the young Count Maximilien de W***, when confronted about his lack of 'reactivity' and unbending elitism by his companion Lucienne Emery. This is one of Villiers's most realistic and subtle stories, in its setting and

psychology, and it reads like a sincere attempt on the author's part to 'explain' his own reactions and behaviour. As such, it is a valuable addition to our picture of the *fin-de-siècle* dandy. 'The Presentiment' is a more classical ghost story in the tradition of Poe, while 'The Desire To Be a Man', despite the dreadful, gratuitous crime it recounts, is more in the vein of Maupassant, dwelling on fears and insecurities that are bred in the mind, and feed off the mind.

'What the Shadow Demands' by Catulle Mendès (1841–1909) is a tour de force in the same vein, in which a terrible crime is committed not through any easily recognizable, externally driven motive like jealousy or greed, but through a type of obsession (we would probably call it a psychosis today) that comes to haunt the afflicted narrator, who in everything else is a respectable, orderly petty-bourgeois in the haberdashery business. Mendès, who resembled, in one account, 'a debauched Christ', was a prolific writer in every genre, and a prodigious 'networker', at the literary epicentre of our period. His star has mysteriously been eclipsed, partly through his own derivative and often torrid style, sometimes verging on the pornographic, and partly, one suspects, through the malign agency of others (like Maupassant and Bloy) who mistrusted him, and later on André Gide, who dismissed his work. In this story, however, which becomes apocalyptic in its monomania, Mendès manages an extended, finely modulated dramatic monologue in which comedy and terror are curiously blended.

Comedy is also to be found in the astonishing *Histoires désobligeantes* by Léon Bloy (1846–1917), but it is of the blackest kind. Bloy is a fascinating figure, possibly the most difficult, touchy, reactive, and reactionary figure in the whole writhing snake-pit; a fundamentalist dogmatic Catholic, the protégé of Barbey, to whom he was attached with almost filial devotion. His hatred of 'filthy lucre' and his championing of the poor and downtrodden (he 'saved' and had a relationship with a young prostitute he picked up off the streets) remind one more of Dostoevsky than of any of the other writers represented here. Bloy's faith was of the most intransigent kind: convinced of man's fallen nature, and seeing evidence of this all around him, Bloy believed that only intense suffering could bring him to salvation (but he did believe in salvation, which was not an option for the 'pessimists' among the Decadents, steeped in Schopenhauer and Darwin). He described himself as the *enragé*

volontaire (the willingly, or readily, enraged); certainly, there was nothing of the emotionally self-controlled dandy about him. If he belongs here, it is because of the venomous and hilarious treatment he metes out to his bourgeois victims, whom he admitted to treating pretty much as the fancy took him. In a preface he wrote to the stories he confesses: 'I cannot remain calm. When I am not out to massacre, I have to be disobliging. It is my destiny. I am a fanatic of ingratitude.'[17] Bloy was so inflammatory (he was a born pamphleteer) that he fell out not only with every editor but with all his friends as well. One of the glories of this writer, in the three nasty little tales of lust and cupidity included here, lies in his style, which has been much admired—a unique mixture of epigrammatic latinate concision and a blatant, almost bullying irony.

No sooner are the palms awarded to Bloy than they have to be taken away again, possibly, and re-awarded to Octave Mirbeau (1848–1917) for the sheer energy of his hatreds. Both writers came from backgrounds they grew to despise; and Mirbeau suffered from a brutal, even abusive, education at the hands of the Jesuits (if his novel *Sébastien Roch* is taken to be autobiographical). When they came to Paris from the provinces, both were obliged to take humiliating jobs—in Bloy's case as an office clerk in the railways; Mirbeau spent years as secretary and general factotum to various conservative politicians, which did little to enamour him to the breed. When he later came out as a full-blown anarchist, defender of Fénéon and a supporter of Dreyfus, the Establishment as a whole became his target. Like so many others here, he also earned money as a prolific, and ferocious, journalist and critic. Mirbeau's brand of anti-bourgeois satire, mixed with a sulphurous, entirely sadomasochistic vision of sexuality, in such novels as *Le Calvaire*, *Sébastien Roch*, *Le Journal d'une femme de chambre* (later made into a film with Jeanne Moreau), and *Le Jardin des Supplices*, have ensured his literary survival. The stories here reflect different facets of this complex personality; 'The Little Summer-House' shows Mirbeau's fascination with crime and its 'metaphysical' consequences, and sketches a memorable portrait of the ordinary-looking personage, Jean-Jules-Joseph Lagoffin, whose eyes are quite dead. 'The Bath' is a little fable about a complacent fool, who opts for marriage as a quick means to ensure his own

---

[17] Léon Bloy, *Histoires désobligeantes* (Talence: L'Arbre Vengeur, 2007), 7.

home comfort. 'The First Emotion' is of interest in that it belongs to a particular type of satire, more Naturalistic than Decadent, which is really an early treatment of what, in the succeeding century, would become a major theme in a writer like Kafka, urban *angst* and alienation. Monsieur Isidore Buche (like Maupassant's Monsieur Leras in 'A Walk', also included here) is an office-worker who has become, through grinding routine, an automaton; but here these figures are the butt of satire. Roger Fresselou, the protagonist of the powerful little story 'On a Cure', is again a type of the melancholic, decadent young man, who withdraws, not this time to a familial chateau, but to a remote mountain village, a victim, literally, of pessimism when adopted as a philosophical position. The narrator recoils from this, reminding us that Mirbeau is too energetic, too politically engaged, and too angry to conform entirely to the Decadent aesthetic; indeed, in some of his work he parodies the type.

Jean Richepin (1849–1926) is possibly less familiar than many here, though he deserves to be known better. Richepin is an incisive, epigrammatic, and at his best an extremely funny writer. He is, so to speak, the joker in the pack. His natural talent is for satire, and few have targeted the dandyish type, and the 'quest to be unpredictable', as brilliantly as he does in his story 'Deshoulières', the tale of an eccentric who pushes this quest to a murderous extreme. Richepin was an extravagantly bohemian, larger-than-life character himself, his wild hair topped by fantastical hats; his family hailed from deeply rural areas of France, Picardy and the Aisne. His first popular success was a poem, *La Chanson des gueux* (1876), which landed him in prison for a month. He pursued his career as a poet, but if he survives today it is thanks to his stories, which are sometimes horrible, and always *piquant*. Like an unexpected, and hilarious, twist in one of his own stories, in 1908 Richepin was elected to the Académie française. The eponymous anti-hero of 'Constant Guignard', on the other hand, suffers from his name—*avoir la guigne* means 'to be dogged by bad luck'—and Richepin is ruthless in his pursuit of the theme. 'Pft! Pft!' is a clever little story, which reads as a parody of stock Decadent misogyny (and as such it comes as something of a relief); for here the target is less the woman—considered by the male so absolutely empty that her sole riposte to the reproaches of her lovers is a kind of charming sulky *moue*, a *tut-tut*, though the noise given here is *pft! pft!*—than the men who fall for her, including a self-styled and

'dandified' cynic who in the end falls harder than the rest of them, and damns himself eternally as a fool.

To pass from Jean Richepin to Guy de Maupassant (1850–93) is to pass from something (relatively) light into something very much darker. Maupassant's great tales of psychic terror, brought on by his own incipient syphilis and the drugs he used to control it, are masterpieces of the type of hallucinatory *fantastique réel* (as opposed to supernatural occurrence) that is self-induced by the disturbed mind. Stories like 'Le Horla' or 'Lui?' are barely fictionalized accounts of his own madness, a form of autoscopy, seeing himself as detached from himself—for instance, as a figure sitting in his chair, seen from the door of his own room (as in the story 'Lui?'). Maupassant's great subject in these stories is in fact not so much madness as the solitude that brings it on. Biographers ponder the consequences of the very strong, and life-long attachment he had to his own morbidly imaginative mother. Compulsive womanizer though he was, Maupassant was a solitary, and love, in the sense of a lasting relationship of trust with one person, was always lacking. Intellectually, he was another 'victim' of Schopenhauer's pessimism, though the little known tale 'At the Death-Bed', included here, which recounts a gruesomely hilarious anecdote relating to the death of the grim-visaged philosopher, would suggest he had put some distance between himself and the German Master. An ultimate solitude, leading to panic and terror, is described here in the famous story 'Night'. Charcot has already been evoked in this Introduction, and Maupassant's fascination with clinical pathologies. It was his interest in fetishism, and the displaced love-object, that led to his story 'The Tresses'. (In another fetishist story, 'A Case of Divorce', the husband, horrified by the conjugal bed, displaces his libido on to exotic flowers.) The elderly office clerk Monsieur Leras, in 'A Walk', is also a lifelong solitary, who puts off marriage until it is too late, feeling he cannot afford to keep a wife; the unusually prolonged stroll he takes one balmy summer night, however, reveals to him, poignantly and terribly, the desert of his own life. Famous, prolific, successful, Flaubert's prize 'pupil', Maupassant must nevertheless go down as one of the most tormented and darkest writers of this group. The syphilis he contracted early in his life, and which brought about his premature death, in the end unhinged his mind and darkened, almost unbearably, his view of the world. At the end of 'The Tresses', the doctor shrugs his shoulders and says: 'The mind of man

is capable of anything,' and Maupassant's stories here give us a fair sense of that.

One of the less well-known writers of the period is Gustave Geffroy (1855–1926). A prolific short-story writer, Geffroy made his name as a brilliant and progressive art critic, a friend of Claude Monet and supporter of the Impressionists generally. He was actually an admirer of Zola, and the story here, 'The Statue', is a nicely turned fable about Idealism and Naturalism, transferred to the realm of sculpture. The story draws in part on the Pygmalion myth, though in reverse; here, the beautiful, well-bred heroine, wife to a fashionable but conventional Salon sculptor, poses for her husband (indeed, she bans from his studio any other female model), and her vanity is flattered when she finds her likeness in the naiad in the fountain or the marble nymph in the park. But then her husband, suffering a severe period of self-doubt, retires from the fashionable art world and devotes himself to becoming a 'realist' with a vengeance—a kind of Courbet of sculpture—insisting that his wife continue as his sole model . . . with complicated results.

Jean Lorrain (1855–1906), who has been evoked already, is probably the most ostentatiously Decadent figure of the whole group—indeed, he did much to incarnate the type, cramming his figure into wasp-waisted evening-wear. He could appear as something like a dreadful caricature of Wilde (whom he met), with his eternal carnation in buttonhole, heavily made-up eyes and sensuous mouth set in a bulging head, and with a face resembling that of a 'vicious hairdresser', in Léon Daudet's phrase, 'his parting touched with patchouli and those globular, astonished and avid eyes'. With his ostentatious homosexuality, and his *penchant* for the low-life of the city, to which he introduced his friend Huysmans, he managed to transform all this experience into some of the most memorable and disturbing tales of the age. Lorrain was also a serious ether-addict (some elegant Parisian hostesses were rumoured to serve strawberry fruit salad soaked in the substance); the nightmare horrors and psychic disturbances caused by the drug recur in his work. He was fascinated by masks, and the freedom disguise allows; the mask permits the other side of the personality to emerge, with the risk that the mask will stick or—horribly, as in one of his stories—there is no face beneath the mask at all, just a gaping black hole. His controversial personality (he provoked several duels) and his rackety lifestyle in

fact repelled the other, more exquisite candidate for the perfect Decadent—the celebrated Comte Robert de Montesquiou, who was the model behind both Huysmans's des Esseintes and Proust's Baron de Charlus. Lorrain is a fluent, accomplished stylist, and in the stories here—as in his important novel, *Monsieur de Phocas* (1901)—he reveals his mastery at grasping the ambivalent and the equivocal in human nature, in particular its attraction to cruelty and sadism, frequently attributes of the criminal mind.

If ever there were an example of the 'cerebral voluptuary' it must be Remy de Gourmont (1855–1915). Gourmont was primarily an intellectual and (like Marcel Schwob) a man of enormous culture and 'curious learning'. Indeed, a legend (perhaps too good to be true) has it that when he was cataloguing the section of the Bibliothèque Nationale known as 'L'Enfer' ('The Hell'), which contained books placed on the index, often pornographic in nature, he contracted a kind of lupus that left him disfigured, and painfully self-conscious about his appearance and his attractiveness to women. His lifelong muse was the fiery and tyrannical Berthe de Courrière, though due to his disfigurement he spent much of his life cloistered in his study in the rue des Saint Pères. He was a distinguished critic—his notions concerning the dissociation of ideas and of impersonality in the artist were to influence Pound and Eliot. Pound even translated Gourmont's curious treatise *The Physiology of Love*, a study of the sexual mores of animals and insects. He brought this analysis to bear in his stories, which are often erotically charged and play once again on the ambivalence of sexual desire—deploying a knowing, unillusioned attitude common, as we have seen, among the Decadent writers. His fables included here, taken from *Histoires magiques* (1894)—'The Faun', 'Don Juan's Secret', and 'Danaette'—retell myths and legends, and are injected with a dose of his own fairly sulphurous fantasy. From *Sixtine*, his novel of the 'cerebral life' (1890), on, Gourmont's work pits Schopenhauerian idealism (and atheism) against Christian respectability. His materialist leanings enable him to write *Le Latin mystique* (1892), a study of the neo-Latin poetry of the early Church, entirely for what he deemed its aesthetic qualities. For Gourmont, the artist was an aristocrat of the spirit. He himself was descended from the nobility, and he too, like his friends Villiers and Huysmans, despised the blurring of difference and distinction brought about by an age of universal suffrage. His unrequited passion for the lesbian

writer and salon hostess Natalie Clifford Barney, whom he called his 'Amazone', opened up new angles on his otherwise fairly conventional, though subtly handled and highly self-conscious, brand of male fantasy. The fourth story here, the Gothic fable 'On the Threshold', is very different, and cuts deeper, recounting a life blighted—two lives, in fact—by infernal pride and a misapplied philosophy of inaction. The Marquis de la Hogue, who owns the crumbling Chateau de la Fourche, is yet another version of the frigid dandy, but this time he is tortured by remorse for his own aloofness.

A different kind of failure, a remorse that comes too late, is at the heart of 'The Time' by Georges Rodenbach (1855–98), a story about a coddled, pernickety, middle-aged batchelor, Van Hulst, who develops a passion for collecting time-pieces from the antique-dealers of Bruges. The passion for collecting, cast as a symptom or as a form of fetishism, fascinated Maupassant, as we have seen, and Huysmans's Des Esseintes is nothing if not a querulous and exigent collector of fine books and *objets d'art*. It is one obvious refuge from mass commodification and vulgarity. Rodenbach was Belgian, and a friend of Maeterlinck. He is best known for the famous portrait of the city he loved, *Bruges-la-Morte* (1892). But he also lived in Paris, and there his wide network of friends included Mendès, Mirbeau, Villiers, the Goncourts, and Mallarmé, who all appreciated his refined manner and his deep, melancholy sensibility. Here, Rodenbach employs great finesse in embroidering into his story the allegorical or even parabolic figures that start to shine through more clearly as it progresses; there is nothing heavy-handed about the way he lays his snare.

The dazzling but cruelly curtailed career of Jules Laforgue (1860–87) is well known, largely thanks to Eliot and Pound, the great Modernist poets, who quickly fastened upon this extraordinary ironic intelligence. Eliot especially fell under his spell, having discovered the poet in Arthur Symons's seminal little book *The Symbolist Movement in Literature* (1899). Symons described Laforgue's poetry and prose as an 'art of the nerves';[18] it is also an art of ascetic, almost inhuman self-consciousness—this well-mannered, polished young man, who looked rather like a benign monk, was in fact crippled by shyness. The invention of the 'Pierrot' persona in his *Complaintes* (1885) was

---

[18] Arthur Symons, *The Symbolist Movement in Literature* (New York: E. P. Dutton, 1958), 60.

an act of genius that allowed him to escape the sub-Baudelairean gloom of his early poetry. As a penurious young man in Paris, Laforgue would work in the unheated 'extension' of the Bibliothèque Nationale, and would then retire to his bedsit, eat a boiled egg, and read Schopenhauer by candlelight. Suddenly propelled into the implausible position of French Reader to the Empress Augusta of Germany, in her gloomy palace in Berlin, it was by developing this ironical persona, and by living his life as it were in front of a mirror— as Baudelaire said a true dandy must—that he survived. While there, he fell in love with an English governess with a name out of Poe—Leah Lee—and lived barely long enough to marry her and return to France, before dying of tuberculosis at the age of twenty-seven. Laforgue was primarily a poet, but his late prose pieces, *Les Moralités légendaires* (1887), show the same ironic style, beautifully modulated into the rhythms of prose. His 'Perseus and Andromeda' is the one story here with a 'mythological' setting; but Andromeda's epic boredom in her island exile, and her growing sexual awareness, the Monster's benign philosophical presence (he spends his days polishing stones, as Spinoza polished lenses), and Perseus's fatuous vanity, are all thoroughly modern creations. In his *Moralités*, the omnipresence of Laforgue's powerful, underlying pessimism, disguised by humour and a style in which Decadent neologism and sophistication reaches its apogee, announces the absurdist literature of the twentieth century.

Seven years his junior, Marcel Schwob (1867–1905) was another highly strung individual whose short life was dogged by illness. He is also one of the most accomplished writers of the whole period. Born into a literary family (his father ran a local newspaper and his uncle was head of the Bibliothèque Mazarine in Paris), Schwob was plunged early into adventure- and travel-fiction, and he wrote his first published critical notice (in his father's journal) at the age of eleven. He read Stevenson's *Treasure Island*, a discovery that turned into a lifelong passion for the Scottish writer, whose reputation he championed in France. So great, indeed, was Schwob's admiration that towards the end of his life, when he was already ailing, he followed in his master's footsteps and journeyed to Samoa. Schwob had a mastery of English (like Paul Valéry, he visited George Meredith), and knew long passages of Shakespeare by heart. His second great passion was for François Villon, whom he researched in detail. A man of wide

learning and tireless curiosity, Schwob was one of the great story-
tellers of the time, in construction and in range of setting—his tales
range from antiquity to the brutish Middle Ages to the brothels and
'retirement homes' of contemporary Paris. He can suggest the spirit
of time and place with elegance and concision—a master of the telling detail. This talent finds expression in perhaps his greatest single
work, the *Vies imaginaires* (1896). In this text he casts his forensic, but
voluntarily unhistorical eye upon a heterogeneous collection of lives,
ranging from classical figures like Empedocles, Erostratus, and
Lucretius, all the way through to (among others) the Jacobean drama-
tist Cyril Tourneur, by way of Nicolas Loyseleur (a searing portrait
of Joan of Arc's murderous judge) and the painter of the *quattrocento*
Paolo Uccello. Declaring in his preface that 'art, opposed to general
ideas, describes only the individual, desires only the unique',[19] in
these brief texts he concentrates his acids on the single, exceptional
trait—taking his cue here from Giorgio Vasari and his *Lives of the
Artists* (1550). Vasari describes, for example, Pontormo as being
reclusive, 'solitary and melancholy', and Andrea del Sarto as exhibit-
ing a certain 'timidity of spirit'. Similarly, Schwob's 'Lucretius',
included here, struggles (and fails) to reconcile a hereditary gloom
and *contemptus mundi* with the extremes of erotic attraction. His
'Paolo Uccello', picking up on Vasari's account of a painter obsessed
with the science of perspective, neglects human needs and comforts
altogether. The stories with contemporary settings show different
powers: 'The Brothel' is a disturbing description of a silent, sealed
house, while 'The *Sans-Gueule*' (surely written with the Franco-
Prussian War in mind, but frighteningly prophetic of the Great War
lying ahead), and '52 and 53 Orfila' are incisive studies in a type of
sadism, conscious or otherwise, with a veneer of black comedy, that
little can match for sheer cruelty, before or since.

The anthology concludes with a comic, and frankly sulphurous,
story by Pierre Louÿs (1870–1925), the youngest of the group.
'A Case Without Precedent' is a mixture of men's talk and legal
jargon, between Monsieur Barbeville, retired judge, bibliophile, and
former ladies' man, and his doctor. Louÿs was an erudite and civil-
ized young man, who began his career writing Parnassian poetry in
the circle of Lecomte de Lisle and José-Maria Hérédia; in 1891 he

---

[19] Marcel Schwob, *Oeuvres*, ed. Sylvain Goudemare (Paris: Phébus Libretto,
2002), 509.

founded the review, *La Conque*, in which he published Verlaine and Mallarmé and some early work by Paul Valéry, who, with André Gide, became a close friend. For better or worse, he made his name with erotic texts set in antiquity, *Les Chansons de Bilitis* (1894) and *Aphrodite* (1896). Louÿs was, in fact, what the French like to call an *érotomane*—he was sexually obsessed—and after his death a mass of pornographic writings (and drawings) were discovered among his papers, including intimate journals and lists recounting in minute detail his numerous and complicated liaisons. The most celebrated of these was with Hérédia's beautiful daughter Marie, who was actually snatched from under Louÿs's nose, so to speak, by a more senior writer, the distinguished *symboliste* Henri de Régnier, who married her. Marie, however, then claimed Louÿs as her lover, and the three of them went on holiday together to Amsterdam. Louÿs, who was an enthusiastic amateur photographer, snapped the married couple; but there existed also a 'secret' dossier of pictures showing Marie in various erotic poses, taken in the writer's batchelor flat in Paris where they would meet.[20]

The dashing Louÿs was in many ways, given his interests and his style, the Ideal Decadent. His star declined in later life, because the literary age to which he belonged, that of the Symbolists and the Decadents, came to an abrupt end, though it had a last, glorious flowering in the *A la recherche du temps perdu* of Proust, a work that originates in the same era but which transcends it. Proust's range is such that he comprehends—notably in the figure of the Baron de Charlus—both the magnificence and the vulnerability of the flawed dandy, with his *recherché* tastes. These are indeed those of Des Esseintes, but Proust's psychological penetration goes far beyond Huysmans. As the age of Decadence came to an end, Proust and Gide between them, in the radical innovations of their fiction, were already forging a style for the new century.

---

[20] See Jean-Paul Goujon, *Dossier secret: Pierre Louÿs–Marie de Régnier* (Paris: Christian Bourgois Editeur, 2002).

NOTE ON THE SELECTION

IN a period teeming with short-story writers, working to supply the insatiable demand for copy of a whole array of newspapers and literary journals, anxious to amuse, divert, terrify, or titillate their readers, the anthologist of the *fin de siècle* is spoiled for choice. By the same token, however, the writers who supplied the copy are uneven in quality—even the best ones could turn out mediocre work—and today's reader has every right to demand 'quality control' in a selection of this kind. It is to this end that I have, for example, avoided the stories set in exotic or classical settings. The Cleopatras in their baths of mare's milk, the implacable Salomés, the sexually voracious Aphrodites—often associated with the painting of Gustave Moreau— I have chosen to avoid. They have become the stuff of cliché, and too much of the writing is over-orchestrated, when it isn't frankly pornographic. I have made an exception for Laforgue, but his 'Perseus and Andromeda' is altogether superior and in a different tonal and stylistic register from the others. Instead, I have opted deliberately for the tales of recognizably 'modern life', because they are, to my mind, not only better but more likely to engage the reader of today, thoroughly versed in types of urban *angst*. Several of the names will be familiar—no anthology of this kind can do without Villiers or Maupassant, Mirbeau or Lorrain—but I have introduced some writers perhaps less familiar to the anglophone reader, such as Léon Bloy, Jean Richepin, or Gustave Geffroy—for the sheer quality of their work. Surprise, mordant irony, and incisive economy of means are the qualities I have particularly sought out.

There are various ways of arranging an anthology of this kind: thematically, chronologically, or alphabetically. The chronological presentation by date of birth that has been chosen is advantageous in that the reader becomes more readily familiar with the style of a particular author when the stories are grouped together. Shifts of tone and emphasis become noticeable—there is a perceptible move from the stately, descriptive sentences of Barbey d'Aurevilly, to the acrid notations of Bloy or Mirbeau, to the cerebral dissociation of ideas in the fierce little tales of Remy de Gourmont. By starting with Barbey d'Aurevilly, who was a contemporary of Balzac and Hugo, and ending

with Pierre Louÿs, a contemporary of Valéry and Gide, I have attempted to cover the whole of the period that might reasonably be characterized as 'Decadent'.

The vast majority of these stories were first published in newspapers and little magazines of all kinds; the authors would then collect them into individual volumes, though sometimes this would be done posthumously. The original source for each story is to be found in the Explanatory Notes at the back of the book. In our own time, several excellent and wide-ranging anthologies of the period have appeared in French, to which I am indebted; details are to be found in the Select Bibliography.

The Decadent writers revelled in *recherché* description and epithet, and in mixing high literary style with snatches of demotic slang, or *argot*. One of them, Marcel Schwob, actually compiled a dictionary of recondite *argot*. Jules Laforgue, on the other hand, pushes preciosity of style to the limit, while never quite (at least in the story here) forging neologisms. They are elegant stylists, especially Barbey or Villiers, whose long, rhythmic sentences contain carefully balanced sub-clauses. The syntax of prose fiction demands a particular kind of fidelity in a way that other genres do not—the freedoms available to the translator are not the same in all mediums. In translating these stories, I have had frequent recourse to the indispensable *Littré* dictionary, dated 1872, which is the one most appropriate to this period, and which the writers themselves would have known. While trying to keep a sprightly pace, I have retained as far as possible vocabulary and usage that would seem appropriate in stories from the same period in English. Nothing dates faster than inappropriate modernization in this kind of prose fiction.

SELECT BIBLIOGRAPHY

Major Anthologies of the Period

Prince, Nathalie (ed.), *Petit Musée des Horreurs: nouvelles fantastiques, cruelles et macabres* (Paris: Bouquins/Robert Laffont, 2008). A full and informative anthology of *fin-de-siècle* short stories, including illuminating extracts from the newspapers of the time recounting *faits divers* and *curiosités* of different kinds.

Bancquart, Marie-Claire (ed.), *Écrivains fin-de-siècle* (Paris: Gallimard/folio, 2010).

Ducrey, Guy (ed.), *Romans fin-de-siècle, 1890–1900* (Paris: Laffont 1999).

Anthologies in English Translation

Hustvedt, Asti (ed.), *The Decadent Reader: Fiction, Fantasy, and Perversion from fin-de-siècle France* (New York: Zone Books, 1998). An important anthology with specialist essays by Charles Bernheimer, Peter Brooks, Philippe Lejeune, Barbara Spackman, and others.

Hale, Terry (ed.), *Dedalus Book of French Horror: The Nineteenth Century*, trans. Liz Hale (London: Dedalus, 1998).

Stableford, Brian (ed.), *Moral Ruins: The Dedalus Book of Decadence* (London: Dedalus, 2001). A selection of poetry and prose fiction.

Gourmont, Remy de (ed.), *The Book of Masks*, trans. Andrew Mangavite, Iain White, Stanley Chapman, and others, Atlas Arkhive 2 (London: Atlas Press, 1995). Gourmont's original essays are supplemented by extracts from the writers he analyses.

Luckhurst, Roger (ed.), *Late Victorian Gothic Tales* (Oxford: Oxford World Classics, 2005). Contains some French material (Jean Lorrain).

Classic Criticism of the Period

Huret, Jules, *Enquête sur l'évolution littéraire* (Paris: Charpentier, 1891; José Corti, 1999).

Kahn, Gustave, *Symbolistes et décadents* (Paris: Vanier, 1901; Geneva: Slatkine Reprints, 1977).

Praz, Mario, *The Romantic Agony* (Oxford: Oxford University Press, 1978). Praz's study (originally published in Italian in 1930) remains unsurpassed in its scope, an analysis of Romanticism (and its continuation in Decadence) from the point of view of the erotic sensibility.

Symons, Arthur, *The Symbolist Movement in Literature*, Introduction by Richard Ellmann (New York: E. P. Dutton, 1958). Symons's classic study, first published in 1899.

General Cultural and Literary Criticism

Baudelaire, Charles, *The Painter of Modern Life and Other Essays* (London: Phaidon, 1995).

—— *The Complete Verse*, trans. Francis Scarfe (London: Anvil Press Poetry, 2012).

Benjamin, Walter, *The Arcades Project* (Cambridge, Mass.: Belknap and Harvard University Press, 2002).

Bonnefoy, Yves, *Sous le signe de Baudelaire* (Paris: Gallimard, 2011).

Carter, A. E., *The Idea of Decadence in French Literature* (Toronto: University of Toronto Press, 1968).

Citti, Pierre, *Contre la Décadence. Histoire de l'imagination française dans le roman 1890–1914* (Paris: PUF, 1987).

Colin, René-Pierre, *Schopenhauer: un mythe naturaliste* (Paris: PUL, 1979).

Constable, Liz (ed.), with D. Denisoff and M. Potolsky, *Perennial Decay: On the Aesthetics and Politics of Decadence* (Philadelphia: University of Pennsylvania Press, 1998).

Dijkstra, Bram, *Idols of Perversity: Fantasies of Feminine Evil in fin-de-siècle Culture* (Oxford: Oxford University Press, 1986).

Dowling, Linda, *Language and Decadence in the Victorian Fin de Siècle* (Princeton: Princeton University Press, 1986).

Freud, Sigmund (with Josef Breuer), *Studies in Hysteria* (London: Penguin Classics, 2004).

Gourmont, Remy de, *La Culture des idées* (Paris: Union Générale d'Editions 10/18 fins de siècle, 1983).

Hansen, Eric, *Disaffection and Decadence: A Crisis in French Intellectual Thought, 1848–1898* (Washington, DC: University Press of America, 1982).

Hanson, Ellis, *Decadence and Catholicism* (Cambridge, Mass.: Harvard University Press, 1997).

Henry, Anne (ed.), *Schopenhauer et la création littéraire en Europe* (Paris: Klincksieck, 1989).

Jacquette, Dale (ed.), *Schopenhauer, Philosophy and the Arts* (Cambridge: Cambridge University Press, 1996).

Juin, Herbert, *Écrivains de l'avant-siècle* (Paris: Seghers, 1972).

Jullian, Philippe, *Dreamers of Decadence: Symbolist Painters of the 1890s* (New York: Henry Holt & Co., 1974).

Ledger, Sally, and Luckhurst, Roger (eds.), *The Fin de Siècle: A Reader in Cultural History c.1880–1900* (Oxford: Oxford University Press, 2000).

Marquèze-Pouey, Louis, *Le Mouvement décadent en France* (Paris: PUF, 1986).

Michelet Jacquod, Valérie, *Le Roman symboliste: un art de l'extrême conscience* (Paris: Droz, 2008).

Nordau, Max, *Degeneration* (1892; Lincoln, Nebr.: University of Nebraska Press, 1993).

Pykett, Lynn (ed.), *Reading fin de siècle Fictions* (London: Longman, 1996).

Pierrot, Jean, *The Decadent Imagination, 1880–1900*, trans. Derek Coltman (Chicago: University of Chicago Press, 1981).

Showalter, Elaine, *Sexual Anarchy: Gender and Culture at the fin de siècle* (New York: Penguin Books, 1991).

Weir, David, *Decadence and the Making of Modernism* (Amherst, Mass.: University of Massachusetts, 1996).

A Rebours *and J.-K. Huysmans*

Huysmans, J.-K., *A Rebours*, ed. Marc Fumaroli (Paris: Gallimard/folio, 1983).

——*Against Nature*, ed. Nicholas White, trans. Margaret Mauldon (Oxford: Oxford World Classics, 2009).

——*Against Nature*, ed. Patrick McGuinness, trans. Robert Baldick (London: Penguin Classics, 2004).

Baldick, Robert, *The Life of J.-K. Huysmans*, foreword by Brendan King (London: Dedalus, 2006).

Further Reading in Oxford World's Classics

Mallarmé, Stéphane, *Collected Poems and Other Verse*, trans. E. H. and A. M. Blackmore.

Maupassant, Guy de, *Bel-Ami*, trans. Margaret Mauldon, ed. Robert Lethbridge.

——*A Day in the Country and Other Stories*, trans. David Coward.

——*A Life*, trans. Roger Pearson.

——*Pierre et Jean*, trans. Julie Mead, ed. Robert Lethbridge.

Rimbaud, Arthur, *Collected Poems*, trans. Martin Sorrell.

CHRONOLOGY OF MAJOR EVENTS
AND LITERARY PUBLICATIONS
OF THE FRENCH *FIN DE SIÈCLE*

1870 Franco-Prussian War; defeat of the French at Sedan. The Emperor, Napoleon III, captured. End of the Second Empire, proclamation of the Third Republic, under Thiers and the Republicans.
Lautréamont, *Poems*
Villiers de l'Isle-Adam, *La Révolte*
Wagner, *Die Walküre*

1871 Defeat of France by the Prussians; armistice with Germany. Thiers becomes President of the Republic. Insurrection in Paris, start of the 73 days of the Commune. Violence on both sides, burning of the Tuileries Palace and destruction of the Vendôme Column. The insurrection is put down with terrible severity and bloody reprisal by the Republican government. Treaty of Frankfurt signed with Germany; France cedes Alsace-Lorraine and has to pay crippling war debt to Germany.
Mendès, *Soixante-treize journés de la commune*
Rimbaud, *Lettre du voyant*; *Le Bateau ivre*
Zola, first novel in his Rougon-Macquart cycle, subtitled *Histoire naturelle et sociale d'une famille sous le Second Empire*

1872 Introduction of compulsory military service and creation of a territorial army.
Nietzsche, *The Birth of Tragedy*
Zola, *La Curée*
Monet, *Impression: le lever du soleil*

1873 Death of former Emperor Napoleon III at Chislehurst, in Kent. Resignation of Thiers, and accession of Maréchal MacMahon as President of France. Institution of the *septennat*, limiting the mandate of the Presidency to seven years. James Clark Maxwell, Theory of electromagnetism. Joseph Glidden invents barbed wire.
Corbière, *Les Amours jaunes*
Rimbaud, *Une Saison en enfer*
Verlaine, *Art poétique*
Pater, *The Renaissance*
Manet, *Gare Saint-Lazare*

1874 Laws regulating public morality, including the re-establishment of

censorship. French commerce expands in Indochina, Tonkin becomes a French protectorate. First Impressionist Exhibition opens in the photographer Nadar's studio.
Barbey d'Aurevilly, *Les Diaboliques*
Ribot, *La Philosophie de Schopenhauer*
Verlaine, *Romances sans paroles*

1875 The Constitution voted, which definitively establishes France as a republic. First explorations in Equatorial Africa, led by Pierre Savorgnan de Brazza, later Commissioner-General for the French Congo. Barbey's *Les Diaboliques* formally withdrawn from public sale, with the agreement of the writer. Zola criticizes Barbey for this, and earns the latter's undying hostility.
Zola, *The Sin of Father Mouret*
Moreau, *Fleur mystique*

1876 Members of the two legislative bodies, elected in accordance with the 1875 Constitution (Chambres des députés and Sénat), take their seats. Alexander Graham Bell patents the telephone. Villiers wins second prize in the Michaëlis competition for drama.
Huysmans, *Marthe*
Mallarmé, *L'Après-midi d'un faune*
Richepin, *La Chanson des gueux*; *Les Morts bizarres*
Wagner, *Siegfried*
Gustave Moreau, exhibits in the Salon, *L'Apparition* and *Salomé dansant devant Hérode*
Swinburne, *Poems and Ballads, second series*
Degas, *L'absinthe*
Rops, *Le buveur d'absinthe*

1877 Chamber of Deputies dissolved. Death of Thiers. Republican victory in legislative elections. Edward Muybridge creates the first moving pictures. Edison invents the cylinder phonograph. Ludwig Boltzmann: statistical definition of entropy. So-called 'Baptism' of the Naturalist school, around a restaurant table: Flaubert, Edmond de Goncourt, and Zola, with their young disciples Alexis, Céard, Hennique, Huysmans, and Mirbeau.
Flaubert, *Trois Contes*
Zola, *L'Assommoir*
Huysmans, 'Émile Zola et *L'Assommoir*'

1878 Universal Exhibition in the Trocadéro; Congress of Berlin (break-up of Turkey, Austria to occupy Bosnia-Herzegovina, Cyprus ceded to the English). Charcot starts clinical experiments with hypnosis at the Salpêtrière.

Duret, *Les Peintres impressionistes*
Zola, *Une page d'amour*

1879 MacMahon resigns as President; succeeded by Jules Grévy. Gambetta elected President of the Chambre des députés. *La Marseillaise* becomes the national anthem again. Reprint of Barbey's *Un prêtre marié* forbidden by the archiepiscopate of Paris.

Maupassant publishes an article, 'Gustave Flaubert', in *La République des lettres*.

Huysmans, *Les Soeurs Vatard*
Redon, *Dans le rêve*, lithographs
Rops illustrates Barbey's *Les Diaboliques*

1880 Anticlerical decrees order dispersion of the Society of Jesus and other congregations not recognized by the state. Final amnesty granted to participants in the Commune. Official institution of Bastille Day (14 July) as the *fête nationale*, and adoption of the *tricolore*. Maupassant is threatened with a court action for offence to public morals, for his poem *Une fille*; in the end no action is taken. Mallarmé institutes his famous salon, *les Mardis*, in the rue de Rome.

Barbey d'Aurevilly, *Goethe et Diderot*
Maupassant, *Boule de suif*, gathered in the volume *Les Soirées de Médan*
Huysmans, *Croquis parisiens*
Mendès, *Les Mères ennemis*
Rachilde, *Monsieur de la nouveauté*
Villiers, *Le Nouveau-Monde*

1881 Jules Ferry presides over the institution of free, secular, and compulsory primary education for all. Law ensuring freedom of the press. Large parts of Tunisia occupied, and France imposes a protectorate upon Tunis. Pasteur discovers anthrax vaccine.

Maupassant, *La Maison Tellier*
Huysmans, *En ménage*
Verlaine, *Sagesse*
Flaubert, *Bouvard et Pécuchet* (published posthumously)
Cézanne, *Autoportrait*

1882 Fall of Gambetta. The *Loi Jules Ferry* for primary education becomes law. The new Hôtel de Ville inaugurated, replacing the one destroyed by the Commune in 1871. Charcot begins studying cases of fetishism. Opening of the Grévin Wax Museum.

Barbey d'Aurevilly, *Une histoire sans nom*
Maupassant, *Mademoiselle Fifi*
Mendès, *Monstres parisiens*

Wagner, *Parsifal*
Redon, *Pour Edgar Poe*
Renoir, *Baigneuse*

1883 Death of the Comte de Chambord, last of the succession claiming divine right to the monarchy in France. Colonial wars in Indochina. Charcot starts his study of Satanism, and gathers documents for his Bibliothèque diabolique at the Salpêtrière.
Villiers, *Contes cruels*
Paul Bourget, *Essais de psychologie contemporaine*
Huysmans, *L'Art Moderne* (praise for Moreau and Redon, and for the Impressionists)
Maupassant, *Une vie*; *Contes de la Bécasse*
Lorrain, *La Forêt bleue*
Mendès, *Les Folies amoureuses*
Ribot, *Les Maladies de la volonté*
Rollinat, *Les Névroses*

1884 Colonial expansion, annexation of Cambodia (Kampuchea) to Cochin-China. Legalization of divorce; trade unions legalized. Lewis Waterman invents the first practical fountain-pen; James Ritty invents the mechanical cash-register.
Huysmans, *A Rebours* (the 'Bible of Decadence')
Barbey d'Aurevilly, *Ce qui ne meurt pas*
Maupassant, *Miss Harriet*; *Les Soeurs Rondoli*; *Yvette* (short stories)
Péladan, *Le Vice suprême*
Rachilde, *Monsieur Vénus*
Verlaine, *Les Poètes maudits* (studies of Corbière, Rimbaud, Mallarmé)

1885 Fall of Jules Ferry's government. Jules Grévy re-elected President of the Republic. Death of Victor Hugo. Harim Maxim invents the machine-gun. Karl Benz invents the first practical automobile to be powered by an internal-combustion engine. Freud studies under Charcot at the Salpêtrière; foundation of the Society of Physiological Psychology under the leadership of Charcot.
Laforgue, *Les Complaintes*
Lorrain, *Modernités* and *Viviane*
Mallarmé, 'Prose pour Des Esseintes'
Maupassant, *Bel-Ami*
Zola, *Germinal*
Pater, *Marius the Epicurean*

1886 General Boulanger becomes Minister of War. Gottlieb Daimler builds the world's first four-wheeled motor vehicle. Anatole Baju

founds *Le Décadent*, a journal that gathers writers who will be associated with the term.

Bloy, *Le Désespéré*
Edouard Drumont, *La France juive* (anti-Semitic tract)
Gourmont, *Merlette*
Maupassant, *Toine*; *La Petite Roque*
Mirbeau, *Le Calvaire*
Rimbaud, *Illuminations* (edited by Verlaine)
Villiers, *L'Eve future*; *L'Amour suprême*
Zola, *L'Oeuvre*

1887 Resignation of General Boulanger; honours scandal forces resignation of President Grévy. Sadi Carnot elected President. Ferdinand de Saussure lecturing on *la linguistique générale* at the Collège de France. Heinrich Hertz invents radar; Emile Berliner invents the gramophone. Construction starts on the Eiffel Tower. Alfred Binet, in 'Le Fétichisme dans l'amour', first coins the term 'fetishism'. Death of Laforgue.

Laforgue, *Moralités légendaires*
Mallarmé, *Poésies*
Maupassant, *Le Horla*
Mendès, *La Première Maîtresse*
Zola, *La Terre*

1888 Wilhelm II becomes Emperor of Germany. Foundation of the Institut Pasteur; Chair of Experimental Psychology established at the Collège de France. John Boyd Dunlop patents the first commercial successful pneumatic tyre. Gauguin and Van Gogh in Arles.

Lorrain, *Dans l'oratoire*
Maupassant, *Pierre et Jean*; *Sur l'eau*
Mirbeau, *L'Abbé Jules*
Rachilde, *Madame Adonis*
Villiers, *Histoires insolites*; *Nouveaux contes cruels*
Wilde, *The Happy Prince and Other Tales*

1889 Inauguration of the Eiffel Tower and International Exhibition in the Centenary Year of the Revolution. The Java pavilion and its dancers cause a sensation (Paul Gauguin executes sketches of them). Failed *coup d'état* by General Boulanger. Sir James Dewar and Sir Frederick Abel co-invent cordite. Opening of Le Moulin Rouge. Anatole Baju publishes last number of *Le Décadent*. The *Mercure de France* journal and publishing house founded by Gourmont, Rachilde, and Vallette. Death of Barbey d'Aurevilly and Villiers de l'Isle-Adam.

Bergson, *Essai sur les données immédiates de la conscience*
Bourget, *Le Disciple*

Huysmans, *Certains*
Janet, *L'Automatisme psychologique*
Maupassant, *La Main gauche*; *Fort comme la mort*

1890 First May-day celebrations, marked by popular unrest. Fall of Bismarck. J. G. Frazer publishes first volumes of *The Golden Bough*.
Gourmont, *Sixtine, roman de la vie cérébrale*
Laforgue, *Derniers vers* (posthumous)
Maupassant, *La Vie errante*; *L'Inutile Beauté*; *Notre coeur*
Mendès, *Méphistophéla*
Mirbeau, *Sébastien Roch*
Villiers, *Axël* (posthumous)
Zola, *La Bête humaine*

1891 Boulanger commits suicide in Belgium. Popular and social unrest marked by strike action. Foundation of the Rosicrucian Society, with Péladan among its leaders. First petrol-powered automobiles (Panhard and Levassor). In *The Man of Genius*, Cesare Lombroso cites mental abnormality and disease as a cause of artistic genius. Gauguin's first period in Tahiti. Death of Rimbaud.
Jules Huret, *Enquête sur l'évolution littéraire*
Huysmans, *Là-bas* (his novel about black-magic circles)
Lorrain, *Sonyeuse*; *Soirs de province, soirs de Paris*
Maeterlinck, *Pelléas et Mélisande*
Schwob, *Coeur double*
Wilde, *Intentions*; *Lord Arthur Savile's Crime*; *The Picture of Dorian Gray*
Zola, *L'Argent*

1892 Factory Acts brought in banning work for children under thirteen and limiting the working day for adults. Anarchist bomb scares. Start of the long-running politico-financial scandal involving the Panama Canal Company founded by Ferdinand de Lesseps; its bankruptcy incurs massive financial losses. In Germany Max Nordau publishes his influential *Entartung* (*Degeneration*), a virulent attack on moral and aesthetic decline, published in France in 1894 as *Dégénerescence*. Wilde's play *Salome* is banned by the censors in England.
Bloy, *Le Salut par les Juifs*
Gourmont, *Lilith*, *Litanies de la Rose*, and *Le Latin mystique* (with a preface by Huysmans)
Richepin, *Cauchemars*
Rodenbach, *Bruges-la-Morte*
Schwob, *Le Roi au masque d'or*

Zola, *Le Débâcle*
Conan Doyle, *The Adventures of Sherlock Holmes*

1893 Anarchist bomb attack on the Chambre des Députés. Trials concerning the Panama Canal scandal. Lombroso's *The Degenerate Female* claims that prostitution is a biologically inherited tendency. Sarah Bernhardt plays the title role in Wilde's *Salome*, translated into French by Lord Alfred Douglas. Verlaine reads in Oxford and London. Death of Maupassant.

Freud and Breuer, *Studies in Hysteria*
Arthur Symons, *The Decadent Movement in Literature*
Gourmont, *Le Fantôme*; *L'Idéalisme*
Lorrain, *Buveurs d'âmes*
Mallarmé, *Vers et Prose*
Rachilde, *L'Animale*
Schwob, *Mimes*
Yeats, *The Celtic Twilight*
Zola, *Le Docteur Pascal* (final volume in the Rougon-Macquart cycle)

1894 Anarchist bombings; French President Sadi Carnot assassinated in Lyon by Italian anarchist Cesario; Casimir Périer elected President. Start of the Dreyfus Affair: Captain Dreyfus is arrested and charged with treason by anti-Semitic, Catholic-dominated military court; found guilty, he is sentenced to solitary confinement for life on Devil's Island. Émile Durkheim publishes *Les Règles de la méthode sociologique*. Havelock Ellis, *Man and Woman*. Founding of *The Yellow Book* by Henry Harland and Aubrey Beardsley in England. Marconi's experiments with wireless. Death of Robert Louis Stevenson.

Bloy, *Histoires désobligeantes*
Geffroy, *Le Coeur et l'esprit*
Gourmont, *Histoires magiques*
Louÿs, *Les Chansons de Bilitis*
Rodenbach, *Musée des béguines, natures mortes et nouvelles*
Schwob, *Le Livre de Monelle*
Conan Doyle, *The Memoirs of Sherlock Holmes*
Kipling, *The Jungle Book*

1895 Félix Faure elected President of the Republic. The CGT (general workers union) founded. Trial of Oscar Wilde. He is found guilty of 'acts of gross indecency between men' and sentenced to two years hard labour. *The Yellow Book* ceases publication. Lumière Brothers patent the first moving-picture *Cinématographe*; first motion picture presented to a public audience. William Röntgen discovers X-rays.

Huysmans, *En route*
Lorrain, *Sensation et souvenirs*
Symons, *London Nights*
Valéry, *Introduction à la méthode de Léonard de Vinci*
Wells, *The Time Machine*
Wilde, *The Ideal Husband; The Importance of Being Earnest*

1896 Tsar Nicholas II makes triumphant state visit to Paris. Kitchener's
expedition to the Sudan. Dreyfus family demand a retrial after the
anonymous letter at the heart of the Affair is attributed to Esterhazy.
Henri Becquerel discovers radioactivity. Henry Ford builds his
first car, the quadricycle. Freud coins the term 'psychoanalysis'.
First modern Olympic Games staged in Athens. The height of Art
Nouveau.
Bergson, *Matière et mémoire*
Gourmont, *Le Livre des masques,* illustrated by Vallotton.
Jarry, *Ubu Roi* (first performances in Paris)
Louÿs, *Aphrodite*
Proust, *Les Plaisirs et les Jours*
Schwob, *La Croisade des enfants; Spicilège; Vies imaginaires*
Valéry, 'La Soirée avec Monsieur Teste'

1897 Félix Faure returns visit to Tsar Nicholas, leading to a renewal of
the Franco-Russian Alliance. A fire at the Bazar de la Charité claims
140 victims.
Barrès, *Les Déracinés*
Bloy, *La Femme pauvre*
Gide, *Les Nourritures terrestres*
Lorrain, *Monsieur de Bougrelon* (a fictional portrait of Barbey
    d'Aurevilly); *Contes pour lire à la chandelle; Lorelei*
Mallarmé, *Divagations; Un coup de dés n'abolira jamais le
    hasard*
Rodenbach, *La Carillonneur*
Rostand, *Cyrano de Bergerac*
Stoker, *Dracula*
Wells, *The Invisible Man*

1898 Zola writes his pro-Dreyfus pamphlet *J'accuse,* published in
L'Aurore, after the acquittal of Esterhazy. Zola is proscuted and
forced to go into exile in England. Height of the 'Affair', France pro-
foundly divided. Foundation of the League of the Rights of Man
(pro-Dreyfus) and of the anti-Dreyfusard League of the French
Fatherland. Pierre and Marie Curie discover radium. Anglo-French
disputes in the Sudan (Fashoda Incident). Start of construction of
the Paris Metro. Havelock Ellis publishes *Sexual Inversion* and faces

prosecution for outrage to public morals. Death of Beardsley, Mallarmé, Rodenbach, Moreau, Rops.

Gourmont, *D'un pays lointain*
Huysmans, *La Cathédrale*
Lorrain, *Ma petite ville*; *La dame turque*
Louÿs, *La Femme et le pantin*
Richepin, *Contes de la décadence romaine*
Nietzsche, *Thus Spake Zarathustra*
Conrad, *Heart of Darkness*

1899 Death of Félix Faure, election of Émile Loubet as President of the Republic. On the insistence of Clemenceau and Jaurès, Dreyfus is given a second trial, found guilty with 'extenuating circumstances', and offered a pardon by the government. Charles Maurras founds the Monarchist-Catholic movement Action Française. Start of the Boer War. Krafft-Ebing publishes *Psychopathia Sexualis*. Marconi's wireless telegraphy transmits successfully across the Atlantic. Arthur Symons publishes his influential study *The Symbolist Movement in Literature*.

Bergson, *Le Rire*
Gide, *Prométhée mal enchaîné*
Gourmont, *Le Songe d'une femme*; *L'Esthétique de la langue française*
Lorrain, *Heures d'Afrique*; *Madame Baringhel*
Mallarmé, *Poésies* (posthumous)
Mirbeau, *Le Jardin des supplices*

1900 Universal Exhibition held in Paris, the most brilliant of its kind to date. Olympic Games held in Paris. Boxer Revolt in China. Reduction of the working week to sixty hours. Paris Metro Line 1 opens. Max Planck defines law of black-body radiation, the basis for quantum theory. Death of Wilde.

Freud, *The Interpretation of Dreams*
Gourmont, *La Culture des idées*
Lorrain, *Histoires de masques*; *Vingt femmes*
Mirbeau, *Le Journal d'une femme de chambre*
Conrad, *Lord Jim*

1901 Second visit of Tsar and Tsarina of Russia to France. Founding of the Radical Socialist Party. Picasso's first exhibition in Paris. Death of Queen Victoria.

Freud, *The Psychopathology of Everyday Life*
Huysmans, *Saint Lydwine de Schiedam*
Jarry, *Messaline, roman de l'ancienne Rome*; *Le Surmâle*
Lorrain, *Monsieur de Phocas*

Mirbeau, *Les 21 jours d'un neurasthénique*
Liane de Pougy, *L'Idylle sapphique*
Rodenbach, *Le Rouet des brumes* (posthumous collection of stories)
Kipling, *Kim*
Gauguin in the Marquesas Islands
Rodin illustrates Mirbeau's *Le Jardin des supplices*

FRENCH DECADENT TALES

FRENCH DECADENT TALES

JULES BARBEY D'AUREVILLY

Don Juan's Crowning Love-Affair

Innocence is the devil's choicest dish.

(A.)

I

'Is he still alive, then, the old rogue?'

'Dear God! Still alive, yes!—and by God's command, Madame—I added, remembering her piety—of the parish of Sainte-Clotilde, the parish of dukes!—The King is dead! Long live the King! as they used to say under the old monarchy before it was broken, like a set of antique Sèvres porcelain. But Don Juan will survive all democracies, he is a monarch that no one will break.'

'In any case, the devil is immortal!' she said self-approvingly.

'He even...'

'Who?... the devil?...'

'No, Don Juan... supped, three days ago, at a cabaret... Guess where?...'

'At your frightful Maison-d'Or,* I suppose...'

'By no means, Madame! Don Juan no longer sets foot in the place... there's nothing there piquant enough for the taste of his Highness. The princely Don Juan has always rather resembled the famous monk D'Arnaud de Brescia* who, according to the chronicles, lived off nothing but the blood of souls. He likes to pink his champagne with it, and you can't find liquor like that anymore among the cabaret *cocottes*!'

'Indeed,' she went on with irony, 'so he supped at the Benedictine Convent, with the ladies...'

'Of Perpetual Adoration, yes, Madame! For once he has inspired adoration, the old devil, it does tend to last forever.'

'For a Catholic I find you full of profanity,' she said slowly, but a little nettled, 'and I beg you to spare me the details of your dissolute

suppers, if this is what you intend to impart to me by harping on so about Don Juan.'

'I'm not inventing anything, Madame! The harlots at that particular supper, if harlots they were, are nothing to do with me... unfortunately...'

'That's enough, Monsieur!'

'Allow me my modesty. They were...'

'The *mille è tre?*...'* she broke in, curious now, altering her manner, almost friendly again.

'O! Not all of them, Madame... Only a dozen. It's quite enough, really, a respectable number...'

'And not quite respectable, either,' she put in.

'Besides, you know as well as I do that you can't fit many people into the boudoir of the Comtesse de Chiffrevas. It has seen great exploits, to be sure, but it *is* a very small boudoir...'

'What?' she exclaimed, sounding shocked. 'They had supper in the boudoir?...'

'Yes, Madame, in the boudoir. And why not? People have supper on the battlefield. They wanted to give a sumptuous supper to Don Juan, and where better to honour him than in the very theatre of his triumphs, the place where memories bloom in lieu of orange trees. It was a charming idea, both tender and melancholic. This was not the *victims' ball*;* it was the *victims' supper.*'

'And Don Juan?' she said, much as Orgon, in the play, says 'And Tartuffe?'*

'Don Juan took it all in good heart, and ate an excellent supper,

...He, alone, in front of the women!

in the person of someone of your acquaintance... none other than the Comte Jules-Amédée-Hector de Ravila de Ravilès.'*

'*Him!* It's true, he *is* Don Juan,' she said.

And though she was too old for such daydreams—a pious bigot in beak and claw—she dreamed nevertheless of the Comte Jules-Amédée-Hector—of the ancient and eternal race of Juan, to whom God did not give the world, but allowed the devil to do so instead.

II

WHAT I just recounted to the old Marquise Guy de Ruy was nothing less than the truth. Barely three days earlier, a dozen ladies, hailing from the irreproachably virtuous Faubourg Saint-Germain* (let them rest easy, I shall not name names!), all twelve of whom, according to the dowagers of gossip, *had been honoured* (to use the piquant old expression) by the Comte Ravila de Ravilès, took it into their heads to hold a supper for him—*at which he was to be the only male present*—to celebrate... what? They didn't say. Giving such a supper was an audacious enterprise; but women, cowardly when alone, become daring in numbers. Probably not one of them would have dared to invite the Comte Jules-Amédée-Hector to a supper *en tête à tête*; but together, and using each other as moral support, they gladly formed a Mesmer chain,* bound by magnetic force to the compelling, to the dangerous, Ravila de Ravilès...

'What a name!'

'And a most fitting one, Madame...'

The Comte de Ravila de Ravilès, who incidentally had always obeyed the directive suggested by his imperious name, was indeed the incarnation in one man of every seducer ever evoked in history or in novels. Even the Marquise Guy de Ruy—who was an old malcontent, with cold, sharp blue eyes, if less cold than her heart, and less sharp than her wit—conceded that in an age when matters concerning women became daily less relevant, then if there *did* exist anyone who resembled Don Juan, it had to be him! Unfortunately, he was the Don of the fifth act. The witty Prince de Ligne* never fully accepted the fact that Alcibiades could ever get to be fifty years old. And by the same token, the Comte de Ravila went on acting like Alcibiades. Like the Comte d'Orsay,* that dandy cast in the bronze of Michelangelo, who was handsome to the day he died, Ravila had the sort of beauty particular to the race of Don Juan—that mysterious race which does not proceed from father to son, like everyone else, but which occurs here and there, at different intervals, within the families of humanity.

His beauty was the genuine article—insolent, joyous, imperious—in a word, it was *Juanesque*: the adjective says it all and needs no further elaboration; and what is more—had he made a pact with

the devil?—he possessed it still... Only, God had now started to stake his claim—the tiger claws of life had begun to furrow the superb forehead that had been so crowned with roses, and by scores of lips; and on his broad, insolent temples the first white hairs were visible, announcing the imminent arrival of the barbarians, and the end of the Empire... In truth, he bore them with the imperviousness that comes from pride magnified by potency; but the women who had loved him observed them with melancholy. Who knows? Did they see their own advancing age reflected in his countenance? Alas, for them as well as for him, the hour had come for that terrible supper with the cold and marble-white Commendatore,* after which there was nowhere left but hell—the hell of old age, waiting for the one to come! Which is why, perhaps, before they came to share with him the bitterness of that ultimate supper, they thought they would treat him to their own, and it would be a masterpiece.

A masterpiece it was indeed, of taste, delicacy, patrician luxury, of inventiveness and resource; it was to be the most delightful, delicious, generous, captivating, and above all the most original of suppers. Just imagine it! Normally, suppers are made of overflowing high spirits, intent on a good time; but this one was animated by memory, by regret, almost by despair, but despair dressed up, hidden behind smiles and laughter, and determined on this final feast or folly, on this last intoxicating return of youth, oh may it never end!...

The Amphitryons* who gave this unbelievable supper, so contrary to the insipid customs of the class to which they belonged, must have felt rather like Sardanapalus* on his pyre, which he heaped with his wives, slaves, horses, jewels, and every luxury he possessed, so they would perish with him. In the same way, these women heaped this blazing supper with every luxury they had. They brought to it everything they had of beauty, wit, resource, ornament, allure, and poured all of it all at once into this supreme conflagration.

The man for whom they draped and enveloped themselves in this final flame was worth more, in their eyes, than all of Asia in the eyes of Sardanapalus. They were more deliciously flirtatious with him than women had ever been with any man, or even with a drawing room full of men; and this flirtatiousness they spiced up with the jealousy which is hidden in society, and which they had no need to hide, for they all knew that this man had been with each one of them, and a shameful secret shared is one no longer... The only rivalry

between them now was, whose epitaph would be graven most deeply upon his heart.

That evening he had the sensuous, sovereign, nonchalant, fastidious manner of a confessor to nuns, or of a sultan. Seated like a king—or the master—at the centre of the table, directly opposite the Comtesse de Chiffrevas, in her peach-tinted boudoir of forbidden fruits, the Comte de Ravila turned his hell-blue eyes—eyes that so many poor creatures had mistaken for the blue of the sky—blazing upon this gorgeous circle of twelve women. Their elegance was touched with genius, and where they sat, around this table loaded with crystal, lighted candles, and flowers, they spread before him, from the scarlet of the full rose to the softened amber glow of the grape cluster, every nuance of maturity.

Excluded from this company were the green young things that Byron* abhorred, the little misses who smell of tartlet and whose figures are still wispy; here were resplendent and delicious summers, voluptuous autumns, lavish and full-bodied, their dazzling breasts at the full, overflowing the corsetry, with shoulders and arms of every plumpness, but powerful too, with biceps worthy of the Sabines who fought off the Romans, and who were ready to intertwine themselves between the spokes of the chariot of life, and stop it dead.

I spoke of pretty ideas. Among the most charming at this supper was to have it served by chambermaids, so nothing could be said to have interrupted the harmony of a feast at which women were the undisputed sovereigns, since they also served... His lordship Don Juan—of the Ravila line—could thus plunge his ferocious gaze into a sea of luminous and living flesh, of the kind Rubens plies in his formidable paintings; but he could also plunge his pride into the elixir—be it clear or cloudy—of these hearts. Because at bottom, despite all indications to the contrary, Don Juan is a masterly psychologist! Like the demon himself, he loves souls more even than bodies, and like the infernal slaver that he is, would rather traffic in the former than the latter!

Witty, noble, and while remaining impeccably Faubourg Saint-Germain in tone, so daring were the women that evening they were like the king's pages, when there was a king with pages; they were brilliantly animated, full of incomparable repartee and *brio*. They felt more invincible than they had ever felt, even at their most triumphant. They experienced an unfamiliar power which came from the

very core of their beings, and whose existence, until that moment, they had never suspected.

The happiness occasioned by this discovery was a feeling that tripled their sense of being alive; added to this, there was the physical ambience, which always has a decisive impact on the nervous system, the brilliance of the lights, the heady perfume of all the flowers that swooned in the close atmosphere heated by these beautiful creatures, the stirring effect of the wines, the very idea of the supper which had about it a sulphurous piquancy, of the kind the Neapolitan required of his sorbet to make it perfect; add to this the intoxicating thought of being accomplices in this *risqué* little supper—a supper that never descended into the vulgarity of the Regency period;* indeed, it remained throughout very much a nineteenth-century, Faubourg Saint-Germain supper, and nothing came loose or undone in those adorable *décolletées*, pressed against hearts that had felt the fire and desired to stoke it even more. In a word, all these things acted together, and strung to the utmost degree the mysterious harp contained within each of these wondrous organisms, as tight as it was possible to string without its breaking, so it produced ineffable octaves and harmonies... It must have been extraordinary, don't you agree? One of the most vibrant pages of Ravila's memoirs, if he ever gets round to writing them?... I ask the question, but he alone can write it... As I explained to the Marquise Guy de Ruy, I was not present at the supper, and if I give these details, and recount the story he told at the end, I am only repeating what de Ravila told me himself; for true to the tradition of the Juan clan, he is indiscreet, and he went to the trouble one evening of telling me everything.

III

BY now it was late—or rather, early! It was dawn. Against the ceiling, and concentrated at a certain spot on the pink silk curtains of the boudoir, which were drawn tight closed, an opal-tinted droplet started to grow, like a widening eye, curious to see what was going on in this fiery boudoir. A certain languor had begun to invade these valiant dame Knights of the Round Table, these carousers, who had been so lively only a moment before. It was that moment, familiar at any dinner-party, when the fatigue which comes with the emotion of the

evening just passed begins to show, in the chignons coming slightly loose, in the burning cheeks, flushed or grown paler, in the wearied looks from dark-rimmed eyes, and even in the thousand flaring and guttering lights in the candelabra, which are like bouquets of flame whose stalks are sculpted in bronze and gold.

The conversation, which had been carried on in a general and lively fashion, a game of shuttlecock in which everyone had batted back and forth, had become fragmented, and nothing distinct could now be heard above the harmonious hubbub made by all these voices, with their aristocratic accents, warbling together like the dawn chorus at the edge of a wood... when one of these voices—a clarion voice—imperious and almost impertinent, just as the voice of a duchess should be—made itself heard above the others, and addressed the following words to the Comte de Ravila, which must have been the logical conclusion to a quiet conversation she had been having with him, and which none of the other chattering ladies had heard:

'Since you are reputed to be the Don Juan of our time, you ought to tell us the story of your greatest conquest, the one that most flattered your pride as a lover of women, and which you consider, in the light of this present moment, to be the crowning love of your life...'

This challenge, as much as the voice that delivered it, cut through all the other conversations, and a sudden silence fell.

The voice belonged to the Duchesse de ***—I shall leave her disguised behind the asterisks; but some of you may recognize her, when I say that she has the palest of pale hair and complexions, and the blackest eyes beneath her golden brows, in all of the Faubourg Saint Germain.—She was seated, like one of the just at the right hand of God, directly to the right of the Comte de Ravila, god of this feast, who had left off using his enemies as a footstool; slim and ethereal as an arabesque, she was fairylike in her green velvet dress with its silvery reflections, whose long train wound around her chair, not unlike the serpent's tail that prolonged the charming posterior of Melusina the sea-nymph.*

'Now there's an idea!' said the Comtesse de Chiffrevas, eager in her role as hostess to second the motion the Duchesse had put forward. 'Yes, the love you place above all the others, whether inspired, or felt—the one, were it possible, you should most like to live through again.'

'Oh! I should like to live through them all again!' answered Ravila with the unflagging appetite of a Roman emperor, or other replete monsters of the type. And he raised his champagne glass, which was not the crude and pagan cup they have replaced it with, but the tall, thin vessel used by our ancestors, known as the *flûte*, perhaps because of the heavenly melodies it pours into our hearts!—Then, looking round the table, he embraced with his eyes every woman in that magnetic chain. 'And yet,' he went on, setting down his glass before him with a melancholy astonishing for a Nebuchadnezzar like him, who had not yet eaten grass except in the tarragon salads of the Café Anglais*—'and yet it is true, there is *one* feeling one has experienced in all one's life, which shines more strongly in the memory than others, as life advances, and for which one would give up the rest!'

'The diamond in the set,' said the Comtesse de Chiffrevas, dreamily, possibly contemplating the facets of her own.

'... And as legend has it in my country', chimed in the Princesse Jable... 'which lies at the foot of the Ural Mountains, there is the famous and fabulous diamond that starts off pink, and then turns black, while remaining a diamond, and still more brilliant black than pink...' She said that with all the strange charm that she has, this Bohemian! For she is a true Bohemian, married for love to the finest prince among the Polish exiles, and as much a princess in her bearing as any born in the palace of the Jagellons.*

This was followed by a veritable explosion... 'Yes!' they all exclaimed. 'Do tell us about it, Comte!' they added with warmth, begging him now, all trembling with curiosity down to the curls at the nape of their necks, and bunching up together shoulder to shoulder, some with cheek in hand, an elbow propped on the table, others leaning back in their chairs, fans in front of their mouths; they challenged him with wide, inquisitive eyes.

'If you absolutely insist...' said the Comte, with the nonchalance of a man who knows how much delay exacerbates desire.

'We do, absolutely!' said the Duchesse, fixing—much as a Turkish despot might the blade of his sword—the golden prongs of her dessert fork.

'Then listen,' he concluded, still casually.

They became as one, staring at him with rapt attention. They drank him and devoured him with their eyes. Women always like a love story—but who knows? Perhaps the particular charm here was

that the story he was to tell would be their very own... They knew he was too well bred and too well versed in social etiquette to name names, and that he would omit certain details that were too compromising; and knowing this made them even more impatient to hear the story. They more than desired to hear it, they placed their hopes in it.

In their vanity, they found themselves rivalling each other, to be the most beautiful memory in the life of a man who must have had so many of them. The old Sultan was once more to throw down the handkerchief... that no one would pick up—but the one for whom he threw it down would assuredly receive it silently into her heart...

And now, in the light of their expectations, this is the little thunderbolt he unleashed on their attentive heads:

IV

'I HAVE often heard it said by the moralists, who are fine connoisseurs of life,' began the Comte de Ravila, 'that our greatest love is not the first, nor the last, as many think, but the second. But in matters of love, everything is true, and everything is false, and in any case, it was not so with me... What you have asked of me tonight, ladies, and what I am about to relate dates back to the proudest moment of my youth. I was no longer exactly what they call a 'young man', but I was young, and as an old uncle of mine—a Knight of Malta—used to say of this stage in life, 'I had sown my wild oats'.* In my prime, then, I was in full relations, as the Italians put it so charmingly, with a woman who is known to you all and whom you have all admired...'

And here, the look which all these women—who were drinking up the words of the old serpent—then exchanged with each other had to be seen to be believed—it was truly indescribable.

'She was a fine woman,' went on Ravila, 'and utterly distinguished, in every sense of the word. She was young, rich, of noble extraction; she was beautiful and spirited, with a broad-minded, artistic intelligence; and she was unaffected—in a way your milieu can produce, when it does... In any case, all she desired then was to please me, to play the role of the tenderest of mistresses, and the dearest of friends.

'I was not, I think, the first man she had loved... She had been in love before, but not with her husband; this was of the virtuous, platonic, utopian type—the kind of love that exercises the heart rather

than fills it; the kind that strengthens the heart for the love that almost always follows soon after—the trial run, so to speak, like the white mass, said by young priests practising for when they come to celebrate the true, consecrated mass... When I came into her life she was still at the white mass. I was her first true mass, and she celebrated it sumptuously and with full ceremony, like a cardinal.'

At this remark, the prettiest of pretty smiles went round that table of beautiful expectant mouths, like a concentric ring on the limpid surface of a lake... It was swift, but ravishing!

'She was a rare pearl!' the Comte went on. 'Rarely have I seen such genuine goodness, such tender-heartedness, such good instinctive feeling, intact even in passion, which as you know, is not always good... I have never encountered less calculation, less prudery and coquettishness—two things often to be found mingled in women, like some material marked with a cat's claw... there was nothing of the cat in her... Hers was what those blasted scribblers who poison our lives by their style call a simple nature, ornamented by civilization; but she was in possession of all the luxuries, and not one of the little vices that come to seem even more charming than the luxuries...'

'Was she brunette?' the Duchesse broke in point-blank, who was growing bored with all this metaphysics.

'Ah! you don't look deep enough!' said Ravila cleverly. 'Yes, she was brunette, brunette to the point of being black as jet, the most luxuriant mirror of ebony I have ever seen shining on the voluptuous curve of a woman's head, but she was fair-complexioned—and it is by the complexion, and not the hair, that you have to judge if a woman is blonde or brunette'—added the great observer, who had not studied women just to paint their portraits.—'She was a blonde with black hair...'

All the lovely heads around the table who were blonde of hair only, stirred imperceptibly. For them, clearly, the story had already lost something of its interest.

'She had the sable locks of Night,' went on Ravila, 'but they framed the face of Dawn itself, a face that shone with a rare and radiant freshness that had lost nothing of its bloom despite exposure to years of Parisian night-life, which burns up so many roses in its candelabra. Hers seemed merely to have been kissed, the pink in her cheeks and lips remaining bright to the point of luminosity. The twofold flush

also went well with the ruby frontlet she usually wore—this was the time women did their hair *en ferronnière,** after Leonardo. With her flashing eyes, whose colour was obscured by the flame that issued from them, they made a triangle whose tips were rubies! Slim, but strong, majestic even, she was built to be the wife of a colonel of dragoons—her husband was at that time merely a squadron-leader in the light cavalry—and she enjoyed, despite her pedigree, the rude health of a peasant-girl who drinks in the sun through her skin. She had the ardour that goes with it, too—she imbibed the sun into her soul as well as her veins, she was always present, and always ready... But here's the strange thing! This powerful and unaffected creature, whose pure, passionate nature was like the blood that fed her beautiful cheeks and gave a pink flush to her arms, was... would you credit it? awkward in a man's arms...'

At this some of his listeners lowered their eyes, but raised them again, mischievously...

'As awkward in love as she was rash in life,' went on Ravila, who did not linger on the tidbit he had just dropped. 'And the man who loved her had repeatedly to instruct her in two things she seemed not to have learned... never to lose control in a world always hostile and always implacable, and in private, to learn the greatest art of love, which is that of keeping it alive. She loved, certainly; but the art of love was lacking in her... In this she was unlike the majority of women, who possess merely the art! Now, to understand and apply the strategies of *The Prince*, you must first be a Borgia. Borgia comes before Machiavelli.* One is the poet, the other is the critic. She possessed nothing of the Borgia. She was a good woman, very much in love; and despite her monumental beauty, she remained naive, like the little girl in one of those motifs above a door who, being thirsty, thrusts her hand impulsively into the fountain and stands there abashed, when all the water pours through her fingers...

'The co-existence of this awkwardness and shame with the grand woman of passion was actually rather endearing. Few who observed her in society had any inkling of it—they would have seen someone who had love, and even happiness, but they would not suspect that she lacked the art to return it in kind. Only I was not then sufficiently detached to be able to content myself with observing the *artistic effect*, and sometimes this made her anxious, jealous, violent—as one is when in love, and she was that!—But her anxiety, jealousy, and

violence simply died away in the inexhaustible goodness of her heart, the instant she had, or thought that she had, hurt one—she was as inept at causing pain as she was at giving pleasure. Strange lioness, indeed! She thought she possessed claws, but when she tried to bare them, nothing emerged from her magnificent velvet paws. Her scratches were of velvet!'

'Where is all this leading?' said the Comtesse de Chiffrevas to her neighbour—for this couldn't, surely, be the crowning love of Don Juan...

None of those sophisticates could conceive of such simplicity!

'And so we enjoyed an intimacy that was sometimes stormy, but never tortured, and in the provincial town known as Paris, it was a mystery to no one... The Marquise... she was a Marquise...'

There were three of them sitting at that table, and they were all brunettes. But they didn't blink. They knew full well he wasn't talking of them... The only velvet they shared between them was the down that one of them had on her upper lip—a beautifully modelled lip which at that moment, I could swear, was curled in some disdain.

'... And a Marquise three times over, just as pashas can have three tails!'* went on Ravila, who was getting into his stride. 'The Marquise was one of those women who cannot hide anything, however they might wish to. Even her daughter, a girl of thirteen, innocent as she was, recognized only too well the feelings her mother had for me. I wonder, has any poet fathomed what these daughters feel about us, their mothers' lovers? The question goes deep! It is one I pondered frequently, when I caught the little girl looking at me out of her huge, dark eyes, a black, spying look, fraught with menace. She was shy, like a wild animal, and usually left the drawing room the moment I entered it, or sat as far away from me as possible, if she was forced to stay... she had an almost compulsive horror of my person, that she would try and hide, but it ran so strong in her she could not help herself... It came out in tiny details, but I noticed them all. Even the Marquise, who was usually quite unobservant, kept saying: "Take care, my friend. I think my daughter is jealous of you..."

'And I did take care, much more so than she.

'But had the little girl been the devil in person, I would still have defied her to see through my game... the thing was, her mother's game was perfectly transparent. That flushed face, so often troubled,

mirrored her every feeling. Judging by her daughter's hatred of me, I could not help thinking she must have sensed her mother's emotion by catching some look of uncommon tenderness in her expression towards me. The girl was, I might add, a skinny little waif, quite unworthy of the resplendent mould she issued from—even her mother agreed she was ugly, for which she loved her all the more; she was a small, scorched topaz... or a little bronze mannikin, but with those black eyes... sheer sorcery! And after that, she...'

At this hiatus he stopped short... as if seeking to erase his last remark, as though he had said too much... His listeners, however, woke up again; anticipation could be read on all their eager faces, and the Comtesse even hissed between her teeth, expressing their collective relief: 'At last!'

V

'IN the early days of my relationship with her mother,' the Comte de Ravila resumed, 'I lavished the kind of fond attention on the girl that we reserve for any child... I would bring her bags of sweets, I called her my "little mask",* and frequently when I was talking to her mother I would stroke the plait of hair at her temple, a plait of black, lank hair, with reddish gleams. But "little mask", who had a wide smile for everybody, recoiled from me, frowningly extinguished her smile, and became truly a "little mask" from screwing up her face, the wrinkled mask of some humiliated caryatid that seemed indeed to bear the contact of my stroking hand as if she were suffering the weight of a stone cornice.

'Encountering the same sullenness every time, which seemed to spring from hostility, I eventually ignored the little marigold-coloured exotic, that would close up if I so much as stroked her hair... I no longer even spoke to her! "She senses that you are taking me from her," the Marquise would say. "Instinctively, she knows you are depriving her of part of her mother's love." And sometimes, truthful as she was, she would add: "The child is my conscience, and her jealousy, my remorse."

'One day, trying to broach the subject of her aloofness towards me, the Marquise received nothing but the broken, stubborn, facetious answers one extracts painfully, like teeth, from a child who refuses to

be drawn—"There's nothing wrong... I don't know"—and noting the hardness of the little bronze figure, she stopped asking, and out of lassitude dropped the subject...

'I have forgotten to mention that this strange child was very devout, with a kind of Spanish, medieval devotion, dark and super-stitious. She would wrap all sorts of scapulars around her skinny body, and plastered over her perfectly flat chest and hung around her sallow neck were stacks of crosses, Blessed Virgins, and Holy Ghosts! "Alas, you are an ungodly soul," the Marquise remarked to me, "and you might have scandalized her by something you said. I beg you to watch your tongue when she is present. Don't magnify my faults in the eyes of the child, I already feel so guilty about her!" And when the child's conduct did not alter or soften in any way: "You'll end up hat-ing her," said the Marquise, worried now. "And I shouldn't blame you." But she was mistaken: I felt merely indifference toward the sulky little thing, when she didn't actively irritate me.

'I had become polite with her, as adults do when they dislike each other. I treated her with exaggerated formality, addressing her as "Mademoiselle", to which she would return a glacial "Monsieur". She refused point-blank to do anything to make herself amiable, or to put herself out in the slightest way for me... Her mother never suc-ceeded in getting her to show me her drawings, or to play the piano for me. Sometimes I would surprise her, practising a piece with intense concentration, and she would leave off immediately, rise from the piano-stool, and play no more...

'Only once, at her mother's insistence (there were guests present), did she sit down at the open instrument, with one of her *martyred* expressions which, I assure you, had nothing gentle about it. She started to play through some piece or other, stumbling horribly, all fingers and thumbs. I was standing in front of the fire, looking at her from an oblique angle. Her back was turned towards me, and with no mirror in front of her she had no way of telling that I was looking at her... Suddenly her back (normally she sat with it curved, so that her mother would often say, "If you keep sitting like that, you'll end up with a weak chest")—her back straightened up, as if by gazing at her I had put a bullet through her spine and broken it. Slamming down the piano-lid, which made a fearful racket in falling, she fled the room... People went to fetch her back; but that evening no one could induce her to return.

'Well, it appears that the obtusest of men can never be obtuse enough, for there was nothing in the conduct of this sombre child, who interested me so little, to lead me to dwell on the nature of her feelings towards me. Neither did her mother. The latter, who was jealous of every other woman in her salon, was no more jealous of her daughter than I was obtuse about her. The girl's feelings were revealed when the Marquise, who was expansiveness itself in private, and still pale from terror at what she had felt, and now laughing hard at herself for having been so, was imprudent enough to impart to me the cause of it all.'

Like a clever actor, the Comte laid just the right stress on the word *imprudent*, knowing that the entire interest of the story must hang upon that word!

And it worked, apparently, for these twelve beautiful women's faces lit up again with a feeling as intense as that reflected in the faces of cherubim before the throne of God. Is not the curiosity of women as intense as the adoration of the angels?... He looked at them, then, with their cherubic faces, shoulders, and so on down—and finding them all ready for what he had to tell them, he resumed quickly and did not stop again:

'Yes indeed, the mere thought of it sent the Marquise into fits of laughter!—as she reported when she told me about it all a little while later; but she had not always found it funny!—"Imagine the scene," she said to me (I am trying to remember her exact words)—"I was sitting where we are now."

'(It was one of those double-backed couches, known as a *dos-à-dos*,* a perfectly designed item of furniture on which to quarrel and make up without moving.)

' "Happily you weren't there when a visitor was announced... can you guess who?... You'll never guess... the priest of Saint-Germain-des-Prés. Do you know him?... No, of course you don't, you never go to mass, which is very wicked of you... How could you know that this poor old priest is actually a saint, who never sets foot in a lady's house except to beg alms for the poor of the parish or for the church? I thought at first this was why he had come.

' "He prepared my daughter for her First Communion; since that time she communicates regularly, and she has kept him as her confessor. Which is why, since then, I have invited him many times to dinner—all to no avail... When he came in, he was extremely agitated.

Seeing his features, that were normally so serene, working with such great and undisguised distress, I realized it was not just his shyness, and I could not prevent myself from this unceremonious greeting:

'"'In heaven's name, what is the matter, Father?'

'"'What is wrong, Madame,' he replied, 'is that you see before you the most embarrassed man in all the world. I have been in holy orders for more than fifty years, and I have never been charged with such a delicate mission, or one that I understand less, as this one which concerns you...'

'"He sat down, and asked me to make sure that no one interrupted us for as long as our interview lasted. You know how much such formalities tend to frighten me... This he noticed.

'"'Madame, do not upset yourself so, you will need all your self-control to hear what I have to say and then explain to me this extraordinary thing, which in truth I cannot bring myself to believe... Mademoiselle your daughter, from whom I have just come, is an angel of purity and piety—you know this as well as I. I know her soul. I have held it in my hands since her seventh year, and I am certain that she is mistaken... perhaps because of her innocence... But this morning she came to tell me in confession that she was—you are not going to believe this any more than I do, Madame, but I must say the word... pregnant!'

'"I let out a gasp...

'"'I gasped just like you, in my confessional this morning,' resumed the priest, 'at this declaration, which she made accompanied by all the signs of the sincerest and most dreadful despair! I know this child through and through. She knows nothing of the world or of sin... Of all the girls in my confession, she is certainly the one I would vouch for most readily before God. That is all I can tell you! We priests are the doctors of the soul, and we are charged to deliver them of all their burdens with hands that neither wound nor stain. And so, proceeding with the utmost caution, I asked her, I questioned her, I pressed her, but once the despairing child had uttered the word, and confessed her fault, which she calls a hellish crime (the poor girl thinks she is damned!)—she said nothing more and retreated into a stubborn silence which she would not break except to beg me to come and see you, Madame, to tell you of her crime—"for my mother will have to know," she said, "and I will never have the strength to tell her!"'

' "I listened to the old priest of Saint-Germain-des-Prés, and I scarcely need describe the mixture of astonishment and anguish his words caused me! Like him, and even more than him, I was convinced of the innocence of my daughter; but often the innocent fall, even through their own innocence... And what she had said to her confessor was not impossible!... She was only thirteen, but she had become a woman, and her precocity had in fact frightened me... I was seized with an access of curiosity.

' " 'I want to know and I shall know everything!' I burst out to the poor old man, who stood before me, patting his hat, speechless with embarrasment.—'Leave me now, Father. She would not speak to you. But I am sure she will tell me everything... I shall drag everything out of her, and then we shall understand what is at present beyond our understanding!'

' "Upon which the priest left—and no sooner had he gone than I went up to my daughter's room, too impatient to ask her to come down and wait for her.

' "I found her before the crucifix above her bed, not kneeling, but prostrated, and pale as death. Her eyes were dry, but red, like eyes that have been crying heavily. I took her in my arms, sat her down next to me, then on my knee, and I told her that I could not believe what her confessor had just told me.

' "But she interrupted me to assure me, with anguish in her voice and expression, that what he had said was indeed true. And then, increasingly alarmed and amazed, I asked her for the name of the man who...

' "I did not finish... What a terrible moment! She buried her head and face in my shoulder... but I could see the back of her neck, which was burning scarlet, and I could feel her shuddering. And then she became stubbornly silent, as she had with the priest. It was a wall.

' " 'It must be someone very unworthy of you, since you seem so ashamed?' I said, trying to provoke her into speaking, since I knew her to be proud.

' "But she stayed silent, her head buried in my shoulder. This went on for what seemed like an eternity, when she said suddenly, without changing position: 'Promise me that you'll forgive me, mother.'

' "I swore that I would, at the risk of perjuring myself a hundred times over; not that I cared a whit! I was boiling over with

impatience... I thought my brain was going to come bursting out of my head...

'"In that case, it was Monsieur de Ravila!' she whispered, and stayed where she was, in my arms.

'"Oh, when she said that name, Amédée! I felt I had been punished with a single blow to the heart, for the great misdemeanour of my life. You are a man so terrible where women are concerned, and rack me with so many jealousies, that the horrible 'and why not?'—when one comes to doubt the man one loves—arose in me... But I had the strength to hide my feelings from the cruel child, who must have sensed that her mother was in love.

'"Monsieur de Ravila!' I exclaimed, with a voice that I felt must betray me completely—'but you never even speak to him!—You avoid him'—I was about to add, my anger rising, I could feel it... 'So you have both betrayed me!'—But I repressed that... Did I not have to pry out, one by one, every detail of this horrible seduction?... And so I asked her for them, with a gentleness that nearly killed me, when she herself released me from the vice-like grip, this torture, by saying quite ingenuously:

'"It was one evening, mother. He was in the big armchair in the corner by the fire, opposite the sofa. He stayed there a long while, then he got up, and I had the misfortune to go and sit in the armchair he had just left. Oh, mother!... I felt I had fallen into fire. I wanted to get up, but I couldn't... I didn't have the strength! And I felt... here, mother, feel here!... that what I had... was a child!...'"'

The Marquise had laughed, said Ravila, when she told him the story; but not one of the twelve women seated round that table dreamed of laughing—and nor did Ravila.

'So there you have it, Ladies, believe it or not,' he added, by way of conclusion, 'the crowning love, the most beautiful I have ever inspired in my life!'

He fell silent, and so did his listeners. They were pensive... had they understood him?

When Joseph was bound a slave to Potiphar's wife, he was so handsome, says the Koran, that the women he served at table cut their fingers with their knives from looking at him. But the age of Joseph is past, and our preoccupations over dessert are less beguiling.

'What a great ninny that Marquise of yours is, for all her wit, to have told you such a thing!' said the Duchesse, who decided to be

cynical, but who still had her golden knife in her hand, and had not used it to cut anything at all.

The Comtesse de Chiffrevas gazed deep into her glass of Rhenish wine, an emerald crystal glass, as mysterious as her reverie.

'And Little Mask?' she inquired.

'Oh, she got married to someone in the provinces—and then she died, very young, before her mother told me this story,' said Ravila.

'That, too...' said the Duchesse thoughtfully.

VILLIERS DE L'ISLE-ADAM

The Presentiment

Attende, homo, quid fuisti ante ortum et quod eris usque ad
occasum. Profecto fuit quod non eras. Postea, de vili materia
factus, in utero matris de sanguine menstruali nutritus, tunica
tua fuit pellis secundina. Deinde, in vilissimo panno involutus,
progressus es ad nos, - sic indutus et ornatus! Et non memor es
quae sit origo tua. Nibil est aliud homo quam sperma foetidum,
saccus stercorum, cibus vermium. Scientia, sapientia, ratio, sine
Deo sicut nùbes transeunt.

Post hominem vermis; post vermem foetor et horror. Sic, in
non hominem, vertitur omnis homo.

Cur carnem tuam adornas et impinguas quam, post paucos
dies, vermes devoraturi sunt in sepulchro, animam, vero, tuam
non adornas, - quae Deo et Angelis ejus praesentenda est in
coelis!

(Saint Bernard, *Meditations*)

ONE winter evening over tea, a group of us, who had in common a
taste for metaphysical enquiry, were gathered round a good fire at the
home of one of our friends, Baron Xavier de la V*** (a pale young
man, whose lengthy spells of military service in Africa, while still just
a youth, had exacerbated a singularly moody and rugged temperament). The conversation came round to a most sombre subject: the
nature of those extraordinary, stupefying, and mysterious coinci-
dences that arise in the lives of some people.

'This is a story,' he told us, 'that I shall tell without further com-
ment. It is true. You may find it striking.'

We lit our cigarettes and settled back to listen to the following
narrative:

'In 1876, at the Autumn solstice,* around the time when the ever-
growing number of shallow burials—expedited far too hurriedly, in
actual fact—began to revolt the Parisian bourgeoisie and set alarm-
bells ringing, one evening, at eight o'clock, after a most extraordinary
spiritualist seance, I went home feeling overcome by that hereditary

spleen I am a prey to, whose black obsessiveness undoes and reduces to nothing any effort of the Will.

'I have, on doctor's orders, frequently but vainly dosed myself on Avicenna's cassia brew,* or imbibed under every preparation extracts of iron, and trampling on all my pleasures, like a second Robert d'Arbrissel,* I have cooled the fiery edge of my passions down to Siberian temperatures, but nothing works!—So be it! It does indeed appear that I'm a person of morose and taciturn temperament! And yet, beneath my excitable surface, I must be made of sterner stuff, as they say, since despite this battery of treatments, I can still, equably enough, contemplate the stars.

'On the evening in question I was back in my room, lighting a cigar by the candles on the mirror, when I noticed that I was mortally pale! So I flung myself into my great armchair, an antique done out in deep red padded velvet, in which the passage of time, during my long reveries, seems to weigh less heavily. My dejection of spirits came on oppressively, until I became almost ill. Judging it impossible to shake myself free of the shadows by going out—especially when the capital was itself assailed by dreadful problems—I resolved to try and get away from Paris altogether, into the fresh air of the country, and lose myself in vigorous exercise, like some good days hunting, to change my mood.

'No sooner had the thought come to me, indeed *at the very instant*＊ I had decided on that plan of action, than there came into my mind the name of an old friend, whom I had not seen for many years, the Abbé Maucombe.

' "Abbé Maucombe!..." I murmured to myself.

'My last meeting with the learned priest dated back to just before he left on a long pilgrimage to Palestine. I had since had news of his return. He lived in a humble presbytery in a little village in central Brittany.

'Surely Maucombe disposed of a spare room or an outhouse of some kind?—Surely he must have gathered, on his travels, some ancient tomes... some curiosities from the Lebanon, perhaps? And I would lay a wager that the country houses in the neighbourhood had wild duck on their lakes... What could be more opportune!... And if I were to make the most of the last fortnight of the magical month of October, among the reddened rocks, before the cold set in; if I really wanted to see the long and resplendent autumn evenings on the wooded heights, then I would have to make haste!

'Nine o'clock chimed.

'I got up; I knocked the ash from my cigar. Then, like a man of purpose, I took my hat, my greatcoat, and my gloves; I took my suitcase and my shotgun; I blew the candles and went out—taking elaborate care and turning the key three times in the secret keyhole that is the pride of my door.

'Three-quarters of an hour later, the Brittany express was transporting me towards the little village of Saint-Maur, where the Abbé Maucombe had his living; I had even found the time, at the station, to post a hastily scribbled letter in which I advised the Reverend Father of my arrival.

'The next morning I was at R***, which is no more than around five miles from Saint-Maur.

'Anxious to get a good night's sleep (I wanted to be out with my shotgun at first light the following day), and judging that a siesta after lunch could possibly affect adversely my chances of getting an unbroken night's rest, to keep me awake despite my tiredness, I spent the day visiting old schoolfriends.—At around five-thirty in the evening, having acquitted myself of these duty-calls, I had them saddle up a horse at the Soleil d'Or, where I had got off, and as twilight fell I arrived within sight of a hamlet.

'As I rode towards it, I brought to mind the priest at whose home I had the intention of stopping for a few days. The lapse of time since our last meeting, the journeys and all the other events of life, in addition to his own reclusiveness, must have changed his appearance and his character. His hair would be greying. But I recalled the astringent conversation of the learned rector—and I allowed myself to anticipate with pleasure the long evenings I would be spending in his company.

'"Abbé Maucombe!" I kept murmuring to myself. "Excellent idea!"

'Enquiring of the old folk pasturing their animals by the path as to the whereabouts of his house, I was convinced of the affection that the priest—as the perfect evangelist of God's pity—was held in by his flock; and when I had been fully apprised of my direction, some way past the hovels and cottages that made up Saint-Maur, I went on my way.

'At last I arrived.

'The rustic aspect of the house, the windows with their green shutters, the three stone steps, the ivy, the clematis and the climbing roses

growing entwined on the walls up to the roof, where a little cloud of smoke escaped from the chimney-stack, filled me with ideas of calm, wholesomeness, and deep peace. Through a trellis gate I could see the trees in a nearby orchard, their leaves showing the rusting of the late season. The two windows of the single storey were burning with the late western light, and between them some saint stood in a niche that was set into the wall. Silently, I dismounted: I tethered my horse to the shutter and raised the door-knocker, casting a look, as travellers will, at the horizon now behind me.

'The horizon was shining brightly on the distant oak-forests and on the wild pines, above which the last birds were flying through the evening, and on the waters of a reed-covered lake, in the far distance, in which the sky was solemnly reflected; and nature herself looked so beautiful in this deserted landscape, in this becalmed moment when silence falls, that I remained—with the knocker still raised —dumbfounded.

'You, I thought, who find no refuge in your dreams, and for whom the land of Canaan, with its palm trees and flowing streams, never appears at dawn, though you have come so far under the hard stars, traveller so light-hearted at the start but now so sombre—O heart made for other exiles than those whose bitterness you share with your bad brothers—look! Here one can sit down on the stone of melancholy!—Here your dead dreams stir to life again, in advance of the moment of death! If you want in truth to experience the desire for death, draw near: here the sight of the sky exalts to the point of oblivion.

'The lassitude I experienced then was of the kind in which the nerves, being so fraught, jangle at the slightest disturbance. A leaf fell close to me; its furtive rustle made me start. And the magic horizon in this place came in through my eyes! Quite alone, I sat down on the doorstep.

'A few moments later, as the evening had suddenly cooled, I came back to a sense of reality. I rose abruptly and raised the door-knocker a second time, and looked at the laughing house.

'But scarcely had I glanced at it than I was forced to stop short again, and this time I wondered if I were not the plaything of some hallucination.

'Was it the same house I had seen just moments ago? But what age would I give it *now*, with those deep fissures visible through the pale

leaves?—The edifice seemed foreign; the windowpanes lit up by the rays of the dying sun glowed with a peculiar intensity; the hospitable porch still welcomed me up its three steps; but, looking more closely at the grey slabs, I saw they had just been polished, and bore the trace of carved letters. I knew then they had been taken from the neighbouring graveyard—its black crosses now quite apparent, close by me, at about a hundred paces. The house seemed so changed it made me shudder, and the knocker, when I let it drop, echoed through the place like a death-knell.

'These kind of *sights*, being more psychological than physical, vanish rapidly. Yes, absolutely no doubt about it, I had been the victim of the kind of intellectual exhaustion I mentioned earlier. Anxious to see a human face that would help dispel the vision, I lifted the latch without waiting and went in.

'The door, with the weight of a large clock, closed behind me.

'I was in a long corridor, at the other end of which, descending the staircase with a candle in her hand, was Nanon, the old housekeeper, smiling broadly.

' "Monsieur Xavier!"... she exclaimed, overjoyed to see me.

' "Good evening, my dear Nanon," I replied, swiftly handing over to her my suitcase and my gun. (My overcoat I had forgotten in my room at the Soleil d'Or.)

'I went up the stairs, and a minute later I clasped my old friend in my arms.

'The mutual affection in our first exchanges, and the melancholy caused by the time that had elapsed, weighed on my friend and I for a few moments.—Nanon came in with the lamp and announced that supper was ready.

' "My dear Maucombe," I told him, giving him my arm as we went down, "intellectual companionship is a lasting joy, and I see that we feel the same about it."

' "There are Christian spirits whose divine kinship binds them closely," he replied. "Yes.—The world has beliefs less 'reasonable' that command adepts to sacrifice, in their name, their own blood, their happiness and their duty. They are called fanatics!" he concluded, smiling. "Let us choose, as our faith, the most useful, since we are free, and we become our belief."

' "The fact that two and two makes four," I replied, "is very mysterious in itself."

'We went into the dining room. During the meal, once he had gently reproved me for neglecting him so long, the Abbé talked to me about the village.

'He told me about the country round about, and a few stories touching upon the local nobility.

'He regaled me with his own hunting stories and his angling triumphs: he was, in short, charmingly affable and lively.

'And all the while, like a swift go-between, Nanon bustled around us, her magnificent coif shaking like a multitude of wings.

'When I rolled a cigarette as we took coffee, Maucombe, who was a former officer in the dragoons, did the same; we puffed away in silence for a while, each thinking his own thoughts, and I observed my host closely.

'The priest was a tall man, about forty-five years old. Long grey hair encircled his lean, firm face. His eyes shone with mystical intelligence. His features were regular and ascetic, his body lithe, unbowed by the years. He moved easily in his long soutane. Steeped in knowledge and gentleness, his words were uttered in a well-modulated voice, issuing from healthy lungs. In short, he seemed to be in rude health: the years had scarcely worn him.

'He invited me into his little study-sitting room.

'The wear of travel and lack of sleep left me feeling shivery; the evening was very cold, a herald of winter. So it was a comfort when my knees were warmed by a fire of vine-shoots blazing between a couple of logs.

'Our feet on the fender, sunk deep in our armchairs of brown leather, we spoke, naturally, of God.

'I was tired: I merely listened.

'"To conclude, then," Maucombe said to me as he rose from his chair, "we are here to bear witness—through our works, our thoughts, our words, and our struggle against Nature—to bear witness *whether or not we weigh in the scale*."

'And he finished with a quotation from Joseph de Maistre:* "Between Man and God, there is only Pride."

'"That notwithstanding," I replied, "we have the honour of living (we children, spoiled by nature) in a brilliant century, do we not?"

'"Let us favour rather the Light of the centuries," he replied with a smile.

'We had reached the landing, candles in our hands.

'A long corridor, parallel to the one below, separated my room from that of my host:—He insisted on settling me in himself. We went in; he looked around to see that nothing I might need was missing, and then, as we shook hands and bade each other goodnight, a lively flare from my candle lit up his face.—This time I shuddered!

'Was it a dying man, standing there near the bed? The face before me was not, could not, be the same as that at supper! Or rather, if I could recognize it vaguely, it was as though I had not really seen it until now. I understood in a trice: the Abbé was giving me, this time in human form, the *second* sensation, that through some obscure analogy I had first experienced from his house.

'The head I now beheld was grave, and very pale, as pale as death, with lowered eyelids. Had he forgotten I was standing there? Was he praying? What was the matter with him?—His whole demeanour became suddenly of such solemnity that I closed my eyes. When I opened them, a second later, the good Abbé was still there—but now I recognized him!—The relief! His friendly smile dispelled my anguish. The impression had lasted less than the time it took to frame a question. It was a seizure, a kind of hallucination.

'For the second time, Maucombe bade me goodnight, and retired.

'Once I was alone: "A deep sleep, that is what I need!" I thought.

'Helplessly, I thought of Death; I offered my soul up to God's keeping and got into bed.

'One of the odd things about extreme tiredness is that sleep does not come immediately. Every hunter is agreed on the point. It is notorious.

'I was expecting to fall asleep, quickly and deeply. I had laid great store on getting a good night's sleep. But after ten minutes had elapsed, I had to accept that this nervous state was not to be tranquillized. I heard groans and creaks coming from the walls and the woodwork. The death-watch beetle,* without a doubt. Every tiny sound in the night found an echo in my being, like an electric shock.

'Outside, black branches thrashed together in the wind. Sprigs of ivy tapped continuously at my window. Above all, my hearing was as strained and acute as that experienced by men dying of hunger.

' "It's because I had two cups of coffee!"

'Raising myself with my elbow on the pillow, I started to stare fixedly at the light of my candle, on the bedside table. I stared at it between my eyelashes, with the expression of someone deeply lost in thought.

'A little stoup of holy water, of coloured china, with its branch of holy boxwood, was fixed above my bed. Brusquely, I splashed my eyelids with holy water to cool them, then I put out the candle and closed my eyes. Sleep was approaching: my fever was calmed.

'I was drifting into sleep.

'Three sharp, urgent taps sounded at the door.

' "What the...?" I said, starting up.

'I realized then that I had already entered my first sleep. I didn't know where I was. I thought I was in Paris. Some types of sleep lead to these foolish lapses of memory. Having almost instantly lost awareness of the principal cause of my waking, I stretched my limbs voluptuously, completely unconscious of the situation.

' "Wait a moment," I said suddenly, "didn't someone knock?—Who can possibly be calling...?"

'It was then that a shadowy notion dawned on me, that I was not in Paris but in a Breton presbytery, staying with the Abbé Maucombe.

'In a flash I was standing in the middle of the room.

'My first impression, along with the sudden cold under my feet, was of a strong light. The full moon, above the church, was shining directly into my window, through the white curtains, and its pale, desert-like flame was playing on the parquet.

'It was past midnight.

'Morbid ideas ran through my head. What was it? The shadow was extraordinary.

'As I approached the door, an ember-light, coming from the keyhole, played over my hand and wrist.

'There was someone behind the door: they had really knocked.

'And yet, at two steps from the latch, I stopped short.

'One thing seemed odd to me: the *nature* of the patch that was running over my hand. It was an icy, blood-red gleam which did not give light.—And how was it that there was no light coming through from the bottom of the door, that led into the corridor?—To speak truly, what was coming through from the keyhole seemed to me something like the sulphurous gaze of an owl!

'At that moment, the church clock struck the hour, outside in the night wind.

' "Who's there?" I demanded, in a hoarse whisper.

'The gleam went out:—I went closer...

'But the door opened wide, slowly and silently.

'Standing opposite me, in the corridor, was a tall, dark figure—a priest with a three-cornered hat on his head. The moon illuminated him entirely, everything except for his face: all I could see was the glare of his eyeballs that looked at me with unblinking solemnity.

'An exhalation from the other world hung about my visitor, and his appearance oppressed my soul. Seized by a terror that was mounting to its paroxysm, I stared at the desolate personage in silence.

'Suddenly, the priest raised his arms slowly towards me. He was offering me something heavy and vague. It was a coat. A large black coat, a travelling coat. He held it out to me, as if he wanted me to take it!...

'I closed my eyes, to avoid seeing that. Oh, I didn't want to see that! But a night bird, with a frightful screech, passed between us, and the breeze from its wingbeats, brushing my eyelids, made me open them. I sensed it was flying about the room.

'Then, with a low groan of anguish—I was too shocked to cry out—I slammed the door closed with both hands stretched out at arm's length and gave a violent turn of the key in the lock, in a state of frenzy, my hair standing up on my head!

'And none of this, strangely, seemed to make the slightest sound.

'It was more than my organism could take. I was fully awake. I sat up in bed, arms braced tensely in front of me; I was chilled; my forehead was soaked in sweat; my heart was beating wildly in my chest.

'"What a horrible dream!" I told myself.

'And yet my unconquerable anxiety remained. It took me a full minute even to *dare* stretch out my arm and grope for the matches. I dreaded the feel, in the darkness, of an icy hand seizing mine and giving it a friendly squeeze.

'I started nervously when I heard the matches rustle under my fingers in the iron candlestick. I relit the candle.

'Instantly, I felt better. Light, that divine vibration, disperses a funereal ambience and comforts night-time terrors.

'Having resolved to drink a glass of cold water to complete my recovery, I got out of bed.

'Passing in front of the window, I noticed one thing: the moon was exactly as it had been in my dream, even though I had not seen it before going to bed; and going to check the door, candle in my hand, I found that the key had been given one turn in the lock, *from inside the room*, which I certainly had not done before going to sleep.

'At these fresh discoveries, I glanced around me. The whole episode seemed to me increasingly unusual. I went back to bed, and reclining against my pillow I tried to reason things through, and prove to my own satisfaction that all I had experienced was a particularly vivid bit of sleepwalking; but I was less and less convinced. Then tiredness came over me like a wave, enfolded my black thoughts, and put me and my anguish to sleep.

'When I awoke, the room was flooded with sunlight.

'It was a gladsome morning. My watch, hanging from the bedpost, showed ten o'clock. There is nothing, surely, that so lifts the spirits as a morning radiant with sunlight. Especially when you feel the call of the countryside outside, all balmy with a light wind in the trees and the thorny thickets, and the ditches grown over with flowers still wet with dew!

'I dressed rapidly, forgetful now of the night's grim beginning.

'Completely revivified by repeated ablutions in cold water, I went downstairs.

'The Abbé Maucombe was waiting for me in the dining room: the table was laid, and he was reading a newspaper.

'We shook hands:

'"Did you have a good night, my dear Xavier?" he inquired of me.

'"Excellent!" I replied distractedly (out of habit and paying not the slightest attention to what I was saying).

'The truth is, simply, that I had a hearty appetite.

'Then Nanon came in with our breakfast.

'During the meal, our conversation was both tranquil and joyful. The man who lives a saintly life, and he alone, knows such joy and how to communicate it.

'All of a sudden, I recalled my dream.

'"By the way," I exclaimed, "I've just remembered that I had a most singular dream, my dear Abbé. It was so strange... how can I describe it? Let's see... striking? astonishing? terrifying?—I leave you to be the judge."

'And as I peeled an apple, I started to recount, in the greatest detail, the sombre hallucination that had visited me as I fell asleep.

'I had got to the moment when the priest was about to make me the *gesture* of offering me the coat, but *before I had started my phrase*—the dining-room door opened. With the lack of ceremony common

to rectors' housekeepers, Nanon came in, walking through the sunbeam, and interrupting me in full flow, handed me a paper:

'"Here is a 'very urgent' letter that the postman has just brought for Monsieur!" she said.

'"A letter!—Already!" I cried, *forgetting my narrative*. "It's from my father. How come?—My dear Abbé, will you permit me to read it?"

'"But of course!" said the Abbé Maucombe, distracted from the story just as I had been, and caught up by my own devouring interest in the letter: "But of course!"

'I opened it.

'So it was that Nanon's arrival, by its suddenness, put everything else out of our minds.

'"Something has come up, my friend: no sooner have I got here than I am obliged to depart."

'"How so?" asked the Abbé, putting his cup down without drinking.

'"I am instructed to return post-haste, to see to a business matter of the very gravest importance. I have to attend a hearing, which I thought would not take place until December: now I am informed that it will take place within the fortnight, and since I alone am in a position to gather the last documents that should prove us in the right, I must go!... What a terrible bore!"

'"Indeed, it is vexing!" said the Abbé, "Most vexing!... Promise me at least, that once the affair is concluded... Our major business is that of our own salvation, and I had hoped to play a part in yours—and now you are to escape me! I was beginning to think that the Almighty had sent you..."

'"My dear Abbé," I cried, "I shall leave you my shotgun. Before three weeks are out, I shall return, to stay for some weeks, if you agree."

'"Go in peace, then," said the Abbé.

'"You must understand, almost the whole of my fortune is at stake!" I murmured.

'"God is our fortune!" Maucombe said simply.

'"But how am I to survive in the future, if..."

'"In the future, we shall be no more," he answered.

'Shortly thereafter we rose from table, the blow somewhat softened by my formal promise to return.

'We went for a walk in the orchard and visited the outbuildings adjoining the rectory.

'All that day, the Abbé, not without some pride, showed me round his humble rustic treasures. Then, while he read his breviary, I walked out alone into the surrounding countryside, delighting in the sharp, pure air, which I breathed in deeply. When Maucombe returned, he spoke at some length of his journey to the Holy Land; by the time he finished it was sunset.

'The evening set in, and after a frugal supper, I said to the Abbé:

' "My friend, the *express* leaves at nine o'clock on the dot. From here to R*** takes an hour and a half. I shall need half-an-hour to return my horse, and settle up at the inn: that makes two hours. I must take my leave of you immediately."

' "I shall come part of the way with you," said the priest. "*The walk will do me good.*"

' "Oh, and by the way," I said, distractedly, "here is my father's address (I'll be staying with him in Paris) if we should need to write to each other."

'Nanon took the card and fixed it into a corner of the mirror.

'Three minutes later, the Abbé and I left the rectory and started up the main track. I led my horse by the bridle.

'Already, we were two shadows.

'Five minutes after starting out, a thin, penetrating, icy rain began to fall, carried by a sudden gust, striking our hands and faces.

'I stopped short.

' "My old friend," I said to the Abbé, "no! Decidedly I cannot accept this. Your existence is precious and this freezing downpour is very unhealthy. Go home. I insist; you could get dangerously soaked. Go home, I beg you."

'After a moment's reflection, and thinking of his flock, the Abbé conceded.

' "But I do have your promise, my dear friend?" he said.

'And as I held out my hand:

' "One moment!" he added; "I am aware that you have some way to go, and this rain is indeed penetrating."

'He shivered. We were standing close to each other, quite still, and gazing at each other intensely, like travellers in a hurry.

'At that moment the moon rose over the pines, from behind the hills, lighting up the woods and moorlands on the horizon. It bathed

us in its sad, pale light, in its cold, pale flame. Our two figures, with the horse, cast huge shadows on the track.—And from out of the stone crosses, back there—from the old ruined calvaries that litter this region of Brittany, from the niches where the birds of ill-omen sit, escaped from the wood of the Dying—I heard in the distance a frightful *screech*. The harsh and alarming falsetto of the rook. An owl with eyes of phosphor, perched on the main branch of an oak, took flight and passed between us, prolonging the screeching sound.

'"Come now!" went on the Abbé, "I shall be back home in a minute; so *take—take this coat!*—I insist! I very much insist!"—he added in an unforgettable tone.—"Have it returned to me by the boy from the inn who comes to the village every day... *I beg you.*"

'As he spoke, Maucombe handed me his black coat. I could not see his face, hidden by the shadow from his three-cornered hat: but I could make out his eyes, which *gazed at me with solemn fixedness*.

'He flung the coat over my shoulders and fastened it with urgency and tenderness, while, completely unmanned, I closed my eyelids. Taking advantage of my silence, he hastened towards his house. At the turn in the road, he was gone.

'By some presence of mind—and half-automatically—I mounted my horse. But I stayed where I was.

'Now I was alone on the track. I could hear the thousand sounds of the countryside. Opening my eyes again, I saw the enormous, livid sky crossed by dark, fast-moving clouds, which masked the moon—nature in her solitariness. But I held myself firm and upright, even though I must have been white as a sheet.

'"Come now!" I said to myself, "Calm down!—I am feverish and prone to sleepwalking. That is all."

'I tried to shrug my shoulders: but a secret weight prevented me.

'And then, coming from the woods on the far horizon, a flight of osprey passed over my head with a loud beating of wings, and screaming their horrible, incomprehensible syllables. They went and settled on the roof of the rectory and on the bell-tower next door; their desolate cries came to me on the wind. Dear God, I was frightened. Why? Who will ever explain it to me? I have seen combat, I have crossed swords on several occasions; I think my nerves are steelier than the most phlegmatic and the bluffest of men; and yet I humbly admit and affirm that at that moment I was seized with fear—with deadly fear.

I even conceived, for my own sake, some intellectual respect for it. Mock at it ye who never felt it.

'In silence, therefore, I spurred the sides of my poor horse cruelly, and with my eyes closed, the reins loose, and my fingers clenched round its mane, the coat streaming out behind me, I felt it galloping as violently as it was able, absolutely flat-out: from time to time it heard my deep groaning as I leaned forward, and I must have communicated to the beast, by instinct, the superstitious horror that possessed me. We arrived in less than half-an-hour. The sound of my horse's hooves on the roads leading into the town made me raise my head—and breathe again!

'At last! I saw houses! Shops lit up! Faces of my own kind behind windowpanes! I saw people in the street!... I had left the land of nightmares!

'At the inn I settled in front of a good fire. The cabbies' conversation sent me into something resembling ecstasy. I had emerged from Death. I looked at the light between my fingers. I gulped down a glass of rum. Bit by bit, I regained control of my faculties.

'I felt I had returned to real life.

'I was even—let me admit—a little ashamed of my panic.

'Also, how calm I felt when I acquitted myself of my errand for the Abbé Maucombe! How easy my smile when I examined the black coat as I handed it over to the hotelier! The hallucination had faded. I could easily have passed for Rabelais's "good companion".*

The coat itself seemed to have nothing extraordinary, or even odd about it—except for its extreme age, and that it seemed to have been re-patched, re-lined, re-hemmed with a kind of obsessive tenderness. The Abbé, being a deeply charitable man, had clearly given away in alms what he might have paid for a new coat: that, at least, is the explanation I gave myself.

' "You're just in time!" said the innkeeper. "The boy is on his way to the village, and he will deliver the coat back to the Abbé Maucombe before ten o'clock."

'One hour later, wrapped in my newly recovered travelling coat, my feet on the foot-warmer, I lit a good cigar and said to myself, as the locomotive gave a whistle:

' "Now I much prefer that sound to the hooting of owls."

'And I rather regretted, truth be told, having given my promise that I would return.

'With that I fell into a deep sleep, forgetting completely what I should from thenceforth consider an insignificant coincidence.

'I had to stop for six days in Chartres, to gather the documents that would, in the event, lead to the successful outcome of our hearing.

'Finally, my mind full of paperwork and chicanery—and in my usual state of nervous dejection—I got back to Paris, on the seventh day after I had left the rectory.

'I arrived home on the stroke of nine. I climbed the stairs. My father was in the drawing room. He was sitting next to a little table, under the lamp, and held an open letter in his hand.

'After a few words of greeting:

'"You cannot imagine the news this letter brings," he said. "Our dear old Abbé Maucombe has died since you left."

'At these words, I felt stunned.

'"What?" I replied.

'"Yes, dead—the day before yesterday, at around midnight—three days after you left the rectory—from a cold he caught on the big track. The letter is from old Nanon. The poor woman seems to have lost her head—she repeats the same thing twice... rather odd... about a coat... read it yourself!"

'He handed me the letter in which the death of the saintly priest was indeed announced—and I read these simple lines:

'"He was very happy—he said at the end—to be wrapped at his last breath and buried in the coat he had brought back from his pilgrimage to the Holy Land, *and which had touched* THE SEPULCHRE."'

The Desire To Be a Man

> ... that Nature might stand up
> And say to all the world: This was a Man!
>
> (Shakespeare, *Julius Caesar*)

MIDNIGHT was tolling from the Bourse,* under a sky filled with stars. At this period, the citizens were still constrained by military law, and under legal injunction relating to the curfew,* the waiters in those establishments where the lights were still burning were anxious to close.

Along the boulevards, and inside the cafés, the flutter of flame in the gaslit lamps went out rapidly in the darkness, accompanied by the clatter of chairs being stacked in fours on the marble tables. It was that psychological moment when every landlord chose to indicate—arm stretched out, ending in a table napkin—the Caudine Forks* of the back door to his lingering customers.

On that particular Sunday a melancholy October wind was blowing. A few yellow leaves, rattling dry and dusty, flew in the gusts, grazed the stones and skimmed the asphalt, and then, like bats, disappeared into the shadow, evoking the spectre of evanescent days gone forever. The theatres along the Boulevard du Crime,* where, during the evening, whole gangs of Medici, Salviati, and Montefeltre had stabbed each other to their heart's content, now rose up like haunts of Silence, with stoppered doors, guarded by their Caryatids. Cabs and pedestrians thinned out, minute by minute, and here and there the wary lanterns of the rag-pickers were already shining, phosphorescence thrown up by the heaps of detritus they were wandering over.

Adjoining the rue Hauteville, under a streetlamp, at the corner of a rather luxurious café, a tall personage with Saturnine physiognomy, smooth-shaven chin, and sleepwalker's gait, sporting long, greying locks beneath a Louis XIII-style felt hat, black-gloved, carrying an ivory-topped cane, and wrapped in an old royal-blue greatcoat edged with rather moth-eaten astrakhan fur, had stopped, as if hesitating automatically, before crossing the road leading to the Boulevard Bonne-Nouvelle.

Was this late straggler on his way home? Was it chance that his nocturnal wandering had led him to this street corner? To judge from his appearance, it would be difficult to say. Whatever the case may be, when he noticed, immediately to his right, one of those tall, narrow mirrors, shaped not unlike his own person—the kind of public mirror that sometimes adorns the front of stylish eating-houses—he halted suddenly and, faced by his own image, he looked at himself up and down, from his boots to his hat. Then, doffing his hat with a sudden gesture that was quite of its period, he bowed, not discourteously, at himself.

His momentary hatlessness revealed the gentleman to be none other than the celebrated tragedian Esprit Chaudval, born Lepeinteur, known as Monanteuil,* descendant of a distinguished family of

seafolk from Saint-Malo. The mysterious workings of Destiny had led him to become the leading man from the provinces, matinée idol and (often successful) rival to our own Frédérick Lemaître.*

While he was pondering in this kind of stupor, the waiters in the adjoining café were helping their last clients on with their coats and fetching their hats; others were turning the nickel cash-boxes upside down and noisily emptying the day's takings onto a round tray. This panic and haste was due to the menacing presence of two city constables, who had appeared from nowhere, and who stood with their arms crossed on the doorstep, glaring with their cold eyes at the dilatory landlord.

Soon the shutters were bolted down into their iron chassis—all except for the mirror-shutter that in the general precipitation had been, through a strange omission, inadvertently forgotten.

After that the boulevard grew silent. All alone, and too absorbed to notice the general dispersal, Chaudval had remained in his ecstatic pose at the corner of the rue Hauteville, on the pavement, in front of the forgotten mirror.

The pale and lunar mirror seemed to give the artist the feeling he would have got from bathing in a pool; Chaudval was shivering.

Alas! The truth must out—which was that in the dark and cruel mirror, the actor had just discovered he was getting old.

He remarked that his hair, pepper-and-salt only yesterday, was now quite white; it had happened just like that! Farewell encores and garlands, farewell roses of Thalia, laurels of Melpomene!* He must take his leave forever, with tears and valedictory handshakes, of the Ellevious and the Laruettes, of the great liveries and the curves, of the Dugazons* and the *ingénues*!

He must climb down rapidly from the chariot of Thespis and watch it disappear, his comrades still aboard! And he must watch the banners and banderoles that fluttered in the morning sun as far down as the wheels, playthings of the joyful wind of Hope, disappear at the turning in the road, twilight all around.

Suddenly conscious of his fiftieth year, Chaudval (who was an excellent man) sighed. A mist passed before his eyes and a kind of wintry fever seized him, and his pupils dilated as if he were hallucinating.

The way he stared so fixedly at the fateful glass finished by conferring on his pupils that ability to magnify objects and saturate them

with solemnity, a phenomenon physiologists have noticed in individuals when under the influence of very intense emotion.

The long mirror became deformed under his eyes, that were
charged now with vague and languid notions. Childhood memories
of beaches and silvery waves danced in his brain. And the mirror,
doubtless due to the presence of stars that deepened the surface,
seemed to him like the still surface of a gulf. And distending even
more, as the old man sighed, the mirror took on the likeness of the sea
and the night, those two old friends of the lonely-hearted.

He feasted on this vision for a while, but the streetlamp which reddened the thin cold drizzle at his back and over his head seemed to
him, reflected deep in the terrible glass, like the gleam of a *lighthouse*,
the colour of blood, which lured to shipwreck the vessel without
compass or future.

He shook off this hallucination and straightened up, to his full
height, and with a burst of nervous laughter that sounded bitter and
false, he startled the two constables under the trees. Most fortunately
for the artist, the two of them imagined it was some inoffensive drunk
or maybe a desperate lover, and continued on their round without
attaching any importance to the wretched Chaudval.

'Well then, let's call it a day!' he said simply and quietly, like a
condemned man who, woken by surprise, says to the hangman: 'I am
all yours, my friend.'

And then the old actor launched into a monologue, carried on in a
kind of bewildered prostration:

'I acted wisely', he went on, 'the other evening, when I charged
Mademoiselle Pinson, my good friend (who has the minister's ear, as
well as sharing his pillow), to obtain for me, between two ardent declarations, the position of lighthouse-keeper that my ancestors occupied on the Ponant coast. And now I come to think of it, I can see why
that streetlamp in the mirror produced such a strange effect on me!...
It was what I had in mind.—Pinson will send me my licence, there's
no doubt of that. And I shall retire to my lighthouse like a rat into a
cheese. I shall give light to the boats, far out at sea. A lighthouse! It
always seemed to me rather like a stage-set. I am all alone in the world:
and that is decidedly the haven best fitted to my declining years.'

Suddenly, Chaudval interrupted his reverie.

'But of course!' he said, patting at his chest underneath his greatcoat... 'that letter the postman handed me, just as I was going out,

that must be the reply?... I went into the café to read it and forgot all about it!—I'm really slowing down!—Ah, here it is!'

Chaudval had just extracted a large envelope from his pocket, from which, once he had torn it open, dropped a ministerial document. Feverishly, he picked it up and ran his eye over it, under the fiery red of the streetlamp.

'My lighthouse! My licence!' he exclaimed. '*Saved*, by God!' he added automatically, as if out of long habit, and in a voice so cracked and falsetto, so unlike his own, that he looked around, as if it belonged to someone else.

'Come now, be calm... and... *be a man!*' he went on after a moment.

But having said this, Esprit Chaudval, born Lepeinteur, known as Monanteuil, stopped short as if changed into a statue made of salt. The expression seemed to have paralysed him.

'What?' He went on after a pause. 'What have I just wished?—To be a Man?... And why not, after all?'

He crossed his arms and thought it through.

'For nearly half a century I have *acted*, I have *played* the passions of other people without ever feeling them—in fact I have never felt anything, myself.—So am I nothing like these "others" except for a laugh?—So does that make me nothing but a *shadow*? Passions! Feelings! Real actions! REAL! They are the things that make up a MAN! Now that age is forcing me to rejoin the human race, I owe it to myself to take possession of the passions, or at least of some *real* feeling... because that is the *sine qua non* for anyone pretending to the title Man. Now that's solidly argued; that's blinding common sense.—So let us choose something most in keeping with the nature I have brought back to life.'

He thought for a moment, and went on in a melancholy tone:

'Love?... Too late.—Glory?... I have known it!—Ambition?... Leave that bauble to the politicians!'

Suddenly he let out a cry:

'I have it!' he said: 'REMORSE!...—that's what my dramatic temper needs.'

He looked at himself in the mirror, pulling a face stretched and convulsed as if by some inhuman horror:

'That's it!' he finished: 'Nero! Macbeth! Orestes! Hamlet! Erostratus!*—Ghosts!... Yes! Now it's my turn to see *real*

ghosts!—like all those aforementioned gents, who were lucky enough to see ghosts round every corner.'

He struck his forehead.

'But *how?*... Am I innocent as the newborn lamb?'

And after a further *pause*:

'Ah, *it depends on that!*' he went on. 'The end must have the means... I must surely have the right to become what I *am meant* to be? Humanity is my right! If I'm to feel remorse, I must commit the crime to go with it! Well so be it, I'll go with crime: what difference does it make, as long as I commit it... with the right intention?—Exactly so...—It's settled!' (And he started to speak in dialogue) '—I shall do atrocious things.—When?—Straightaway. Don't put off till tomorrow...—What crimes?—Just one!... But huge!—An atrocity, an enormity! Something to bring all the Furies forth from hell!—What, then?—The most dazzling, of course... Bravo! I have it! FIRE! Time is pressing! I must start my blaze and pack my trunks! And then return, duly muffled behind the window of some cab, to enjoy my triumph among the desperate crowds! I must harvest the curses of the dying—and then take my train to the north-west, with enough remorse on my plate to last the rest of my days.

'And then I shall go and hide out in my lighthouse! In the light, out at sea! Where the police will never find me—for my crime will be *disinterested*.* And I shall lament all alone.'—Here Chaudval straightened up, practising this line, absolutely worthy of Corneille:*

'Washed of Suspicion by th'Enormity of the Crime!

'It is spoken.—And now,'—concluded the great actor, picking up a cobblestone and looking around to make sure he was quite alone—'and now *you*, you will never reflect anyone again.'

And he hurled the stone against the glass, which shattered into a thousand dazzling shards.

This first duty expedited, he hurried away—satisfied with this initial, but nonetheless energetic and striking act—and rushed towards the boulevards where, a few minutes later, he hailed a cab, jumped into it, and disappeared.

Two hours later the flare of a huge catastrophe, leaping up from large depots of petrol, oil, and matches, licked against all the window-panes in the district of Le Temple. Soon there were squadrons of firemen rolling and pushing their machines, rushing in from all sides,

their bugles sounding sinister blasts, waking with a start the citizens of that densely populated area. The sound of numberless running feet echoed on the pavements, and the crowd assembled in the large Place du Château d'Eau and the neighbouring streets. People were already being organized into water-chains. In less than quarter of an hour the soldiery had closed off the area, and policemen kept the crowds moving, by the ruddy light of torches, away from the fire.

Carriages came to a standstill, gridlocked. Everyone was shouting. Further off, cries could be heard coming from the terrible crackling of the fire. Victims trapped in that hell were screaming, and burning roofs caved in on top of them. Around a hundred families, from the burning workshops at the centre of the blaze, were trapped, deprived of relief or refuge.

Some way off, a solitary carriage, with two stout trunks on its roof, was stationed behind the milling crowd in the Place du Château d'Eau. And there in the carriage sat Esprit Chaudval, born Lepeinteur, known as Monanteuil; from time to time he parted the blind to contemplate his handiwork.

'Ha, ha!' he muttered to himself, 'now I feel an object of horror to God and man!—Yes, that is indeed the look of one rebuked!...'

The good old actor's face looked radiant.

'O wretch!' he hissed between his teeth, 'what dreadful avenging insomnia I shall suffer, a prey to the ghosts of my victims! I feel mingling within me the souls of Nero, burning Rome with an artist's exaltation! Of Erostratus, burning the temple at Ephesus to immortalize his name!... Of Rostopschin,* burning Moscow for love of his country! Of Alexander, burning Persepolis for love of his immortal Thais!... But I, I burn out of DUTY, having no other means of *existence*!—I burn because I owe it to myself... I acquit myself! What a Man I shall be! Now at last I shall know what it feels like to have a tormented conscience! What sumptuous nights of horror I shall have!... At last, I can breathe... I feel born anew... I exist!... To think that I have lived as an actor!... And now I am no more, to the vulgar eyes of common mortals, than fodder for the scaffold—let us flee at the speed of light! Let us shut ourselves away in our lighthouse, to enjoy our remorse at leisure.'

Two days later, in the evening, having travelled without hindrance, Chaudval reached his destination and took possession of his old, abandoned lighthouse, situated along our northern coasts: an

obsolescent lamp atop a dilapidated structure, that an act of ministerial compassion had relit on his behalf.

It was hardly as if the beacon were of any use to anyone: all that was
nothing but a superfetation, a sinecure, a dwelling with a flame on its
roof which everyone could do without, except for Chaudval.

So it was that the worthy tragedian, having brought with him bed-
ding, victuals, and a tall mirror with which to study the effects of all
this on his physiognomy, shut himself up without more ado in his
lighthouse, out of reach of human suspicion.

All around him murmured the sea, where the old abyss of the heavens
dipped its starry points. He watched the waves breaking on his tower,
driven by the squalls, much as the Stylite* might have watched the sand
scatter against his column, driven by the gusts of the desert storm.

He watched distractedly, in the distance, the vapour from the
steamboats and the sails of fishing boats ply back and forth.

And every moment, the dreamer forgot about his fire.—He went
up and down his stone staircase.

On the evening of the third day, Lepeinteur—shall we call him?—sat
in his room, sixty feet above the waves, rereading a Paris newspaper in
which the events surrounding the great disaster were recounted.

'An unidentified miscreant is reported to have thrown some lighted
matches into a petrol depot. The monstrous fire that ensued in the
area of the Faubourg du Temple kept the firemen and the surrounding neighbourhoods at their exertions all night.

'There were close on one hundred casualties: unfortunate families
plunged into the blackest despair.

'The whole area was in mourning, and still smoking.

'The name of the wretch who did this deed is unknown, as is the
motive for the crime.'

On reading this, Chaudval jumped for joy, and rubbing his hands
with delight exclaimed:

'What a huge success! What a wonderful villain I am! Shall I be
sufficiently haunted? What ghosts I shall see! I was sure that I would
become a Man! Ah, I admit that the way was hard! But it had to be
done!... It had to be done!'

Turning back to the newspaper, which continued with the
announcement that a charity performance was to be given to raise
money for the victims of the fire, Chaudval murmured:

'Well, well! I should have deployed my talent and come to the aid

of my victims!—It would have been my final performance. I would have declaimed *Orestes.** I would have been extremely lifelike...'

And with that, Chaudval began living in his lighthouse.

The evenings fell, and after them the nights, in succession.

Something which stupefied the artist came to pass. Something appalling.

Contrary to his hopes and expectations, his conscience dictated nothing resembling remorse. No ghost made its appearance.—He felt *nothing, absolutely nothing!*...

He could not believe the Silence. It dumbfounded him.

Sometimes, scrutinizing himself in the mirror, he noticed that his cheery countenance had not changed in the least!—In fury, he dashed up to the beacon and tampered with it, in the radiant hope of luring some steamboat onto the rocks—anything to help activate or stimulate his stubborn remorse!—To bring on his ghosts!

All to no avail!

A complete waste of time and effort! He felt *nothing*. He saw not a single threatening spectre. He couldn't sleep any more, stifled as he was by despair and *shame*. Until one night, suffering a cerebral attack in his luminous solitude, in torment he cried out—accompanied by the sound of the ocean and the gales howling round his tower standing out there in the infinite: 'Ghosts!... For the love of God!... Just one, let me see just one!—*I have earned it!*'

But the God he invoked refused to grant this favour—and the old ham expired, declaiming in his florid style his ardent desire to see ghosts—*not realizing that he had himself become that which he sought.*

Sentimentalism

> I esteem myself but little when I look at myself; highly, when I compare myself to others.
>
> (Mr Everyman)

ONE evening in spring, two well-brought-up young people, Lucienne Emery and the Comte Maximilien de W***, were seated under the tall trees of the Champs-Élysées.

Lucienne is that beautiful young woman who always wears black, whose face has a marble pallor, and whose past is obscure.

Maximilien, whose tragic end we heard about, *was* a wonderfully talented poet. Further, he was attractive, and elegant in his manners. An intellectual light shone in his eyes that were charming, but, like precious stones, a touch cold.

The two had been intimate for six months at most.

On that evening they sat in silence and watched the dim silhouettes of cabs, shadows, passers-by. Suddenly, gently, Madame Emery took her lover's hand.

'Does it not seem to you, my friend, that as the result of being ceaselessly excited by artificial, and, in a manner of speaking, by abstract impressions, great artists—like yourself—end up by blunting their capacity *really* to undergo the torments or the pleasures that Destiny puts in their way! At the very least, you have difficulty in expressing—something which people might take for lack of sensitivity—the personal sentiments that life bids you feel. Judging from the cold deliberation of your movements, people might think that you only throbbed as a matter of courtesy. A preoccupation with Art, no doubt, pursues you constantly, even in love and grief. From the habit of analysing the complexities of these feelings, you fear too much not being perfect in your responses, is that not so?... You can never rid yourself of that niggling thought. It paralyses your noblest flights and tempers all natural expansiveness. It's almost as if—being princes of a different universe—an invisible crowd surrounds you ceaselessly, ready to praise or blame.

'In short, when you experience some great joy or misfortune, what stirs in you first of all, even before your mind has really taken anything in, is the obscure desire to seek out some retired actor to ask *how you should be carried away* and what gestures are appropriate for the circumstance. Does the pursuit of Art then lead to a certain hardening?... That worries me.'

'Lucienne,' replied the Count, 'I once knew a singer who stood by his fiancée's death-bed, and listening to his sister's convulsive sobbing, could not restrain himself from commenting, despite his own affliction, on the defects of her vocalizing. He even thought of certain exercises that would give her sobs "more body". Does that seem horrible to you?... And yet, it was the singer who died of his grief, while the sister came out of mourning at the first prescribed opportunity.'

Madame Emery looked at Maximilien.

'Listening to you,' she said, 'it would be hard to define in what true feeling consists, and by what outward signs it might be recognized.'

'I should be glad to enlighten you on the subject,' replied Monsieur de W*** with a smile. 'But the technical... terms... er... are unpleasant, and I rather fear...'

'Stop that! I have my bunch of Parma violets, and you have your cigar; so please go on.'

'Very well, then! I shall obey,' replied Maximilien. 'The cerebral fibres affected by the feelings of joy or pain appear, you seem to be saying, distended in the artist, by the excess of intellectual emotion required on a daily basis by the cult of Art.—In my opinion, these mysterious fibres are merely sublimated!—Other men seem content with more predictable shows of tenderness, and with passions more openly expressed, more *serious*, in fact... My own view is that the placidity of their organisms, still somewhat occluded by Instinct, causes them to present, in lieu of supreme expressions of emotion, mere overflowings of animality.

'I maintain further that their hearts and brains are served by nervous centres which, enveloped in the torpor of habit, send out infinitely fewer and more muffled vibrations than our own.

'These leaden natures are what the world calls acting "in character"—their hearts, their beings—are violent and empty. Let us refrain from being duped by the dullness of their cries. To broadcast weakness in the secret hope of rendering it contagious, in order to benefit, at least in one's own eyes, from the real emotion that one has provoked in others—thanks to a shadowy pretence—is really only suitable for fragmentary beings.

'By what right can they claim that their writhings, of a more than dubious alloy, are required in the expression of life's sufferings or ecstasies, and how dare they accuse those who have the discretion to abstain from them of being insensitive?* Is the ray that strikes a diamond in the raw state more truly reflected than in one properly cut in which the essence of fire enters? In truth, those men and women who let themselves be carried away by such crude expressiveness are of the type that prefer confused noises to deep melodies: that is all.'

'Excuse me, Maximilien,' interrupted Madame Emery: 'I am listening to your rather subtle analysis with very real admiration... but would you be kind enough to tell me what hour is chiming?'

'Ten o'clock, Lucienne!' replied the young man, consulting his watch by the light of his cigar.

'Ah!... That's all right, then.—Do go on.'

'Why all of a sudden this anxiety about the time?'

'Because our love affair has one more hour to go, my friend!' replied Lucienne. 'I have a rendezvous with Monsieur de Rostanges at eleven-thirty this evening; I have put off telling you this till the last moment.—Are you angry with me?... Please forgive me.'

If the Count turned a little paler at these words, the ambient darkness veiled his emotion; not a flicker betrayed the effect of this announcement on his being.

'I see!' he said in an even and well-modulated tone. 'A most accomplished young man who well deserves your affection. Then I shall say my *adieux*, dear Lucienne.'

He took his mistress's hand and kissed it.

'Who knows what the future may have in store?' replied Lucienne with a smile, even though she was rather taken aback. 'Rostanges is merely an irresistible caprice...—and now,' she went on after a brief silence, 'go on, my friend, I beg you. I should like to know, before we take our leave of each other, *what is it that gives great artists the right to be so scornful of the behaviour of ordinary mortals?*'

There was a pause, silent and terrible, beween the two lovers.

'We experience, to put it simply, ordinary feelings as intensely as the next man,' Maximilien went on. 'Yes indeed, the natural, *instinctual* fact of an emotion we experience physically, just like everyone else! But it's only at the very *outset* that we experience it in that human way!

'It is the near impossibility of expressing its immediate *repercussions* that makes us, almost always, seem paralysed, in so many circumstances. By the time most men have got over and forgotten such emotions, through a failure of vitality, in us they get louder, rather like the sound of roaring as you approach the sea. Such perceptions and their hidden repercussions, such infinite and marvellous resonances, these alone are the things that establish the superiority of our race. This is the source of the apparent discrepancy between thought and act when one of us tries to express, in the conventional manner, what he feels. Think of the distance that separates us from those early ages of Feeling, buried so long ago in the depths of our spirit. The flatness of the voice, the inappropriateness of the gesture, being lost

for words, all of this is in contradiction with the sincerities and banalities of current usage, tailored to the way the majority experiences emotion. We ring false: people think us cold. Observing us, women can't believe their eyes. They imagined that we too would be moved, at least a little—and drift off into our "clouds" where, according to a saying which suits the Bourgeoisie, we "poets" are meant to take refuge. They are astonished to see quite the contrary! The disdainful horror they feel, discovering this, for those who duped them on our behalf, is excessive—and would procure us some amusement, if we were vengeful.

'No, Lucienne, it does not do for us to travesty ourselves with the false and extroverted performances that people put on. It is vain for us to try and wear the old human cast-offs that have lain forgotten in our antechamber since time immemorial!—People identify us with the essence of Joy! With the living idea of Grief! That's how it is.—We alone among men have come into possession of an almost divine aptitude: being able to translate, simply from our contact with it, the transports of Love, or its torments, into a form that has immediate universality. That is our deep secret. Instinctively, we keep it hidden, to spare our neighbour, as far as possible, from the shame of not understanding us.—Alas! We are like those potent crystals that enclose, in the Orient, the pure essence of dead roses, which have been hermetically sealed by a triple envelope of wax, gold, and parchment.

'A single teardrop of this essence—an essence kept in the precious amphora (which represents the fortune of the whole race and is handed down as a sacred treasure with the blessing of the elders)—a single teardrop, I tell you Lucienne, is enough to infuse volumes of clear water! And the latter can perfume dwellings and tombs for years on end!... But we are not the same (and therein lies our crime) as these flasks filled with dull perfumes, sad and sterile phials that people mostly neglect to stopper and whose virtue therefore sours or disperses on every passing wind.—Having conquered a purity of feeling inaccessible to the uninitiated, we would become liars in our own eyes if we were to participate in the "expected" mime-shows and expressions that satisfy the vulgar. Indeed we would hasten to disabuse him if he took upon faith the first cry that a happy or fatal event sometimes draws from us. It is from a very exact notion of Sincerity, precisely, that we owe it to ourselves to be sober in our movements,

scrupulous in our language, reserved in our enthusiasms, and self-contained in our despairs.

'Is it therefore the *quality* of our emotional faculties which earns us the imputation of callousness?... In truth, my dear Lucienne, if we were anxious (God forbid) to cease being misunderstood by most individuals—or to require from them any other form of homage than indifference—it would effectively then be desirable that a good actor, placing himself behind us and passing his arms under our own, spoke and gesticulated on our behalf. Then we would indeed be certain to touch the masses by the only means accessible to them.'

Deep in thought, Madame Emery pondered the honourable Monsieur de W***.

'But really, my dear Maximilien,' she exclaimed, 'soon you won't be able to say "good morning" or "good evening" for fear of stooping to the level... of mere mortals!—You do have your exquisite and unforgettable moments, and I am proud of having inspired them in you...—Sometimes you have dazzled me with the depths of your heart and with the sweet, sudden accesses of your tenderness; yes, and there have been indescribable, troubling ecstasies that I shall never ever forget!... But what can I do?... For then you slip beyond me—with a look I cannot fathom!—and I shall never be entirely persuaded that you actually feel yourself, except through the imagination, what you inspire in others.—And this is why, Max, I have no alternative but to leave you.'

'I shall therefore resign myself to not being *ordinary*, even at the risk of provoking the scorn of the good folk who (perhaps rightly) consider themselves better organized than me,' replied the Count. 'In any case, these days everybody seems proof to feeling anything whatsoever. I hope that soon there will be four or five hundred theatres per capital in which, the ordinary events of life being played out markedly better than they are in reality, no one will bother very much about living anything through for themselves. When they feel like being stirred or impassioned, they'll simply book a seat.—Surely that would be a thousand times better, from the common-sense point of view?... Why exhaust oneself in passions destined to oblivion?... And what is not half-forgotten, over the course of one season?—Oh, if you only knew the silence we bear within ourselves!... But forgive me, Lucienne: ten-thirty has just gone, and it would be indecorous of me, in the light of your earlier confidence, not to draw your attention

to the fact,' murmured Maximilien, getting to his feet with a smile.

'And your conclusion?...' she said. 'I still have time.'

'I conclude', replied Maximilien, 'that when some nobody, beating the outer casing of his chest as if to daze himself on the emptiness he feels within, yells out: "He is too intelligent to have a heart!" it is, first of all, very probable that the said nobody would fly into a rage if one replied that he himself had "too much heart to be intelligent!"; which in itself rather proves that our choice is the more valid, given his furious involuntary reaction. And what becomes of that phrase, when submitted to critical scrutiny? It is like saying: "That person is too well brought-up to have good manners!" In what do good manners consist? This is something the vulgarian, and the man who is truly well brought-up, will never know, despite all the puerile and worthy codes governing the subject. In fact, what that phrase really betrays, naively enough, is the instinctive jealousy, and even the *melancholy* in certain natures that comes out when confronted with our own. In fact, what separates us is not a difference: it is an infinity.'

Lucienne got up and took the Count's arm.

'I shall take this axiom away from our discussion,' she said. 'That however contrary your words and your actions seem sometimes to be, in the dreadful or joyful circumstances of your life, this does not in any way prove that you are...'

'—Made of wood!...' finished off the Count with a smile.

They watched the lighted cabs go past. Maximilien hailed one of them down. When Lucienne was safely seated, the young man bowed to her, silently.

'Goodbye!' cried Lucienne, blowing him a kiss.

The cab drove off. The Count watched it for a while, as usual. And then, still smoking his cigar, he walked back up the Avenue to his home, which was at the Rond-Point.

Alone in his room, seated at his desk, he took a little file out of a box of toiletries and was soon apparently absorbed in polishing the ends of his fingernails.

Then he wrote a few lines on... a Scottish valley, in response to a memory that had come to him, rather strangely, from some corner of his mind.

Then he cut a few pages of a new book, glanced through them—and threw it down.

A clock chimed two in the morning: he stretched.

'Really, this heartbeat is unbearable!' he murmured.

He got up, released the heavy curtains and hangings so they fell to, went to a little desk, opened it, took a small hand-pistol out of a drawer, went to stand by a sofa, put the weapon to his chest, smiled, shrugged his shoulders, and closed his eyes.

A dull shot, muffled by the draperies, rang out; and a little blueish smoke came from the chest of the young man, as he fell among the cushions.

Since that time, when they ask Lucienne why she wears such mourning colours, she answers her lovers gaily:

'Oh, I don't know! Black suits me so well!'

But then her dark fan starts to tremble on her breast, like the wing of a moth over a gravestone.

CATULLE MENDÈS

What the Shadow Demands

THE scene is the prison of La Roquette,* in the cell of a condemned man.

'Gentlemen, I thank you. You have brought me paper, envelopes, a pen, an inkwell' (he arranged these objects before him on the table as he spoke), 'thank you indeed. Thanks also to Monsieur le Directeur, governor of the prison, for allowing me to keep a light burning for a part of this night. I have a letter to write. This will take me a little while; and I believe, yes I believe' (and here he chuckled, almost mischievously) 'that I only have a few hours left me. So I bid you good evening, gentlemen. Sleep well, sleep well, while I write. I sense that we shall be woken early tomorrow morning. And so goodnight.'

One of the warders left the cell, followed by a heavy scraping sound as the bolt was shot to in the thick wall. The other warder stretched out on a camp-bed placed directly in front of the door. He was soon snoring away peacefully. The prisoner caused them no concern whatever. He was a sickly, prematurely aged little man, whose fingers continually trembled. He was always cooperative and gentle in manner, notwithstanding the atrocity of his crime. They had never once had to use the straitjacket on him. And he would assuredly be as gentle as a lamb when they led him to the guillotine, a lamb who knew where he was going, but who would offer no resistance. In that whiteish and brownish cell, where the candle flame burned absolutely straight, the little man, with his nose pressed up against the paper, scraped away with his pen, the only sound to be heard between the snores.

In the way of methodical people, he began by adddressing the envelope: 'For the Attention of the Chaplain, Prison of La Roquette.' And he underlined an instruction: 'Not to be opened before my death.' Excellent. Now for the letter. And he began to write, carefully, but without undue haste—he was used to the slight trembling

in his fingers—like a conscientious clerk calmly copying out a report. His writing was very close and small.

'Reverend Sir, I must ask you to forgive me for having so long postponed, despite your charitable enquiries, revealing to you the motive behind the abominable murder I have committed. I *could not allow* the cause of my crime to be known before its perpetrator found himself beyond the reach of all absolution or mercy. For my salvation would have been a disobedience. But today—this afternoon, this very evening—I knew by some infallible signs that the decisive moment was near, in the instants when, given the positioning and height of the two narrow windows, my appearance in the shadow projected on the wall seemed to flout every natural law... Just now, for instance, while I was speaking to my warders, seated not behind, but in front of the candlestick, the *trenchant* absence of what I still possess was so clear-cut in the shadow cast, I knew the time was close when all would be resolved, and my appearance corrected. I knew that just before dawn, Monsieur le Directeur, governor of the prison, would come in here, accompanied by others, and tell me that I must resolve to die. Which gives me just time to write this letter of explanation...

'It is indeed extraordinary that a man like myself, not wicked, not demented, but a straightforward fellow, born of decent folk, well brought-up and respectably employed—I was, you will recall, a haberdasher in Rémy-sur-Oise—that a man like myself, I say, should be guilty, and without any hatred to motivate it, as if I did it for pleasure, of such a dreadful and calculated murder. I can imagine the stupefaction of the members of the jury, of the court, of the doctors appointed to report on my mental health. (I have been careful not to reveal the truth, they would have taken me for a madman! I would have been acquitted, and therefore unable to fulfil my destiny.) I can also well understand your bewilderment before me, Chaplain. Because you know no more than the others.

'But I know...

'One thing that surprises even me, however, is that I was not aware of this thing immediately, I mean even after I had attained the age of reason. Was it because, as a child, with undisciplined mind and eyes, I simply didn't notice the strangeness of my condition, or possibly I believed that everyone shared it? No, instinct alone would have informed me that I was somehow afflicted. Could it be, then, that the

places where I worked and played—the schoolroom, the little vegetable garden behind my parents' neat house—simply prevented my noticing the anomaly? No again, because light plays through the bars of a schoolroom window as freely as it does elsewhere; and the garden wall was a good deal taller than I was at shoulder-height. Having pondered the question for a long time, I have come to the conclusion that in my boyhood and early adolescence I was—as far as conformity to natural laws goes, and especially as concerns the one whose eventual disfunction compelled me to murder by way of expiation—I was, I repeat, in every particular constituted like the other boys. The thing that was to alter the direction of my life developed only later, with the onset of manhood proper. And in a way, is it not normal, is it not in fact logical, that given the most unbelievable involution of eternal rules, an irregularity that implied for the person concerned—such was my case—some fatal demand, some ineluctable duty—should make itself manifest at a time in life when a person finds himself able to act on this demand, to fulfil this duty?

'Let me now outline for you, Reverend Father, how and when I first understood the nature of the necessity that I have obeyed with horror, but also with resignation, and even, perhaps, with pride! For is a man that, even through crime, has assuredly rescued both humankind and nature from unimaginable disorder and disaster—is such a man, I repeat, not entitled to feel a little pride in himself?

'Since my father deemed unsatisfactory the education I was receiving at the school of Saint-Rémy-sur-Oise (the teacher, who was a very pale young man, down from Paris, cared little for teaching the scriptures or arithmetic, but spent most classes reading aloud texts concerning death and eternity, texts I didn't understand, and that terrified me); and since the trade of hatmaker does not require any great erudition, my father, who intended to pass the business on to me, decided, after my fourteenth birthday, to keep me with him. I never saw the schoolmaster again, and if I remember rightly, he was asked to resign, the authorities deeming him a little mad. I made a very docile and contented apprentice. I grew, though not much, but I enjoyed good health, despite my slightly stunted appearance. I thought no more of the dark and disturbing hocus pocus fed to us by the wild-eyed young teacher, with his hair standing up on end. My parents were very good to me. In my hours off work they would let me play as I liked in the garden or the street. I ate well, I slept well.

I already had a taste of what my life would always be, a calm vista stretching ahead. Even at fifteen, I scarcely felt the disturbances associated with the onset of puberty. My mother rejoiced at my placidity. And yet I have to confess that, from sixteen on, I would steal more glances than were strictly appropriate at the new apprentice, a young girl, still a child almost, who came daily and worked in the back of the shop, sowing on hatbands and the peaks for caps. She would end up with scores of little black pinpricks on her fingertips. But she had such pretty eyes, glowing with life, under her mop of unruly red curls! And between her freckles, her skin was so white.

'She was the daughter of our neighbour, the village druggist. She was a bit skinny, and had long arms that she didn't quite know what to do with—they would hang down awkwardly when she had stopped working. I found her charming, just as she was. When I gazed at her, seated on the other side of the table, she would laugh, or else she would cry; and when she cried she was prettier still. You must forgive me, Reverend Father, for recounting these follies, perhaps not entirely untainted by sin. My excuse is that I did intend to marry her, when I came of age and got established.

'We used to meet on spring mornings, in the clump of willows by the river. We would hold hands, but not stand too close; we didn't say anything and we didn't look at each other. But I could hear her breathing, which like my own came strong and rapid, as though we were out of breath. Then it was summer. I was seventeen. Now, when we walked, I drew closer to her. I didn't dare declare myself yet, but I would draw her close, as if to whisper something in her ear. She turned her head to look at the trees, or lowered it to the sandy path. And then, on one occasion—the air was on fire and the bees were loud and dragonflies darted about us—I drew her brusquely towards me, and hugged her close, and scarcely knowing what I was doing, I pressed my lips to hers. We stopped, astonished, delighted, lost! And I kissed and kept kissing her beautiful hot mouth which she could not close.

'Why was it, at the very instant my child's heart was flowering into that of a man's—and while I kissed her still—I drew slightly to one side to examine our two shadows, our two slender and lengthened shadows, clearly outlined on the pale narrow path?

'I could make out her body next to mine, I could see our arms entwined, and a little higher than her shoulder I could see my own,

slightly inclined, and higher still, there was her forehead, and the pretty tousle of her hair... but as I was breathing in her own breath, I did not see... no, no, I did not see, on the pale path, my own face, I did not see my forehead, I did not see my hair. My own lips were upon her lips! But, from the neck upwards, my own shadow had no mouth, no forehead, no hair!... My shadow was without a head.

'It would be difficult indeed, Sir, to express my agitation on discovering that my shadow had no head! A little later on, I rushed back to the spot in the track where my image had been cut off, supposing there must be some abrupt hollow or hole into which my head had fallen, cut off by the edge. But there was no such hollow. The ground was smooth and unbroken. And there, in front of me, stretched my decapitated shadow! Out of some instinctive terror, I brought my hands up to my cheeks and my temples: I touched, and touched again my fleshy, downy, living skin: and on the road I saw the black shadows of my palms sketching the contour of the nothing that was between them.

'I succumbed to a fever that confined me to my bed for fifty days. Once in convalescence, my eyes looked wildly, and I said not a word; people started to wonder whether my illness—it was typhoid fever—had not left me mad or simple. Neither was true. My reasoning was entirely intact. But I could not help thinking of my unfinished shadow. And I thought about it obsessively, with fear and with rage. I was both terrified and consumed by the desire to know whether, after my illness, the thing was as before. Today, perhaps, my shadow had a head! How I wished it were so! In the end, my curiosity triumphed over my apprehension. One morning when I was alone in my bedroom, sunk deep in my valetudinarian's armchair, I rose up slowly between the window and the wall, I turned around slowly... above the chair-back rose my shoulders, my neck—and nothing else! I fell back in a dead faint.

'For days, weeks, months I was morose, and sat with staring eyes, which alarmed my mother. It is very hard to give an idea—unless one has experienced it oneself—of the anxiety that borders on terror, of the shame that turns into torture, which in the early days afflict a man who is in any way sensitive and who is persuaded—a conviction confirmed at every moment—that his shadow lacks a head. It might even be easier to get used to not having a head oneself; in that case, to keep the mind calm, it would simply mean not touching the face or the

skull, and carefully avoiding mirrors. Perhaps one might even forget that one was headless. But how is it possible, without living in unbroken darkness, to prevent one's shadow appearing on the wall, on the parquet, on the pavement? My suffering was all the more acute, in that I dared tell no one of my trouble. If I had been able to confess to my parents or my friends, I might have lessened the torment. But some instinct—and since then I have come to understand the wisdom of this instinct—warned me to remain silent, and that I should keep secret the deviance from natural law that was embodied in my person, or at least in the apparent incompleteness of my person. What proved to me that I *had* to keep it secret, is that, thanks to the operation of some mysterious and higher will, I was the only one to notice it. No one ever evinced the least surprise at seeing, next to his shadow complete with a head, my own that was not. The fact is that everybody else—through a *necessary* illusion—saw a head there. But this remained something between me and... someone. In addition to this, I was helped because time, which accustoms us to most things, and repetition of the fact, ended by taking the edge off my anguish. First my astonishment and then my fear became less acute, confronted with this neck that supported nothing. My father died the year after my mother, and I had to busy myself—after the shock of the double loss—with putting some order into our business affairs, which had become somewhat chaotic. To keep my clientèle, I had to make visits and advertise in the local newspaper of Saint-Rémy-sur-Oise. Then I got married, to the little apprentice, daughter of our neighbour the druggist, who had turned out tall and beautiful; I had children, two boys and a girl, and all of this took my mind off my troubles. There remained just the slight hesitation in my speech, and a slight constraint in my movements, which fitted with the amiable reserve of my character. I nearly stopped noticing my anomaly, or at least I acknowledged it without pain; sometimes I even treated it with familiarity and good humour. On one occasion—it was so comic, I shall never forget it—I was showing our range of silk top-hats to the owner of the Hôtel des Trois Empereurs; not knowing where to put one which was much too small for my client, the tables and chairs being cluttered, I put it on my own head—and I doubled up, I literally doubled up laughing! Why? Because on the wall I saw the shadow of the hat, which was so narrow that a child's head could scarcely have fitted it, with its rim, resting rather shakily, right on the shadow

of my shoulders! I can assure you, my dear Sir, it was really very droll; even you would have split your sides, despite your grave and saintly character. And on occasion my "infirmity" actually afforded me some joy. It was when I used to take my children for a walk in the countryside, on Sundays in summer, after closing the shop. As they were already quite tall, and I was fairly small, the shadows we cast in front of us were almost the same size, because I was shorter by a head. I derived some pleasure from that.

'In this way I might have just gone on, and come to the peaceful end of a very happy life—unless I had been destined to fall victim to the universal disaster from which I have, God be thanked, saved humanity and the world! But some very strange and disturbing signs started to manifest themselves in the winter of this present year, enough to set anyone with a modicum of intelligence pondering. From the fifteenth of January onwards—as I am certain you will recall—a sun appeared, burning more hotly even than is customary in July, a sun that would have maddened a brain less stable than my own, and it dried up the fields and the paths, drank up the rivers, forced the trees into leaf and the roses into flower. Long islands of sand, like the yellow backs of beasts, emerged from the shrunken waters, and one day I saw the apple tree in the courtyard covered in a thousand pink-and-white flowerlets! No doubt about it, nothing like it had ever been seen in Saint-Rémy-sur-Oise, nor in any country of the world: this was a complete inversion of the seasons! I could only agree with my wife when, looking through the window at the sky from which not a snowflake nor a raindrop had fallen for a month, she suddenly said: "Of course, there must be something awry in the world."

'Her remark came as no surprise, but I was singularly affected by it.

'And since, at that very moment, my headless shadow was projected against the wall, I repeated, almost in a whisper, between my trembling lips: "Yes, there is something awry. There is something awry in the world."

'I would be lying, my dear Sir, if I said to you that from that moment on I fully and wholly perceived there might be a connection, that there really was a connection (as I came later on to recognize!) between the prodigious summer-in-winter we were living through, and my own truncated image. No, initially the connection between

them did not strike me at all—and the relation of cause and effect between the two anomalies even less. But just as one can scarcely make out the tendrils of creeper stretched from one side of the track to the other, in the growing light of dawn, it seemed to me that there were links, albeit light, tenuous, vague, more guessed at than averred, which connected the two phenomena. Yes, I felt that I was not a stranger to the strange thing that was happening, and that the transgression of one of nature's laws, in me, corresponded in some mysterious way with the transgression of another of nature's laws...

'Nevertheless, the suspicion—which remained in any case very vague, uncertain, scarcely hinted at—that the headlessness of my shadow was not unrelated to the anomaly of a winter so burningly summerlike, soon faded as the season, in accordance with unalterable law, cooled down to its seasonal norm; and I think that the suspicion which troubled my mind would have vanished for good, had it not been for the fact that, quite a while later, at the beginning of April, the papers carried reports, often recounted in great detail, of the sudden and appalling cataclysm which had overwhelmed the island of Java, nearly wiping it off the map.*

'The few survivors of this prolonged disaster gave descriptions of what seems to have been more than a week of unparalleled horror. To the backdrop of a terrifying and ceaseless barrage of thunder, and an enveloping darkness on which the sun rose no more, lit only by lightning flashes, mountains crashed into abysms that were suddenly opened at their foot, cascades of rock and molten metal surged up through lakes or from the plains; what had been mountains were swallowed up in an instant, and a vast, thinly spread, torrential surface, not of water but of lava, roared over the whole island, like some gigantic scythe, and cut down everything—hills, forests, houses—on its path, and left nothing but heaps of ruins behind it. The whole thing represented a formidable inversion of the laws that govern matter: huge rocks were seen flying off, carried by a wind that did not come from the sky. Meanwhile, mysteriously weighted, swarms of doves and swans were seen plunging down in rockfalls. Contrariety triumphed in the great hullaballoo of the end of the world! True, it was a limited world—not even a continent—but a world nonetheless. And the inhabitants of this whole globe of ours—without ever interpreting it as a sign—were dumbfounded by this upheaval, and trembled.

'But *I* understood: it was a sign, a warning. I understood that the Destroyer—who was originally the Creator—had announced, by this concentrated ruin, the universal ruin to come; that the partial annihilation of an island was a trial run for the total catastrophe of the galaxies.

'But why should the sign have been given precisely when it was? Why should it be my own epoch that witnessed the imminent reversal of all the laws of matter which had hitherto governed the Creator's handiwork of six days? Why should the end of the world be nigh, during my lifetime?

'It was then that the vague suspicion which had nagged at me during our strange sultry winter returned, but more pressing, more precise, and with a terrible urgency. And so it was that, after a time of long and painful meditation, I acquired this certainty: "The world is going to end, because my shadow has no head."

'As I write now, the truth of this proposition appears to me so irrefutable, my dear Sir, that I feel it would be an insult to the subtlety of your intelligence were I to rehearse at any length the arguments that convinced me; a learned man like you will understand instantly what it took a simpleton like me so long to grasp.

'Everything in nature is interconnected. Nothing can become disordered, that does not shake the whole. Everything that exists may be considered like a castle made of cards; the almost infinite length of its existence persuades us of its solidity—the fond illusion of the guests on this ephemeral dwelling-place; remove a single card, and the whole edifice collapses and scatters. To speak more bluntly, a single process that is turned aside from its normal completion, a single supporting strut withdrawn from the unique and multiple balance, a single law in the universal order transgressed, can involve—what am I saying!—must of necessity involve the breakdown of the whole enormous edifice. And my head, without its shadow, meant the collapse of everything into nothing.

'No sooner had this conviction taken hold of my mind than I became a prey to a terrible and unceasing melancholy. Not because I mourned for my own life, soon to be pitched headlong into the general disaster; nor for my wife and children, doomed to the most dreadful end. Although I had some kindness to myself, and for them I had all the tenderness that the heart of a husband and a father can hold, I was importuned by a wider, more encompassingly human, anxiety.

Concern for my own welfare was the least of the things that caused me grief. I was filled with compassion for the whole beautiful earth, and for all the happy beings that dwell therein. What! Could it be true, could it be certain, that dawn would no longer smile upon the calm blue sea, or on the green and flowery meadow? There would be no more sun, because there would be no more sky? There would be no more stars, for night itself would no longer be? Oh my God, to think that after that terrible hour no birds will sing in the withered trees, and nowhere, nowhere at all, would roses flower. And all the men and women who love each other will love each other no more. The highest and most glorious aspirations will be worthless in the decomposition attendant upon the funeral. The day before the universal catastrophe, engaged couples, he twenty, she sixteen years of age, will still exchange their vows...

'An immense pity for all things and for all living beings wrung my heart repeatedly; as my lashes were continually wet with tears, people around me surmised that I must have developed some weakness of the lachrymal glands, and this was the cause of the great, slow tears that swelled and trembled... Not a bit of it! I was weeping because the end of the world was nigh! I also felt a certain amount of remorse. It was certainly not my fault that the terrifying cataclysm was so near at hand! But it was still in my own person, however guiltless I may be, that the first sign was made manifest, announcing the cause, and the final disaster.

'A remedy? Was there some remedy against the imminent evil? My pity convinced me that there must be a remedy...

'The world was going to its perdition because the law that governed it had been broken in me—because my shadow had no head! I began to wonder if there were not a way I could furnish my head with a shadow. If only I could obtain this result, then all things, necessarily, would return to their old order—and the universes would continue to live. I cannot begin to tell you, kind Sir (and I am somewhat confused on the matter), how much time I devoted to inventing some ruse whereby I might correct my abnormal shadow on the wall. I recall only that, more than once, I experimented with wearing masks, with several wide and very dark masks, in fact, hoping that increased darkness, greater opacity, would infringe upon the light. Alas! The masks covering my face had no more shadow than my own face...

'Then it was that God, who has shown pity on his worlds and on his peoples, sent me inspiration... for which I thank him on my knees!

'So that the danger should be averted, for the present at least, and that everything should be restored to the state demanded by natural law, it was not necessary (why did I not think ot it before?) that my head appear on the wall; it was enough that my shadow correspond to my person. So, if I ceased to have a head, if, somehow or other, I no longer had a head, my shadow would no longer be in disharmony with my form, the universal law would no longer be trans-gressed*—and the eternal stream of life, naturally, would pursue its course!

'I can promise you that, when the idea came to me, I let out a cry of joy. Humanity was saved! I didn't waste a second, I seized my razor and standing there, before the narrow mirror, by the window—without for a moment thinking of my wife and children, in grief behind the funeral car—I set about cutting my own neck... But no, the separation of the head from the trunk could not be completed, when attempted by a hand that trembled, inevitably, and the ensuing pain would weaken its resolve. I could only be beheaded usefully—by which I mean entirely—I could only become an identical match to my shadow with the steady, methodical, even mechanical aid of someone acting without passion and without grief. Only the execu-tioner could render me identical to my image on the wall or on the path, only the executioner could accord me the joy of rescuing from nothingness, universal life!... Oh, the sweet hope! My corpse, if it were raised, would be in conformity with its shadow.

'But only the most hideous murderers are guillotined...

'Ah! Kind Sir, I loved my children so much; especially my daughter—I loved her so tenderly and with such pride. She was very pretty. When we walked out together, the looks we drew swelled my heart with pride. She was blonde, with a little fringe. For a long time I had hesitated to let her marry, because I was so happy to have her around the house. Nevertheless, the following month, her wedding was due to take place. She loved her young man. They had promised me that they would come often to see me, and they promised not to put the children they would have out to a wet-nurse in the country. The little ones were to remain at Saint-Rémy-sur-Oise. I was to go to my son-in-law's every morning, to see how they were getting on, and

bring them rattles, and in time, toys. And my wife, who teased me a little, but kind-heartedly, was pleased at the arrangement. We said to each other: "Well, we shan't be all alone in our old age. The boys will come down from Paris, marry, and settle down nearby. We'll have a large and happy family about us. In the evenings, the sitting room on the first floor will hardly be large enough to hold everybody, there'll be such laughter, such amusements and story-telling, and all of us, all of us, shall be happy…"

'Ah, Reverend Sir, I do not repent of my own excessive barbarism; it is, however, dreadful that I had to kill my family in such an atrocious way as to be sure that they would not send me to prison, but rather to the guillotine, so that my neck be cleanly cut, that my shadow be correct at last, that the world should not end, and that for a long, long time to come there should be roses, and loving couples to be wed…

LÉON BLOY

A Dentist Terribly Punished

'So what may I do for you, Sir?'

The person addressed by the printer was absolutely unexceptional, as insignificant and vacant as it is possible to be, one of those men that seems to exist in the *plural*, so utterly do they belong to the collective and to the indivisible. He might have said *We*, like the Pope, and resembled an encyclical.

His face, turned out by the shovelful, belonged to that numberless category, the thick-set Southerner, that no breeding can ever refine, and about whom everything is false, even the grossness...

He was unable to reply immediately, for he was in a state, and trying hard, at that moment, to be a somebody. His large, vacant eyes rolled in their sockets, like those games of chance in which the marble seems to hesitate, before falling into the numbered hole that decides the destiny of an imbecile.

'Well, dammit all,' he exclaimed at last, in a strong Toulouse accent, 'I haven't come to your shop in search of fire and brimstone. I want you to print out a hundred wedding invitations.'

'Very good, Sir. Here are some models for you to choose from. Would Sir care for our luxury option, printed on Ivory, or on Japanese Imperial?'

'Luxury? What else! One doesn't get married every day of the week. I did assume you wouldn't print it out on toilet paper. The most imperial stuff you've got, understood? But whatever you do, don't for God's sake do it out with a *black border*!'

The printer, who was a simple fellow from Vaugirard, fearing he was in the presence of a lunatic who must be humoured, simply protested calmly that such an act of gross negligence would be unthinkable.

When it came to filling in the names, the client's hand started trembling so violently the printer had to take them down at his dictation.

'*Monsieur le docteur Alcibiade Gerbillon has the honour of announcing his marriage to Mademoiselle Antoinette Planchard. The nuptial blessing will take place at the parish church of Aubervilliers.*'

'But Vaugirard and Aubervilliers are miles apart!' thought the printer, who calmly drew up the bill.

They are indeed miles apart. Doctor Alcibiade Gerbillon, dentist by profession, had been wandering about Paris for fifteen hours.

He had accomplished all the other tasks preparatory to his wedding—which was to take place in two days—quite calmly, like a somnambulist. But this business of the invitation had completely overwhelmed him. Here's why.

Gerbillon was a *murderer* who got no sleep.

Explain this as you will. Having perpetrated his crime in the most cowardly and ignoble manner, without emotion, like the brute he was, remorse had only begun to bite when he received the notice of death, broadly framed in black, in which the entire family, bereft, implored him to attend the obsequies of his victim.

This masterpiece of typography had horrified and destabilized him. He pulled three perfectly good teeth, filled mere chips copiously with gold, attacked perfectly healthy gums, dislocated jaws that time had respected, and generally inflicted upon his patients tortures as yet unheard of.

His lonely orthodontist's couch was visited by dark nightmares, in which full sets of dentures, made of vulcanized rubber according to his own design, and which he had built into the orifices of trusting citizens, would grind and clatter all around him.

The cause of all this disturbance was the same printed message that the certified burghers roundabout had welcomed with untroubled souls, Alcibiade being one of the worshippers of the Moloch of imbeciles, who received such printed notices.

Could it be credited? He had murdered, truly he had murdered, *out of love.*

Justice would have to conclude that such a crime was due to the dentist's reading-matter, the only such matter that fed his murderer's brain.

Having read a stream of cheap novels in which amorous entanglements ended tragically, he ceded little by little to the temptation to suppress, in a single act, the purveyor of umbrellas that stood in the way of his happiness.

This young businessman, whose dentition was superb, and whose jaw he had no opportunity to massacre, was about to take to wife Antoinette Planchard, daughter of Planchard, the big ironmonger. Gerbillon had smouldered in silence for the girl, ever since the day when, having broken off a tubercular molar in her mouth, she fell fainting into his arms.

They were about to publish the banns. With the lightning decisiveness that marks out great dentists, Alcibiade had schemed for the extermination of his rival.

On a morning of torrential rain, the purveyor of umbrellas was found dead in his bed. A medical examination proved that a rogue of the worst stripe had strangled the wretched man as he slept.

The diabolical Gerbillon, who knew better than anyone what happened, had the effrontery to confirm the scientific validity of this finding. In fact he had covered his tracks so well, that after an inquiry as vain as it was meticulous, the authorities had to abandon their hunt for the culprit.

The bloodthirsty dentist was saved, but he did not go unpunished, as you shall hear.

As his crime had always been a means to an end, no sooner was the umbrella-seller under the sod than the dentist began to lay siege to Antoinette.

The dignity and superiority he had shown during the inquiry, the light he had shed upon this obscure crime, and above all, the delicate way in which he had made his compassion felt for the young person so cruelly afflicted, eased the access to her heart. It was not, truth be told, a heart that was difficult to take; it was no Babylon of a heart. The ironmonger's daughter had a steady head on her virginal shoulders. She was doing all right, and her plunge into grief was altogether a shallow one.

She had no pretensions to eternal, vainglorious lamentation, and made no show of being inconsolable.

'Let the dead bury the dead, lose one husband, find ten more, etc,' murmured Alcibiade. A few more sentences plucked from the same abyss soon revealed the nobility of this raptor, who appeared quite transcendent to her.

'It is your heart, Mademoiselle, that I should like to extirpate,' he told her one day. That clinched it.

At this charmingly turned phrase, which was one that the girl—who was educated—could savour, she made up her mind. Besides, Gerbillon was an acceptable husband. They soon came to terms and the marriage went ahead.

But why should this dearly bought happiness be poisoned by the memory of the dead? The black-bordered letter, the memory of which had begun to fade, returned to haunt the mind of the murderer: he felt roundly denounced by it. Two days before his wedding—as we have seen—the obsession had returned stronger than ever, driving him almost to madness, and he wandered about for a whole day, in parts of Paris he didn't know, until the terrible moment when he at last summoned the courage to order his marriage invitations from the printer in Vaugirard, who had surely guessed he was a murderer.

It was all very well to have been so clever and so cunning; to have put justice off the scent; to have won the hand, against all the odds, of the woman he adored—all of this, just to have his life poisoned by guilty dreams!

The ecstasy of the first days was a mere respite. The fine horns of the newlyweds' crescent honeymoon had not even ceased to pierce the azure when the first sign of trouble appeared.

One morning Alcibiade found a portrait of the purveyor of umbrellas. Oh, just a simple photograph that Antoinette had innocently accepted from him as a gift, shortly before they were due to be married.

Beside himself with rage, the dentist smashed it into pieces before the eyes of his wife, who was appalled by his violence, even though the relic meant precious little to her.

At the same time—it being impossible to destroy anything—the threatening image which up till then had existed only on the paper, like the visible reflection of one of the fragments of that invisible photographic film that envelops the universe, ended up by fixing on to the suddenly *suggestible* memory of Madame Gerbillon.

From then on, she was thoroughly haunted by the memory of the deceased she had almost forgotten; she lived only for him, she lived him perpetually, she breathed him through all her pores, and through all her exhalations, which flooded her poor husband, who was at first surprised, and then desperate, upon finding that cadaver perpetually interposed between him and his wife.

At the end of the first year they had an epileptic child, a monstrous male child with the face of a thirty-year-old, that bore an uncanny resemblance to the man Gerbillon had murdered.*

The father fled the house, uttering dreadful cries, wandered like a madman for three days, and then, on the evening of the fourth, he bent sobbing over the cradle of his son, and strangled him.

The Last Bake

When one is dead, it lasts for a long time.

(An Inheritor)

MONSIEUR FIACRE-PRÉTEXTAT LALBARIE had retired from business at the age of sixty, having amassed considerable riches from his coffin-making.

He had never once disappointed his clientèle, and the aristocracy of Geneva, that had placed so many orders, were unanimous in celebration of his loyalty and care.

The excellence of his handiwork, which passed muster even in scrupulous England, had also obtained the plaudits of Belgium, Illinois, and Michigan.

His retirement had thus been met with bitter regret in both worlds, when lamenting international dispatches announced that the famous artisan was leaving the rites of the shop-counter to devote his august white hairs to his beloved studies.

Fiacre was, in truth, a contented old man, whose philosophical and humanitarian vocation did not emerge until the very moment at which his own fortune, less blind and less mean than the vain multitude might suppose, had heaped its benefits upon him.

In no way did he despise, like so many others, the infinitely honest and lucrative business which had raised him from almost nothing to the pinnacle of his ten millions.

On the contrary, he used to recount, with all the naive enthusiasm of an old soldier, the numerous campaigns waged against his competitors; and he liked to recall the heroic rolling fire of his inventories.

He had simply abdicated, like Charles V,* from his empire of the invoice, to devote himself to the higher life.

Having amassed, in short, enough to live on, and now too elderly to keep his beady eye much longer upon his business—that flare for spontaneity which knows how to forestall and disarm the competition—he had the wisdom to dispose advantageously of his commercial empire before the star of his patent began to pale.

From this moment on, he devoted himself to the pleasures of the human species.

With touching lucidity, he had grasped the fact that a crowd of nincompoops had failed in all their efforts to improve the condition of the poor; and convinced as he was, moreover, of the *usefulness* of the poor, he concluded that he had better things to do than to put his financial and intellectual resources at the service of the unwashed masses.

Instead, he resolved to dedicate the last glimmers of his genius to alleviating the sorrows of millionaires.

'Who ever thinks', said he, 'about the sufferings of the rich? I alone, perhaps, along with the divine Bourget,* whom my clientèle all adore. Because they fulfil their mission, which consists in slaving for the sake of business, people think too hastily that they must be happy, forgetting the fact that they have a heart. People have the effrontery to set against them the crude tribulations of the wretched, whose duty is to suffer, after all, as if hunger and rags could be put in the balance against the dread of dying. Such is the law. No one really dies, if they possess nothing. The possession of capital assets is an indispensable condition of giving up the ghost, this is what no one seems to grasp. Death is nothing other than to be separated from one's money. Those without money, are without life, so how can they know what it is to die?'

Heavy with such thoughts—that went deeper than he supposed—the coffin-maker set his whole soul to abolishing the pangs of death.

Monsieur Lalbarie had the signal honour of being among the first to conceive the generous invention of the Crematorium.* To his thinking, the traditional horror of death was in large part caused by the dreadful image of the corpse in decomposition. The Guild of Incinerators elected him their president, and it was to them he described the stages of putrescence—that subterranean chemistry—with an eloquence fuelled by fear; the idea of turning into a flower, for example, was repellent to his accountant's soul.

'I do not want to end up a corpse!' he bellowed. 'As soon as I die, I demand to be burned, I insist on being carbonized, reduced to ashes, purified by fire, etc.'

His wish was fully granted, as you shall see.

The excellent man had a son, which is something to be wished on everyone who knows the value of money.

And here I must beg permission to launch for an instant into dithyrambic mode.

Dieudonné Lalbarie was, if possible, even more admirable than his father. Conceived in a most auspicious hour, one that saw his father triumph over impertinent competitors, he was the very model of all the solid virtues that a serious house of credit requires.

At the age of fifteen he had already invested his savings, and he kept his own person as tidily as his account book. No instrument could detect in him the slightest trace of frivolity.

It would have been a gross injustice to charge him with giving way to a moment of enthusiasm, or with an access, even repressed, of gratuitous tenderness for anyone, or over anything whatsoever.

When he spoke, his happy father was obliged to lean against the counter or the till, such was his pride at having spawned such a son.

This blessed child is alive and prospering. He has already doubled his wealth since losing his parents, having contrived to make himself loved by a hugely wealthy keeper of tortoises, to whom he is married; many there are who will know of whom I speak, but I fear I would offend his modesty if I sketched him out more fully.

I shall let you guess. Perhaps it is already saying too much, if I add that he has the face of a handsome reptile, and is usually accompanied by a hound of monstrous size.

What follows is the little-known story of his father's death and funeral. Lovers of mild emotions are advised to stop reading here.

One morning the coroner declared that the great Fiacre had ceased to exist.

Instantly, Lalbarie *fils* went into action. Without wasting a moment on useless tears, without wearing out the precious 'fabric' of his own life, by which is meant 'time', to adopt Benjamin Franklin's expression,* which he quoted endlessly, he set to and got things ready.

At ten thirty-five the papers were apprised that he had gone into mourning, and his words of sorrow were scattered on the winds in a thousand copies—the card announcing the sad news having been judiciously designed and executed a long time in advance.

The same thing was true of the black marble slab destined for the 'Columbarium',* which showed a phoenix beating its wings amidst the flames, and, on the orders of the deceased, the following terrifying inscription:

I SHALL RISE AGAIN

To blow away the cobwebs, Lalbarie *fils* went for a bicycle ride, lunched copiously, received a few mourners, made his ritual devotions at the Bourse, executed, towards evening, some profitable placements, and spent the night on the town, as a token of his extreme grief.

The next day a sumptuous funeral carriage loaded with flowers, and followed by an unprayerful crowd, bore the remains of the deceased to the Crematorium.

'Ha! You will rise again!' said the amiable Dieudonné to himself, who entered alone into the terrible inner sanctum, with the two men whose job it was to commit his father to the furnace. 'We shall see if you rise again!'...

The bier had been fashioned out of thin planks, according to the correct administrative norms, so it would combust instantly once introduced into the oven that was heated to seven-hundred degrees; it rested on a mechanical trolley, whose two sprung-metal handles, thrust with force, hurl the dead into the furnace, and then return with a squeal, in a diastole–systole movement lasting twenty-five seconds.

So things stood, and Dieudonné had reached this climactic moment of filial grief, *when a sound was heard, coming from inside the coffin*...

Oh, a vague and muffled sound, to be sure, like a corpse come alive and stirring in its shroud. The coffin seemed to shudder, even...

At that very instant the oven door, manoeuvred with precision, opened wide.

The three faces, reddened by the atrocious flame, looked at each other.

'It's the body deliquescing,' said Dieudonné placidly.

But the two men hesitated still.

'Well get on with it, in heaven's name!' screamed the parricide suddenly. 'I tell you it's the body deliquescing.' And he thrust a bundle of banknotes into the hand of the man nearest him.

The handles leaped forward, and leaped back...

The door slammed shut, but not quite fast enough, it seems, because Dieudonné, planted square in front of it, thought he saw, in the instantaneous combustion of the coffin, his father, with a petrified face and his arms stretched out.

The Lucky Sixpence

MONSIEUR TERTULLIEN had just reached his fiftieth year; his hair was still admirably black, his business successful, and his influence growing daily, when he had the misfortune to lose his wife.

This was a terrible blow. It would have been sheer perversity to imagine a more pleasing companion.

She was twenty years younger than her husband, with the most winning looks and a character to go with it, so sweet that she never let an occasion pass without dazzling.

The magnanimous Tertullien had married her, even though she didn't have a penny to her name. In this he was like most merchants who get tired of celibacy, but who are too busy to set about seducing exigent virgins.

He married her 'between two cheeses', as he liked to remark skittishly. For he was in fact a wholesale cheese merchant, and he had undertaken the solemn act of matrimony between a memorable delivery of Cheshire and an exceptional delivery of Parmesan.

But the union, I regret to say, was not blessed with offspring, and this cast a shadow over the gracious picture.

Who was to blame? It was a weighty matter, still undecided among the fruiterers and grocers in the neighbourhood. A hare-lipped butcher's wife who had been passed over by the handsome Tertullien accused him openly of impotence, overriding the objections of a spotty mattress-seller who claimed to have empirical evidence.

The pharmacist, however, declared it was too early to form an opinion, and the benevolent crowd of concierges, quite uninterested in the matter, approved the circumspection of this thoughtful man.

The crowd of them laid down the law as follows, saying that Paris wasn't built in a day, that all's well that ends well, that you spread your relish thinly if it's to go a long way, etc., etc., and that in consequence there was every reason to suppose that the happy event would arrive, which would add the finishing touch to the dazzling prosperity of the cheeseman.

They might have been speaking of the Heir Apparent.

News of this sudden death, which cut down so many legitimate hopes, was met with real sorrow.

Unless Tertullien were to remarry rapidly—a hypothesis that in his grief the cheese merchant did not entertain for an instant—the future of his business, the work of his own hands and by now so richly endowed, though it had started from nothing, would falter, and his clientèle pass into the hands of a younger rival!

The perspective, indeed, looked black, and it must have added a tinge of bitterness to the regrets of the grieving spouse, who seemed on the point of plunging headlong into a gulf of despair.

I do not know to what extent anxieties about not having an heir for his cheese business exercised him, but I myself was witness to his bellowing grief and the unrepeatable anathemas he cast upon himself for having to process behind Clémentine as she was borne to her grave, and in short order too, though he could not bring himself to set a date.

Ten years of business dealings with him had enabled me to observe at length the character of this amiable man, and there was a trait in particular that I noted, admirable but little known.

He lived in terror of being made a cuckold. All his ancestors had been, dating back two or three hundred years, and the tenderness he had for his wife was based essentially on the unshakable certainty that he was safe on that front, and her honesty entire.

His *gratitude* had about it something deeply unusual and touching. The more I thought about it, it came to seem almost tragic; and I sometimes wondered if Clémentine's notorious sterility was not in some peculiar way brought about by Tertullien himself, whose doubts concerning *his own identity*—and a sublime fear of cuckolding himself—prevented him from impregnating her.

But it was all too perfect, too far above the common herd, and the banal thing occurred that was bound to occur.

Clémentine had given up her soul to the Lord, and the unfortunate widower had given way, vigorously, to the groanings and bellowings of grief, as nature will have it.

When he had paid this first tribute—to employ one of his own favourite expressions—and before the whole crowded business of the funeral which he dreaded, he desired to put some order into the papers and relics of his beloved.

And it was thus that his destiny, like a cruel stepmother, struck him; the ridiculed standard of the Tertulliens was raised above his head.

In a secret drawer deep in a private desk, which the most jealous husband would never dream of suspecting, he found a whole correspondence, whose volume and variety held him absolutely riveted.

All his friends and acquaintances were represented. With the exception of myself, all had been cherished by his wife.

His own employees—he found letters from his own employees written on pink paper—had been simultaneously gratified.

He now knew with certainty that the dear departed had betrayed him night and day; at any time, and practically everywhere. In his bed, in his cellar, in his attic, in his shop, under the very eye of the Gruyère, and in the effluvia of the Roquefort or the Camembert.

I need hardly add that throughout the whole unedifying correspondence he himself was scarcely spared. He was unremittingly mocked from the first line to the last.

An employee from the post-office, renowned for the sharpness of his wit, ridiculed his business in the most disobliging way, and went as far as to make some allusions, and to give some *bits of advice*, that are quite unpublishable.

But there was something else—extraordinary, excessive, fabulous— enough to send a shudder through the constellation of the Goat.

Next to this mortifying bundle was an endless series of little wooden sticks. These astonished and baffled him, at first. But then, with the wisdom of a subtle Apache with his ear to the warpath, the light flooded in upon him, when he realized that the number of sticks tallied exactly with the number of admirers encouraged by his faithless spouse, and that each of them was scored with a multitude of nicks made by a penknife, much in the manner of a baker's account book.

Clearly, this Clémentine was an orderly woman, who kept her account books up to date.

Crushed and humiliated, the husband asked, quite naturally, to be left alone with his dead spouse, and shut himself in with her for two or three hours, like a man who wants to give himself up unconstrainedly to his grief.

A few weeks later Tertullien held a sumptuous dinner to celebrate the feast of the Epiphany.

Twenty carefully selected male guests gathered around his table. There was a quite unparalleled spread. Exquisite, abundant, unexpected. It semed like the farewell feast given by an opulent prince who is about to abdicate.

A few of the guests, however, felt a tinge of unease at the funereal aspect of the decor, a product of the now somewhat sombre imagination of the cheese merchant, borrowed from some half-remembered melodrama.*

The walls, even the ceiling, were draped in black, the tablecloth was black, the lighting came from black candles burning in black candelabra. Everything was black.

The man from the post-office, completely unmanned, wanted to leave. A jolly pig-breeder stopped him, saying that no one was to 'let the side down', and that he himself found it all 'a good joke'.

After a moment's hesitation, the others resolved to spit in the eye of death. Soon enough, the bottles began to go round, and the meal became quite riotous. By the time the champagne came out the pun reigned supreme and the smutty stories were beginning, when a gigantic cake was brought in.

'Gentlemen,' said Tertullien, rising, 'we must lift our glasses, if you will, to the memory of our dear departed. Each one of you knew and loved her heart. You cannot have forgotten, can you? Her kind and tender heart. I would ask all of you therefore to let yourselves be infused—in a quite *particular way*—with her memory, before we cut into this cake which she would have liked so dearly to share with you.'

Having never been the lover of the cheese merchant's wife, probably because I had never met her, I was not invited to this dinner, and I never found out who got the lucky sixpence.

But I do know that Tertullien got into trouble with the law, for having inserted, into the swollen sides of this almond cake, the *heart* of his wife, the little, putrefying heart of the delicious Clémentine.

OCTAVE MIRBEAU

On a Cure

BEFORE quitting the Pyrenees, I wanted to see my friend Roger
Fresselou, who has lived for years and years in Le Castérat, a small
village in the Ariège.*

It was a long, hard journey. After six days of tough walking and
steep climbing, aching and exhausted, I arrived at Le Castérat as
night was falling. Picture in your mind thirty or so houses clustering
on a narrow plateau surrounded on all sides by black mountains with
snowy summits. To begin with the view is majestic, especially when
the mist softens somewhat the closed horizon, turning it milky and
covering it with gold dust. But this feeling soon vanishes, and faced
with these lofty walls of rock, it is replaced by an invasive and dreary
sadness, and by a horrid sense of imprisonment.

The village is at such an altitude that the trees are stunted and the
only bird is the heavy ptarmigan with his feathery claws. Only a
few meagre rhododendrons survive in this stony soil, and the dwarf
thistle which opens its large yellow flowers with their pointed and
wounding spines only in the noonday sun. On the slopes below the
plateau, to the north, grows short, greyish grass, grazed over in summer by cows and sheep and goats, whose bells tinkle incessantly, like
the tinkling of the priest's bell in our native countryside, that sounds
in the evening as he bears viaticum to the sick. Nothing is sadder, and
nothing is less flower-like, than the rare species that scrape a living
out of this mean and joyless corner of nature; poor stunted plants
with whiteish, hairy leaves, and coarse corollas that have the discol-
oured, clouded look of dead pupils. Winter with its snowfalls, and all
the surrounding gulfs filled with snow, cuts the village off from the
rest of the world, from the rest of life. The herds move down to the
low valleys, the sturdy men of the village seek work or adventure
elsewhere, sometimes far away; the post doesn't even get through…
For months and months there comes no news from the other side of
the impassable snows. No one living is left, merely the half-alive, the

old men, and the women and children who go to earth in their houses, like marmots in their holes. They only come out on Sundays, to hear mass in church, which is made up of a little square tower, its stone fissured, with a kind of lean-to up against its side, shaped like a barn. Oh! The sound of that bell muffled by the snow!

This is, however, where my friend Roger Fresselou has made his home for twenty years. A little house with a flat roof, a small, stony garden, and with rough, silent, jealous men for neighbours, miserable and complaining, clad in coarse homespun and mountain headgear. Roger has very little to do with them.

How did he end up here? And above all, how can he live here? In truth I have no idea, and I don't think he really knows either. Every time I ask him why he has exiled himself like this, he replies with a shrug: 'How would I know?... That's how it is...' offering nothing further by way of explanation.

One curious thing: Roger has scarcely aged at all. Not a single grey hair, not a wrinkle on his face. And yet I scarcely recognize him under his mountain apparel. His eyes have gone dead, not a spark comes out of them. And his face has taken on the ashen colour of the soil. It's a totally different man from the one I used to know. There is an entirely new life within him, about which I know nothing. And I try in vain to puzzle it out.

He used to be enthusiastic, charming, and full of life. Never exactly exuberant in words or acts, he had a melancholy common to all young people who have tasted the poison of metaphysics. In our little circle in Paris, we were fairly confident of his future. He had contributed some literary essays to small magazines which, while not absolute master-pieces, showed ambition, real seriousness, and a curiosity about life. Thanks to his clear mind and his solid, forthright style, he seemed to be one of those destined to break free of the narrow cliques (in which talent can shrink) and reach a wider public. In the domains of art, literature, philosophy, or politics he had nothing of the intransigent sectarian about him, even if he held firm both in radicalism and in beauty. There was nothing morbid about him, no abnormal obsessions, no intellectual bugbears... His intelligence was built on solid foundations... And then we learned, a few months later, that he was living in the mountains.

Since I have been with Roger we have not once spoken about litera-ture. Many times I have tried to steer the conversation round to a

subject he used to love, but every time he has avoided it ill-temperedly. He has asked after no one, and when, pointedly, I mention certain names, once dear to us, and now famous, he betrays not the slightest inner emotion, not so much as a flicker. I sense within him no trace of bitterness or regret. He seems to have forgotten all that, and his former passions and friendships are nothing but dreams, long since blotted out! Of my own work, of my own hopes in part fulfilled, in part disappointed, he has said not a word. And in his house—impossible to find a book, a newspaper, or any kind of image. There is nothing here, and he himself is as empty of intellectual life as his mountain neighbours.

Yesterday, as I pressed him one last time to impart to me the reason for his baffling renunciation, he said:

'How would I know?... That's how it is... I came here by chance, during a summer holiday... I liked the place because of its unspeakable wretchedness... or rather, I thought I liked it... I came back the following year, with no set plan... I thought I would stay just a few days... I ended up staying twenty years!... That's it!... There's no more to say... It's quite simple, as you see...'

This evening, Roger asked me:

'Do you ever think about death?'

'Yes, I replied... And it terrifies me... so I try to banish the dreadful image...'

'It frightens you?...'

He shrugged his shoulders and went on:

'You think about death... and you come and you go... and you torment yourself... and twist and turn in all directions?... And you work on ephemeral things?... And you fondle dreams of pleasure, maybe... and even of glory?... Poor little thing!...'

'Ideas are not ephemeral things,' I protested... 'they can prepare the future, they can steer progress...'

With a slow, sweeping gesture he motioned at the circus of black mountains:

'The future!... Progress!...* How can you possibly, faced with that, utter such meaningless words?...'

And after a short pause he went on:

'Ideas!... Just wind, wind, wind... They pass over... the tree stirs for an instant... its leaves tremble... and then they have passed... the tree becomes still again... nothing has changed...'

'You're wrong... The wind is full of cells, it carries pollen and winnows seed... it fertilizes...'

'And creates monsters.'

We remained silent a while...

And then I felt, coming from the black mountains opposite us, all around us, with their implacable walls of slate and rock, a stifling, oppressive weight... I truly felt the weight of those blocks on my chest and on my skull... Roger Fresselou went on:

'When the idea of death suddenly took hold of me, I felt at the same time the pettiness and the vanity of all my endeavours which were using up my life... But I procrastinated... I would say: "I've taken a wrong turning... perhaps I can do something else with my life... art is corrupt... literature all lies... philosophy mere mystification... I shall seek out simple men, rough, good-hearted men... There must somewhere exist, in pure, remote parts, far from cities, human material from which one might strike a spark of beauty... Let us go... let us find it!..." Alas, no, men are everywhere the same... Only their actions differ... And even here, on this silent peak where I see them, these actions are disappearing. There is nothing more than a teeming herd which, whatever it does and wherever it goes, jostles on towards death... You speak of progress?... But progress, swifter and more conscious, is just a big step forward towards the ineluctable end... And so here I have remained, where all is ash, charred stone, dried-out sap, where everything has already entered into the silence of dead things!...'

'Why didn't you just kill yourself?' I let fly, exasperated by my friend's voice, and seized in my turn by the horrible obsession with death which floats on the mountains and around the summits, gliding over the gulfs towards me, borne along to the sound of those tinkling bells, those tolling bells, on the slopes of the plateau.

Roger answered calmly:

'You don't kill what is already dead... I have been dead these twenty years, since coming here... And you've been dead for a long time too... Why struggle against it?... Stay where you are now!...'

I summoned the guide who was to lead me back to the world of men, to life, to light... Tomorrow, at first light, I shall be gone...

The Bath

AROUND his fortieth year, on a rainy evening when he stayed home, alone and ruminating, Joseph Gardar decided he would get married. Why had he taken this sudden decision? He hardly knew. Was he in love? No. Was he ruined, or ill? No. How could it possibly be, then, that rich, fit, and not in love, he should want to marry? Was he mad? It may be so. It may be also that he felt vaguely weary of all his happiness and his freedom. And then, on the evening in question, it happened that he had wanted to look at an album of *japonaiseries* that was on a table the other end of the room, and this led to the following consideration: 'I want very much to look at the album; on the other hand, I don't want to get out of my chair. If I were married, I would ask my wife to fetch it for me.' He noted also that a woman with blonde hair, who was tall and svelte, a woman wrapped in light-coloured material, in smooth, silky chiffon, seated in the armchair facing his, would make a pretty sight, a pretty splash of colour... Also, the silence of his apartment weighed on him. The door never opened brusquely, no ornament was ever broken, no rancorous reproaches, never a voice raised in anger! His papers always odiously in order on the desk!... Oh, just once, not to find a letter he needed!... To know that a poem barely begun, or a novel nearly finished, had been torn up, burned, destroyed, by an unconscious, foraging little hand! He fell asleep with this consoling idea and dreamed of novel and exquisite sensations.

The last time I saw him, he spoke to me thus:

'Woman is a marvellous animal,* equipped with marvellous instincts. She is quite clearly the masterpiece of terrestrial fauna. Much have I travelled, and nowhere, in the forests or the steppes or in the mountains of the wildest countries, or in the remotest palaeolithic, have I come upon the spoor of a more complicated, a more startling, a more absurd creature, or one with a softer coat, or one more mutinous than woman! But how remote she is from me! I could never make her the companion of my intelligence, the sister to my thought, the ideal spouse to my enthusiasms and my passions. Which is why I shall never marry. At the very most I would set her on a perch, like a parrot, with a golden chain attached to her foot; or else I'd shut her up in a birdcage. Each morning and evening I would

bring her, instead of seed and millet, the hearts of young men, warm and bleeding hearts, and I would listen to her sing. What's the point? I can observe the same spectacle at any salon I choose to go to... Look, I have a cat. My cat is wonderful too, with those mysterious green eyes that spell the hours! The entire occult world is concealed within them... Yet I can understand my cat, I can fathom it; I know what it wants and what it dreams. Its dream is much the same as mine, and of its language, which remains unarticulated, I can seize every nuance, every inflection, every subtle nuance. Of woman, I know nothing; her forehead is a wall; her eyes are walls, and the sensual beauty of her body is a wall, behind which is the void... Very often, stretched out on a couch, I smoke, and send blue rings floating up to the ceiling; next to me my cat, stretched out on a cushion, pricks his ears, shivers and quivers along his back, and watches the smoke-rings as they rise, grow longer, undulate, float in light skeins, dissolve and vanish in the air, like a poet's ideas. Sometimes an insect with gauze-like wings comes buzzing by, and my cat follows its mad, capricious flight, watching it with wide, sad, solemn eyes, as if it traced the distressing passage of a soul. But no woman has ever been interested in the smoke from my cigarette, or in the flight of my pet insects. As the smoke drifts up into the air, and even higher beat the quivering antennae of the sphingids,* I would say to the woman: "Look." She would lower her eyes and look at the ground, eyes like the muzzles of tracking dogs, and she would ask: "What's under this carpet?—The floor.—And under the floor?—The cellar.—And under the cellar?—The sewer." She would clap her hands: her swollen nostrils seemed to sniff out the subterranean smells, and she would kiss me, exclaiming, "The sewer!... That's where I want to go!... Come." And then, suddenly all sulky, she would push me away: "No, not with you...You stink of tobacco!"

*   *   *   *   *   *   *   *   *   *

So Joseph Gardar got married. Not to just anyone, I assure you. He had searched long and hard. And he had found the most beautiful, the best, most intelligent, and most poetic among women. Her name was Clarisse. Everyone was jealous of him.

Eight days after his marriage, as they were finishing lunch, just the two of them, Clarisse said gently:

'Dearest, wouldn't you like to have a bath?'

Gardar was startled.

'A bath!... Now!... Why on earth?'

'Because I want you to, my dearest.'

'Am I dirty or something?'

'No, no!... I just want you to take a bath, right now.'

'But this is madness!... This evening, yes!... But now!'

'Oh but I want you to so much... so much!... so much!...'

She clasped her little hands together, and her voice became imploring.

'But my darling, what you're asking me is madness... And what's more, I tell you, it's dangerous!'

'Oh! Do it for me!... I want you to, my love...'

She came and sat down on his lap, kissing him tenderly and murmuring:

'Please, please!... Right now!'

They went into the bathroom. Clarisse set about getting the bath ready herself, laying out soaps and brushes and gloves and pumice on a table...

'And I shall do the scrubbing!... It'll be heavenly, you'll see!'

Even as he got undressed, he kept complaining:

'What a queer idea!... And it's dangerous too, so soon after lunch... People have died of it you know!...'

But she just laughed her clear frank laugh.

'Oh, people! Anyway, when they want to be nice to the little woman, no one ever dies.'

But he went on.

'And I'm extremely clean... I had a hot tub this morning! I'm spotless!'

'Now, now, don't be naughty.'

Still startled, he got into the bath and slid into the water...

'There!' said Clarisse... 'Isn't that lovely? Go right in, my darling! Like that!... Deeper!...'

After a few minutes, Joseph Gardar didn't feel well at all. Even though the water was very hot, it seemed to him that his legs were turning cold. He was finding it hard to breathe; his head, which had gone scarlet, was burning hot... There was a ringing in his ears, as if he were deafened by a violent pealing of bells.

'Clarisse!...' he shouted, 'Clarisse... I feel awful... awful... *Clarisse!*'

And suddenly his staring eyes showed their bloodshot whites. He tried to raise himself, his hands beating the water with a feeble, convulsive movement, and then he collapsed, sliding in a great gurgle to the bottom of the bath.

Clarisse pursed her lips a bit and murmured:

'My darling, don't do that, that's not nice of you at all!'

The First Emotion

HE was an old man, rather bowed, very mild, very silent, very clean, who had never, ever, thought about anything.

His life ran more regularly than clockwork, for even clocks can sometimes stop or go wrong. He had never known the eagerness of being a little ahead, or the worry of being a little slow, or fancied he heard bells ringing madly in his soul.

His name was Monsieur Isidore Buche, employee at the Ministry of Education.* Strange to relate, he retained, as an old man, the same rank and the same emoluments, the same office and the same work as he had had as a young man, when he first joined the civil service. A promotion would have upset his routine; he couldn't have brooked the idea, even had the idea come to him. But no idea ever did come to him. The eruption of anything new into his existence would have been worse for him, and would have scared him more than death.

Monsieur Isidore Buche rose at eight o'clock, winter and summer alike, walked to his office by the same streets, without once pausing to look in a shop window or look round at a fellow pedestrian, or waste time following the light step of a lady, or admire a pretty poster on a wall. Same thing at six in the evening: he went home, via the same streets, with the same measured, mechanical step. He would take his frugal, indescribably bland meal in his room, brought up to him by the concierge; then go out and buy the *Petit Journal** from the same place and with the same formalities, bring it home under his left arm, and then read it in bed, until nine o'clock. Then he went to sleep.

He was good, which was easy, since he had no one to love; no wife, no child, no relation; no friend, dog, waif, or flower! He was good, by which I mean he never spoke ill of his superiors; he had never spoken out against a colleague, and had always sat under every insult and

attack without ever answering back. People said of him, using a singular euphemism: 'Ah, old Isidore Buche, he's a brick!' He worked all day Sunday—for his emoluments were modest—balancing the account books of an old lady in Clichy, who owned five working-class dwellings. He was sixty years old and had never thought about anything.

*   *   *   *   *   *   *   *   *   *

He had never thought about anything. But suddenly, one day, he was astounded to see something in the sky on his way to the office, something very tall which he didn't know. He didn't know Notre-Dame, he didn't know the Obelisk or the Arc de Triomphe or the Pantheon or the Invalides; he didn't know anything. He had passed all these monuments without seeing them, and consequently without wondering why they were there or what they signified. He did, however, have a vague notion of their proximate presence. The sculpted façades, the domes, the spires, the great masses of cut stone, the arches under the dreaming sky, the squares, the horizons, the breaches made by the streets, all these things melted into the great nothingness that included, in his mind, the city, the countryside, all things and all beings, except for his office, his room, the clerks at the Ministry, his concierge, and the *Petit Journal*. But the sudden eruption of this unfamiliar thing which blocked the sky and which disturbed the nothingness—this he was compelled to see, and having once seen it, he was compelled to think about it. His *Petit Journal* informed him that it was the Eiffel Tower.*

And then, his mind went to work.

Every morning he experienced tortures of perplexity, he wondered what the Eiffel Tower really was, what function it could serve, and why its name was Eiffel. This was the only moment in his life when, inside his brain, there laboured something resembling intellectual excitement. He became dimly aware that there might be some life outside of his own, a life that existed beyond his concierge; he came to some vague and groping consciousness in which embryonic forms took shape, and larval movements corresponding to them. But he got such a headache thinking of all these things. In terror, he would exclaim every morning to the clerks at the Ministry: 'I saw the Eiffel Tower again!' And in the evening, with the same terror sharpened by some remote biblical memory, he would say to his concierge: 'I saw

the Tower of Babel again!' And then he started to get distracted as he
read his *Petit Journal*. Several times he stopped short in the street, in
front of a poster; and one day he had been surprised by the strange
gaze of a passer-by. Sensing the approach of various undefined fantasies, combined with an insidious need to break through the narrow
walls of his room and the blackened ceiling of his office, he became
terrified. But soon this remarkable convulsion within his breast
calmed down, and the crisis passed. Gradually he stopped speaking
again, he stopped seeing and hearing, he no longer stopped to look at
a poster or notice the commotion in a human gaze. The regular tick-
tock of his inner life was re-established. And the Eiffel Tower became
blended with the Louvre, Notre-Dame, the Obelisk, the Arc de
Triomphe, the Pantheon, and the Invalides in the thick mist attendant upon the death of his mind and the death of his eyes. He started
once more not to think about anything.

* * * * * * * * * *

He started once more not to think about anything. But then something unexpected and stupefying happened to him.

One night, he had a dream!

He dreamed he was on a riverbank, fishing.

Why that dream? He had never gone fishing.

Why any dream? He had never dreamed.

His nights were as empty of dreams as his days. He slept as he
lived: in nullity. Day and night, the same moral shadowiness went on.

To him, the thing was serious, it was terrible, the eruption of a
dream into his nocturnal life, as terrible as the eruption of a thought
in his diurnal life. But he did not seek to explain the wherewithal of
this new mystery.

The next night, he dreamed again.

He dreamed he was fishing. Yes, he saw himself thus, sitting, on a
bank amongst fragrant flowery grasses. In his hand was a long, thin
fishing-rod. From the far end of the rod hung a horsehair attached to
a red float that was bobbing on the water. From time to time the float
twitched on the still, hard, mirror-like surface. Then he tugged with
all his might and with both hands on his end of the rod. The line was
taut, the rod bent, and he spent hours trying to land the invisible fish.
Then he would wake up, all in a lather, panting and exhausted, and
for some minutes in the darkness of his room, which seemed to be lit

with the fantastical and phosphorescent carcasses of fish, he was held
by the horror of the bent rod, the taut line, and the stony surface of
the water which showed no jumping minnow or cruising pike, or
indeed any ripple around the red float.

The dream recurred every night, for a period of several months.

'Shall I never bring it in?' he exclaimed to himself in horror.

He thought about his dream all day. And he would have preferred
not to think about anything.

*   *   *   *   *   *   *   *   *   *

He would have preferred to think about nothing. But from thinking
so hard about his dream, he developed a passion for fishing.

To reach his office, Monsieur Isidore Buche made detours, wandered along the quays, and lingered to watch the fishermen. On his
way home in the evening, he stopped in front of a shop where rods
and lines and every kind of attractive accessory were displayed in the
window. He didn't know what they were for, but he should have
liked to possess them. He experienced a glow of pleasure when
he looked at the carp made of golden card, hanging high up in the
window, attached to a silk thread. And he said to himself again, with
beating heart and a rush of hot blood through his veins: 'I'll never
bring it in!'

One Saturday evening he steeled himself and went into the shop,
spent lavishly, and went home, prey to a most unusual excitement. At
dawn the next day he made his way towards the Seine, furnished with
rods, lines, landing-nets, pockets stuffed with tins and little cases.
He followed the Seine to Meudon, and at Meudon he picked a spot
where the water looked deep and the grass soft. As he prepared his
line, according to the instructions they gave him in the shop, he kept
murmuring: 'Come now!... Come now!... I'll never bring one in!'
Then he cast his line on the stream...

The morning was festive, the water sang gently by the banks, in a
clump of reeds. Walkers dawdled on the towpath, and picked flowers.

Monsieur Isidore Buche stared at the red-and-blue float bobbing
on the quiet surface of the water. His lips were pursed and his heart
riven with anxiety. Something hard and burning seemed to be
clamped over his skull, which was covered by the inevitable straw hat.

Suddenly the float tremored, and around it appeared a growing
series of ripples...

'Oh! Oh!' said Monsieur Isidore Buche, who had gone very red…
The float moved more rapidly on the water, and then disappeared
in a small trail of bubbles.

'Oh! Oh!' he said, very pale.

And he felt a shudder… Pulling up, he saw the line go taut and the
rod bend; his heart started beating like an Easter bell… Cold sweat
broke out on his temples… he collapsed on the bank… stone dead!

The Little Summer-House

I HAD suffered serious losses in enterprises, alas less solid but quite
as honourable as the Panama Syndicates,* the Southern Railways,
and suchlike. So the day came when I was forced to make my assets
'earn their keep', as they say. There are moments in life when one
misses not having some Reinach to hand, or some Yves Guyot,* which
would ease things a great deal. But stop this whingeing! I'm not
writing these lines out of self-pity.

So I cut down on my expenses and reduced my service to the bare
minimum—a butler and a cook—which as it turned out represented
no great saving, since the two loyal retainers began to rob me as much
as the other five I had dismissed. I sold my horses and my carriages,
my collection of paintings and Persian porcelain, a section of my wine
cellar, alas! and my three greenhouses, which contained some rare
and splendid plants. In the end, I resolved to rent out a little summer-
house, a delectable little place, set apart from the main property.
I had done the place up specially so that I might receive clandestine
visits, which cost me a lot of money, so I had to renounce those too.
Thanks to its isolated position in the grounds and its comfortable
furnishings, it could serve as a country retreat for a member of either
sex who, for the three summer months, felt inclined to vary their
celibacy or hide their adultery, depending on their situation.

Titillated by the suggestive wording of my advertisements, many
people—strange and hideous people, mostly—came to have a look.
To them I vaunted the excellence and the security of this refuge, with
its exterior covered in Virginia creeper, though not its interior, for
that wouldn't do at all—ho! ho!—there must be no creeper on the
inside, and no virgins either. But these people demanded I do so

much work on the place—they wanted the cellar in the attic and the attic in the cellar—that in the end we couldn't come to terms. I began to despair of renting the summer-house, by now it was well into the season, when one afternoon a little gentleman, clean-shaven, upright, extremely polite, and somewhat advanced in years, arrived, hat in hand, to inspect the place. He was wearing garments of an old-fashioned cut, unpressed, with a long watch-chain hung with strange charms, and on his head a wig, greenish-blond in tint, whose shape recalled the worst days of the Orléanist Monarchy.*

The little gentleman found everything to be perfect... quite perfect!... and spoke of the place in such glowingly complimentary terms I scarcely knew what to say. In the bathroom, which was decorated with mirrors and licentious paintings on alternating panels, his wig shifted and nearly came adrift, and he exclaimed:

'Aha! Aha!'

'They're by Fragonard,'* I explained, uncertain whether his 'Aha!' signalled disapproval or pleasure. But I was soon enlightened.

'Aha!' he said again... 'Fragonard?... Really?... Wonderful!'

And I saw his little eyes blink weirdly in response to a definite sensation.

After a short silence, during which he scrutinized the panels more closely, he said:

'Very well... it's agreed... I shall take the perfect summer-house.'

'Which is so discreet...' I added in a suggestive way, gesturing eloquently through the window at the tall, thick, impenetrable wall of greenery that surrounded us on every side.

'Discreet indeed... perfectly so!'

Noting the respectful and probably slightly 'twinkly' enthusiasm of my accommodating tenant, I found various ingenious reasons to increase the rent, which was already exorbitant, by adding a few hundred francs on to the advertised rate. But this is by the by and of no significance, and if I mention it, it is only to pay homage to the perfectly good grace of the little gentleman, who even declared himself charmed by the way I had received him.

We returned to the house, and there I hastened to draw up a short contract, under private agreement, for which I required his surname, first names, and civil status. I learned that his name was Jean-Jules-Joseph Lagoffin, formerly a property lawyer at Montrouge. To complete the contract in due and proper form, I asked him if he was

married, widowed, or single. Instead of replying he placed upon the table in front of me a wad of banknotes, which obliged me to write him a receipt and put an end to my questions. 'He's obviously married,' I thought... 'But he is embarrassed to admit it, because of the... Fragonard paintings.'

Then I looked more closely at him, and at his eyes, which might perhaps have been gentle ones if they had been anything. But at that moment they were quite expressionless, and quite dead, as dead as the skin of his face and cheeks, which was slack, wrinkled, and entirely grey, as if it had been cooked and re-cooked in boiling water on a low flame.

After accepting a glass of orangeade, out of politeness, Jean-Jules-Joseph Lagoffin took his leave, with an effusive show of gratitude, salutation, and deference. He advised me that—if it were not inconvenient—he should like to settle into the summer-house the very next day. Upon which, I gave him a key.

The next day, he didn't come. Nor did he come the day after. Eight days, fifteen days went by without news from him. This was strange, but certainly explicable. Perhaps he had fallen ill—and yet, such was his excessive politeness, he would have written to tell me so. Or had the companion he was to have brought with him to the summer-house refused to come at the last moment? This seemed altogether more likely, for I didn't doubt for an instant that Jean-Jules-Joseph Lagoffin had rented this discreet and perfect summer-house with a mistress in mind, for the way his eyes blinked at the sight of the Fragonards and the way his wig had gone awry was proof enough of his concupiscent designs. In any case, I felt I had no need to be unduly preoccupied, since he had paid me generously, beyond all expectation.

One morning I went to open up the little summer-house in order to air it, since it had stood closed since Lagoffin's visit. I crossed the hall, the dining room, the salon, and at the entrance to the bathroom I let out a scream and backed away in horror.

There on the cushions was a naked body, the corpse of a little girl, stretched out and horribly stiff, her limbs all twisted and convulsed, like those of a torture victim.

To call for help, call my servants, call everyone—that was my first impulse. But once I had got over the first flush of horror, I decided it were better that I should examine things by myself first of all, and

with no witnesses. I even took care to triple-lock the door to the summer-house.

It was indeed a little girl, with the slender figure of a young boy. At her throat were marks of strangulation; and on her chest and belly were long, thin, deep incisions, made with fingernails, or with cutting and pointed claws. Her swollen face had turned black. On a chair lay her pauper's clothes, a wretched little dress, frayed at the edges and all muddy, and a ragged petticoat, folded almost punctiliously. On the marble-topped bathroom table I saw a bit of paté and two green apples, one of which had been nibbled, as if by mice. And an empty bottle of champagne.

Nothing was altered in the other rooms, which I scanned one after the other. Each piece of furniture, each object, was in its usual place.

Rapidly, feverishly, and in no logical order, my mind started racing:

'Should I alert the police, the law?... Never... The magistrates would come and I would not know what to say to them... Accuse Jean-Jules-Joseph Lagoffin?... Obviously the man had given me a false name, and there was no point in going to Montrouge to find out he had never lived there... What then?... They would not believe me... They would think I'd invented it... They would never believe that this man had committed an atrocious crime almost on my doorstep, in a strange house that belonged to me, without my seeing or hearing anything... Tell us another!... You can't tweak the nose of the Law like that... And then, suspicious, with hyena-looks, they would examine me, and of course I would fall into the snare laid by their insidious and sinister questions... They would ransack my whole life, looking for clues... Fragonard would be held against me, Fragonard would scream out the grossness of my pleasures and the shame of my routine lusts... They would want to know the names of every woman who had come here, and of all those who had not... And then I would be calumnied by the servants I had dismissed, by the grain merchant I had boycotted, by the baker I had accused of using false measures, by the butcher whose poisoned meat I had sent back... all of them would be ready, under the protection of the Law, to sully me with their vengeance and their rancour!... And finally the day would come when my hesitation and reticence and embarrassment in response to their questionings would be taken as a confession of my guilt, and they would charge me with murder... No!... There

must be no judges, no gendarmes, no policemen here!... Nothing... Nothing but a little earth to cover this poor little corpse, and a bit of moss over the earth, and silence, silence, silence... on all of this!...*

I took the frayed and muddied dress, the ragged petticoat, and in them I wrapped the little body of the unknown girl, like a shroud... Afterwards, once I had ascertained that everything in the summer-house was hermetically closed and sealed against the indiscreet or accidental curiosity of my servant, I went out. I wandered around the summer-house for the whole day, waiting for nightfall.

That evening was the village fête. I sent off my servants, and when I was alone, completely alone, I set myself to burying the little girl in the grounds, deep in the earth at the foot of a beech tree...

Yes! Silence, silence, silence, and earth, earth, earth, over all that!...

Yesterday, in the Parc Monceau, I spotted Jean-Jules-Joseph Lagoffin. He still had the same slack, grey skin, the same dead expression, the same greenish-blond wig. He was following a little flower-girl, who was selling sunflowers to passers-by. Near me, a municipal policeman was waddling along, ogling a girl... But the stupidity of his face made me turn on my heel... I foresaw nothing but complications, the Whats?... and the Hows?...

'Ye gods! Let them work it all out,' I said to myself. 'It's none of my business...'

With a light step, I fled in the opposite direction to the municipal policeman, to Jean-Jules-Joseph Lagoffin, and to the little flower-seller... that someone else may have to bury in his grounds, under a beech tree, and at night!...

JEAN RICHEPIN

Constant Guignard

THE Guignard spouses, married for love, longed passionately for a son. As if the little soul who was so desired had hastened to fulfil their wishes, he arrived prematurely. His mother died in childbirth and, unable to bear the loss, his father hanged himself.

* * * * * * * * * *

Constant Guignard had an exemplary but an unhappy childhood. He spent his time at school doing detentions he didn't deserve, receiving thrashings meant for others, and being ill on the days when all the important exams were held. He completed his studies with the reputation of a cockroach and a dunce. When it came to the Baccalaureate, he did his neighbour's Latin translation for him. His neighbour passed, but Guignard was expelled from the exam for copying.

* * *

Such inauspicious beginnings in life would have turned a lesser nature vicious. But Constant Guignard had a soul of the higher type, and convinced that happiness is the reward of virtue, he resolved to conquer his ill-fortune by sheer force of heroism.

He entered a house of commerce, which burned down the next day. As the fire raged, he noticed the distress of his employer, and plunged into the flames to retrieve the safe. His hair burned and his limbs suppurated, but he managed, at peril of his life, to break the safe and take the contents out.

But the fire consumed them in his hands. When he emerged from the furnace, two constables grabbed him by the collar. A month later he was condemned to five years imprisonment for having tried to steal, at the opportune moment offered by the fire, a fortune that was quite safe where it was in a fireproof strongbox.

* * *

A riot broke out in the high-security prison where he was held. In his attempt to come to the rescue of a warder being attacked, he tripped him accidentally and left him to be massacred by the rebels. So they sent him to Cayenne* for twenty years.

Driven by the knowledge of his innocence, he escaped, made his way back to France under an assumed name, and truly believed he had shaken off ill-fortune, and once more set about doing good.

* * *

One day, during a fair, he saw a runaway horse dragging a cab straight towards the edge of the rampart. He flung himself at the head of the horse, got his wrist twisted, his leg broken, and had several ribs stove in, but he managed to prevent the dreadful fall. Except that the horse turned round and charged into the middle of the crowd, crushing an old man, two women, and three children. There had been no one in the cab.

* * *

Wearied by these acts of heroism, Constant Guignard took instead to doing good quietly, humbly devoting himself to alleviating everyday hardships. But the money he gave to families in need was spent by the husbands on drink; the woollens he distributed to poor workers, used to the cold, made them catch pneumonia; a stray dog he rescued gave rabies to six people in the neighbourhood; the military substitute* he purchased to get an interesting young man out of the army sold pass-keys to the enemy.

* * *

Constant Guignard came to believe that money did more harm than good, and rather than spreading wide his philanthropy, he decided to concentrate it on a single person. So he adopted a young orphan girl, not in any way beautiful, but graced with the most loveable nature, and he looked after her with all the tenderness of a father. Alas! He was so good, so devoted, and so kindly towards her, that one evening she flung herself at his feet, declaring that she was in love with him. He tried to make her understand that he had always considered her as his daughter, and that it would be a crime were he to succumb to the temptation she presented. He made her understand, in his fatherly way, that what she took to be love was in fact the awakening of her

senses, and he promised her that, taking note of this sign of nature, he would not delay in seeking a husband worthy of her. The next day he found her lying against his door, a knife in her heart.

* * *

With that, Constant Guignard decided to give up his missionary role, and swore that from now on he would seek satisfaction simply in trying to prevent evil.

Some time after this, he was apprised by accident of a crime that one of his friends was going to commit. He could have denounced him to the police; but he preferred to try and prevent the crime, and save the criminal. So he became closely involved with the planning, understood all the details, and waited for the precise moment when, having set everything up, he would scupper the whole plan. But the rascal he was trying to save saw through his game, and managed to outwit him, in such wise that the crime was perpetrated, the criminal got away, and Constant Guignard was arrested.

* * *

The public prosecutor's requisition against Constant Guignard was a masterpiece of logic. He recalled the defendant's whole life, his miserable childhood, with its punishments and expulsions, the audacity of his first attempted theft, his despicable treachery in the prison riot, his escape from Cayenne, his return to France under an assumed name. From this moment on, the orator rose to the greatest possible heights of legal eloquence. He scourged the hypocritical virtue of the man, who was a corrupter of decent families, who for his own pleasure had sent honest husbands out to drink his money; this false do-gooder who contrived, by giving presents, to attain an unmerited popularity, this monster hidden in the habit of a philanthropist. He dwelt in detail upon the refined perversity of a wretch who rescued rabid dogs only to let them loose on society, of a demon who, in love with evil for its own sake, was prepared to injure himself in order to stop a runaway horse, and why? For the unspeakable pleasure of seeing the animal plunge into the crowd, crushing to death old men, women, and children. Such a man would stop at nothing! And there were certainly other crimes to his name as yet unknown. All the evidence pointed to the fact that he was the accomplice of the mercenary who had betrayed France. And as for the orphan he had raised, and who had been found

one morning dead at his door, who else but he could have murdered her? This crime was undoubtedly the bloody end to one of those family dramas made up of shame, debauchery, and filth, the like of which was hard to contemplate. After such a list, it was scarcely necessary to dwell on this latest crime. In this case, and despite the impudent denials of the accused, the evidence was incontrovertible. It was necessary, therefore, to condemn this man with the full rigour of the law. The punishment was just, and no punishment could be heavy enough. The defendant was not only a great criminal, he was one of those geniuses of crime, one of those monsters of malice and hypocrisy that make one doubt the existence of virtue and despair of humanity.

Before such a crushing indictment, Constant Guignard's lawyer had no alternative but to plead that his client was mad. He did his best, spoke learnedly of the *compulsion to evil*, portrayed his client as an irresponsible monomaniac, as a kind of unconscious Papavoine,* and concluded by saying that such behaviour was more appropriately treated in the asylum at Charenton* than on the Place de la Roquette.*

The verdict was unanimous: Constant Guignard was sentenced to death.

* * *

Men of virtue, driven wild by their hatred of crime, went into transports of joy, and cried hurrah.

* * *

The death of Constance Guignard, like his life, was exemplary but unhappy. He mounted the scaffold without fear and without pretence, his face as calm as his conscience, and with a martyr's serenity about him which onlookers took to be the indifference of a brute. At the final moment, aware that his executioner was poor and with a family, he whispered to him that he had left him his entire fortune. The executioner was so moved by this that it took him three attempts to sever his benefactor's neck.

* * *

Three months after this, one of Constant Guignard's friends, returning from a long journey, learned of the honest man's sad end. Knowing only the man's merits, he set about trying to repair as best he could the injustice meted out by fate. He purchased a permanent concession,

ordered a fine marble tombstone, and composed an epitaph for his friend. The next day he died of a stroke. Nevertheless, the expenses had been paid in advance, so the guillotined man got his sepulchre. But the stone-carver employed to execute the epitaph took it upon him to correct a letter that had been badly written on the manuscript. And the poor virtuous man, misjudged in his lifetime, lies in death with the following epitaph for all eternity:

Here lies Constant Guignard
A Zero

Deshoulières

His name was Deshoulières and he didn't like it.

In this he was wrong, for it was doubtless in large part his name, and the banalities associated with it, that led to his singular obsession with being original.

He was indeed, as far as originality goes, a species apart, rare and whole.

Having dabbled in nearly everything—arts, letters, pleasures—he had forged for himself an ideal, that consisted in being *unpredictable* in everything.

At first sight, this wasn't anything strange, the theory merely indicating a curious soul, the enemy of the commonplace, a seeker of the new—in common with all true creators. But where things became unusual was that Deshoulières made of this theory a rule of conduct in his daily life and in his dealings with the world, pushing it to the point of extreme eccentricity.

He had become the dandy of the unpredictable.

* * *

So it was that, finding originality only in change, he invented the following axiom: one should never look like oneself, physically, especially. It is this that explains his extraordinarily varied clothes, manners, voice, and even physiognomy. Making ample use of make-up and false hair, he emerged each day with a different head, and lived like a veritable Proteus.*

His mind was as various as a kaleidoscope, showing up paradoxes like coloured glass, mingled with the most monstrous truisms, which made in reality for a dazzle of words, ideas, images, arguments, quite blinding for those who wanted to take the measure of this fantasmagorical intelligence.

* * *

He was, moreover, extremely gifted.

Robust and well-built, he was two feet longer than the verses of his deplorable homonym,* and one could discern a modern beauty under all his borrowed facets. He had marvellous facility in assimilating every virtue and every vice, all the sciences and all the arts. He was known for his acts of heroism and his acts of cowardice, for his *tours de force* and his swoonings, for incomparable fragments of verse and prose, for snatches of novel melody, for sketches which showed the marks of a future master. Potentially, he possessed every human genius.

But he never took anything further, claiming that it would be too banal to do so. It sufficed him to say that he had all the power necessary to become a great man, poet, musician, painter—but he renounced such things, such grandeurs being altogether too vulgar and below him.

It's all as old as the hills, he would say. There is no point in my being the god of my century, since I already am. It might amuse me to be that god, if I were a mere brute! But even that has been done before!

Mostly, people wrote him off as a lunatic. But some men thought of him as a kind of Antichrist.

But this Antichrist was much too subtly eccentric to believe in himself.

If God did exist, he said one day, and if I were He, I wouldn't be so stupid as not to prove to myself I did not exist.

* * *

Holding such theories, it is obvious that Deshoulières could exist only in Paris, and only in our own times; and he would surely have lived on there quietly, for many years to come, a source of anxiety to a few friends, but mostly an amusement to the crowd, no more nor less than a simple clown, had he not in fact been the man of genius that he was.

An ordinary original would not have had the idea of carrying out the extreme eccentricity that cost him his life.

He contrived to murder his mistress, have her embalmed, and to continue as her lover.

The crime was carried out with such skill, and with such *novelty* in the manner of concealing it, that it remained undetected.

But it was the fact that this monstrously sadistic crime was a secret, this is what seemed banal to Deshoulières. He considered that there was no great originality in being a monster and escaping the exactions of the law. He confessed to the crime himself, showing not the slightest remorse, which was, indeed, essentially *unpredictable*.

The whole of Paris cried out in horror, and every eye was riveted upon Deshoulières.

* * *

This was the moment, if ever, to be unusual, and his task now was to find a way of being *unpredictable*, while surrounded by the vulgarities of prison, the assize court, and the guillotine. Deshoulières remained true to his *mission*.

In prison, he busied himself not with his defence, nor with his notoriety, but with classifying and codifying the mysteries of animal magnetism, and of transforming this dense philosophical treatise into a sequence of monosyllabic sonnets. After writing three he gave up, having satisfied himself that the thing was *possible*.

* * *

In the dock, he was magnificent.

His barrister, an illustrious member of the profession, was tickled by the challenge presented by the difficulty of the case and the indifference of his client; his speech for the defence was extraordinary, and he succeeded in shaking the jury and wrong-footing the public prosecutor. Numerous irrefutable proofs, a powerful current of pity, and a winning eloquence combined to establish Deshoulière's innocence and ensure his acquittal.

The judge had tears in his eyes when he asked the accused if he had anything else to say in his own defence.

'Gentlemen,' said Deshoulières, 'I should first of all like to offer sincere congratulations to my lawyer for his masterly piece of

eloquence in the tradition of French justice. There is only one passage I could perhaps improve upon.'

And he commenced to rework one of his advocate's arguments, in a way that shed new light and conquered the sympathy of the court.

'Alas,' he went on, 'I cannot say the same of the honourable gentleman the Public Prosecutor, who seems unfit for the grave task entrusted him by the Republic.'

The judges looked startled, the prosecutor furious, the jury baffled.

But this was as nothing to the effect produced when Deshoulières, having enumerated all the weak links in the Prosecutor's argument, undertook to rebuild from the beginning the case for the prosecution. And he did so with such fire, such energy, such power! He showed in their true light all the hideousnesses of his crime, he took the defence apart brick by brick, and concluded by proving his own guilt so comprehensively that no possible doubt could remain. The verdict that had seemed so certain was reversed by him like a glove, and he obtained what he wanted: the *unpredictable* result of having himself, by his own volition, condemned to death.

* * *

He spent the last hours of his life inventing a new dance-step and an oyster sauce.

When the prison chaplain came to hear his confession, as his final hour drew near, Deshoulières refused to comply, unless the priest first confessed to him. That done, he confessed nothing, but rather spoke to the priest thus:

'In your speech just now, you quoted a phrase of St Augustine's. It is from Tertullian, the ninth paragraph of his *De cultu foeminarum.** Go in peace, my son, and quote no more!'

In spite of these capricious attitudes and his force of character, Deshoulières grew anxious when he saw the guillotine.

Not that he was afraid! But he dreaded coming to a banal end after a life of unremitting eccentricity. It displeased him to think that he was to have his neck severed like any Tom, Dick, and Harry. So he contrived a way of being guillotined in an *unpredictable* fashion.

He must have found one. For his face, as he mounted the scaffold leading to the Widow,* was lit up by a smile of joy.

And he offered no resistance when they strapped him down on the sinister plank.

But at the instant it tilted into place, he made a gigantic effort, broke his bonds with his Herculean strength, and thrust himself backwards so his head was no longer engaged up to the neck in the lunette of the machine.

The spring was released, nothing could stop the blade, and Deshoulières had his skull topped like a boiled egg.

* * *

He was *unpredictable* on the guillotine.

It chopped his head, *page-boy style.**

Pft! Pft!

ONCE upon a time, exactly where I could not say (for in truth, the land has been called by every name and exists at all times), lived a woman whose exact appearance I cannot sketch either.

Every man saw her differently and each was right, because he found her appealing like that.

To which must be added the fact that she herself did nothing to try and appear in a certain light. She was content to be in reality everything that people thought she was, not knowing herself exactly what she was.

Some wise heads implied that she was in fact nothing; others, wiser still, added that this was precisely the source of her charm. They compared her to the clouds, whose magic depends on the dreamer that contemplates them, and to the symphonies of the sea, whose music is governed by the music one sings to oneself.

Certainly the said wise heads were not far wrong in their comparisons. But like all great sages, they were quite wrong. For this nothing, that they treated so disdainfully as nothing, was indeed something. The proof being that they were unable to let it alone, and kept trying to explain the reason for it.

Wiser still perhaps were the self-confessed madmen who did not seek to understand, and who simply took the mysterious woman for what she was, or at least for what they believed her to be. Thus they would live through her and within her.

Live, yes, and die too, alas! And they would die having first suffered the thousand deaths known as broken trust, shattered hope,
sexual jealousy, and love betrayed.

But why say, *alas?* Do not these thousand deaths constitute what is
called life? And the lovers went gaily to their doom, and savoured it,
as if they had the poet's words for a motto:

> Come, take my life; it is yours, I give it you.
> Write what you will on the great white sheet.
> Tear, if you will, every page of the book.
> Eat my flesh, pierce my side, drink my spirit.
> But this is life! It is living still
> To watch your own life-blood spill.

It must be said in favour of the mysterious woman that she never
once made them suffer out of deliberate cruelty.

She was no more wicked than she was, in particular, anything
else. She was even, on occasion, prone to accesses of tenderness
and compassion. She felt sincerely sorry for those she was about
to make unhappy. She would often warn them, in all honesty, by
saying:

'You know that I am not in love with you.'

To which nearly everyone replied:

'So what? I adore you.'

Well, and after that, what right did the men she betrayed and
tortured have to complain?

To others, assuredly, she would sigh breathlessly:

'I love you!'

Then she would betray them too, using this excuse:

'I made a mistake. I thought I loved him. It's not my fault. And
now I am paying for my mistake!'

And she would say this so gently, and so reasonably, that anyone
not biased would be sure to agree with her.

What is more, she would end by turning everything into a joke, her
own sufferings, and those of others even more. The basis of her philosophy (for this *nothing*, despite what the wise heads thought, had
her own philosophy) was that one should never attach too much
importance to anything whatsoever.

She was not hard-hearted, and she did have a heart, and sometimes
she would cry; but once she had turned her back she thought no more

of her suffering, shrugged her shoulders, and *moved on to other things*, making a little noise with a winning pout of her lips:

'Pft! Pft!'

She did this so often that a sharp-tongued wag ended by calling her *Madame Pft! Pft!*

She wasn't angry. On the contrary, it tickled her vanity. The nickname amused her. She even, on reflection (for this *nothing* also engaged in reflection), found it could come in useful.

Now, instead of trying to find excuses for her conduct, and explanations to those who questioned her like the sphinx, she answered simply:

'Pft! Pft!'

At which the wag with the sharp tongue scratched his head and congratulated himself on his inventive genius:

'Ye gods! Have I made a huge discovery? Have I stumbled upon the answer to the riddle?'

He thought, and then thought some more, so much so that he ended falling head over heels in love with the mysterious woman, whose mystery he thought he had solved.

To tell the truth, since he was a wise and learned man, *id est* one of those proud souls who are cleverest at deceiving themselves, he would not admit that he was in love, but nursed the fantasy rather that he was undertaking a scientific inquiry.

'No,' he would remind himself complacently, 'I have not been seduced by this doll. I just want to study her, that is all.'

So, exactly like the commonest of mortals, he set about studying her by courting her, desiring her, thirsting for her; and with the pretext that he was examining her soul in the crucible, he in fact contrived quite naively to melt into the depths of her bed, as so many others had melted before him.

And melt the poor sage did, no more nor less than other men. And the experience of melting thus taught the incompetent sage absolutely nothing at all.

He did not even know if he was loved.

She could have told him that he was not, as she had, with admirable frankness, others before him. But in his case, because he affected to be so haughty and knowing, she allowed herself to be a little less than honest. When he questioned her, out of his wits with passion, she would reply with a little smile, looking away:

'Pft! Pft!'

It goes without saying that she was unfaithful to him. But this time she put a little malice and cruelty into it, or so one might believe. The man she chose to be his lucky rival was a complete imbecile.

The learned man was coward enough to promise he would forgive her, if only she would admit her faithlessness. If need be he would have analysed this depravity in her taste, his thorough understanding would itself have led to forgiveness and absolution. Is it not natural for a woman to want to alternate between a brute and a man of refinement? To please her, he would have given her a dazzling lecture to demonstrate the matter.

But she refused to allow him even this consolation. When, in tears, he would ask her if this rival really existed, and when, abjectly, he offered to proclaim the guilty party innocent, she would turn on her heel and murmur:

'Pft! Pft!'

So he suffered all the agonies of jealousy and despair. He began to harbour murderous ideas. These he did not hide, and threatened to put the blame for them on her.

'Yes,' he screamed, 'I shall kill this rival that you flay me with!'

She would just shake her head, indicating that she didn't believe a word of his bloodthirsty plan; and then she added:

'And in any case, it would all be too pft! pft!'

Driven to distraction, the sage proved even more of a brute than the brute who was loved. One evening he ambushed him, cut his throat, slashed him to pieces, and tore the heart out of his breast; and he flung this horrible trophy, still beating, at the feet of the woman.

This time she really was horrified, somewhat. But catching a gleam of triumph in the eye of the murderer, she refused him this victory. Mastering her horror, she gazed quite calmly upon the hideous morsel of red meat, prodded it with the point of her parasol, and with a winning pout went:

'Pft! Pft!'

'Oh! The monster, the monster!' shrieked the learned man. 'I shall kill you too! Yes, I shall kill you too. I want to know if you actually have a heart, and if so, what is in it. And I shall know. I shall, I shall!'

He looked wildly, and his hands trembled.

'What is in my heart?' she answered placidly. 'I shall tell you what there is. It's quite simple. It is this:

'Pft! Pft!'

At this he took leave of his wits completely. With both hands he seized the woman's neck, and closing his fingers upon it, upon the smooth white neck that he adored, he throttled her long and hard, and showed no pity.

She did not have the strength to scream. She scarcely struggled, like a strangled bird. But with her dying breath, exhaled like a final answer, came an almost imperceptible sigh:

'Pft! Pft!'

'At last,' roared the sage, once she was well and truly dead. 'At last! There'll be no more of your damnable *pft! pft!* You shall mock at my love no longer, nor at my learning. And since I studied you when you were living, valiantly shall I study you dead.'

And he set about dissecting her in his mind, hoping to find the *nothing* that she was, and he became convinced that she really was that *nothing*, for in no part of her did he find the soul whose existence he denied.

This made him joyful.

To perpetuate his joy, and to keep a proof of his victory always near at hand, the implacable sage started to scheme. Or, to put it another way, the inconsolable lover conceived the fantastic idea of *embalming* the mysterious woman to re-endow her with a living form.

He was still in love with her!

Indeed, once he had had the horrible corpse tanned, he loved her more than ever. In the perversity of his adoration he found her beautiful, and kneeling before her, he implored her forgiveness.

Of what is madness not capable?

Deeply deranged and lost, desire rose in him once more for this mannikin filled with air. In an access of lust he flung himself upon the horror to possess it.

Suddenly, as his amorous arms pressed the thing hard against him, and as he bit into it with his kisses, there was a tearing sound, and from the monstrous lips, in a long whistle, horribly against his face in posthumous irony came:

'Pft! Pft!'

GUY DE MAUPASSANT

At the Death-Bed

HE was dying, after the fashion of the tubercular. Every day, at around two o'clock, I would see him sit down beneath the windows of the hotel, facing the calm sea, on a bench along the promenade. For a while he would remain quite still, in the heat of the sun, and contemplate the Mediterranean with a forlorn expression. From time to time he would glance up at the high mountain with its cloudy summit, that surrounds Menton; then, very slowly, he would cross his long legs, so thin they resembled two bones, with the ample trouser cloth draped over them, and he would open a book, which was always the same.

And then he would move no more; he read, he read with utter concentration; his whole wretched, dying body seemed to be reading, he read with his whole soul, that seemed to sink and disappear into this book, until the air which had cooled made him cough lightly. Then he would get up and go in.

He was a tall, light-bearded German, who took lunch and dinner in his room, and spoke to no one.

A vague curiosity drew me to him. One day I sat down next to him, and so as to appear occupied, I brought with me a volume of Musset's poetry.

And I started to flick through 'Rolla'.*

Suddenly my neighbour addressed me, in good French:

'Can you speak German, Monsieur?'

'Not a word, Monsieur.'

'A pity. Since chance has placed us side by side, I would have lent you, I would have shown you, something of inestimable worth—the book I have here.'

'What is it?'

'It is a volume by my master, Schopenhauer, annotated in his own hand.'

I took the book into my hands with care, and contemplated its words that were to me incomprehensible, but which revealed the

immortal thought of the greatest debunker of dreams that ever walked the earth.

And these lines of Musset came to me:

> Do you sleep content, Voltaire, and does your hideous smile
> Hover still above your fleshless bones?

Involuntarily, I compared the childish sarcasm of Voltaire towards religion to the irresistible irony of the German philosopher, whose influence from now on will never be eradicated.

One can protest or get angry, one can deplore or rejoice, the fact is that Schopenhauer has branded humanity with the iron of his disdain and his disenchantment.

Disabused joker, he has overturned hopes, poetries, chimeras, he has destroyed aspirations, ravaged trusting souls, killed love, cast down the cult of the idealized woman, punctured the hopes of hearts, and generally carried through the most gigantic labour of scepticism ever attempted. Nothing has escaped his mockery, he has emptied everything out. And today, even those who loathe him seem to bear within their minds some vestiges of his thought.*

'So you knew Schopenhauer personally?' I asked the German.

'Until the day he died, Monsieur.'

And he started to tell me about him, he described the almost supernatural effect this strange being had on all those who frequented him.

He described the interview between the great dismantler and a French politician, a convinced republican, who sought out this man and found him in a crowded bar, sitting in the midst of his disciples, dry, wrinkled, laughing his unforgettable laugh, tearing and biting through ideas in a single phrase, as a dog will tear the cloth he's worrying with his teeth.

He repeated to me what the horrified Frenchman had exclaimed on leaving:

'It was like spending an hour with the devil.'

Then my German companion went on:

'He did indeed have a dreadful smile that frightened us, even after his death. There is an almost unknown anecdote concerning this that I could recount if you like.'

And he began, with a weary voice, broken from time to time by fits of coughing:

'Schopenhauer had just died, and it was decided that we should watch over the body in pairs, in turn, until morning came.

'He was laid out in a large room that was austere, cavernous, and dark. Two candles burned on the bedside table.

'Our turn to watch came at midnight; the two friends left, and my companion and I took up our places at the foot of the bed.

'The face had not changed at all. It was laughing. The wrinkle we knew so well furrowed the corner of his lips, and he seemed about to open his eyes, stir himself, and talk. His thought, or rather his thoughts, enveloped us; more than ever we felt ourselves in the atmosphere of his genius, invaded and possessed by it. His mastery seemed if anything even more Olympian now he was dead. There was mystery mixed in with the power of that incomparable mind.

'The bodies of such men may disappear, but they themselves remain; and in the night their heart stops beating, I can tell you, Monsieur, they are terrifying.

'In a whisper we spoke of him, recalling his phrases, his sayings, his startling maxims which, in so few words, seemed to throw forward rays of light into the darkness of the unknown Life.

' "I think he's about to speak," said my companion. And with an anxiety bordering on fear, we looked at that motionless face with its rictus of laughter.

'In a little while we felt ill at ease, oppressed, almost faint. I muttered:

' "I don't know what's wrong with me, but I assure you I am ill."

'And then we realized that the corpse smelled bad.

'So my companion suggested we remove to the neighbouring room, leaving the door open; to this I agreed.

'I took one of the candles that was burning on his bedside table, leaving the second where it was, and we went to sit at the far end of the other room, so that we could see, from where we sat, the bed and the corpse, fully lit.

'But we were still transfixed; it was as though his immaterial being, disengaged, free, dominating, and all-powerful stalked around us. And sometimes we caught the vile whiff of the decomposed body, penetrating, nauseating, indeterminate.

'Suddenly, a shudder passed through us to the marrow: a noise, a small noise reached us from the dead man's room. Our eyes were instantly riveted on the corpse, and we saw, yes, Monsieur, we both

saw, clearly, with our own eyes, something white run over the bed, drop down to the carpet, and disappear under an armchair.

'We were on our feet in a trice, in terror, minds empty, and ready to flee. Then we looked at each other. We were both horribly pale. Our hearts were beating fit to lift our clothes. I spoke first.

' "Did you see?..."

' "Yes, I saw."

' "Does that mean he's not dead?"

' "But hasn't he started to decompose?"

' "What should we do?"

'My companion replied falteringly:

' "We must go and see."

'I took our candle and went in first, my eyes darting into every black corner of the room. All was still; then I went up to the bed. But I stopped in my tracks, shocked and horrified: Schopenhauer was smiling no longer! He was grimacing in a most dreadful way, his mouth puckered, his cheeks deep hollowed. I stammered:

' "He isn't dead!"

'But the dreadful smell assailed my nostrils, and sickened me. I stayed where I was, staring in horror at the figure on the bed, as if before a ghost.

'Meanwhile my friend, who had taken the other candle, bent down. Then he touched my arm without a word. I followed his gaze and there, on the ground, under the armchair next to the bed, all white on the dark carpet, open as if ready to bite—Schopenhauer's false teeth.

'The rot setting in had loosened his jaws, and they had sprung from his mouth.

'I had a real fright that night, Monsieur.'

And as the sun neared the glittering sea, the tubercular German bade me good evening, and returned to the hotel.

A Walk

WHEN old Leras, bookkeeper with Labuze & Co., left the shop, he was momentarily blinded by the brilliance of the setting sun. He had worked all day under the yellow gas in the back office, which gave

onto a courtyard as narrow and as deep as a well. The little room in which he had spent the best part of forty years was so dark, even at the height of summer, it had to be lit artificially throughout the day, except on occasion between eleven and three.

It was perpetually cold and humid in there; and through the window, which gave onto a kind of gutter, came the smell of damp and the nauseating whiff of drains.

For forty years Monsieur Leras had arrived in this prison at eight in the morning and worked until seven in the evening; bent over his books, he wrote away sedulously like the model employee that he was.*

He was now earning three thousand francs a year, having begun at fifteen hundred. He had remained single, since his modest emoluments would not allow him to take a wife. And because he had never much enjoyed anything, there was very little he desired. From time to time, however, weary of this monotonous and unceasing toil, he allowed himself a secret wish: 'Lordy, if I had five thousand in rents, I would take it easy.'

But he had never taken it easy, having never earned more than his monthly salary.

His life had passed without event, without emotion, almost without hope. The capacity to dream, which we all carry within us, had scarcely developed within the banality of his ambitions.

He was twenty-one when he had gone to work for Labuze & Co. He had never left.

In 1856 his father died, and then he lost his mother in 1859. Since then he had moved lodgings once, in 1868, when his landlord raised the rent.

Every day his alarm clock woke him, at six o'clock on the dot, its dreadful noise of a dragged chain making him jump out of bed.

On two occasions this mechanism had gone wrong, in 1866 and 1874, but he never found out why. He would get dressed, make his bed, sweep his room, dust down his armchair and the top of his chest of drawers. All these chores took him an hour and a half.

Then he would go out, buy a croissant at Lahure's bakery—he had known eleven different owners, but it still went under the same name. Then he set off, eating his croissant as he went.

His entire existence had in fact been spent in this dark office, which had never been repapered. He was a young man when he first

went in, as assistant to Monsieur Brument, whom he had hoped to replace.

He had replaced him, and he now expected nothing more.

The great harvest of memories gathered by other men throughout their lifetimes, unpredictable events, sweet or tragic love affairs, eventful journeys, all the chances of a free existence, had completely passed him by.

Days, weeks, months, seasons, years had all seemed identical. At the same time each day he would get up, leave the house, get to the office, have a break for lunch, leave the office, have supper, and go to bed, and nothing had ever interrupted the regular monotony of these repeated acts, facts, thoughts.

In former times he would look at his fair moustache and his curly hair in the litttle round mirror left behind by his predecessor. Every evening now, before leaving, he contemplated his white moustache and his bald head in the same mirror. Forty years had gone by, long and swift, as empty as a day of melancholy, and as relentless as the hours of a sleepless night. Forty years of which nothing remained, not even a memory, not even a misfortune, since the death of his parents. Nothing.

That particular day, Monsieur Leras stood for a moment at the street door, dazzled by the brilliance of the setting sun; and rather than go straight home, he thought he would take a little walk before supper, which was something he did about four or five times a year.

He reached the big boulevards, which were packed with people walking under the greening trees. It was an evening in springtime, one of the first evenings of real warmth, the kind that infuses the heart with a lust for life.

Monsieur Leras walked spryly on, like the elderly gent he was, with a twinkle in his eye, happy to be a part of this universal joy, promenading in the balmy air.

He reached the Champs-Élysées and walked on, animated by the exhalations of youth that were carried on the breeze.

The whole sky was aflame; and the Arc de Triomphe stood out starkly against the burning horizon like a giant in the middle of a fire. When he came level with the monstrous monument, the old book-keeper felt a pang of hunger and went into a bistrot to get some supper.

They gave him a pavement table, and he dined on leg of mutton, lettuce, and asparagus. It was the best dinner Monsieur Leras had

had in a long time. He washed down his brie with a carafe of decent claret; then, unusually for him, he followed this with a small cup of coffee, and finished up with a glass of fine champagne.

When he had paid he felt all light-hearted, skittish, a little flushed even. And he said to himself: 'Well, this *is* an evening out! I shall walk on to the beginning of the Bois de Boulogne. It will do me good.'

He set off again. An old song he had heard one of his lady neighbours sing kept running through his head:

> *Quand le bois reverdit,*
> *Mon amoureux me dit:*
> *Viens respirer, ma belle,*
> *Sous la tonnelle.**

He hummed this endlessly, starting over and over again. Darkness had fallen over Paris, it was a close night, with no wind. Monsieur Leras continued down the Avenue du Bois-de-Boulogne, and watched the carriages go by. They came on, with their brilliant lamps, and for the space of a second he had a glimpse of a couple entwined, the woman in a light dress, the man in black.

It was one long procession of lovers, driving out under the burning starry sky. They kept on coming. Couples kept passing by, deeply reclined in their carriages, silent, pressed to one another, lost in the hallucination and the excitement of desire, in the thrill of the next embrace. The warm shadow seemed full of kisses that fluttered and flew. There was a tender softness about the air which made it even more stifling. All these clasping couples, all these people drunk with the same anticipation, the same thought, generated something feverish around them. All these cabs, filled with caresses, left a subtle and troubling aura in their wake.

Monsieur Leras, now rather weary from walking, sat down on a bench to watch the procession of love carriages go by. Almost instantly, a woman came up and sat next to him.

'Hallo, little man,' she said.

He said nothing. She went on:

'Come on, a little love don't do no harm, my darling! I'm nice, you'll see.'

He answered:

'You are mistaken, Madame.'

She took his arm:

'Come on, don't be a silly, listen to me...'

He stood up and moved away, feeling very uncomfortable.

Fifty yards on, another woman accosted him:

'Will you come and sit by me a moment, pretty boy?'

He replied: 'Why do you do this kind of work?'

She stood foursquare in front of him and said, in an altered voice that sounded harsh and crude:

'Jesus, don't go thinking it's what I always wanted!'

Then he enquired, in a gentle voice:

'So what is it drives you to do it?'

She groaned: 'Got to live, ain't I!'

And she moved off, singing to herself.

Monsieur Leras felt bewildered. More women came up to him, calling and beckoning.

He felt that something black, something wretched, was unfurling over his head.

He sat down again on a bench. The carriages kept on coming.

'I should never have come here,' he thought. 'Here I am, feeling all strange and upset now!'

And he started thinking about all the love, whether passionate or venal, and all the kisses, bought or freely given, that was being paraded in front of him.

Love! He scarcely knew anything about it! He had only ever had two or three women in his life, that had come his way by chance, and by surprise; his purse had never stretched to anything more. And then he started to think about the life he had led, so different from that of others, his shadowy, dreary, boring, empty life.

Some beings really do have no luck. And as if a thick veil had been torn away, he saw now the wretchedness, the infinite, monotonous wretchedness of his existence: past, present and to come. His latter days identical to his first, with nothing to look forward to, nothing to look back on, nothing around him, nothing anywhere.

The procession of open carriages kept on coming. And he was presented, as each passed by, with a glimpse of a silent, embracing couple. It seemed to him that the whole of humanity was passing before his eyes, drunk on pleasure, happiness, joy. And he was alone watching it all, entirely alone. He would still be alone tomorrow, always alone, more alone than anyone could possibly be.

He rose, took a few steps, and then almost collapsed onto the next bench along, suddenly exhausted, as if he had been walking for miles.

What was he looking forward to? What was he hoping for? Nothing. He thought how good it must be, when one is old, to return home to a house full of grandchildren. Growing old is softened when one is surrounded by the beings that owe you life, who love you and caress you, and who lisp the sweet and sentimental nothings which make the heart swell and spread balm on every hurt.

Then he thought of his own empty room, his little room all clean and forlorn, where no one ever came except for him. And he felt almost strangled by a wave of despair. His room seemed more woeful even than his little office.

Nobody ever came; nobody ever spoke. It was dead, mute, no human voice ever sounded there. Walls seem to take on something of the qualities of the people who live within them, something of their attitude, their countenance, their words. Houses lived in by happy families are gayer than those lived in by the wretched. His room was empty of memories, like his life. And the thought of returning, all alone, to that room, of lying down in that bed, and of repeating the movements and the chores that were identical every evening, appalled him. As if to put more distance between himself and that sinister room, and to put off the moment when he would have to go back to it, he got up, and finding himself alongside the first path that led into the forest proper, he started down it, and then walked into a copse, where he sat down on the grass...

Around him, above him, coming from every direction, he heard a muffled, immense, and ceaseless sound, made of numberless different noises, a dull sound, both near and far, a huge throb of life: it was the very breath of Paris, inhaling and exhaling like one colossal being.

*   *   *   *   *   *   *   *   *   *

The sun, already high, was pouring a flood of light over the Bois de Boulogne. A few cabs were out, and exuberant riders were beginning to arrive.

There was a couple walking slowly up an empty path. Suddenly the young woman raised her eyes, saw something brown in the branches; she lifted her hand, startled and alarmed:

'Look... what is that?'

Then, with a cry, she collapsed into the arms of her companion, who had to stretch her out on the ground.

The foresters, rapidly alerted, came and took down an old man who was hanged from a branch by his braces.

The hour of death was established as the evening of the day before. Papers found on the body revealed that the man was a bookkeeper with Labuze & Co., name of Leras.

The cause of death was recorded as suicide, without discoverable motive. Possibly a sudden attack of madness?

The Tresses

THE walls of the cell were whitewashed and bare. One narrow window, with bars, placed high up so as to be out of reach, lit the pale and sinister little room. The lunatic, sitting on a straw chair, stared at us unblinkingly, his gaze haunted and vague. He was extremely thin, with sunken cheeks, and his hair was almost white, and would be so entirely in a few months. His clothes hung too large on his withered limbs, his sunken chest, his cavernous stomach. One could sense that the man was ravaged, and eaten out by his thoughts, or by a Thought, like a worm-eaten fruit. His Madness was there, lodged inside his head, obstinate, persecuting, all-devouring. Little by little, it was eating out his body. This invisible, impalpable, ungraspable, insubstantial Idea was eating the flesh, drinking the blood, draining the life.

What a mystery he was, this man killed by a Dream! He was possessed, and it was pitiful and terrifying to behold. What kind of strange, dreadful, lethal dream was it, that made such deep wrinkles, which moved unceasingly over his forehead?

The doctor confided to me: 'He has frightening accesses of rage; he is one of the strangest lunatics I have ever come across. He's in the grip of a kind of macabre, erotic passion. Something like necrophilia. In fact we have his diary, which shows quite clearly the onset of his mental illness. You can almost feel his madness. If it's of any interest, I can let you read it.' I followed the doctor into his surgery, and he gave me the wretched man's diary. 'Read it,' he said, 'and tell me what you think.'

This is what the notebook contained:

Up to the age of thirty-two I lived quite peacefully, and free of love. Life to me seemed very simple, very good, and very straightforward. I was wealthy. I enjoyed so many different things, that I couldn't feel passion for any particular one of them. It was good to be alive! I woke gladly every morning, ready to do things that gave me pleasure, and I went to bed satisfied, in the hopes of a peaceful morrow and an untroubled future.

I had had a few mistresses, but never felt my heart maddened by desire or my soul bruised by love, after possession. It is a good way to live. It is better to love, but more terrible. Those who love in the usual way must feel ardent happiness, though less than mine, perhaps, since love came to find me in the most incredible fashion.

As a rich man, I collected furniture and antiques; I would often think of the strangers' hands that had stroked these things, the eyes that had admired them, the hearts that had loved them—for we do love things! Sometimes I would spend hours and hours contemplating a little watch from the last century. It was so moving, and pretty, with its goldwork and enamel. And it worked, as it had worked on the day it was purchased by a woman, delighted to own such a gem. Since the last century it had never stopped ticking, or living its mechanical life. Who was the first to have worn it against her breast, where it lay amidst the warmth of her satins, the heart of the watch beating against the heart of the woman? What warm hand had held it, what fingers had turned it over and over, and then wiped off the china shepherds, misted for a second by the contact with warm skin? What eyes had watched the flowery dial, waiting for the cherished hour to arrive?

How I should like to have known her, the woman that had chosen an object so exquisite and so rare! She is dead! I am haunted by a desire for these dead women, and from a distance, I love them for having loved!—All their tenderness fills my heart with regret, for it cannot come again. The beauty of those smiles, those first caresses, and all the hopes that went with them! All that should last forever!

Whole nights have I wept, over these women, who were so beautiful, so tender, and so gentle, and whose arms opened to receive a kiss, and who are dead! The kiss itself is immortal! It is passed on, from lip to lip, from century to century, from age to age.—Men receive it, they return it, and they die.

I am drawn to the past, while the present terrifies me, since ahead lies only death. I yearn for everything done, I weep for those who are gone; I want to halt time in its tracks. But on it flows, it passes, and is passed, and every second a piece of me is gnawed away, in preparation for the void ahead. And I shall never live again.

Adieu! ladies of yesteryear, ladies that I love.

But I am not to be pitied. For I have found the one I was waiting for, and together we have tasted unbelievable joys.

One sunny morning I was strolling through Paris, high-spirited and light of step, looking through shop windows with the vague interest of the *flâneur*.* Suddenly I spotted in the window of an antique-seller's an Italian piece from the seventeenth century. It was very fine, and very rare. I attributed it to Vitelli, a Venetian craftsman who was famous at the time.

Then I walked on.

But for some reason the memory of this piece haunted me, so much so that I turned back. I stopped in front of the shop to have another look. I felt it was tempting me on.

Temptation is a strange thing! You look at an object, and little by little it seduces you, disturbs and invades you, much as a woman's face can. Its charm enters into you, a strange charm that comes from its form, its colour, and the way it looks; you already love it, you desire it, you must have it. You are invaded by the need to possess, a mild, almost shy need to begin with, but one that grows, until it is fierce and overweening.

And shopkeepers seem able to read that gleam in the eye, and note the secret, growing desire it betrays.

I bought the desk and had it taken home immediately. I placed it in my bedroom.

How I pity those who know nothing of that honeymoon period, spent between a collector and his latest find! You caress it with eye and hand; as if it were living flesh; you keep passing close to it and it remains in your thoughts, wherever you are, and whatever you do. The sweet thought of it goes with you, out walking or in company. And the first thing you do on getting home, before even removing your hat and gloves, is to go and look at it with a lover's tenderness.

I truly did adore this desk. For eight days I could not stop myself from opening its drawers and little doors; I kept handling it, delightedly, enjoying the full extent of possession.

One evening, as I was testing the thickness of a wooden panel, I realized there must be a secret place behind it. It set my heart beating, and I spent the night trying without success to find the secret mechanism.

But I did succeed the next morning, by inserting a blade into the woodwork. A panel slid back, and there I saw, lying on black velvet, a wonderful mane of hair!

Yes, a whole mane of woman's hair, a thick plait of reddish-blonde tresses, which must have been cut off at the scalp. It was bound together with a golden ribbon.

I stood aghast, moved and trembling. An almost imperceptible scent, so old it seemed to be the ghost of a scent, rose from the mysterious drawer with its singular relic.

I took hold of it gently, religiously almost, and drew it forth from its hiding-place. Instantly it unfurled, a thick, light, supple golden stream that reached to the floor, shining like a comet's tail.

A strange emotion seized me: what did this mean? When? How? Why had the hair been hidden in the desk? What affair, what tragedy, lay concealed in this relic?

Who had cut the hair? A lover on the day of separation? Or was it a husband's act of vengeance? Or did she to whom the hair belonged shear it off herself, in a moment of desperation?

Did she hide this treasure, like a love-token left for the living, on the day she entered the nunnery? Or did the beauty die young, and did her lover take this from her before the coffin was nailed up, as the sole thing not destined to rot, the sole thing he could still love and caress, and smother with kisses in the spasms of his grief?

And was it not strange to think that her hair had lain there all this time, while nothing at all remained of her body?

It ran through my fingers, and tickled my skin, with a peculiar caressing feel, a caress from the dead. My heart dilated with tenderness, and I was close to tears.

I held it for a long, long time in my hands, until it seemed to stir, as if a trace of the soul it belonged to remained lodged within it. Then I laid it back on the faded velvet, shut the drawer, locked the desk, and went out to walk the streets and think.

I walked in a daze, full of sadness, and with the kind of emotion that lingers in the heart, after a loving kiss has been bestowed on one. I felt I had lived before, and that I must have known this woman.

Like a stifled sob, Villon's lines rose to my lips:

Dictes-moy où, ne en quel pays
Est Flora, la belle Romaine,
Archipiada, ne Thaïs,
Qui fut sa cousine germaine?
Echo parlant quand bruyt on maine
Dessus rivière, ou sus estan;
Qui beauté eut plus que humaine?
Mais où sont le neiges d'antan?

*   *   *   *   *

La royne blanche comme un lys
Qui chantoit à voix de sereine,
Berthe au grand pied, Bietris, Allys,
Harembouges qui tint le Mayne,
Et Jehanne la bonne Lorraine
Que Anglais bruslèrent à Rouen?
Où sont-ils, Vierge souveraine?
Mais où sont les neiges d'antan?*

When I got home, something compelled me to have another look at my strange discovery; I took it out again and felt, as I handled it, a long shudder pass through my limbs.

For a few months my state of mind remained normal, even if the thought of the mane of hair remained active, and never left me.

Whenever I returned home I had to get it out and handle it. I would turn the key in the lock with the same emotion one might turn the doorhandle leading to the loved one, for lodged in my hands and my heart was a confused, peculiar, sustained, and sensual need to dip my fingers into that lovely stream of dead hair.

And when I had finished caressing it, and closed up the desk, I still felt its presence, as if it were a living being, but sealed up like a prisoner. I felt it and I desired it once more, and the same imperious need to take it and feel it came over me, to feel against me that cold, slippery, irritating, maddening, delicious thing, until I almost fainted away from nervous excitement.

I continued like this for a month or two, I no longer recall exactly. The hair obsessed and haunted me. I was in that state of blissful and torturing anticipation known to lovers, after the avowals and before consummation.

I would shut myself away with it, so as to feel it on my skin, to

plunge my lips into it, to kiss and bite it. I rolled it over my face, I drank it in, I covered my eyes with its gilded wave so the world was fair when I looked through it.

I was in love with it! Yes, I loved it. I could no longer be without it, not even for a single hour.

And I waited... and I waited... what for? Did I not know?—For her.

One night I woke with a start, persuaded that I was not alone in my room.

I was alone, however. As I was unable to fall asleep again, and a feverish insomnia had taken hold of me, I got up to go and touch the hair. It seemed to me to be softer than usual, and more animated. Do the dead return? The kisses I bestowed upon it made me faint with happiness; I took it with me into bed, where I lay with it, pressing my lips against it, as if it were a mistress, before the act of love.

The dead do return! She came to me. Yes, I have seen her, I have held her, I have possessed her, as she was, tall, blonde, voluptuous, with cold breasts and haunches shaped like a lyre; I have run my lips the full length of that divine and wavy line that runs from her throat to her feet, and followed every curve of her flesh.

Yes, I had her, every day, and every night. She came back to me, the Dead Lady, the beautiful Dead Lady, the Strange, Mysterious, Adorable one, she was with me every night.

So great was my happiness, I could not hide it. With her I felt superhuman delights, and the deep, inexpressible joy of possessing the Impalpable, the Invisible, the Dead! No lover has ever tasted such keen and terrible pleasures.

I could not conceal my happiness. I loved her so much I could not leave her. I took her with me everywhere. I walked about with her in town as though she were my wife; I took her to the theatre with me, and sat with her in a closed box, as though she were my mistress... But people saw her... they guessed... and they seized me... And they cast me into prison like a criminal. And they took her away from me... Oh misery!...

The manuscript ended at this point. And as I raised my horrified eyes to the doctor, a dreadful cry, a scream of impotent fury and longing, sounded through the asylum.

'Listen to him,' said the doctor. 'We have to stick him under the

shower at least five times a day, the filthy lunatic. It isn't only Sergeant Bertrand* who loved the dead.

Beside myself with shock and horror and pity, I stammered out: 'But... the hair... did it really exist?'

The doctor got up, opened a cupboard full of instruments and flasks, and tossed in my direction, across his consulting-room, a long tress of blonde hair that flew towards me like a golden bird.

I shivered as the light, caressing thing landed in my hands. My heart was beating with disgust and desire, the disgust associated with criminal exhibits, the desire to probe deeper into something vile and strange.

With a shrug of his shoulders, the doctor went on:

'The mind of man is capable of anything.'

Night

I LOVE the night with a passion. I love it as one loves one's country, or one's mistress, with an instinctive, deep, invincible love. I love it with all my senses, with my eyes that can see it, with my sense of smell that can breathe it, with my ears attentive to its silence, with my whole body, caressed by its darkness. Larks sing in the sun, in the warm air, in the light air of fine mornings. The owl plunges into the night, a black form crossing the blackness, and delighted, intoxicated by the black immensity, he gives his resonant and sinister hoot.

Daytime wearies and bores me. It is noisy and brutal. I find it hard to get up, I dress wearily, go out regretfully, and each step, each movement, each action, each word, each thought wearies me, as if I were under the burden of a crushing load.

But when the sun starts to sink, my whole body comes alive with an intense joy. I wake up, I come alive. As the shadows lengthen I feel a different person, younger, stronger, more alert, and happier. And I watch it, the great soft shadow falling from the sky, I watch it growing thicker: it drowns the city, like a thick and immaterial wave; and it hides, blots out, destroys colour and form; houses, beings, and monuments are smothered under its lightest of light caresses.

It is then that I want to utter a shriek of pleasure like the owls, and

bound from roof to roof like the cats; and an imperious desire for love starts running through my veins.

So I set off, walking vigorously; either in the darkened suburbs or in the woods adjoining Paris, where I can hear my sisters the creatures, and my brothers the poachers.

What you love too violently finishes by killing you. But how can I explain what has happened to me? How can I plausibly even relate this story? I do not know, I do not know, all I know is that this is how it is.—That's all there is to it.

So, yesterday—was it yesterday?—yes, no doubt it was, unless it were before that, a different day, a different month, a different year—how should I know? But it must be yesterday, because day has not come since, the sun never reappeared. But how long has the night lasted? Since what time?... Who can say? Who will ever know?

So, yesterday—I went out as I do every evening, after dinner. It was very fine, very mild, very warm. As I walked down to the boulevards I looked at the black, star-filled river above my head, cut into sections by the rooftops which, in a way resembling a veritable river, turned and guided this rolling stream of stars.

Everything stood out clear in the light air, from the planets to the gas-jets. With so many fires burning up there, and down below in the city, the darkness itself seemed luminous. Such brilliant nights are more joyous than long sunny days.

Café lights were blazing along the boulevard; there was laughter, conviviality, drink. I stopped by a theatre for a few moments, which one I no longer recall. But it was so bright in there I found it oppressive, and I came out rather cast down by the brutal glare of the naked light striking the gilded balcony, the false brilliance of the enormous chandelier, the footlights, and the melancholy at the heart of all this superficial and showy glister. I reached the Champs-Élysées, where the café-concerts seemed like fires seen through the foliage. The chestnuts, refulgent with yellow light, were like painted, phosphorescent trees. The electric globes, like pale and glinting moons, or moon-eggs fallen to earth, or monstrous, living pearls, projected a whiter light through their nacre shells, turning the gas-jets, the dirty gas-jets into something royal and full of mystery, and brightening the garlands of coloured glass.

I stopped beneath the Arc de Triomphe to gaze down the avenue, the splendid starry avenue that heads into central Paris, with its twin

streams of lights, under the stars! The remote, distant stars in the heavens, the unknown stars cast randomly in the galaxy where they form the strange patterns that set men dreaming and wondering.

I went into the Bois de Boulogne, and stayed there for a long, long time. A strange excitement had taken possession of me, a powerful and unexpected emotion, an exaltation of thought which bordered on madness.

I kept walking, on and on and on. Then I turned back.

What time was it when once again I passed under the Arc de Triomphe? I do not know. The city was going to sleep, and clouds, great black clouds, were streaming slowly over the whole sky.

Then, for the first time, I felt that something new and strange was about to happen. It seemed cold suddenly, and the air was thickening, my own beloved night came to weigh upon my heart. The avenue was by now deserted. Only two city constables were patrolling past a line of stationary carriages, while on the road, now barely lit by the gas-jets, which seemed to be running low, was a line of vehicles loaded with vegetables heading for Les Halles.* They were moving slowly, loaded with carrots, cabbages, and turnips. The drivers were sleeping and invisible, and the horses moved steadily, following the coach in front, silent on the wooden surface. As they passed under each lamp on the pavement, the carrots lit up red, the turnips white, and the cabbages green: and they moved one behind the other, these coaches, red as fire, and white as polished silver, and green as emerald. I followed them, then turned up the rue Royale, and rejoined the boulevards. There was not a soul about, no lighted cafés, just a few late stragglers, hurrying home. I had never seen Paris so dead or so empty. I pulled out my watch. It was two o'clock.

Some force was propelling me onwards, so I kept walking. I went as far as the Bastille. And it was there I realized that I had never seen a night so dark, I could scarcely make out the Column, and the golden Hermes was concealed by an impenetrable darkness. A vault of clouds, thick as immensity itself, had engulfed the stars, and seemed to be bearing down upon the earth as if to destroy it.

I turned back. Now there was no one near me. Except, at the Place du Château d'Eau, a drunk nearly careered into me, and then vanished. For a moment I could still hear his loud, unsteady footsteps. I kept on. At the junction with the Faubourg Montmartre a carriage went by, heading down towards the Seine. I hailed it. The driver

didn't respond. A woman was hanging about near the rue Drouot: 'Please Monsieur, listen to me.' I quickened my pace to avoid her outstretched hand. Then nothing again. In front of the Vaudeville a rag-picker was working the gutter. His little lamp was held at ground level. I called out: 'What time is it, good fellow?'

He growled back: 'How should I know. Don't 'ave a watch.'

Then I noticed that the gas-jets had gone out. I knew that they were put out early in this season, to economize; but daybreak was still a long way off, a very long way off.

'I'll go to Les Halles,' I thought, 'there's bound to be people there.' I set off, but I could hardly see where I was going. I moved forward carefully, as if I were in a thick wood, counting off the streets.

A dog growled at me in front of the Crédit Lyonnais. I turned up the rue de Grammont, and then got lost. I wandered on, and recognized the Bourse by the iron railings surrounding it. A cab went by in the distance, a single hansom, perhaps the one that had passed me a little while ago. I tried to catch up with it, heading towards the noise of its wheels, plunging through the lonely streets, that were black, black as death.

I got lost again. Where was I? What folly to cut off the gas so soon! Not a single pedestrian, not a single straggler, not a rodent, not even the scream of a cat in heat. Nothing.

Where were the town constables? I thought: 'I shall shout, then they'll come.' I gave a shout. No one answered.

I shouted louder. My voice faded out, and gave no echo—weak, stifled, crushed by the impenetrable night.

I screamed: 'Help! Help! Help!'

But my desperate call found no answer. What time was it now? I pulled out my watch, but had no matches. I listened to the light ticking of the clockwork with a strange, intense joy. It seemed to be alive. I felt less alone. It was all a mystery! I started off again, tapping the walls with my stick, like a blind man, and I raised my eyes continually to the sky, hoping for the first trace of daybreak; but the space up there was black, blacker even than the city.

What time could it possibly be? I felt as though I had been walking for an eternity; my legs trembled under me, my chest was heaving, and I felt a terrible hunger.

I resolved to ring at the next doorway. I pulled on the copper bell, and it rang throughout the house, but strangely, as if it were the only

sound in the whole house. I rang again, and waited some more—still nothing!

I was frightened now. I ran to the next house, and twenty times pulled on the bell in the dark corridor where the concierge should be sleeping. But he did not wake—so I went on, tugging on every bell-pull I could find, kicking and beating with my cane on doors that remained stubbornly closed.

Suddenly, I realized that I had come to Les Halles. Les Halles was empty: there was not a sound, not a movement, not a single coach, or man, not a stick of celery or a single bunch of flowers.—The place was empty, motionless, abandoned, dead!

Terror seized me. What was going on? My God! What was happening?

I started off again. But what was the time? Who would tell me the time? The bells in the clock-towers and monuments had fallen silent. I thought: 'I shall open the glass front of my watch and feel for the hands with my fingers...' But it had stopped. There was nothing now, nothing at all, not the slightest gleam, not the whisper of a sound in the air. Nothing! Not even the sound of a cab passing in the distance—nothing at all.

I had reached the quay, and a glacial chill rose from the river.

Was the Seine still flowing?

I wanted to find out, so I found the steps, and went down... there was no sound of water flowing fast under the arches of the bridge... More steps... now sand... and mud... now water... it was flowing, but cold... cold... so cold... almost frozen... almost stopped... almost dead.

And I knew then that I would never have the strength to climb back up... and that I would die there... I would die—of hunger—of exhaustion—of cold.

GUSTAVE GEFFROY

The Statue

THROUGHOUT the engagement, the preparations, and the day itself, when the young woman formally contracted to marry the young sculptor, she had a fairly clear idea of the uncommon existence that she would lead from then on. As a young *débutante*, she had moved easily in the brilliant world of fashion, with all its excitements, and in the literary and artistic milieu that contained the principal actors of Parisian social life. It was the sort of milieu in which everything can be said, or at least suggested, in the malicious, gossipy, *blasé* conversations that are its very being. Some girls understand little—others know exactly what is going on. Some can live through the most scandalous times, and hear the most scabrous things, and still lose nothing of their flower-like freshness, their virginal candour, their childlike naivety. Then there are those who seem to grasp everything straightaway, in a manner that is as mysterious to others as it is to themselves, and they come into possession of the finest keys that open the most secret locks. This latter type is no more to be censured than the former is to be praised, and the difference can only be laid at the door of physiological chance and the mystery of the instincts.

The young woman in question belonged to the latter type, and when she moved from girlhood into womanhood she believed that she would be able not only to order her existence and her future in accordance with the desires of her heart and mind, but would be able also to foresee any obstacle that might arise, and by turning it to her advantage, secure her lasting happiness.

And it was precisely here, in her pragmatism, that her romanticism appeared, and the qualities one might have thought suppressed—virginal candour, childlike naivety—came into play.

She had wanted to be an artist; she frequented museums and enrolled in the painting schools. She had also wanted to be a writer; she read a great deal and contrived to converse with men of letters. In the end,

she gave up on the idea of producing art herself, and curbed her ambition, which was now to become wife to an artist.

This she achieved. She was wife to a fashionable sculptor, who was busy all day with official commissions and producing busts for the Salon; he was much in demand, and liked to receive guests himself, in his sumptuous house near the Parc Monceau.* And besides all this, he was intelligent; he knew that his work was a little glib and superficial—but he was curious, he was likeable, and he was in love.

Jeanne was in love too, and very attached to this husband of hers; her passion would flare up easily, and she was jealous. With her head full of novels and memories, determined that her future should continue as idyllic as her present, the first change she implemented concerned the role of the female model in the work of the artist.

How many novels and stories had she not read in which the model played a role in the lives of painters and sculptors—one that was detrimental to the tenderness of the husband and the security of the wife! That is not how things would be in her marriage, and she intended to start where stories of the printed variety usually ended. In the course of romantic days, and the passionate nights that follow upon marriage, she had no trouble in obtaining from her spouse a promise that no other woman should cross the threshold of his studio. The studio itself would become as intimate and sacred as the boudoir, because the legitimate spouse herself, sovereign to this artist and his art, would come there to undress, and pose for him on the dais.

The sculptor willingly agreed to her loving involvement. It was an amiable arrangement, having his wife there all the time, always ready to pose, in addition to which she was superior in grace and expression to the models he had used before.

He did not tire her, either, by overwork. He made ample use of photographs and etchings, he referred to the art of Antiquity and the Renaissance, and sought inspiration in the immense storehouse of the past, as he had been enjoined to do by his teachers at the Beaux Arts and the Villa Médicis.* He purchased plaster casts that he believed showed the truth in its fugitive passage. And he would ask his wife to pose for a few minutes, just to verify a particular angle or a fall of drapery, or to get a view of the whole arrangement.

She fulfilled her chosen role to perfection. She posed, draped or nude, standing, reclining, seated. She accepted every incarnation, just as her husband accepted every commission. She saw herself at the Salon, in the aisles, where white statuary alternates with decorative green pot-plants. She contemplated her own form as a Greek mythological divinity in the Luxembourg Museum, and in the gardens and squares as a naiad drenched by a fountain or a nymph running over the green lawn. She saw herself as Fame, placing laurels on the heads of great men, at the centre of public squares. She encountered her likeness in provincial cemeteries and cathedrals, a muse to adorn the tombs of the rich and famous. She played her role in representing France, at an exhibition in St Petersburg; she was even cast in bronze for a huge commercial and industrial fair in Chicago.

And so the years went by until, suddenly, this life underwent a change.

The sculptor became troubled. The artist, who was prosperous, productive, contented, became prey to a desire. He was shaken by some glories that appeared, rose above the horizon, and invaded the artistic heavens, where they shone like tranquil suns. The sculptor, acknowledged for his commercial success, prizewinning medallist, honoured, tipped for the Institut, now experienced a vast emptiness. He surveyed his life so far, as he approached forty; and in a minute of dreadful clarity he saw the legions of his puerile statues, the hollowness of his artistic conception, the nullity of his work.

He stopped working for a while, crushed and undecided. His placid forehead became lined with thought, and his hair slightly silvered.

With a nervous excitement that was mingled with melancholy, he informed his wife he had new projects for his work; he confided to her his ambitions and his hopes, and won her approval.

And so it was he withdrew from society, left the fashionable quarter, and moved into a provincial-style house on a silent road, the other side of the river. Now his fellow sculptors were of the type that live like working men, who take their meals in the little bistrots on the Boulevard Montparnasse and on the Boulevard de Vaugirard, who promenade their great beards in melancholy comings and goings, between the studio and the ministry. He frequented the artistic communes, with their houses full of studios, like cells in a monastery or a barracks. He listened to their confidences and their theories.

Then he shut himself up in his studio, and set out to be a realist.

His wife continued to support him, until the day she became aware that a very singular and unexpected torture had begun for her.

The sculptor did become realist, and with a vengeance. He laboured over the motif, drawn direct from nature.* He wanted to render everything, to express everything, and transform his vague vision of former days into an imperious, near-sighted scrutiny.

Now the posing sessions went on until exhaustion set in. Worldliness was a thing of the past, official approval was withdrawn. A new existence replaced the old one. And it seemed to Jeanne that another woman had been substituted for her, and had taken her place in her husband's work. And yet there was no mistaking, it was he who sculpted, and she who posed. So how come no trace remained of Fame, or of the nymph and the naiad, in these creatures that were sculpted with such violent application?

She no longer recognized herself in this graceless stranger, with its plumpness, its slightly sagging breasts, its prominent stomach.

'I sculpt what I see,' came the reply to her first shy, tentative objections.

Another time she found herself really too fat, her body too ample and uncorseted:

'What can I do, my dear friend, the body continually changes. I must sculpt what I see before me.'

So this was it, the new line! Alas! Why had he not conceived of it before, in the days of her dazzling youth? Perhaps, if he had, he would be less concentrated than he was today, and so much the better. Life was unbearable, if it had to be lived under the magnifying glass and then exhibited in the public place, bearing all the stigmata of the years, all the blemishes of age.

The blemishes got worse, they looked grievous, pitilessly rendered by the artist's fingers—he who had been such a clever charlatan, and was now a ruthless practitioner of the art. He showed everything of the woman, her irritation, then her exaltation and her suffering, everything, from the tiniest natural defects, unnoticed until then, to the ravages wrought by childbirth and motherhood. He catalogued her wrinkles, he drew up the inventory of her fleshly existence.

She wanted to stop posing for her husband, and she told him to go back to using models. He refused, and then, after a violent row,

consented; but soon he was back, pleading, making such a fuss that too often she was forced to relent. For it was his wife and no one else the sculptor wished to copy from nature. He had found his inspiration in her subtly ageing, ripening body. As an artist, he was in love with her autumnal plenty.

With a gentle smile, he even said things to her like, 'well, it was filling out'. He looked at his old anatomical drawings, and pointed out the faults of design and structure in the body of his beloved life companion. He adored these faults, they were 'so interesting!', and 'so amusing!' Yes, he found his wife to be 'interesting!' He would show his drawings, statues, fragments, to his spade-bearded friends; with fervour he explained what he was after, glorying in the sagging and wrinkled flesh that did indeed win approval among the beards, but distressed the poor woman terribly, confronted with the idea of her own decrepitude. The idea started to obsess her, and she felt the piercing, critical gaze of her husband upon her, morning, noon, and night. Walking in front of him, she began to dread the feel of her husband's heavy gaze upon her back.

The denouement was logical enough. Desiring some violent distraction, some proof from life that would tell her whether or not her youth was finished, and whether she was still desirable—she took a lover. He was a poet, and he reassured her by portraying her in his books, but only through a haze of infinitely decorous language.

JEAN LORRAIN

An Unsolved Crime

'THE things that can happen in a furnished hotel room on the night of Mardi Gras!*—So horrible they beggar the imagination!' And having filled a large glass, a soda glass, with Chartreuse, de Romer gulped it down in one and began:

'It was two years ago, at the height of my nervous troubles.* I had come off ether, but was not free of its morbid side-effects—trouble hearing, trouble seeing, night-time dreads and nightmares: solfanol and bromide had cured me of most of these, but the dreads persisted. They clung on chiefly in the apartments I had lived in with her, on the rue Saint-Guillaume, the other side of the river, where her presence seemed to have impregnated the walls and the hangings with some indefinable spell. Everywhere else I enjoyed unbroken sleep and quiet nights, but no sooner had I crossed the threshold than the indefinable unease of the old days poisoned the whole atmosphere around me; irrational terrors froze and strangled me by turns. Strange shadows gathered in the corners of the room, and ambiguous folds in the curtains and the doorways were suddenly filled with some terrifying nameless life. At night it became intolerable. Something strange and horrible lived with me in that apartment, some invisible thing that I felt was squatting in the shadow and watching me, some inimical thing whose breath I felt pass over my face, as it almost brushed against me. It was a dreadful feeling, Gentlemen, and if I had to relive that nightmare I think I would rather... but let us not dwell on that...

'Anyway, I had reached the point when I could no longer sleep in that room, or even live in it, but since there was still a year to run on the lease, I took to living in hotels. But of course I couldn't stay put, and quit the Continental for the Hôtel du Louvre, then quit the Louvre for smaller establishments, driven on by an exhausting compulsion to keep moving and changing.

'Why was it that after eight days spent in the lap of luxury at the Terminus, I elected to remove to that seedy hotel on the rue

d'Amsterdam?—The Normandy, the Brest, or the Rouen—or some such name—they're all called that round the Gare Saint-Lazare!

'Was it the incessant movement of arrivals and departures that attracted and held me there, rather than elsewhere?... I can't exactly say... My room was large and light, on the second floor, with two windows looking out onto the main station exit on the Place du Havre. I had been living there for three days, since the Saturday before Mardi Gras, and was very comfortably installed.

'It was, I repeat, a third-class hotel, but perfectly decent, for travellers and provincials, who felt less lost staying near their point of arrival than in the heart of the city; a respectable hotel, deserted from one evening to the next, but in fact always full.

In any case, the faces I met on the stairs or corridors were the least of my preoccupations, until that is, on the evening in question, at about six o'clock, when I returned to the hotel (to change for a dinner in town) and was getting my key from the office, I couldn't stop myself from staring more curiously than is polite at two travellers who were there too.

'They had just arrived; a black leather overnight bag was at their feet, and standing in front of the reception desk they were negotiating the price of rooms.

'"It's for one night," explained the taller of the two, who also seemed the older; "we're leaving tomorrow—any room will do."—"With one bed or two?" asked the manager.—"Oh, if we sleep at all—we're going to a masked ball." "With two beds," interrupted the younger.—"Right! Have we got a room with two beds, Eugène?" The manager called one of the waiters who had just come in, and after a brief discussion: "Put these gentlemen in number 13, on the second floor; you'll be very comfortable there, it's a big room. Will the gentlemen be going up now?" And when they shook their heads to say no—"Will the gentlemen be dining? We have a *table d'hôte*."—"No, we're dining out," answered the taller of the two, "and we shall come back at around eleven o'clock to change for the ball; but have the suitcase taken up."—"And a fire in the room?"—"Yes, a fire for eleven o'clock," and they were already on their way out.

'I realized then that I had been standing there staring at them, with my candle in my hand; I blushed like a child caught red-handed, and went quickly up to my room. The boy was making up the beds in room 13, which was next to mine, and that too intrigued me.

'Passing once more through the lobby on my way out, I couldn't help asking the manager about my new neighbours. "The two men with the overnight bag? Well, they've filled in the forms, you can have a look!" And glancing rapidly, I read: "Henri Desnoyels, thirty-two years old, and Edmond Chalegrin, twenty-six", both of them butchers.

'Bowler hats and travelling coats aside, they were both very elegantly dressed for butcher-boys, I thought. I recalled the tallest wearing gloves, and having a haughty, aristocratic air about him. There was, moreover, a certain resemblance between them: the same very dark blue eyes, slanted, with long lashes, and the same long, reddish moustaches emphasizing the sharp profile. But the taller man was much paler than the other, with something languid and bored about him.

'An hour later I had forgotten all about them, it was Mardi Gras, and the streets were in uproar, full of people in masks. I got back around midnight, and went up to my room. I was already half-undressed, and was going to bed, when I heard a voice raised in the room next door; my butchers were back.

'Why did the curiosity that had seized me before in the hotel lobby return now, irrational and imperious? In spite of myself, I started listening. "So you're not going to get dressed and come to the ball," came the cutting voice of the taller man; "and after all that trouble; what's wrong with you? Are you ill?" And as the other said nothing: "Are you drunk, have you been boozing again?" went on the older man. Then came the other voice, thick and whining: "It's your fault, why did you let me drink? I'm always ill when I drink that wine."—"All right, that's enough, go to bed," grated the other, strident voice, "get your nightshirt." I heard a key scrape in the lock of the overnight case. "So you're not going to go to the ball either?" went on the slurred voice.—"A great night out that will be, wandering the streets alone and all dressed up! I'm going to bed, too." I heard him plump his pillow and mattress violently with his fist, and then the sound of clothes falling came from the room; the two men were undressing. I held my breath and listened—I was barefoot, listening at our adjoining door; the taller man's voice broke the silence again: "And such lovely costumes, it's a shame!" And then I heard the rustle of silks.

'I bent my eye to the keyhole. My candle prevented me from obtaining the darkness around me necessary for seeing into the

next-door room, so I blew it out. The younger man's bed was right opposite my door. Collapsed on a chair next to the bed, he was immobile, extremely pale and with a vague expression; his head had slid from the back of the chair onto the pillow; his hat was on the floor, and with his waistcoat unbuttoned, his tie removed, and his shirt open, he looked as though he had been asphyxiated. The elder man, whom I could make out only with difficulty, was in his undershorts and socks, pacing round the table which was piled with light materials and spangled satins. "Be damned! I must try it on!" he exclaimed aloud, without taking the slightest notice of his companion. And standing in all his svelte and muscular elegance in front of the looking-glass, he slipped on a long, green, hooded cape lined with velvet. The effect was so sudden, so horrible and bizarre, that I only just stopped myself from crying out in shock.

'I no longer recognized the man, who seemed to be taller, swathed in the light green cloak which made him even thinner. His face was now covered by the metallic mask, and half-hidden under the dark velvet hood. It was no longer anything human that swayed about, but the horrible nameless thing whose invisible presence had poisoned my nights at the rue Saint-Guillaume, and that had now taken form and was alive.

'Slumped in a corner by his bed, the drunken man had been witness to this metamorphosis and was staring aghast; he had been seized with a trembling-fit, his knees knocked together with terror, his teeth chattered, and he had brought his hands together in an imploring gesture. He was shivering from head to foot. The thing in green revolved in the middle of the room in a slow and spectral way, lit up by two candles, and beneath the mask I could sense two fearfully watchful eyes. Then it went and stood right over the other, its arms crossed over its chest, and from beneath the mask it gave him an unspeakable, suggestive look. It was then that the other, apparently seized by a fit of madness, fell from his chair and, lying belly-down on the parquet, tried to gather in and embrace the cape in both arms. He buried his head in its folds, stammering out incomprehensible words; he was foaming at the mouth and rolling his eyes.

'What was the mystery that joined these two men, and what irreparable event in his past had the spectre in cape and icy mask conjured up in the eyes of the mad wretch? O ye gods, the pallor of those imploring hands, rolling about in ecstasy in the folds of that larval

cape! What kind of Sabbath was this, taking place in a drab and dreary furnished room? And as the strangled crying went on, issuing from the black hole of the drunkard's wide-open mouth, the thing stepped back, drawing the hypnotized creature that lay crawling on its belly along after it.

'How many minutes, hours, did this scene go on? Then the Ghoul stopped moving, placed a hand on the forehead and on the heart of the man who had fainted at its feet; then, gathering him up in its arms, propped the body upright back on its chair by the bed. The man was slumped there motionless, eyes closed and head hanging. The thing in green now bent over the suitcase. What was it searching for so avidly, by the dancing light of the fire? Even though I could no longer see, I knew it had found what it was seeking, for I could hear the clinking of glass phials above the sink, and then there was a famil-iar smell, which invaded my head and sent my brain into a swoon: the smell of ether. The shape in green reappeared, and moved silently towards the unconscious man. And what was it he was carrying so carefully in both hands?... Oh, horror! He was carrying a hermeti-cally sealed glass mask, without eye- or mouth-holes, and the mask was filled to the brim with ether, with liquid poison. And then the thing in green leaned over the defenceless, inanimate creature and clamped the mask over his face, fixing it tightly with a red scarf knot-ted behind. Some kind of laughter seemed to convulse the dark velvet hood: "That's shut you up for good," I thought I heard it murmur.

'The butcher boy now slipped out of mask and cape, and wandered around the room, a vague form in his undershorts. He put his city clothes back on, his overcoat, his clubman's dog-skin leather gloves, his hat on his head—and then, in silence, packed away, in slightly feverish haste perhaps, the carnival costumes and the glass phials into the suitcase, clicked the nickel fasteners to, lit a cigar, took the case and his umbrella, opened the door, and went out... And I didn't utter a sound, I didn't ring, I didn't call.'

'And it was all a dream, as usual!' said Jaquels to de Romer.

'Oh yes! I dreamed it so clearly in fact, that there is today, in the asylum at Villejuif, an incurable ether addict, whose identity they have never been able to establish. You merely have to check the register: found on Wednesday, 10 March, at the Hotel..., rue d'Amsterdam, nationality French, probable age twenty-six, probable name Edmond Chalegrin.'

The Student's Tale

In the hotel where I was then lodging on the rue du Faubourg Saint Honoré, I became aware of a suspicious-looking client. I was at that time a penniless law student, and very self-involved, so for this woman to attract my attention, she must have cut a figure which contrasted violently with the grey uniformity of the other lodgers.

She was... how shall I put it?... an intermittent guest at the hotel... and even though she rented her room by the month, she rarely slept there; on the other hand, not a week went by without her coming to spend a couple of hours shut up in her room, and she was never alone. Sometimes she would bring a man, sometimes a woman, and at other times her girl-friends in a group. In winter there were hearty fires and she had bowls of punch brought up; in summer, lemonades and soda.

She was treated with the greatest deference at the hotel. The manager and his wife were lavish in their praise of Madame de Prack: she must have tipped very generously.

She was not a prostitute, as I had first thought. Early on, seeing her come in with someone different each time, I took her for a vulgar tart of the worst kind, since she apparently took up with anybody. But not a bit of it, and on further reflection I supposed her to be a member of some secret society, a creature hunted by the police, hiding out in Paris under assumed names: the wife of an anarchist, a ringleader, or just a common criminal belonging to a gang—of the sort that operates in the big department stores—giving tip-offs to denizens of the murky underworld, and indulging in the handling and resale of stolen goods. And then other notions flitted across my mind: perhaps this woman was nothing more than a degenerate, seeking distraction in debauchery and secret orgies from the daily boredom of conjugal life in a bourgeois setting.

From the well-heeled bourgeoisie, in any case, since Madame de Prack's expenses were considerable by the standards of the other lodgers, who were hard-up students or office clerks. She would always arrive in a carriage and leave the same way, and the men she brought in were usually shabbily dressed and seemed to belong to the lower classes: little bowler hats, long rumpled overcoats, grubby scarves. But often they had something remarkably debonair and lively

about them, and carried themselves like gymnasts or acrobats—so much so that I began to entertain the idea that Madame de Prack was some kind of theatrical agent, working for circuses and music-halls in the provinces.

The women she brought with her were more elegant, with their red henna'd hair, their eyes made up, and their mouths heightened by lipstick. They seemed to belong to the same family of small-time actresses, or waitresses on the night-shift, and their loud voices, gaudy clothes, and histrionic gestures were in stark contrast with the excessively sober appearance of their friend.

Madame de Prack was perfectly turned-out. Always in black, wrapped in soft furs for winter or in tulle and silk muslins for summer, which made her figure look even slimmer, she hid beneath thick veils a remarkably pale face, and eyes that seemed dashed with kohl between their purple eyelids, the whole not without charm, but for a slightly long nose. An over-large mouth also rather spoiled the face, but it opened scarlet onto some wide-set, brilliant little teeth. Shadow dwelt at the join of the lips, and her wide smile, flecked with scarcely perceptible down on the upper lip, was not without a certain *piquant*. With her narrow face, her pointed chin, and horse-like profile, she looked a little like an elongated grasshopper, with the slow and then sudden movements to match.

Madame de Prack must have had a strong character—to judge from her appearance at least—for if she was neither a thief nor from a theatrical agency, she remained a fine-spun net of lust; and judging from the prey she caught, fish or fowl, all was grist to her mill.

More than once I brushed past her on the stairs of the hotel; she was coming up, I was coming down, or vice-versa, and each time I had the audacity to trail my hand along the banister in an attempt to meet her own, because that shadowy, enigmatic mouth and those inviting eyes pierced me through. But it was each time in vain. I cannot have been her type, and her strangely insistent eyes never once met mine. For a time I resented this. The svelte woman with the melting eyes would have made an exquisite and obliging mistress—sex and mystery within my grasp! The hotel staff never said a word about their guest, and they refused to be drawn. As I have suggested, Madame de Prack must have been very generous. My pride was hurt, and for a while I was base enough to try and dream up some trick to play on my neighbour, and then I just forgot about it.

Chance, that great agent in human affairs, was to help me solve one part of the mystery. It was the end of winter, during a performance at the Français, where I had a cheap seat in the last row of the stalls. They were playing repertory, and the actors were going through the motions; indeed, they dozed so deeply that I had stopped listening to their droning, riveted as I was by a whispered conversation two women were having in one of the boxes just above and behind me. Here are the fragments I heard|

'No, I wouldn't dare!' said one voice. 'And how could I leave my house in a carnival cape? There's the coachman. I can trust my own maid, but the footman and the housekeeper are devoted to the Marquis. I am watched over—spied on—don't you see! Yours puts up with everything, lucky you.'—'And what a mistake!' exclaimed the other woman.—'The fact is his trust does him credit. No, Lucie, there's no question of it, and yet heaven knows how dearly I would love to go to that ball! To wander about for a whole night in disguise, free to come alongside and brush past every kind of debauchery and vice, including those one never imagined—certain of not being recognized!'—'Indeed! It's all quite pungent, and you'll never imagine the kind of thing people get up to on those nights.' At this point a whispered confidence ended in stifled laughs, and then the more hesitant voice came through again clearly: 'But how do you manage? What about the servants? Is your lord and master jealous?'—'I dine out on those evenings, of course, and I sleep at my mother's. You really are too innocent, Suzanne. I indulge all my fantasies. Life is short and I want to live it. Renting a room by the month at the hotel, under a false name, like I do, isn't ideal either, I can tell you...'—It was the end of the act; the audience got up to the sound of shoes scraping and seats springing back. I heard no more that night.

Ten days after this the hotel manager died. Influenza carried him off in less than a week, and it was in the little furnished reception room, transformed into a chapel of rest, that the gloomy wake was held. The devastated widow sat near the body, weeping the loss both of her husband and her business partner. The shutters had been closed, and there in the darkened room the poor woman, helped by two relatives, tried to find some solitude in the middle of the incessant coming and going of the hotel; in spite of her grief, she remained professionally attentive to noises coming from the street and the hotel itself. With another of the lodgers, I had gone in to pay my respects

to the widow. After exchanging the usual formalities we fell silent, rather embarrassed, and not knowing quite how to take our leave. Suddenly there came the sound of a carriage stopping in front of the hotel, followed by hurried steps on the stair, and in a bristling mass of astrakhan Madame de Prack burst into the room. She was not alone; another woman, young, elegant, and heavily veiled, was with her.

The newcomers were taken aback—they knew nothing of what had happened, and were shocked at the funereal scene; but Madame de Prack soon recovered her sang-froid. After murmuring a few words, and having pressed the hand of the widow: 'I am so sorry, and I feel wretched, my dear Madame! But I must ask of you a service. Where have you stored my capes and wigs and costumes?' When the hotel-keeper, rendered speechless, gestured helplessly, Madame de Prack went on: 'You see, Madame here (and she indicated the stranger), Madame is to accompany me to the ball tomorrow, and I am lending her a costume, and we want to try it on. Am I disturbing you?' The widow's eyes suddenly filled with tears, and she pointed to a cupboard on the far side of the corpse. The dead man had been placed right in front of it.

'It is indeed very inconvenient, but what can I do? None of this is my fault, and my friend is in rather a hurry.' The widow, who had stood up, now fell back into her chair and started sobbing in silence, her hands on her knees, and with an imploring expression on her face; but Madame de Prack just stood there, her long, pale visage imperious and wicked. The widow made an effort, and removing her trousseau of keys from her belt, stepped over the coffin, and with her legs apart, straddling the corpse, opened the cupboard and passed over a whole mass of satins, velvets, and lace to her implacable client.

A wig that was hanging out loose nearly caught fire in the candle-flame; we looked on in dread. 'Thank you,' said Madame de Prack, flattening down the dresses and capes with the back of her hand; then, turning towards her companion: 'Are you coming, Suzanne?'

The Man with the Bracelet

OCTOBER: the ambiguous and sinister aspect of certain outlying streets during these rainy and livid days of the late season, especially

at dusk when, once the sickening grind of the daily task has been acquitted, the bestial instincts inside us come to the fore, emboldened in the general stew of lust as the brothels light up, and provoked by the multitude of skirts trailing along in the gloom.

Voici le soir charmant, ami du criminel... *

It's that moment in the evening when the bars are ablaze, and between the tall vessels of polished copper, like those in a laboratory, a ragged, hollow-eyed crowd made up of old working men and young toughs fraternize and banter: outside the anxious silhouettes of the tarts keep watch, especially on pay-day, when any man a bit the worse for drink is prey. There they are, working the pavement, black-rimmed eyes set in faces white as plaster, looking like masks in the wan light of the streetlamps. And there, on the other side, is a crowd of worn overalls and resigned expressions—they belong to the legitimate spouses and the mothers of these working men in the grip of vice—and they wait for their menfolk at the wine-seller's door... there, at the dark, damp crossroads they wait, timidly and pitiably, for the week's earnings; deformed, worn out, and ugly, like pathetic ghosts of virtue—they have come to bargain for food on the table for the brats, competing against alcohol and sex.

Further on, where the crowded street leads down towards the ramparts, it becomes less well lit, and the storefronts of the wine-sellers, half-concealed by curtains, are engulfed in mystery; the voices of the customers become hushed and the tarts more spaced out along the empty pavements; the footsteps of the last stragglers ring out more rapidly, and along the tall fences that close off the newly built blocks of flats there are groups of three or four at the most, standing together in the dark, holding dubious council.

Slang words are exchanged in whispers—*pognon* and *rousse**—a guttural and sinister slang, like the sound of a steel blade rasping in the dark; then the group disperses, and at the windows of the new blocks and the old slums the vaguely gleaming forms of women in petticoats emerge, leaning their pallid flesh on the lintels.

These are the prostitutes who work from their windows, the most refined and shameful of such practices, and also the most troubling for the client—for the woman thus glimpsed seems far off, idealized in her squalor or by the mystery and crudeness of the decor, the promise of unimagined pleasures, the danger of a strange house, the

thrill of the ambush lying in wait in the black stairwell, the terror of
the blackmailer—who knows?—squatting behind the alcove curtains!… and the alluring face, the made-up face appearing high up in
the darkness, out of the blind façade, that might conceal the ageing
flesh refurbished by creams and powders, or the pretty oval of a little
immature virgin offered as bait by Poverty to Vice. All this contains
uncertainty, and doubt, and gives off a whiff of risk irresistible to
the sated or the daring… It's the heady rush towards the abyss, the
ineluctable magnetism of the chasm, the old symbol rejuvenated,
modernized, and even more deadful in its new context than the smiling
head of Scylla,* the supernatural head swimming and singing above
the blue Sicilian gulfs, with the puerile charm of over-red lips and
wide, glassy eyes; a bodiless head, and all the more enticing as men's
lust bodied forth for this head torso, arms, legs, and haunches. In
their madness, they picture all this beauty below the dangerous head;
all the more desirable in that it is the smile set in the façade of the dull
brick house, like a mask.

Ah, the woman at her window in the houses of the dreary streets,
golden apple of infernal pleasures, placed there on the window lintels, just as Scylla's head, once upon a time, emerged, revolving on
the waves, a lethal flower from the abyssal depths.

Outside, there are puddles and mud reflecting the gaslight, rain
pattering and dripping from gutters, the muffled footstep of cut-
throats in the night; and high, high up, set in the top storey of the
blind façade, like a fleshy orange in lamplight, juicy and full of
flavour, shines the painted face.

The fascination exerted by the window, the power of glimpsed
flesh and muslin gown, seen as luminous from the cold and dark of
the street, their hold on the senses of modern man, the city-dweller
especially, with his overstretched and morbid imagination, has been
described by Banville in a wonderful story entitled 'You Will
Return'.*

In one of those cities dear to Baudelaire's muse:

> *Je vois un port rempli de voiles et de mâts,*
> *Encor tout fatigués par la vague marine…*

Barcelona, Bilbao, Antwerp, Saigon, or Marseilles, as the traveller
strolls at leisure through the popular district of the town, he lets himself be distracted by a pretty, childlike head leaning out of the skylight

of a squalid house. No sooner has he entered than the story, boldly sketched in, introduces some romantic characters: a negress with a yellow madras on her head welcomes the young man and leads him in; on the first-floor landing there's a white parrot, a monstrous pink-crested macaw that watches him from his perch; on the fifth floor the staircase gleams under a covering of splendid rugs, and at last he is introduced to the attic room, which is done out like the boudoir of an oriental princess, all in silk, lacquer, and soft, silvered furs; inside is a Sicilian Greek, her profile could be struck on a medal, her bronze nakedness statuesque, she's a child-bride, scarcely fourteen years old; and all shivering and swooning, she offers him her supple body... They make love on white and yellow cushions; they drink wine from Samos out of cups of jade, and to the intoxication of their kisses is added that of burning perfumes rising from old silver tripods... Silks and spices, the style is one of sparkling goldwork, vision of an artificial paradise, the dream of an opium addict or an *habitué* of the Hôtel Pimodan:* the whole Baudelairean aesthetic is brought to life again. But it's only a dream, because when the traveller comes to his senses and wakes up, he is outside a bar full of sailors. He tries to find the enchanted house; he wanders for nights and days! All to no avail. Then he leaves, quitting the town of masts and yardarms, and sets off on his travels once more. Ten years pass, when suddenly, in some port or other, he recognizes the long-desired doorway. The negress in her madras is standing in the hall, and the giant parrot on his perch. The staircase is still as slippery in its cage of damp walls, the Asian carpets blaze as before on the final steps up, and the ebony-faced madame opens the door to the tiny room... but, alas! The Greek has aged... Deformed, coarsened, enormous, her breasts hang ripe, her belly is slack, and through the stink of creams and unguents, the spectre of his love proffers slavering, gap-toothed kisses. The stew is covered in rags, the velvet cushions are falling to pieces, the perfume-pans have gone out... Deeply distressed, his nausea rising in his gorge, the traveller comes clattering and stumbling down the stairs of the vile house. Sick to his stomach, he laments his lost dream and swears never ever to return. But as he falls through the door, 'You will return,' cries a harsh, strident voice. *You will return*, and the shattered man bows his head, for he knows inside him that he will return to the hideous sink, and that he will do so despite the slack flesh, the rancid lips, and the shapeless bust all oily with waxes.

For the giant parrot knows the heart of men, and he has known it these hundred years, ever since he first saw them filing up and down that staircase; and what he cries out on that threshold is the very form of their destinies: *You will return*, and they do indeed all return, since we return to our vice, as the dog in the scriptures returns to its vomit. Once we have met the fourteen-year-old Greek, with her cool, firm flesh, we never stop returning to the house of ill-fame, knowing that we shall meet none other than the aged tart with the drooping breasts; but the illusion, the hope that we might once again recover the Greek we encountered first, draws us inexorably back. We are always hooked, and always ready to be so, because what compels us is lust.

> *Ah! malheur à celui qui laisse la débauche*
> *Se planter comme un clou sous sa mamelle gauche!**

sobbed Alfred de Musset in two of his finest lines; and as he knew about Vice, and about the vicious with their complex, credulous, and quivering souls, the terrible *man with the bracelet* is the one fantastical and criminal shadow missing from Canler's *Memoirs.**

In one of the most frequented streets of Paris, not far from the Wagram dance-hall,* a meeting point for thieves, cut-throats, and pimps, some twenty years ago the police managed in the end to see through the racket—simple and complex at once—of one particular lady at her window. She never appeared entirely, but from four in the afternoon in winter, and seven in summer, a bare arm, a very white bare arm, beautifully modelled, emerged from behind a curtain and swayed like a swan's neck; it would remain there for hours on end, either folded so as to show a glimpse of the soft down of the armpit, or else it dangled down, languid and supple, reaching with desire towards the street. The arm and nothing more. The woman never showed herself. No one had ever seen her face; a gold bracelet encircled the wrist, and passers-by would stop and gaze up at the motionless arm, that moved very occasionally, and languidly when it did so, a hairless, powdered arm, so cold and white it seemed to be carved from marble. Men went up, mostly elderly men, and wealthy men, serious clients with refined requirements, and they came down again almost immediately, terrible-eyed and staggering; this went on for nearly ten months, when vague rumours started to circulate in the locality. Rumours of traps to snare old libertines for their salacity; eminent

names were bruited, the names of captains of industry and landed gentry, who had all been lured into a room and then threatened and robbed. But since no formal complaint had ever been made to the police, the vice-squad itself began its own enquiry. When the time came for a census to be taken of the girls living in the house, they found that the room belonging to the bare arm was inhabited by a painter, a young man who had won a Prix de Rome, who had now been back from Italy for a year-and-a-half, and who was living in considerable comfort on undeclared resources. The very evening of this discovery, when the bare arm was already deployed from behind the red curtain, a policeman disguised and made up as an old man rang discreetly at the studio door. After some whispered negotiations through the keyhole, and a few lascivious words pronounced by a feminine voice, the door half-opened, to be slammed shut instantly behind the speechless detective: a turn of the key in the lock, and the agent found himself face to face with a vigorous young man in shirt-sleeves, with one sleeve drawn right up to the shoulder. He grabbed the policeman's throat with one hand, and with the other brandished a long butcher's knife: 'Let's be having you, you dirty old wretch, and no nonsense... Your watch, your jewellery, and everything you have on you or I'll have you arrested! You have the effrontery to come calling on a man! So come! Your money, your rings, or I'll turn you in!'

It was the man with the bracelet, who was detained that evening by the police. For ten months he had been operating with impunity. Out of perhaps two hundred victims, not one had dared report him. The fear of ridicule, fear of the police, the thought of the scandal that might ensue as a result of a suspect liaison—all these had made them hold their tongues:

> *Ah! malheur à celui qui laisse la débauche*
> *Se planter comme un clou sous la mamelle gauche!...*

The Man Who Loved Consumptives

'AH, here's a new one!' said an elegant black suit sitting in front of me in the orchestra stalls, during the second act of Legendre's play.* Smiling into his moustache, he trained his glass on a box to the side,

where a slender young woman had just taken her place, extremely pale, in a beautiful dress of light blue tulle which made her look even paler.

It was the middle of the second act, the scene in the chapel, during which Lord Claudio, frowning craggily, his hand on the pommel of his sword, insults Leonato and the candid Hero in the famous Shakespearean apostrophe:

*Garde ta fille, elle est trop chère!**

Rapt as the audience was by the drama of the scene, and by the dazzling Roybet costumes against the wonderful Ziem watercolour that Porel* had mingled with the set design, every eye, and every lorgnette, followed the lead given by the opera-glass, so that the fragile creature, leaning now on the red velvet of the box, seemed to reflect, in her disturbing and spectral pallor, the gaze of all the men and women that had turned their eyes upon her.

Her face was oval, but drawn, with a languid, suffering expression: her eyes, that seemed enlarged, were ultramarine bordering on black. They were unnaturally bright, deep-set in their bruised and blueish rings, spotted with pearl: her delicate nose, with its arched and quivering nostrils, breathed rapidly and shallowly, as if in an atmosphere too thin to sustain her in life, and with her great feathered fan resting against her flat chest, from time to time, with her teeth that shone bright against the red of her mouth, she would bite at the burning purple of her lips, hard enough to draw blood. A man had now taken his place next to her; he was tall and strongly built, flourishing in the prime of health, and very smartly dressed; with the wide silk ribbon of his opera-glass threaded through his white evening waistcoat, his sartorial elegance was reminiscent of the Prince de Sagan. He leant towards the pale, fragile woman, whispering in her ear, and now and again offering her, from a soft silk bag, crystallized Parma violets, which she would nibble at, half-smiling, half-choking.

'She's not long for this world,' sniggered my black-clad neighbour. 'Two months at the outside. That little woman is suffocating, she must be coughing up lungfuls of blood, but I bet she's fired up with fever between midnight and two. She's extremely pretty too, if a little on the thin side.'

He took the lorgnette from his friend's hands, and with both lenses fixed on the box, he described every contraction of the pale blue dress, and every attention proffered by the large white waistcoat.

'All the same, he's got damned strange taste,' the lorgnette went on, 'going for skeletal women; he's a fervent adherent of love's funeral rites.'

'Good old Fauras, I never see him except with funereal Venuses, and they're always different. How many mistresses has he expedited by now?'

'At least three or four in the last two years. It's a kind of monomania, almost as if he collects them from the hospital; illness excites him, especially consumption. We have seen the *hangman's mistress*, now we have the *lover of doomed ladies*; in love with tears and the elegiac, the excellent Fauras, who keeps himself in such good trim, loves only those who are close to death. The frailty of their existence makes them all the dearer and more precious to him. He chokes with their spasms, shivers with their fevers, and listens out for the slightest sigh; attending to their stifling, he spies, like a broken voluptuary, on the progress of their disease, and lives their dying agonies—he's a sybarite, that's what he is!'

'Yes, I know. He's a beast, a kind of sadist, prey to macabre ideas, the next thing to a necrophiliac, seeking the last warmth in a cadaver, and in death the last piquancy of love. The Saint-Ouen horror crime* relived every evening in the privacy of the boudoir. The quest for novel sensations, proof from the sanction of the law because the victim is still just alive.'

'My dear fellow, you could hardly be more wrong! Fauras is a tender-hearted, elegiac soul, obsessed with the exquisite manifestations of sadness, besotted with mourning; he wears black crêpe in his thoughts and has a funeral urn in place of a heart. Deliciously distressed, and delighted to be so, he is forever fingering the evergreen cypress of his regrets above his latest loves—a phoenix eternally rising from the ashes!'

'I must confess, I am completely lost.'

'What a lumpish man you are! To love a woman who is doomed to die, to know that with every kiss and caress time is running out, to feel with the rasping of her breath everything ebbing away forever; to know oneself condemned to despair and yet exalted, to be aware that each fresh pleasure is one step closer to the grave, and that with one's own hands, shaking with horror and desire, one is hollowing out within the love-nest the pit wherein you will lay your love to rest, *that* is the piquancy of the thing! A man can never have known the

bitter appeal of stolen assignations which may never be repeated, not to understand a passion of this type, with its piercing melancholy, hatched in relationships like this, marked indelibly by Pleasure and Sin!'

'But that's monstrous!'

'And yet absolutely true. Frailty is the great appeal of beings and things, the flower would scarcely move us if it never faded; the faster it perishes, the sweeter the scent, its life is exhaled with its fragrance! The doomed woman is exactly the same; dying, she abandons herself frenziedly to pleasures that fill her with burning life even as they hasten her death; her time is running out; her thirst for love, her need to suffer burns and flames within her, and she clings to love with the final convulsions of the drowning; and desiring still, she redoubles the force behind her last kiss. Twisted under the hand of Death, she would kill the object of her desperate adoration, were she not expiring herself; and his long, crushing, and furious embrace makes her swoon, and die.'

'Voluptuous!'

'Voluptuous, indeed! And Fauras has another advantage; with these consumptive women of his the relationship is never broken off brutally, there are no disagreeable scenes, unavoidable even for a gentleman, there is no vitriolic and sordid settling of accounts: tactful and clear-sighted, Fauras escapes all the predictable disgust and lassitude at the end of such affairs, the dull and wretched conclusion to all such liaisons in which satiety and boredom succeeds passion. His love affairs come to an end with the clean white, silver-threaded winding-sheet in a young woman's coffin, amidst violets and roses in clusters, by candlelight, to the sound of anthems and organ music, with the dead girl laid out like Ophelia. A modern Hamlet, he follows the procession of his own love, and if his heart is wrung, at least it is so within a beautiful setting, with flowers and incense, with music and priestly psalms, in an uplifting scene of apotheosis. His is an artist's grief, in short, but an artist who is also practical and clear-headed, for he has taken death as his notary and his counsel, and he charges the keeper of Montparnasse cemetery with the disposal of his feelings. What is more, the tears he sheds for his mistress are real; now she is dead, he brings her favourite flower to the graveside, and arranges it carefully, and wins the hearts of the family standing by; and so, with a sweet melancholy, embellished with the adored images

and the light ghosts of women, his life flows on, between the beloved friend of yesterday and *the one who is to come*, already perfumed with regret, trembling with echoes, beating with hope, nuanced with memories!'

'The man's a monster, a vile wretch, a...'

'... great sensualist and a wise man, my dear fellow, for he has contrived to get Death to work for him in the amorous exploits of his life, and he has given body to his dreams by idealizing that nuisance known as Memory. And whatever anyone may say, he is our superior, for he is the only man who mourns his mistresses sincerely, the only man who savours genuine loss, which is the the philtre and the poison that killed the legendary lovers of yesteryear. Very few of their kind remain, and they are stranded in this century, this century of unbelief and lucre, in which tuberculosis remains the only killer.'

GEORGES RODENBACH

The Time

'BARBE, what is the time?'

'A quarter to five,' answered presently the old servant, who had gone to the mantel where, between two old-fashioned vases, stood a small Empire-period clock with four little columns of white marble, bearing aloft a short pinion embellished with gilt bronzes in the form of sinuous swans' necks.

'But I think our clock is slow,' she went on. And with the steady, deliberate tread of people in the provinces who aren't in a hurry, she went to the window, lifted the muslin curtain, and stared out at the nearby tower, the dark tower of the Halles de Bruges, to which is affixed, like a great crown, a vast dial which declines the hour unceasingly to the deserted streets around it.

'Oh, yes! It is slow: it's about to strike five o'clock,' she went on. 'The hands are already in place.'

Sure enough, one minute later the peal went out, and sent a kind of carolling, flustered nest effect into the air; less a song than a plaint, less a snow of flying feathers than a rain of iron and ash... Then the great bell struck five times, at regular intervals, slow and solemn, and each time it struck the nimbus of melancholy in the silence expanded, as a stone thrown into the waters of a canal makes rings that shimmer outwards until they reach the banks.

'How long it goes on!' said Van Hulst, falling back among his pillows, wearied from sitting up, even for these few instants, on his bed, to which for weeks now he had been confined by illness.

He had recently entered upon his convalescence, after the attack of typhoid fever which had laid him low. But at least the accesses of the fever had taken from him the sense of time, prostrating him until he lost consciousness, or exalting him in delirium and nightmares whose melting imagery absorbed him. It was only now, when things had grown calmer, that the days had started to drag, divided into the minutes that he had to live through and, as it were, tell out one by one.

And movement, occupation of any kind, was forbidden: and no company was to be admitted to the empty house, to this solitary bachelor's world, crossed only by the silent tread of the old servant, faithful Barbe, who had got him up and seen to his needs, watched over him and restored him with an almost maternal solicitude.

But she could do nothing now to divert him a little: she could not converse, or try reading aloud. And he felt so alone, a prey to the slow, sad passage of time. Especially in the leaden northern twilight, in this late autumn on the quays of Bruges (he lived on the Quai du Rosaire), where a contagious melancholy came in through the windows, settled on the furniture in pallid tones, afflicted the mirrors with a kind of valedictory light...

And then there was the impartial little clock in his room, telling out its rosary of minutes without end! During his enforced inaction, empty of event and thought, the patient had little by little become obsessed with the time. He worried about the clock as if it were a living presence. He looked at it like a friend. It made him learn patience. It distracted him with its moving hands and the noise of its workings. It alerted him to the arrival of cheerier moments, when his light meals were served, milk or broth; best of all, to the return of darkness, and with it a good stretch of oblivion, which helped shorten the time. Mesmerizing dial! Other patients use their eyes to count out, mechanically, the number of flowers on the wallpaper or on the cretonne curtains. He engaged in calculations based on the clock. He sought the day when he would be cured, which was already imminent—but still imprecise... He consulted the clock, he checked the time, since often, like today, there was a discrepancy between his timepiece and the ancient clock on the tower. When it pealed, he compared one with the other. It became a small diversion for him, seeking the same time on the two dials, as one might a resemblance beween two faces.

When Van Hulst was better, he carried over from his sickness this preoccupation with the *right time*. In a town as calm and circumscribed as his own dead Bruges, the tower can be seen, or at any rate heard, in every district, even as far as the suburbs. So the correct time, the official time, so to speak, was given out by this clock. Elsewhere, time is never more than approximate. Everyone keeps their own, and makes do with it. Van Hulst had set his watch against the dial on the belfry, and through the entire period of his illness had

never altered it; now, every time he went out, he would check it, and became almost vexed if he remarked it were slightly fast or a tiny bit behind. His timetable, his meals, when he went to bed, when he got up, always at the same time, were synchronized to the minute.

'Gosh! I'm five minutes slow,' he would say sometimes, as if dismayed.

He made sure that his watch and the clocks in his home were always synchronized, not just the little Empire-period clock with the swan's neck bronzes, but the kitchen clock with its dial decorated in red tulips, which old Barbe would consult for her housework chores.

One Friday, market day, Van Hulst, who was still convalescing, was out on one of his gentle strolls; he lingered among the stalls in the main square, and noticed a rather strange Flemish clock. It was half-hidden, almost buried, in the miscellaneous chaos covering the pavement. They sell everything at this market: canvas, cotton stuffs, objects in metal, agricultural implements, toys, antiques. A pell-mell patchwork, a turning-out of the centuries. The market is not limited to the stalls, where the sellers display their wares elegantly, underneath pale canvas awnings, shaped into hoods, rather like the winged coifs worn by nuns. Frequently the merchandise is piled or stacked anyhow on the ground, still covered with grey dust, as though issued straight from some inventory, the sale of some missing person's goods and chattels, brought out of a house long since deserted and closed-up. Everything is old, dusty, oxidized, rusted, faded, and would look plain ugly were it not for the intermittent northern sun, which suddenly lights up patinas, or Rembrandtian russet golds. It was among such ruins, where occasionally a surprise lies hidden—a piece of furniture, an old jewel, some lacework—but of fine workmanship, that Van Hulst found the Flemish clock, which he instantly wanted to possess. It was made up of a long oak case with sculpted panels, warmly coloured by time, in varnishes and sheen; but its most original feature was the dial. Made of copper and pewter, wrought with taste and imagination, a whole playful cosmography was affixed to it, with a laughing sun, a gondola shaped like a crescent moon, stars that browsed with the bodies of lambkins, moving over the numerals as though they wanted to pick them out like flowers in the grass.

Van Hulst was delighted with this antique clock, which wore its date of birth triumphantly: '1700', incised onto the original metal.

But had the mechanism survived, after counting out innumerable years? This was Van Hulst's chief concern, for he desired it less as an antique curiosity than as one more clock which, old as it was, would synchronize with the young clocks in his house.

The merchant assured him that the clock worked perfectly, that even the chiming mechanism functioned accurately; in short, that it had never once gone wrong, throughout all its long years of telling the time.

And chime it did, loudly! Strong-voiced clock, it sang out the hour, in its new home at Van Hulst's. And how thin, by comparison, were the little chimes of the Empire clock and the clock with the red tulips. Rather like children's voices, issuing from clocks that had not yet come of age. But their venerable ancestor lived in harmony with them. Each kept slightly different time; but by an amusing anomaly, it was the old clock that struck the hour first, ahead of the others, as though enjoining them to follow suit. Was this grandmother more solid and indefatigable than her children?

Van Hulst smiled, cheered by the family of clocks that brought his home to life. Nevertheless, it troubled him rather that they were not perpetually in unison. When one lives together, is it not better to think as one!

The obsession with the *right time*, which had come over him during his illness, became stronger since he had added the Flemish clock to his collection. One was fast, the other was slow... which was right? He synchronized them all with the dial on the tower, that he could see from his windows. Especially when the hour struck. It displeased him that one should ring for longer than the other. When this happened, it was as though they were running after each other, calling each other, losing and seeking each other at all the variable intersections of time.

Little by little, Van Hulst developed a taste for pendulums and clocks. He had acquired others, from the Friday market, from jewellers and auctioneers. Without intending to, he had started a real collection, an interest that started to consume him. No man is ever really happy without an *idée fixe*.* It fills his time, the vacancies of his thought, startles his boredom, gives direction to his aimlessness, and sends a brisk, revivifying breeze over the monotonous water of his existence. Van Hulst had access to a subtle joy and to incessant surprises.

Now he had a veritable hobby. In the heart of morose Bruges, in the life of this bachelor, which had been free of incident, in which every day had been the same and of the same grey tone as the air of the town, what a change had come about! Now his life was intent, always on the alert for some new treasure! He experienced the collector's lucky find! The encounter with the unexpected, that swells his treasure! Van Hulst already had some expertise. He had studied, sought, compared. He could see at a glance what period a clock was from. He could tell its age, sort the genuine article from the fake, appreciate a beautiful style; and he came to know the signatures of master clockmakers, whose products were works of art. By now, he possessed a whole series of different clocks, scarcely noticing he had done so. He had haunted the antique shops of Bruges. To swell his collection, he had even travelled to nearby towns. He followed auction sales, especially when estates were being sold off, for then one could pick up rare and curious items that had been forever in the possession of dynastic families. His collection became impressive. He had clocks of every type: Empire clocks in marble and bronze, or in bronze gilt; Louis XV and Louis XVI clocks, with curved panels in rosewood, with encrustations and marquetry, showing romantic scenes which enlivened the woodwork like a fan; he had mythological, idyllic, warlike clocks; clocks made out of biscuit, of costly and fragile pastes; Sèvres and Saxe clocks, where time laughs among flowers; Moorish clocks, Norman, or Flemish, with oak or mahogany casings, and chimes that whistled like blackbirds or squeaked like well-chains. Then there were the rarities: maritime water-clocks, in which water-drops compose the seconds. Finally, he possessed a whole panoply of little table clocks, and ceremonial clocks as delicate and as finely wrought as jewels.

Van Hulst considered that he needed more still. Is this not the subtle pleasure of the collector, that he can perpetually prolong his desire? It is infinite, and meets no limit, and knows nothing of that total possession which can disappoint by its very plenitude. And then there is the excitement caused when he cannot obtain the object he ardently desires! There was, in fact, just such an object, a very old clock that Van Hulst had spotted one day at Walburge's, the richest antique-seller in Bruges, whose shop is situated on the rue de L'Âne-aveugle,* and well known to collectors, and to foreigners who find it mentioned in guides. But the old antique-seller was connoisseur and

merchant in equal measure; if he had something special, he would refuse to sell it unless he got a good price. The old clock coveted by Van Hulst was in fact a very rare piece indeed, unique of its kind, marvellously carved, and adorned with painted scenes from the gospels, in the style of prayerbook illumination, and signed by the artist whose name was prized by connoisseurs. Walburge was asking a great deal of money for this clock. Van Hulst would bargain, leave, and then come back. He would have to dig deep, and he hesitated. The merchant stuck to his guns. With his shrewd eye, he could tell how much his client wanted the clock. Every time he entered the shop, Van Hulst would set to and examine the precious thing once more, with the excitement, the feeling in his fingertips that is a kind of pleasure; he had the nervous, sensitive hands of the collector, who are *tactile* by nature, and he would touch, handle, stroke the object of desire. It was as though he already half-owned it. But the embrace was incomplete, a half-possession: the caresses of the fiancé who dreams of a full consummation.

Van Hulst had done his sums. He really could not afford the clock. He would never be able to raise the sum against his income, which barely covered his expenses. And he had already used the remainder on his previous purchases. His methodical lifestyle was such that he would never allow himself to eat into his capital, however strong the temptation. He simply had to bargain the price down.

Old Walburge would never have given in; he was one of those hard-headed Flemish types, who digs in his heels for no particular reason, and refuses to budge, rather than be seen to compromise. But by going again and again to the shop, and showing so openly his disappointment and dismay at not being able to buy, he won the heart of Walburge's daughter, a girl of tender age called Godeliève.* She was the fruit of a late marriage, somewhat too delicate and pale, and she adorned the old widower's home like a large virgin lily.

Van Hulst soon got Godeliève on his side. He had started to engage her in conversation, leaning over the loom she worked at to examine the fine lace, playing over it with his fingers as though on a keyboard.

Soon they were joined in a silent, friendly conspiracy against old Walburge. The latter could refuse nothing to his daughter, whom he adored. And the combined force of their two willpowers went to work.

And so it was that one day, pressed yet again by Van Hulst, the antique-seller gave way and accepted his offer. The collector was

overjoyed, especially when he took possession of the precious clock and placed it on an old oak table, where it gleamed in a direct ray of light from his windows in the vast room on the first floor which housed his singular clock museum. No sooner was it placed there than the newcomer added its humming, like a small metal bee, to all the others; the strange room was like Time's Beehive.

Van Hulst was not, however, merely interested in having a collection of rare clocks. He treasured them, but not just as still-lifes. Of course, their appearance mattered to him, their structure, mechanism, and artistic merit. But there was another motive behind his assembling so many clocks, and it had to do with his concern for the right time. It was not enough that they should be beautiful. He wanted to consider them as the same, as being of one mind, to think like him, and to keep time, without ever deviating, from the second he had synchronized and set them running. But such a degree of harmonization was a miracle he would never have thought possible up till then. As well ask the pebbles on the beach, come from every corner of the horizon and rolled in the sea by such varying tides, to be identical in size. Yet try he did. Having been initiated by a clock-maker, he now knew the secrets of the wheels, the springs, the cogs, the diamond pins, the workings, links, and circuits, every nerve and muscle, the complete anatomy of this gold-and-steel beast whose steady pulse gives the universe its rhythm... He had acquired all the right tools: the eyeglass, the tiny saws and files, all the minuscule implements needed to take apart, polish, correct, and restore such sensitive and delicate organisms. With observation, patience, punctiliousness, by slowing this one and accelerating that one, attending to the weak point in each, he might just attain what was now his obsessive dream: to see them all in unison; to hear them, if only once, strike the hour at the same time, synchronized with the clock-tower; to attain his ideal of harmonizing time.

Van Hulst's compulsion lasted a long while. He never got discouraged. Every afternoon he put in long hours, trying to synchronize all his dials. Whenever he had to go out, he would give careful instructions to his old servant that under no circumstances was she to enter the closed room, where she might upset the weights, brush against the chains, or generally disturb the clocks and thereby upset the result he so desired, which was to get all his clocks to strike the hour

in perfect unison. He would remind her of all this, every time he went out. And these days he went out more often. He continued his quest, he remained on the look-out. He was also a frequent visitor at old Walburge's shop, in the rue de l'Âne-aveugle, to see if a new clock had come in. Mostly it was the gentle Godelième who greeted him. She was always sitting in her place by the window, where the grey day, filtered through curtains, darkened her honey-coloured hair... She was like a Memling Madonna,* with eyes like little mirrors in which you could see yourself, amidst the blues of the sky. She worked unceasingly at her lace-making, and the spindles of the loom played with her fingers, animated her fingers, gave themselves up to her fingers, as though she had tamed them.

When old Walburge was out doing errands, Van Hulst engaged Godelième in long and restful conversations. As a committed collector, he returned to the shop frequently. Little by little, however, he realized that he went there not only in the interests of his beloved museum, but also in part for the girl, who had become dear to him too. Especially since once again she had been unwell. She had grown pale, and thinner still, even though she was already as slender and incorporeal as the Saint Ursula in the Hospital reliquary. Van Hulst was deeply stirred by Godelième's frailty. What was wrong with her? Was there some hidden malady? Or a lack of vitality, something like a death-wish?

Before long, he became anxious as well. Perhaps she was fading away from some deep hurt, unavowed even to herself, from some secret too heavy for the delicate soul to bear. She surrounded herself in the mystery of it, in the nimbus of something that was divine in her. And seeing her melancholic, Van Hulst fell in love with her. He had to confess as much to himself. It was for her, to gaze upon her, and to hear her gentle voice—the mysterious voice that canal water has under the bridges—that he stopped by so often at the antique shop. The clocks were merely an excuse. By now he was neglecting his own, being so taken up with Godelième. Is love not an obsession too, one that annihilates all the others, that makes one happier than all the others? And is the lover also not in pursuit of a breathtaking collection of wonderful little nothings: looks, the lowered gaze, the squeeze of a hand, words, declarations, letters, pledges, kisses, that are similarly inventoried and set in order like a treasured collection? And when it is first love, a whole museum comes into being!

Van Hulst, who was already greying, had in fact never experienced real passion. It was as though his heart had lain dormant, dulled by the dead city, with its aimless waters, its empty quays, its silence, Bruges the mystic, given up entirely to the sky.

No access of tender feeling had ever troubled his single life. But here was the old bachelor, chronically stuck in his ways, a victim of his tics and the mad devotion to his clocks, here he was about to betray that devotion, and become someone tender, ardent, and loving.

And it was all the more ardent this time, in that his passion could not so easily find satisfaction. Collecting had been child's play, almost instant gratification. But how could he satisfy his passion for the sweet and delicate Godelième! So delicate! She constantly fell ill, and sometimes weeks would pass before he saw her again. But he went on stopping by the antique shop, asking after her, discussing her with her father. The latter was also worried now, concerned by the mysterious malady that no doctor seemed able to fathom. Van Hulst dared not go every day to the rue de l'Âne-aveugle. But even when he stayed home his sole thought was for Godelième, completely taken up as he was by the girl he had once hoped to make his. He grew alarmed. Perhaps the nameless illness that was eating away at her would end up killing her! The idea sent him into a panic. What if she should slip through his fingers! The collector's instinct within him rose up once more, whetted by the challenge, and he came to desire the object all the more ardently as it escaped him. She was now the wonderful clock that was his heart's whole desire; it was the ticking of her heart that he wanted to hear; it was her face he wanted to set as a guide to his life, that soft dial of flesh with its eyes in enamel, which had gradually led him into neglecting his clocks. The long vigils in his museum were all over, like the dream of synchronized time, the diverting sessions of clock-restoration, identifying all the little malfunctions in the cogs and the springs before him on his bench, with the glass fixed in his eye, pursued with all the patience of laboratory science. He still wound up his clocks and pendulums, but he did it mechanically, merely out of habit, raising the weighted chains, turning the keys, but he was no longer concerned with the dials or the time they showed, he abandoned them to themselves, scattered like a flock the shepherd has set loose, his eye suddenly distracted, gazing from star to star...

His single thought was for Godelièvë. Would he win her one day? He had never dared declare himself. And anyway, what was the good? She seemed reserved for death, rather than as someone's fiancée. On his latest visits to the antique shop he had not seen her. She had taken to her bed. Was it not his great misfortune, to have met Godelièvë, to have conceived this unattainable love for her, a love that was enough to have spoilt all his earlier joys?

Van Hulst started to brood; he scarcely spoke; his old servant Barbe scarcely recognized her master. It was as though he were always waiting for something. His thoughts grew dark; he imagined the worst.

His fears, as it happened, were only too justified. One Sunday, towards evening, a messenger arrived at his house, sent by Walburge the antiques merchant, one of those messengers they have in Bruges who go from door to door, sent by families when they have to announce a bereavement. Godelièvë was dead. She had suffocated in a sudden coughing fit that had brought up blood. Hurrying immediately over to his shop, Van Hulst had learned this from old Walburge himself.

And there on a white bed, with a few lilies scattered round the pillow and with her face framed by rivulets of hair, now stilled, in the light of a calmly burning candle, he suffered the grief of gazing one last time upon the young woman he had hoped one day to win, but in a different white dress, and with other lilies.

Returning home fairly late in the evening (he had stayed a good while at Walburge's), Van Hulst was startled to find there was still a light in the corridor. Barbe was waiting up, she of all people, who was usually in a hurry to get to bed. He could hear her walking about. Her footsteps seemed to be coming from the first floor, apparently from the room that housed the clock museum. What had happened? Did she not obey him? Did she thus dare to handle and disturb what he had expressly forbidden her to go anywhere near when he was out? But the moment she heard him come in, Barbe leaned over the banister and cried out from the stairwell:

'Monsieur! Monsieur!'

Her voice had a slight quaver in it, as if she had some serious news to impart, which frightened him rather.

Van Hulst hurried up the stairs. Barbe cried out from further off:

'Monsieur! The clocks have struck!...'

'What? How?' Van Hulst was baffled.

The servant explained that her master had left open the door of the museum, no doubt accidentally. In the stillness of the house she had suddenly heard a loud noise. As the great clock-tower struck ten, all the chime mechanisms from all the clocks began to strike, all together and at the same time. The result was tumultuous, a strange coppery sound breaking the silence. She had entered the room. All the clocks stopped at the tenth stroke, perfectly in unison, as if in measure, with not a single voice out of line or going over; they were all juxtaposed, and superimposed, and they all sounded as one. And on all the dials all the hands were opened at exactly the same compass angle... Shocked, Van Hulst looked hard. Most of the clocks still showed exactly the same time. A mere twenty minutes had passed since the incredible moment he had dreamed of for so long, and that had come to pass. It would never come again. Little disharmonies were already creeping in. The old Flemish clock began running fast; the little Louis XV pendulum, with its romantic panelwork, was going slow.

Strange skulduggery! The clocks had synchronized themselves, for the space of a minute. They had coalesced, just this once, and they had done so *against him*, to avenge his neglect of them; the very evening that Godelième had died, together they had struck, or rather they had sung the hour, like a conspiracy of abandoned mistresses whose reign, from that moment on, began once more.

The truth dawned on Van Hulst: his plan to harmonize time had been realized, but without him, and without his having been able to enjoy it, punished as he was for coveting love, for having cherished and mourned Godelième, for having abandoned the ideal for reality. The ideal is always jealous, and demands, if it is to be attained, immense, single-minded purpose. Is it not our renunciation of Life itself, that alone makes us fit to attain our Dream?

REMY DE GOURMONT

Danaette

As she was getting dressed after lunch, in her special and even mysterious dress, the snow started to fall.

Below the curtains which glowed like stained glass, lifted and pinned back to let in a bit of light, she watched it falling, the beautiful snow falling and falling—and it was sad and it was solemn; it gave the impression of some ironic and occult force, of some divine soul, terrible and cold, that in disdain spread wide its light layer of crystal ice over the panoply of human pretentiousness that analyses everything and understands nothing.

'There's a great battle going on in the sky,' her old Breton chambermaid said to her. 'The angels are tearing out each other's feathers—and that is why it's snowing. Madame should know that.'

There was no arguing with this assertion, and Madame did not try. Every year, and sometimes several times each winter, her old Breton maid confided the same secret, always completed by a 'Madame should know that', expressed as an irrefutable and slightly threatening fact. The old servant had a neat, short, ready-made answer for everything—quaint explanations delivered as manifest truths.

Madame did not reply, but as soon as her hair was dressed she dismissed the old maid.

She desired to be alone—alone with the Snow.

She was not properly dressed, she had lost interest halfway through, and sat on a divan near the fire, watching fascinated by the spirals of angelic snowy fluff and feather.

Getting dressed! Oh what a bore it was, two or three times a week! Adultery is highly pleasurable at the beginning—it's a journey into the unknown, you're spread like a sail on the stiff but delicious breeze that drives you on to new embraces, you're filled with curiosity, and there's nothing in your head but the anticipation of a fresh and ever-more gratifying pleasure: sin feels like a baptism to the inventive mind of the female sinner. But for any little delinquent, however

intense the sense of rebirth afforded by the thrill of lying, the feeling does not last, and its detestable twin brother, Boredom, tags along behind.

What a bore! You have to remember so many things, and experience is there to nudge you to remember the thousand humiliating and discouraging measures that must be taken.

'For example,' she mused (without taking her eyes off the snow), 'I have to wear pumps and not boots. He dropped a heavy hint to that effect. The first time, he rebuttoned them innocently and worshipfully, drawing my leg upon his knees; the second time he took a button-hook from his pocket and gave it to me; and the third time he didn't even think of bringing that, and I was most unhappy.

'Same thing for the corset and the dress. Monsieur is impatient. He tears at my stays, he tangles the laces. I've had to design a special bodice that comes undone in one go, and I have replaced the corset with a kind of halter you put on babies, that unbuttons much the same way as a bodice. In a flash, I am naked, or very nearly.

'Yes, naked, because he makes me wear petticoats rather like soutanes, which fall open like curtains once one has undone the tiny buttons that hold them together; and the costumes affect the way I behave.

'Come on! I must put on the baby-halter and lock away my corset, so that my scandalized maid doesn't blurt out to my husband, on my return, "Madame went out without her corset. And Madame knows it."

'The snow is so beautiful!...'

They went on falling, the fine, soft, white angel plumes. The mutinous adulteress became childlike; the fascination exerted upon her by the subtle and monotonous snow, the perpetual and apparently infinite snow, acted on her sensibility. The peremptory nonsense of the little Bretonne came back to her, and she felt sorrow for the angels who had lost their feathers!

A featherless angel must be an odd sight, rather like those plucked geese you saw in farmyards in Normandy, the poor geese who gave their plumage to stuff the pillows of fussy adultresses.

It was a foolishly childish image, but plucked angels are still angels—and angels are very beautiful creatures.

Snow went on falling, and it was getting thicker, so thick that the air now seemed condensed into a polar ocean of white stars, or into an

immaculate flight of gulls that a gust would occasionally disturb and throw in tumult against the panes.

Forgetting all about her classic rendezvous, the little darling became obsessed by these sudden gusts, but she was even more delighted when the crystalline cloud crumpled slowly and majestically with the sovereign calm of certainty. But her eyes kept closing and she could scarcely keep them open, resolved as she was not to give way, but to watch the snow fall for as long as the snow would fall.

She was overcome: her eyes closed and did not open again until after she had fallen into a long semi-trance. But behind her eyelids the snow kept falling. The windowpanes no longer kept out the rain of limpid flakes. It was snowing in her room, on the furniture and on the carpet, everywhere; it was snowing on the couch where she lay, overcome by fatigue. One of the cold stars fell on her hand; another on her cheek; another on her breast which was half-uncovered: and these were, especially the last, new and exquisite caresses.

Other stars fell: her pale-green dress was lit up like a meadow by a host of simple daisies; her hands and her neck were soon all covered, and her hair and her breasts. This unreal snow did not melt on contact with the heat of her body, nor of the fire: it remained flowering, like a beautiful gown.

Deliciously icy, the snow kisses passed through her clothes, and in spite of all her defences they found her skin and gathered in the declivities: it was wonderfully gentle, and procured her a voluptuous pleasure she had most certainly never felt before!

In fact this was a rape, the snow possessed her—and Danaette put up no resistance, curious about this novel adultery, entirely given up to the unspeakable and almost terrible pleasure—of being the willing prey of a divine caprice, and the lover elected by a few angels suddenly turned perverse.

The snow kept on falling, and penetrated so deeply into her prone body that she had no other feeling than that of wanting to die, buried under these adorable snow kisses, to be embalmed in the snow—and then to be swept off, in a final gust, to the land of eternal snow, to the fabled infinite mountains where the darling little adultresses lie in a perpetual swoon, ceaselessly and firmly caressed by all the perverse angels.

The Faun

SHE had retired early after dinner, believing herself ill but in fact merely sad, and weary of the innocent chiming laughter of the smaller children, of the good-hearted conviviality of the poor relations enjoying a bit of a holiday, that wretched seasonal pantomime dictated by the calendar.

Most of all she was depressed and almost indignant at the hypocritical tenderness that shone in the dull eye of her husband when they had people round: like other women, she would have preferred to be beaten in public and loved in secret.

She dismissed her maid, bolted the door, and began to feel properly alone, and free, and less unhappy.

She undressed slowly, adopting poses, glancing at herself in the mirror, simulating languors, as if she were making ready to fall artfully into beloved outstretched arms, and receive a delicate compliment on her shoulder or even her knee, and a reminder that one has a beautiful soul and beautiful skin... She played at all this—it was merely harmless fun—with the confidence of a woman who does not fear the surprises of her own imagination.

Her ingenuous little acts of daring were tempered by her modesty. She knew how far to raise her skirts, she knew the level fixed for dry weather and wet weather, and just like Arlette, when favoured by the attentions of Robert le Diable,* she would have torn her gown rather than raised it. So she felt rather ashamed and, smothered in a fur, she knelt down chastely in front of the fire.

She poked at the fire, built up blazing structures, almost burned her face, got bored.

Would it not have been better to respond to the opportunistic caresses of her husband? With a few provocations she could dominate him, and the evening would end in some really rather calming exercises—instead of which here she was restless, enervated, angry—and she could become melancholy to the point of tearfulness, and prey to that extreme sobbing which no one can calm, sobbing that shakes the heart like a ship in the storm!

Oh! The sad and stupid business of Christmas Eve! Must there be dates, and magical days, during which it is a crime to be alone, during which human contact is prescribed almost under duress and the

threat of remorse! Ideas of this order crossed her weak and flitting brain, but soon it all grew too complicated to ponder and she summed it all up under one word—Christmas!

And there she was again, a little girl, going to midnight mass—and tucked up in bed falling asleep, dreaming of how the Baby Jesus would spoil her with goodies...

... No, that's such a cliché! Everyone has these visions of the past, every year the tender memories of the child's Christmas returns. Mediocre dreams, these, for mediocre folk, they're two a penny! Wretched, conformist, sentimental dreams!

In rebellion against the snow-white purity of her memories, she fell into sensual imaginings. The heat from the logs that were blazing still tickled her, brazenly: it set her dreaming—she imagined a series of startling kisses coming down the chimney like so many wingless little angels, hotter and nimbler than the sparks that played among the burning embers like amiable demons.

She dreamed on, and imagined a lavish act of fornication, of being debauched suddenly and unexpectedly, to which she gave herself as willing victim, here on the soft rug, and with this fine beast, this loving and devoted he-goat...

The scattered atoms of the incubus in the warm room started massing together... and a shadow, like that of a young faun, darkened the mirror, mussed her hair, and blew hot upon the nape of her neck.

She was frightened, but she wanted to be more frightened; and yet she dared not turn round or raise her eyes to the mirror. What she had felt was piercingly sweet; what she had seen was troubling, strange, curiously absurd: a hard, blond head, with ravenous eyes and a large, almost obscene mouth, with a pointed beard...* She shivered: the being that was going to take her must be tall and strong and handsome! How she would tremble in his arms! But she was trembling already, possessed already, prey already to the amorous monster who was staring at her and coveting her so.

The fur slipped off her shoulders, and instantly a violent kiss burned into her naked flesh—a kiss so violent and so ardent that the mark would undoubtedly stay with her, like that from a red-hot iron. She tried, in that movement women have when being undressed, to regather her cloak around her and preserve some vestige of modesty, but the Being was having none of it and he seized both her arms with his hands. His violence was not displeasing to her, she rather expected

it as a form of homage. Her back and shoulders were fashioned to be seen, and to accommodate such kisses, was it not their duty as well as their delight?

But the assault was hurried and the incubus was breathing as hard as a bellows, which made her laugh lightly: 'What a performance!' she thought. 'He's clumsy... I shall steal a look at him out of the corner of my eye...'

As she turned her head the beast thrust forward his muzzle, and his wide, obscene mouth crushed her lips.

She closed her eyes, but too late; she had seen the monster face to face, and no longer in the complacent reflections of a mirror fashioned by her dream. She had seen him, no longer forged by desire, but disfigured by the most uncompromising of realities: he was so ugly, with his cruel goat's face—so ugly and so bestial and drunk on a desire so singlemindedly base—that she was revolted and stood up.

... She saw herself naked in the long mirror at the far end of the room, naked and all alone in the dreary room.

Don Juan's Secret

... Et simulacra modis pallentia miris.

(Virgil, *Georgics* 1.477)

I

VACANT-SOULED and greedy for flesh, from adolescence on Don Juan prepared to accomplish his vocation and fulfil his legendary role. Subtle, foresightful spirits showed him the way, and he entered upon his career armed and embellished with this motto:

'*To please, you must take what pleases from those that please.*'

From a fainting blonde he imitated the gesture of pressing a dainty hand to his absent heart;

From another, he took the ironic blinking of eyelids which seemed to be impertinence but was in fact the flickering of a weak eye exposed to the light;

From another he took the act of raising the little finger and scrutinizing it carefully, like a rare jewel;

From another he took the subtle, pretty, impatient tapping of her foot;

From another, pure and languid, he took the smile in which, as in a magic mirror, you see, before the act, the pleasures it procures, and after the act the reanimated joys of desire;

From another, no less pure, but lively and without languor, and continually restless like a cat during a storm, he took a different smile, the smile in which there are kisses so strong they disarm the hearts of virgins;

From another he took the sigh, the long, broken sigh which is the shy brother of the sob, the stirring sigh that precedes the storm like the hurried flight of a bird;

From another he took the slow and languid movements of those who have been sated with love;

From another he took the loving way of murmuring sweet nothings and lisping 'It's raining', as if it were raining angels.

He took these looks, every look, the gentle, the imperious, the docile, the astonished, the compassionate, the envious, the subtle, the proud, the devouring, the look that kills, and he took a lot of others, among them the entire rosary, bead by bead, made up of the looks which fascinate. But the most beautiful look taken by Don Juan, the ruby among the corals, the sapphire among the turquoise, was that of the cornered animal, vouchsafed him in the gaze, dying of love and despair, of a girl he had raped. This look was so touching that no one at all could resist it, not even the wildest, and eternal vows melted in its light like sin under a ray of grace.

II

DON JUAN made an even greater conquest, he conquered a soul—a soul that was ingenuous and proud, tender and haughty, the soul of a seductress by gentleness and of one by violence, and of a soul that did not know itself, a soul full of instinctive desires, a soul deliciously naive.

He came near, adorned in all his seductions, the grieving attitude attenuated by an ironic gleam in the eye and a certain joy playing over

the lips; his movements slow, as of one sated by love but corrected with a proud lift of the head; and the first long, broken sigh that escaped his breast was accompanied by a subtly impatient tapping of his foot—which said: 'You have wounded my heart, but I cannot help myself from loving you, and yet I feel some anger.' Next, he put on the gaze of the cornered animal; and then, he played at observing his little finger.

After a short silence, he lisped lovingly, 'It's a beautiful evening'—and it was then the young woman answered: 'It is my soul you are after, Don Juan! Have it then, I give it you!'

Don Juan accepted this soul so deliciously naive, and so feminine, that the instantly subjugated had offered him along with her skin, her hair, her teeth, every one of her beauties and the fragrance of all her concealments: and having had his fill of her, he went his ways.

Out of this soul he fashioned a limpid and invincible cape in which he draped himself, as though in folds of white velvet. Equipped with such a soul, and more triumphant than a Moorish killer, more adored than a pilgrim from Compostella or a crusader returned from Palestine, he multiplied his conquests to the number of a thousand and three.

All of them! All who might give a new pleasure, a new frisson of joy, all were seduced by what he had taken that pleased them about their sisters. They passed before him, they kissed his hands, they bowed before him, a whole lovesick people already vanquished by the approaching conqueror.

Soon they fought among themselves as to who should be the first to fall, and who the most subjugated. Drunk on their slavery, they would die of love before having tasted it.

In the towns and in the castles, and even in the cottages, their cry went up: 'O my dearest! O my deepest! He is irresistible!'

III

BUT Don Juan started to fade. The sap which had bloomed in luxuriant force fell back down in a rain of dry leaves, and though it still stood tall, the tree was no more than a shadow.

Don Juan expended, from a few late flowers, the last of his pollen; as long as there was a trace of seed in his blood, he loved—and finally,

no longer able to love, he lay down to wait for what must come, the only one he had not yet conquered.

And when she arrived, Don Juan set out to seduce her, offering all that pleases, all that he had taken from the pleasers.

'I offer you the power of seduction,' said Don Juan, 'I offer you, O ugly one, my attitudes, my looks, my smiles, my various voices, everything, even my coat which is made from a soul: take all this and go! I want to relive my life in memory, for now I know that the true life consists in remembering.'

'Live your life over again,' said Death. 'I shall return.'

Death vanished and the Simulacra rose up in crowds from out of the shadow.

They were young and beautiful women, all of them naked and all of them silent, and anxious, like beings who were seeking for something they lacked. They were arranged in a spiral around Don Juan, and while the first of them placed her hand on his breast, the last was so remote that she was mingled with the stars.

She who put her hand on his breast took back from him the action of holding in the emotion from an absent heart;

Another took back from him the ironic fluttering of his white eyelids;

Another took back from him the grace involved in examining the nail of his little finger;

Another took back from him the impatience of his tapping feet;

Another took back from him the complex smile of satisfaction before and of desire after;

Another took back from him the smile that, as in an alcove, leads to a swooning;

Another took back from him the sigh of a fearful bird.

And then he was stripped of his languid movement as of one who has been sated with love; and of his loving way of saying 'It's raining', as if it were raining angels; and from the rosary of gazes, one after the other: the imperious like the astonished, the docile and the fascinating were taken back from him;—and the gentle one he raped came in her turn and took back from him the gaze of the cornered animal, the gaze of love and of despair.

And finally another took back from him her soul, that deliciously ingenuous soul from which he had fashioned a cape in white velvet; and of Don Juan there remained nothing but a hollow ghost, a rich

man with no money, a thief without arms, a dreary human grub
reduced to its reality, and giving up its secret!

On the Threshold

AT the Chateau de la Fourche, everything was melancholy and gran-
diose: the gallows name,* to begin with, redolent of a more severe
and primitive justice, meted out in seigneurial times; the four dark
avenues whose lamentations sounded like an ocean; the moats in
which black swans swam amongst the broken reeds, the threatening
hemlocks, the multitude of blooming yellow flowers, that were like so
many dead suns; the chateau, with its storm-coloured walls, its roof
undulating like furrows of ploughland, its narrow, ogived, trefoiled
windows, its broken tower swarmed over by ivy so thick it seemed as
perennial as life itself.

Having mounted the steps and crossed the threshold, one entered
a series of huge, cold, and lofty rooms, hung with greensward on
which one gazed once more at the slanting reeds of the moat, the
melancholic flowers and the hemlock, sheltering in their shade the
royal procession of mourning swans. Simple straw matting was all
there was in the way of carpeting; everywhere were sleeping dogs,
muzzles between their paws, and a strange, spectral vision (which
I could never get used to): moving from room to room, snapping its
beak every time a door was opened, was a tame heron. This funereal
creature went everywhere; it followed us at mealtimes, pecking at a
large pan that contained its feed; at regular intervals the bird would
make a noise like a loose tile clacking in the wind against an old wall.
It was called the Missionary, because of its resemblance, with its
benevolent, sidelong look, to a Capuchin monk who had come to
preach at La Fourche. The death of the monk, a few days after, coin-
cided with the appearance of the bird, which had been shot and
wounded, and was found on the moat by a gamekeeper.

When, on my first evening at La Fourche, I heard this story, I had
been amused, even though my host told it without a glimmer of
humour. The next day, however, I started to find the Missionary
unsettling, less for its ugliness than for the absolute assurance with
which the creature had taken sovereign possession of the place; as if

it really were there to accomplish some supernatural design. No one ever shooed it away or shut it in; as soon as its beak clacked against a door, someone would get up to let it enter, and if it left a room with us, it would always go first, walking gravely, with the expression, not of some Capuchin, but of an old, incorruptible, and gently implacable judge.

The Missionary: privately, I had already rechristened it, Remorse.

One evening, when we had risen from table, having dined on venison in juniper-flavoured cider, I nearly tripped over the bird near the door, and in my annoyance I rather hissed at it:

'Well go on through, Remorse!'

'Why did you not call it Missionary?' the Marquis de la Hogue asked me sharply, seizing my arm and looking at me with eyes alive, not with anger as I had first thought, but with terror.

He went on in a strangled voice, hardly able to get the words out:

'How did you know its name is Remorse? Who told you?'

'You did!'

By risking this, which was a shot in the dark, for I was almost as disturbed as Monsieur de la Hogue, I had made myself privy to more confidences.

When we entered the room reserved for our nightly conversations, the bird was there in front of the fireplace where huge logs were flaming, standing on one leg, its beak under its wing. Hoping our conversation would continue, I enquired casually, as I sat down in one of the wooden armchairs that resembled a stall in a cathedral:

'Is it asleep?'

'It never sleeps!' replied Monsieur de la Hogue—and sure enough, at that moment, in a brighter light cast by the fire, I saw the cold, ironical eye of the old judge, fixing me with the muddied gleam of a star reflected in a frog-pond—the incorruptible and gently implacable eye.

'It never sleeps,' went on Monsieur de la Hogue, 'and neither do I. My heart never sleeps. I know sleep, but I know nothing of the unconscious. My dreams are a seamless continuation of my evening thoughts, and come morning, I join my dreams with equally seamless logic to my thoughts. It seems to me that I have swum for a single hour in full intellectual clarity for thirty-odd years. And what is it I dream about during the endless hours of my life? Of nothing, or rather, of negations—what I have not done, what I shall not do, what

I should not do, even if my youth were granted me a second time. For that is who I am, I am the man who has never acted, who has never lifted a finger to further the fulfilment of a desire, or a duty. I am the lake no wind has ever ruffled, the forest that has never soughed, the sky untroubled by any clouds of action.'

After uttering these rather solemn, even lapidary, phrases he was silent for a few seconds, and then:

'Do you know about my life? No, you are too young, and in any case what people say about me is not me. I have never told my story, and if you had not, by chance—or by some providential perspicuity—uttered a word—a name!—that (I confess) fills me with dread—then you should not have heard my confession either.

Here it is:

'I was eight years old, when my mother brought home from her far-flung travels a little girl of about my own age, our cousin, at least by name, whom the death of her parents had left as vulnerably alone in the world as a lamb lost at night in a wood. This adorable little thing instantly became the spoiled child, and an ideal sister, or even a future fiancée for me, an angel fallen from the heavens for my eternal consolation. At twelve, I was a precocious, stout-hearted lad, grown up in the country; even then I loved Nigelle infinitely, and in consequence, until the day I lost her, my love was such that it could neither grow nor decrease. She loved me in return, with the same ardour; I knew it, too, and her dying confession taught me nothing I didn't know, except my own wickedness.

'As soon as the first glimmer of reasoning inhabited my infant brain, I had arrived at a singular conception of life, which I now feel to be criminal. Having, one hot noon, picked a rose whose scent exasperated and whose purple smile made me want to possess it, I wandered about the garden paths with my rose forgotten between my fingers; I noticed that within an hour it was all crumpled and wilted, wounded by the arrows of the sun. And I thought, it is permissible to desire roses, but one must not pick them.

'And I thought, when Nigelle came up to me, one can desire women, but one must not pick them.

'Following on from this primordial discovery, I was besieged by a host of thoughts, and slowly I came to elaborate a whole philosophy of the negative, a religion of nirvana took root in my proud and

shallow mind. One day, I summed the whole thing up in a phrase:
' "Man must remain on the threshold." '

'A few books came to my assistance, ascetic treatises, a summary
of Plato, some fragments of the German metaphysicals,* but to all
practical intents and purposes the doctrine was my own. I was
very proud of it, and I plunged resolutely into the darknesses of
inaction.

'I applied myself to accomplishing only the simplest of acts, and
certainly only those which, while procuring me no great pleasure,
could never lead to my experiencing any disappointment.

'I had violent desires, and I enjoyed them, I wallowed in them,
I got drunk on them. My heart expanded, until it contained the
world. Wanting everything, I had everything, but not in the way you
hold something between your two small, trembling hands. I took
everything, but nothing of its own accord gave itself to me; I had
everything—but lovelessly!

'It was only later, at a particularly solemn moment, that I understood the existence of love. Until that time, my pride had sustained
my illusion, and my days passed happily; I was proud of having
escaped from the disenchantment consequent upon any action when
carried through.

'Even today, and now that I know, now that suffering has made me
wise, I would still be unable to pick the rose. What purpose would it
serve? This is the terrible refrain that runs perpetually through my
head, and it has never been so imperative as now.

'For twenty years Nigelle and I lived side by side: she became
shyer and sadder by the day, overawed by my fortune, while she,
poor thing, possessed only the treasure of her blonde hair. For my
part, I became increasingly proud, and formidably uncommunicative.

'I loved her as much as it is possible to love, but I loved her only as
far as the threshold.

'And I never did cross that threshold, and nor did my shadow; and
not so much as the shadow of my heart ever walked about in that
palace of love.

'Tender and welcoming, the door had been open always, but I
turned aside my head, when I passed in front of it, to contemplate my
own desire, to commune with my own desire, to confide to my desire
the dreams I sought never to realize.

'To cross the threshold? And what then? That palace was possibly

a palace like any other—but the palace of my dreams was unique, and no one will ever see its like again.

'She died for love of me, I who loved her, and I say it again, with infinite love. She died with these words: "I love you!" And I replied nothing.'

The heron changed leg, snapped its beak, and this time buried it under its left wing: now the mournful, ironic eye was fixed upon Monsieur de la Hogue.

'I think that this bird', went on my host, 'seems to you ugly and ridiculous, doesn't it?'

'Above all, grim.'

'Ridiculous and grim. I endure it as a punishment. It frightens me, it pains me, and I wish it thus. You do understand, of course, that if I wanted I could wring its neck in no time at all!'

'Have you thought of doing so?' I asked. 'Wringing the neck of Remorse?'

'I have thought of it,' answered Monsieur de la Hogue. 'But what would be the point? There is no meaning whatever in this grim and ridiculous bird, except that which I choose to give to it; all I need to do is to withdraw that, and it would be as dead as a stuffed bird. Do you really think I am duped by its inanity? Do you think I'm mad?'

The old man had risen, shaking out his long, grey locks that fell upon his pallid, hollow cheeks; and then, suddenly relaxed, he fell back into his armchair.

He asked me again, but now quite at ease, and with a touch of mockery:

'At least, I presume you don't think I'm mad?'

As I looked back at him with a smile, and moved my hand unthinkingly towards the feathers of the motionless bird, he jumped up again:

'Do not touch the Missionary!'

And he uttered these words in the tone of voice Charles I must have used to a bystander on the scaffold: 'Do not touch the axe!'

JULES LAFORGUE

Perseus and Andromeda

or The Happiest of the Three

I

O MONOTONOUS and ill-favoured country!...

The solitary island, done out in yellow-grey dunes; under meandering skies; and everywhere the sea blocking the view, and the cries of hope and of melancholy.

The sea! From whatever angle you look at it, hour after hour, whatever moment you surprise it: it is always itself, nothing is ever missing, always alone, empire of the unclubbable, weighty matter in process, ill-digested cataclysm;—as if the liquid state we witness were no more than a destitution! And then there are the days it starts to stir up that liquid state! And even worse, the days it takes on those injured tones that have no face of its quality to look into it, who has no one! The sea, always and unfailingly present and correct, every instant! And in short, not the slightest skirt-tail of a friend. (Oh, really! We must be done with the idea of sharing grudges after confidences, however lonely we have been together all this time.)

O monotonous and ill-favoured country!... When will it all end?—And even, where infinity is concerned: space monopolized by nothing but the indifferently limitless sea, time by nothing but skies in their seasonal transitions marked out by the passage of grey migrant birds, shrieking and untameable!—What on earth can we make of all this, of all this enormous and ineffable fit of the sulks?* It were better to die forthwith, blessed as we are from birth with a good and feeling heart.

The sea, this afternoon, is quite ordinary, uniformly and extensively dark green; it is an endless enchainment of white foam lighting up, going out, lighting up again, it is a legion of sheep swimming,

drowning, bobbing up again, and never arriving, until they are ambushed by darkness. And over their heads frolic the four winds, frolicking for the love of art, for the pleasure of killing the afternoon, whipping it up into prismatic particles, cresting the foam. And should a sunbeam strike, there's a rainbow running over the wavebacks like a rich gold lining—that rises for a moment and then dives back down, foolishly untrusting.

And that is all. O monotonous and ill-favoured country!...

Into the inner reaches between two grottoes, downed with eider feather and pale beds of guano, the vast and monotonous sea comes panting and streaming. But its lament does not cover the little moans, the little sharp and raucous moans of Andromeda, who, flat on her belly and propped on her elbows, stares without seeing at the mechanical waves, swelling and dying as far as the eye can see. Andromeda is moaning over herself. She moans; but suddenly she becomes aware that her lament is in chorus with that of the sea and the wind, two unsociable beings, two powerful ringmasters that don't so much as look at her. So she stops abruptly; and then looks around for something to take it out on. She calls out:

'Monster!'

'Poppet?...'

'Hey! Monster!...'

'Poppet?...'

'What are you doing now?'

The Dragon-Monster, squatting at the entrance to his cave, turns round, and in turning all the rich, sub-aquatic, jewelled impasto along his spine shines out, and with compassion he raises his multi-coloured cartilaginously fingered eyelashes, to reveal two large, watery-glaucous orbs, and says (in the voice of a distinguished gentleman who has fallen on hard times):

'As you can see, Poppet, I am breaking and polishing stones for your train; further flights of birds are forecast before sunset.'

'Stop it, the noise gets on my nerves. And I want to stop killing the birds that fly by here. Oh, let them pass and see their homelands.—O migratory flights that pass me oblivious, O legions of waves that come in and die, bearing me nothing, how bored I am!* And this time I am truly ill...—Monster?...'

'Poppet?'

'Why have you not brought me any more of those jewels? What have I done to displease you, my nuncle?'

The Monster gave a sumptuous shrug of his shoulders, scratched in the sand to his right, lifted a pebble, and extracted a fistful of pink pearls and crystallized anemones, that he had kept in reserve for a caprice of this kind. He waved them in front of Andromeda's pretty nose and laid them down before her. Andromeda, still flat on her tummy and propped on her elbows, sighed without moving:

'And what if I were to refuse them, and refuse them with inexplicable stubbornness?'

The Monster took his treasure back and flung it away, where it sank to its aquatic Golconda depths.

At which Andromeda rolled groaning on the sand, twisting her hair about her face in tragical disarray:

'Oh! My pink pearls! My crystal sea-anemones! Oh, I shall die! And it will be all your fault; can you conceive the irreparable?'

But brusquely she stopped her wailing and took up her wheedling, crawling in her usual way underneath the Monster's chin and encircling his neck, his purplish-striped and viscous neck, with her white arms. The Monster gave a sumptuous shrug of his shoulders and, always kind-hearted, started to secrete wild musk from every pore over which he felt brushed by those plump little arms, the little arms of the dear child, who soon took up her plaint:

'O Monster, O Dragon, you say you love me and yet you can do nothing for me. You can see that I am dying of boredom and yet you do nothing. How much I should love you, if you could only heal me! Do something!...'

O noble Andromeda, daughter of the king of Ethiopia!* The reluctant dragon can only answer you in a vicious circle:—'I cannot cure you until you love me, for it is in loving me that you will be cured.'

'Always the same conundrum! But when I tell you that I do love you!'

'I don't feel it any more than you do. It's no use; I remain just a little monster of a dragon, just an unhappy Catoblepas.'*

'But you could at least carry me on your back, and bring me to a country where there might be some company. (Oh, I do so want to go into society!) Once we got there, I'd gladly give you a little kiss for your trouble.'

'I have already told you it's impossible. It is here that we must live out our destinies.'

'Oh yes? How can you possibly know that?'

'I know nothing more than you do, O Noble Andromeda of the orange hair.'

'Our destinies, our destinies! But I'm getting older every day! I can't go on like this!'

'Do you want to go on a little sea-trip?'

'Oh, I know all about your little sea-trips! Find something else.'

Andromeda flung herself down on her belly on the sand, that she scratched and furrowed all the way down her legitimately hungry flanks, and started up her little groans and whimpers again.

The Monster thought it a good moment at which to adopt the falsetto voice of the poor child who was growing up, to make fun of her histrionic grievances, and he began to recite, in a neutral tone:

'*Pyramus and Thisbe.** Once upon a time...'

'No, please, no! Any more of your worn-out stories and I shall kill myself!'

'Now, now, what's all this? You must pull yourself together! Go fishing, go hunting, make up rhymes, blow the conch at the four points of the compass, renew your collection of shells; or, I know—carve symbols onto recalcitrant stones (that *really* passes the time!)...'

'I can't, I can't; everything bores me, I've told you.'

'Oh! Look up there, poppet! Shall I get the sling?'

It was the third group of autumn migrants to pass over since morning; their triangle went away with the same pulsing regularity, and no laggards. They passed over, and this evening they would be far away...

'Oh! To go where they go! To love, to love!...' cried poor Andromeda.

And the little fury leaped up in a single bound and, screaming into the squalls, went galloping through the grey dunes of the island.

The Monster smiled indulgently and returned to polishing his pebbles, much as the sage Spinoza* must have polished his lenses.

II

LIKE a small, wounded animal, Andromeda goes galloping, galloping like a long-legged stilt through the gravel pits; and further maddened, as she has forever to be shaking back her long red hair the

wind blows in her eyes and mouth. Where can she be going like this, puberty, O puberty! through the wind and the dunes, keening like one of the wounded?

Andromeda! Andromeda!

Her perfect feet are shod in espadrilles of lichen, there's a necklace of wild coral attached by a twist of seaweed round her neck, and otherwise immaculately naked, naked and austere, she has grown up like this, through squall and sun, bathing in the sea and sleeping under the stars.

Her face and hands are neither more nor less pale than the rest of her body; the whole of her little person, her silky red hair falling to her knees, is the same shade as rinsed terracotta. (Oh those leaps and bounds!) All toned and springy and tanned, this wild adolescent on ususually long and slender legs, with proud, straight hips cambering into a high waist just below the breasts, a childish chest with the merest bud of breasts, so meagre that her breathlessness scarcely lifts them (and when and how might they have formed, always driven against the salty sea-wind and the fierce, cold drenching of the waves?) and the long neck and the small babyish head, all drawn under its red fleece and her eyes either flashing like the seabirds or as dull as the waters of the everyday. In short, an accomplished girl. Oh those leaps, those bounds! And the mews of the wounded little thing whose life is so hard! Thus has she grown, I tell you, naked and toned and tanned, with her red fleece flying through gallops and squalls, sea-dips and starlight.

But where can she be going like this, puberty, O puberty?

At the end, part of a promontory, is a singular cliff; Andromeda scales it by means of a labyrinth of natural ledges. From the narrow platform she overlooks the island and the moving solitude that encircles it. Into the centre of this platform the rains have worn a basin. Andromeda has tiled this with pebbles of black ivory, and she keeps it filled with clean water; for since the spring this has been her mirror, and the only secret she has in all the world.

For the third time today she returns to look at herself. She does not smile into it, she looks sulkily rather, trying to deepen the depths of her eyes, and her eyes never relinquish their depth. But her mouth! She never wearies of admiring the innocent flowering of her mouth. Oh, but who will ever comprehend her mouth?

'I really am very mysterious!' she ponders.

And then she runs through all her airs.

'So that's it, that's me, nothing more and nothing less; you must take it or leave it.'

Then she falls to thinking that she is really nothing special at all!

But she comes back to her eyes. Her eyes are beautiful, touching, and very much hers. She never wearies of meeting them; she would like to remain there quizzing them until the dying of the light. How can they remain in that infinity of theirs? Or why can she not be someone else, to spy on them, and to ponder their secret while making no noise!...

But she admires herself in vain! For her face, just like her, remains expectant and serious and remote.

Then she attacks that red fleece of hers, trying out twenty different hairstyles, but they all end up too heavy for her little head.

And now the storm-clouds come over, they will blur her mirror. She also keeps there, under a stone, a dried fish-skin that she uses as a nail-file. So she sits down and does her nails. The storm-clouds arrive and they break in a tremendous sounding deluge. Andromeda zigzags down the cliff and resumes her gallop to the sea, keening through the shower:

> O who can cure
> Poor little Andromeda
> Naughty naughty
> Naughty thing

Tears run down her childish breast, the song being so sad. The shower has already passed and now the wind ruffles her hair, and it's squalling everywhere...

> Naughty naughty
> Miaow miaow
> Since no one comes to help me
> I'll throw myself in the water!

But it's just a dip, she's running to take a dip in the sea, that's all. And just as she's about to plunge in, she turns back. Sea-bathing, endless sea-bathing! She is so weary of playing with the waves, with her swollen, uncouth sisters the waves, whose manners and surface she knows inside out. So she lays herself out, star-wise on her back, on the wet sand, facing the unfurling waves. It's better this way, all

she needs to do is wait for a great packet of water. After a few men-acing approaches, a rearing breaker runs in and deluges her. With her eyes closed, Andromeda receives it full on, with a long throaty scream, and she wriggles all her limbs to keep the icy moving pillow of water over her, though it runs off and leaves her with nothing between her arms...

She sits up, dazed, and contemplates her runnelled, streaming body, and plucks some shreds of seaweed from her tresses that the wave brought with it.

And then she plunges decidedly into the water; beats the waves like a water-mill, dives and comes up again, gasps for breath, floats; a new front of waves comes in, and now watch the little demon, knocked over at first but then jumping like a carp to straddle the breakers! She catches one by the fringe, and beats it for an instant with cruel yells; a second unbalances her by stealth, but she grabs hold of another. And then the whole lot gives way beneath her, unable to wait. But the sea, warming to the game, becomes uncontrollable; so Andromeda plays dead, and lets herself be thrown up sprawling on the sand, crawls up the beach a bit and flops down on her belly on the moving sand.

And here comes a fresh bundle of showers passing over the island. Andromeda doesn't move; and whimpering under the great deluge, she receives the shower, the yelping shower, which gurgles and bub-bles in the small of her back. She feels the sodden sand give way a little beneath her, and she wriggles herself further into it. (Oh sub-merge me, bury me alive!)

But the storm-clouds pass on just as they had come, the roar dies away, leaving the island to its Atlantic loneliness.

Andromeda sits down and gazes at the horizon, that is clearing, still with nothing to report. What can she do? When the wind has dried her, she runs off to scramble up her cliff again, where at least some intelligence, in the form of her mirror, awaits her.

But the wicked rain has clouded the surface of her mournful mirror!

Andromeda turns away, on the brink of bursting into tears, but now there's a great seabird arriving, all sails flying, heading straight for the island, towards the cliff, coming for her perhaps! She lets out a prolonged and pleading ululation, and backs up against a rock, her arms outstretched, her eyes closed. Oh let the great bird marry itself

to her little Promethean person, offered up by the gods; and perched on her knees, let it, with its implacable, salutary beak, peck out the place where it burns and hurts!

But she feels the flight of the great bird cover her, then opens her eyes, and already it is far away, its mind on other, differently intriguing carcasses no doubt.

Poor Andromeda, it is clear that she doesn't know where to turn for relief from her own being.

What to do? If not stare once more at the sea, so blinkered and yet alone so open to hope... And more than this, what a cry-baby her own torment is compared to this unlimited solitude! With one breaker, the sea can soothe her unto death; but how can she, slender little body, soothe and comfort the sea! She would gladly stretch out her arms, but in vain!... And anyway, she is so weary! In days gone by she would roam about her domain, but now, with these palpitations about her heart... And here's another of those big seabirds passing over. She would so like to adopt one, and to rock it in her arms! But none ever lands on the island. You'd have to kill them with a sling to get anywhere near them.

To rock, to be rocked, the sea does not rock obligingly enough.

The wind has dropped, and now it's the doldrums, and the horizon is wiped clean in preparation for the ceremony of sunset.

To rock, to be rocked!... And Andromeda's weary little head fills with maternal rhythms; and the only human rhyme that she knows, the legend *The Truth About Everything,** comes back to her; it was the little sacred poem with which her guardian the Dragon lulled her to sleep as a child.

In the beginning was Love, the universal organizing Law, unconscious, infallible. And it is, immanent within the solid-forming whirlpools of phenomena, the infinite aspiration to the ideal.

The Sun is for the Earth—Keystone, Reservoir, Wellspring.

Which is why morning and springtime are about happiness, and why twilight and autumn are about death. (But since there is nothing that tickles superior organisms more than feeling they are about to die, when there is no danger of it, twilight and autumn, the drama of sun and death are aesthetic emotions par excellence.*)*

The ideal Will has always been in action and always in infinite space it formulates into countless worlds that solidify, the acme of their organic

evolution attained as far as their elements permit, and then they disinte-
grate into further novel formulations.

As for the primitive unconscious, all it has to do is busy itself with the
higher world, it has its particular tasks and watches over certain livelier
and graver worlds; nothing could ever turn it away from its dream of
futurity.

And the planets which, having attained the degree of evolution already
possessed by the unconscious, serve as a laboratory for the Life of futurity,
with these the Unconscious is not concerned: their minor evolutions hap-
pen of necessity, following on from the given drive, like so many identical
and negligible proofs of an exhausted threadbare cliché.

And so it is that just as the necessary human evolution, in the womb
of the mother, is a miniature reflex of the whole of terrestrial evolution,
terrestrial evolution is only a miniature reflex of the Gigantic Unconscious
Evolution in time.

Elsewhere, elsewhere, within infinite space, the Unconscious is more
advanced. What larks!...

The Earth, even if she is to produce superiors to Man, is but an identical
and repetitive cliché of trial and error.

But the goodly Earth, come down from the Sun, is everything for us,
because we have five senses, and the whole Earth fits in with them. O suc-
culence, sensory wonders, smells, noises, ravishing visions as far as the eye
can see, Love! O my own life!

Man is but an insect under the heavens; let him but respect himself, and
he is a very God. One spasm from the creature is worth the whole of
nature.

This is what Andromeda chants to herself miserably as yet another
evening falls; nothing but the weariness of lessons learned. Ah! She
groans and stretches.

Ah! For how long must she stretch and groan?...

And then she says aloud from out of the Atlantic solitude of her
island:

'Yes, but when I do not know what sixth sense may open—and
nothing, but nothing, may respond to it! Ah!—the real point is that I
am alone, and isolated, and I don't quite see how all this is going to end.'

She strokes her arms and then, furious, clenches her teeth and
scratches long stripes in her arms with a piece of flint she found lying
there.

'But I can't end my life if I want to see what happens to me, O gods!'

She bursts into tears.

'No, it's too much, I have been left too much alone! And even if anyone does come to fetch me now, I shall be bitter about it all my life, I shall always retain a little bitterness.'

III

YET another evening about to fall, another preening sunset; the classic programme, the programme even more than classic!

Andromeda tosses back her red mane and sets off for home.

The Monster does not come out to meet her. What can this mean? The Monster has gone! She calls out:

'Monster! Monster!'

No answer. She blows on the conch. Nothing. She returns to the cliff that dominates the island and blows and calls, my god!... There's no one there! She returns to the house.

'Monster! Monster!... Oh disaster! What if he has dived underwater forever, what if he's gone, leaving me all alone, saying that I tormented him too much and made his life unbearable!...'

And now the island seems all of a sudden extravagantly and impossibly lost! She flings herself down on the sand in front of the cave, and lets out a long, long moan, as if she might die there, as if that is indeed all she can expect...

When she gets up the Monster is there, in his usual murk, busy piercing holes in one of the shells he uses as an ocarina.

'So there you are,' she said. 'I thought you'd gone.'

'I've no choice. I am your gaoler, which I shall be for as long as I live, fearless and faultless.'

'What did you say?'

'I was saying that for as long as I live...'

'Yes, yes, we know all that.'

Silence and horizon; the horizon over the sea swept clean by the sunset.

'Why don't we play draughts,' sighs Andromeda, visibly exasperated.

'Let's play draughts.'

The board, inlaid with white-and-black mosaic, is encrusted at the entrance to the cave. But no sooner has the game begun than Andromeda, visibly exasperated, sweeps the board clean.

'Impossible! I'd lose; I can't concentrate, and it's not my fault. I am visibly exasperated.'

Silence and horizon! After all the turbulence of the afternoon, the wind has calmed and the sky is hushed as the Star performs its classic withdrawal.

The Star!...

Over there, on the dazzling horizon where the mermaids hold their breath.

The sunset sends up its scaffolding;

From footlight to footlight the theatre stalls rise up;

The artificers give the last nudge;

A series of golden moons blossom out, like the embouchures of cornets from where phalanxes of heralds would thunder out!

The slaughterhouse is ready, the hangings taken in;

On beds of diadems, harvests of Venetian lanterns, on spreads and garlands,

Dammed by banks of alloy already strafing,

Pasha Star,

His Scarlet Eminence,

Toga'd with catastrophe,

Fatally triumphal, descends

For minutes on end, through the Heavenly Door!...

And now it lies upon its side, marbled all over with atrabilious stigmata.

Quick, someone come and squash this punctured pumpkin with their foot!...

Farewell baskets, the grape harvest is in!...

The row of cornets are lowered, the ramparts collapse with their brilliant prismatic carafes. Cymbals fly, the whole army breaks camp, its followers tripping over the draped standards, the tents folded away, and occidental basilicas, wine-presses, idols, chopping-blocks, vestals, offices, ambulances, whole choirs in their ranks and all the official auxiliaries.

And they vanish in a puff of pink gold.

Well! It all went off perfectly!...

'Fabulous, fabulous!' gushes the Taciturn Monster in ecstasy; his huge watery eyeballs still lit up by the last streaks in the west.

'Farewell baskets, the harvest is in,' sighs Andromeda in crepuscular fashion, and her red mane seems quite dull after such fires.

'Well, now we just have to light the evening lamps, take a little supper, and bless the moon, before going to bed, to wake tomorrow and begin an identical day.'

So, silence and horizon readies for the mortuary Moon—when! Oh blessed be the gods who sent, and just at the right time too, a third personage.

He comes in like a rocket, the hero in diamond on a snowy Pegasus whose wings are tinted with the trembling sunset, and he is cleanly reflected in the immense melancholy mirror of the Atlantic on a gala evening...

No doubt about it, it's Perseus!

Andromeda, palpitating all over with her girlish palpitations, rushes to crush herself under the Monster's chin.

And big tears brim at the Monster's eyelids like flower baskets at balustrades. And he speaks with a voice we have never heard before:

'Andromeda, O noble Andromeda, do not be afraid, it is Perseus. It is Perseus, son of Danaë and of Zeus in the shower of gold. He is going to kill me and rescue you.'

'No, no, he won't kill you!'

'He will kill me.'

'He won't kill you if he loves me.'

'He can only rescue you by killing me.'

'No, no, we'll come to an agreement. We always do. I'll settle this in your favour.'

Andromeda got up from her usual place and stared.

'Andromeda, Andromeda! consider the value of your priceless flesh, the price of your fresh soul, a mismatch is so easily entered into!'

But what is this that she hears! Face held high, elbows into her body, fingers clenched at her sides, she stands on the beach, so forthright and feminine, still.

Perseus draws near, miraculous and very polished, the wings of his hippogriff slowing down;—and the closer he gets, the more provincial Andromeda feels, not knowing what to do with her lovely arms.

Within a few yards of Andromeda, the well-schooled griffin halts, plunges up to its knees in the waves, while keeping itself upright with

a pink vibration of its wings; and Perseus bows. Andromeda lowers her head. So that is her fiancé. What will his voice sound like, and what will be the first thing he says?

But he's off again without a word, and taking to the air, he passes and repasses in front of her, describing a series of ovals, cantering along the miraculous sea-mirror, narrowing his eyes and staring at Andromeda, as if giving the little virgin time to admire and to desire him. He is in truth a most remarkable sight!...

This time he passes so close to her, still smiling, that she could almost have touched him.

Perseus rides side-saddle, his feet crossed coquettishly in their yellow linen sandals; from the pommel of his saddle hangs a mirror; he is beardless, and his pink and smiling mouth might be described as an open pomegranate, the hollow of his chest is lacquered with a rose and his arms are tattooed with a heart pierced by an arrow; a lily adorns the swell of his calves and he sports an emerald monocle and several rings and bracelets; from his gilded cross-belt hangs a little sword with a mother-of-pearl dagger.

Perseus wears Pluto's helm, that makes him invisible, he has the wings and ankle-wings of Mercury, the divine shield of Minerva, and from his belt hangs the head of the Gorgon Medusa, who petrified the giant Atlas into a mountain with a single look, as everyone knows, and his griffin is Pegasus, the same Bellerophon rode when he killed the Chimaera.* The young hero is beautifully equipped for the job.

The young hero halts his griffin in front of Andromeda and, smiling all the while with his pomegranate mouth, he starts fencing movements with his adamantine sword.

Andromeda doesn't move, almost crying with uncertainty, and seems only to wait for the sound of this person's voice to abandon herself to fate.

The Monster stays coyly at a distance.

In one graceful movement Perseus turns his mount, and without disturbing the water-mirror, it kneels before Andromeda and presents its flank; the youthful cavalier joins his hands to make a stirrup and, bowing towards the young captive, says with an inveterately affected lisp:

'Let'th be going! Off to Cythera!...'

Ah well, there's nothing for it; Andromeda places her rough foot in the delicate stirrup and turns round to wave farewell to the Monster.

Ah, but the Monster has plunged between them, underneath the hippogriff, and emerges all reared up, with his front paws braced before him and his purplish furnace of a mouth issuing a rapier of flame! The griffin recoils in terror and Perseus withdraws to give himself room, and lets fly a stream of braggadocio. The Monster hears him, Perseus rushes in, and then stops short:

'I shan't give you the pleasure of killing you in front of her,' he yells; 'fortunately the just gods have equipped me with more than one string to my bow. I'm going to... petrify you!'

The gods' little darling unbuckles the Gorgon's head from his belt.

Severed at the neck, the famous head is still alive, but poisonously and stagnantly so, blackened with apoplexy, the white and bloodshot eyes staring fixedly, the mouth stuck in the rictus of decapitation, nothing moving except the hair of snakes.

Perseus seizes the head by that mass of snakes, whose writhing gold-studded black bodies are bracelets to his wrist, and shows it to the Dragon, yelling at Andromeda:

'Close your eyes, you!'

But wonder of wonders, the magic doesn't work!

The trick has failed!

What has happened is that, by some incredible effort, the Gorgon has closed her petrifying eyes.

The good Gorgon recognized our Monster. She recalled those rich and breezy days when she, with her two sisters, lived hard by the Dragon, who at that time kept watch over the Garden of the Hesperides,* the wonderful Garden situated somewhere near the Pillars of Hercules.* No, no, a thousand times no—she will not petrify her old friend!

Perseus waits meanwhile, with his arm stuck out, having noticed nothing. Between the masterful bravura of his gesture and its totally ineffectual outcome the contrast is a little too grotesque, so much so that wild little Andromeda cannot suppress a smile—which Perseus notices. Our hero is dumbfounded—what's wrong with his Medusa's head? And even though in principle his helmet makes him invisible, he is still a little fearful when he hazards a glance at the Gorgon's face, to see for himself what's going on. It's all too simple: the petrifying power has failed because the Gorgon has closed her eyes.

Perseus, enraged now, replaces the head and brandishes his sword with a victorious snicker. Clasping the divine shield of Minerva close

against his heart, he spurs on his griffin (at the exact moment the moon rises over the Atlantic Mirror!) and charges straight at the Dragon, now a poor wingless huddle. With a vertiginously rapid snicker-snack of sword, he cuts him to the left, he cuts him to the right, and forcing him back against a rock, he plants his sword so wonderfully, square in the Dragon's forehead, that the poor creature collapses and expires, with this final croak:

'Farewell, noble Andromeda; I loved you, and lastingly, had you wanted me; adieu, you will think of that often.'

The Monster is dead. But Perseus is overexcited, despite the comprehensive nature of his victory, for it seems he must butcher the corpse! Till it is striped with gashes, and its eyes pierced through! He massacres it until Andromeda stops him.

'That's enough, now: you can see that he's dead.'

Perseus replaces his sword in his belt, rearranges his blond curls, swallows a pastille, and, dismounting from the griffin as he strokes its neck:

'And now, my little lovely!' says he in a syrupy voice.

Andromeda, standing there irreproachably and inflexibly naked, with her black gull's eyes, asks:

'So you love me, you really love me?'

'Do I love you? But I adore you! Life without you would be unbearable and full of darkness! Of course I love you! Just look at yourself!'

He offers her his mirror, but Andromeda, looking perfectly amazed, gently refuses it. He pays no attention, adding rapidly:

'We must make sure we look our best!'

He removes one of his necklaces, made up of gold coins (a memento from his mother's wedding), and tries to place it around her neck. This too she refuses gently, but he takes advantage of this to take her waist in both hands. The wounded little animal wakes up! Andromeda lets out a cry, the cry of a gull on the worst days, that rings round the darkened island:

'Do not touch me!...—Oh, forgive me, but it's all a bit sudden! I beg you, let me alone a bit to wander and say a final goodbye...'

She turns round, and with a sweeping gesture that embraces the island and her favourite cliff, on which night is falling, the serious night, serious for a lifetime! So serious, indeed, that she turns back straightaway towards he who is about to snatch her from the past and towards her future. And she surprises him! He was giving a little

yawn! An elegant little yawn, that he tried to transform into that pomegranate smile.

O night on the island of the past! Monster bestially slaughtered, unsepulchred Monster! O landscapes too refined of the future... Andromeda lets it all out in a single cry:

'Begone! Begone! You are horrible to me! I'd rather die alone! Begone from here, you've made a mistake.'

'Well that's gratitude for you! Listen my little lambkin, no one from where I'm from talks to me like that! You're not that smooth-skinned, you know.'

With a twirl of his adamantine sword, he remounts and vanishes into the enchantment of the rising moon, without a backward look; with a yodel, he zooms off like a meteor, towards the elegant and easy lands...

O night on the poor banal island!... What a dream!...

Andromeda remains, head bowed, bewildered now in front of the horizon, the magic horizon she has just turned down, which she could not but turn down, O gods, having a heart as big as hers.

She goes to see the Monster, still lying in his corner, violet and limp and wrinkled, and miserable so miserable! It would have been worth it after all, it's true!...

As always she goes and curls up under his chin, though now it is a dead weight that she must lift, and she puts her little arms around his neck. He is still warm. Curious, she lifts one of his eyelids with her index finger, to reveal the pierced eyeball, before the lid falls back. She parts the strands of his mane and counts the bleeding gashes made by that wicked diamond sword. And tears for the past and for the future, silent tears, start streaming down. How beautiful life had been with him on the island! And as she wiped her eyes with automatic hand, she remembered. She remembered the good friend he had been, the accomplished gentleman, the busy sage, the fluent poet. And she is shaken by heartfelt sobs under the slack chin of the Monster she never appreciated, and hugging him round the neck, she implores him, but too late.

'Oh my poor, poor Monster! Why didn't you say anything earlier? And then you wouldn't have been slain by that vile hero out of comic opera. And now I'm all alone in the dark! We had beautiful days ahead of us. You should have seen that for me it was no more than a passing crisis, a case of idle curiosity. O triply damnable curiosity!

I've killed my friend, my only friend! My nursing father, my mentor! With what lamentations can I now move these insensible shores? Noble monster, his dying words were for me: "—Farewell, Andromeda; I loved you, and lastingly, had you wanted me!" Now how I recognize the sincerity of your great soul! And your long silences, and your afternoons, and everything! But too late, too late! O gods of justice, take one half of my life and restore him to me, so that I might love him and serve him from now on with loyalty and tenderness. O ye gods, do that for me, ye that read in my heart and know how much I loved him, even when blinded by capricious adolescent cravings, I've never loved anyone but him, and I'll love him always!'

And noble Andromeda moves her adorable mouth gently over the Dragon's closed eyelids. And suddenly recoils!

'I thank you, noble Andromeda. The time of trial is over. I shall be reborn, and reborn in a form more appropriate for our love. And nothing will be able to describe your happiness. But learn first who I am, and what my destiny. I was born of the cursed race of Cadmus,* condemned to the Furies! I preached the pettiness of being and the grandeur of nothingness in the groves of Arcady. To punish me, the gods of life condemned me to watch over, in my present form, the treasures of the Earth, until a virgin would come to love me, in my monstrous form, for my own sake. As a three-headed dragon, for many years I guarded the golden apples of the Hesperides; Hercules came and cut my throat. To Colchis then I came, where the Golden Fleece was destined to be. Riding on the ram with the golden fleece came Theban Phrixus and his sister Helle.* An oracle had prophesied to me that Helle would be the promised virgin. But she drowned on the way, and gave her name instead to the Hellespont. (I have learned since that she wasn't very pretty.) And then came those strange Argonauts, whose like we shall see no more!... Heroic times! Jason was their leader, Hercules came after, and his friend Theseus, and Orpheus, who tried so hard to charm me with his lyre (and who was to come to such a sorry end!), and then the two Twins: Castor, breaker of horses, and Pollux the gifted boxer. Such times of yore!... With their tents, and their nightly campfires!—Finally I had my throat cut in front of the Golden Fleece of the Holy Grail, tricked by the potions of Medea, who burned with immodest passion for the sumptuous Jason. And the cycles started over, I knew Eteocles and

Polynices, and pious Antigone;* and how improvements in weaponry put an end to the age of the Heroes. And finally there was the strange and fearful Ethiopian, and your father and you, Andromeda, noble Andromeda, beautiful above all others, whom it is my duty to make happier than any word can say.'

Having uttered these dazzling words, the Dragon, without warning, turned into a highly polished young man. Leaning against the entrance to the cave, the moonlight playing over his human skin, he speaks of the future.

Andromeda dares not recognize him and, half-turning away, smiles into the void, with one of those stabs of sadness that presages with her those inexplicable follies (her soul being so rapidly overwhelmed).

But life must be lived, whatever the eye-popping astonishments it has in store for you at every turn.

The morning after this night essentially devoted to nuptials, a pirogue was hollowed out of a tree-trunk and launched on the sea.

They drifted, avoiding the coasts dotted with casinos. What a honeymoon, under the sun and the open stars!

And on the third day they made landfall in Ethiopia, where Andromeda's inconsolable father was king. (His joy I leave you to imagine.)

'Now really, dear Monsieur Amyot de l'Épinal,* you've left us open-mouthed with your story!' exclaimed the Princess of U... E... (drawing in her shawl a little, for the night was cool). 'I had set my heart on a quite different acount of Perseus and Andromeda. I shan't quibble with the way you have travestied poor Perseus. (You are excused that because you have flattered me in a masterly way, classical of course, disguising me under the features of Andromeda.) But the ending! Why all this fuss about the Monster, whom no one even considered before? And dear Monsieur Amyot de l'Épinal, I advise you to lift your eyes to the celestial night-chart. That couple of star-clusters over there, just along from *Cassiopeia*, are they not known as *Perseus and Andromeda*? Whereas that twisting tail of stars, all the way down there, do we not call that constellation the *Dragon*, flickering between the *Great Bear* and the *Lesser Bear*, his shaggy familiars?...'

'My dear U..., that proves nothing. The skies are calm and conventional; one might as well say that your eyes are merely brown (you

wouldn't like it). Look elsewhere, down there, near the *Lyre*, is that not the *Swan*, which is Lohengrin's constellation and the form of a cross in memory of Parsifal? And yet you maintain that my *Lyre* has nothing to do with Lohengrin and Parsifal?'*

'It is true, it is analogically true. But it's impossible to discuss or learn anything with you. Let's go in for tea. Oh, and what's the moral of the tale? I always forget the moral...'

'Here it is:

> Young ladies, look most carefully
> Before scorning a poor Monster.
> As this tale of mine should show
> —He was the worthiest of the three.'

MARCEL SCHWOB

The Brothel

IT was a strange house, grey and shuttered, and it seemed to blink from its windows, reclining sleepily as it was on the slope of a long street. Its deep-set door was stained white, and there was no keyhole, bell, or knocker. As if in times gone by it had carried the double stroke of the red cross and the inscription: 'May The Lord Have Mercy Upon Us'* as a warning that plague was within. It may be that Morgiana had marked it in chalk, to deceive the brigand.* But time had worn away these signs; the nonchalant patches of whitewash on the wood spoke of neither crime nor plague; and the door seemed immured in silence.

The windows were sealed against sunlight and darkness alike by close-fitting shutters. Even on very hot days, when we put our fingers between the slats we could feel the cold, as if we had felt the shadow oozing from the house. Sometimes, during thunderstorms, when lines of dazzling rain beat on the pavement, two shutters would yawn open as if to breathe in the storm and a red curtain swelled in the deep darkness of a strange bedroom.

During the day the house was terribly silent. No milk-girl and no postman came knocking at the door. It was so situated that at all times, like that town in Upper Egypt, Syène, where no body, at noon on the summer solstice, sheds any shadow. Its walls never impinged on the sunlight, and at night it was completely smothered in darkness.

It was said that children, after beating incessantly at the door, had sat down to wait. Suddenly, they had heard a dreadful oath coming from inside. Then silence again. And despite their hammering on the door with boots and sticks, and the sand and mud they flung against the shutters, nothing more was heard.

The lights in the house came on regularly. Around nine in the evening a reddish light filtered through one of the shutters. At midnight it went out, and an hour after that several yellow lamps shone confusingly. At crack of dawn, on the dot, all lights went out.

We imagined the house occupied by forgers, and we tried to spy on them. But we never saw a soul coming out or going in. And besides, crucibles would have been needed, and metal and plaster and moulds, as well as accomplices to circulate the new coins.

So we came to dread the brothel, without knowing why. One night we stopped in front of it. From the edge of the pavement we could hear some heavy breathing, regular and continuous, which seemed to come rumbling straight out of the façade. As if a heavy sleeper were lying spread out up against the inner wall. We listened to this breathing for more than an hour. And abruptly we took to our heels, imagining that the white door would open and something would leap out at us.

Rather than casting its shadow on the sunlight, the brothel absorbed it. The house could not have been more silent, or its white-stained door more mute, if lepers had lived there. But bit by bit, the idea came to obsess us. We walked past the shutters in terrible suspense, thinking that some fleshless hand would come thrusting out. Crossing the street we would hold our breath, to avoid inhaling dreadful vapours. We would wake in our beds (for our house was almost adjoining) with the sound of ratchets and bells in our ears. We had read how lepers used to cloister themselves like this, wearing scarlet hoods, and with two joined pieces of wood dangling on a straw from their hands, and we became convinced they tolled their passing-bell in the night.

One day of torrential rain, falling in a seamless sheet, we finally saw a face behind the swollen red curtain. It was not the face of a leper. It was the pinched face of a little girl, with golden hair. She was crying and shivering in the gusting wind. When she saw us she made a dreadful grimace and shouted insults. But a hand dragged her back inside and pulled the shutters to.

At night we were wakened in our beds by a squeaking noise. Then there were screams and the crash of furniture falling and mirrors smashing. We got up half-dressed and slipped outside. Now there were several lights in the brothel, and they were moving about. A red lamp seemed in pursuit of a yellow one, at another window a yellow lamp was in flight; behind one shutter a reddish light was circling slowly.

In the midst of the moving lights, we heard terrified pleas and stifled sobs. We dashed at the white door, full of horror and courage,

and beat on it violently. There came two long groans, like the death-rattle. And then silence, the same oppressive silence as before. And then the lights went out, one by one, and not all together at daybreak. And all our calls brought no response.

We went to bed until dawn. As shredded red clouds breached the sky we opened the window. One of the brothel shutters gaped open. Rapidly we came downstairs. In the rising sun the little golden-haired girl was laughing. When we questioned her, she laughed and said nothing. I took her little hand: it was soiled, and under her nails there were traces of blood

But when we informed the police, the little girl had vanished, and we found the brothel clean and completely bare of furniture. The agents there showed us a notice: *For Rent*, nailed to the white door—and laughed in our faces.

The Sans-Gueule

THEY found them lying next to each other on the burned grass, and gathered them both up. Their clothes had been blown off in shreds. The explosion had burned out the numbers and shattered the metal identity tags. They were like two pieces of human clay. The same fragment of shrapnel, flying slantwise, had sliced off their faces, so that they lay on the tussocks like a couple of trunks with a single red top. The Major who had loaded them into the ambulance did so mostly out of curiosity: for the effect was, in truth, most singular. They had neither nose, cheeks, nor lips. Their eyes had sprung out of their shattered sockets, their mouths gaped open in a bloodied hole where the severed tongue still wagged. What could be odder: two creatures of the same height, and *faceless*. Their skulls, covered in close-cropped hair, now had two red sides, simultaneously and identically carved out, with cavities where the eyes had been and three holes for mouth and nose.

In the ambulance they were dubbed *Sans-Gueule* no. 1 and *Sans-Gueule* no. 2. An English surgeon, who was working there voluntarily, was intrigued by the case and took it on. He anointed and dressed the wounds, extracted the splinters of bone, stitched and modelled the mass of meat, fashioning two red, concave hoods of flesh,

identically perforated towards the base, like pipes emerging from some exotic furnace. Lying in adjoining beds, the two *Sans-Gueule* stained the sheets with a twin wound, round, gaping, and meaningless. The eternal stillness of the wound was frozen in silent suffering: the severed muscles did not even pull against the stitches; the dreadful shock had annihilated the sense of hearing, so the only sign of life left was in the movement of their limbs, and by a twin rasping cry, emitted at intervals from between their gaping palates and the stumps of their tongues.

And yet they started to heal. Slowly and surely they began to control their movements, to develop their arms, to fold their legs so they could sit down, move their hardened gums that still fleshed out their wired jaws. They had one pleasure, which was signalled by some sharply modulated sounds that still had no syllabic content: it was procured by smoking pipes—the stems were held in place in their mouths by pieces of oval rubber, fitted to the dimensions of their mouths. Curled in their blankets, they stank of tobacco, and plumes of smoke escaped from the orifices in their skulls: from the double hole of the nose, from the dark caverns of their eye-sockets, and through the torn mouth, between the remains of their teeth. And each plume of grey smoke was accompanied by an inhuman laugh and a sort of gurgling that came from the uvula while the rest of the tongue wagged feebly.

There was a stir in the hospital when a little woman with a mass of hair was brought by the intern to the bedside of the *Sans-Gueule*; she looked at them one after the other, with a terrified expression, and then burst into tears. Sitting in the office of the head doctor, she explained, between her sobs, that one of the two must be her husband. He had been listed among the casualties: but these two mutilated soldiers had no identifying marks, and belonged to a special category. The height, the width of shoulder, and the hands recalled the lost man infallibly. And yet she was in a terrible perplexity: which of the two *Sans-Gueule* was her husband?

The little lady was kindness itself: her cheap gown moulded her breast, and due to the way she put up her hair, in the Chinese style, she had a sweet, childlike face. Her straightforward grief and her almost absurd uncertainty mingled in her expression and contracted her features in a way reminiscent of a child that has broken its toy. So much so that the head doctor couldn't stop himself from smiling; and

because he had a crude way of talking, he said to the little woman looking up at him:

'Well, what of it! Take them both home! You'll recognize which is which when you try them out!'

At first she was scandalized, and averted her head, like a child blushing for shame: then she lowered her eyes and looked from one bed to the other. The two red mugs rested in their stitches on the pillows, with the same lack of meaning that constituted the whole enigma. She leaned down towards them, and whispered in the ear, first of one, and then the other. The heads did not react at all—but all four hands started to shake—undoubtedly because these two poor bodies whose souls had fled had a vague feeling that a very gentle little woman was close by, who had an endearing manner, and who gave off the sweet smell of a baby.

She hesitated some more, and then asked if they would let her take the two *Sans-Gueule* home for a month. They were transported in a big padded ambulance, and the little woman, seated opposite, wept hot tears unceasingly.

When they got to the house, a strange life began for the three of them. Tirelessly she went to and fro from one to the other, looking for a clue, waiting for a sign. She observed the red surfaces that would never stir again. Anxiously she contemplated the stitches, as one would the features of a beloved face. She examined them in turn, as one might consider different photographs, without being able to choose.

Little by little the sharp grief that wrung her heart, in the early days, when she thought about her lost husband, ended by dissolving into an irresolute calm. She lived like someone who has renounced everything, but goes on by sheer force of habit. The two broken pieces that between them represented the loved one never joined together in her affections; but her thoughts went regularly from one to the other, as if her soul were continually tilting like a balance. She regarded them as her red 'puppets'; they were the two comical dolls that peopled her existence. Smoking their pipes, sitting in the same attitude on their beds, blowing out the same plumes of smoke, and uttering the same inarticulate cries, they resembled more those gigantic puppets brought back from the East, those scarlet masks from overseas, than beings possessed of conscious life that had once been men.

They were her 'two monkeys', her red mannikins, her two little husbands, her burned men, her meaty rascals, her bloodied faces, her holey heads, her brainless bonces. She mothered them in turn, arranging their blankets, tucking in their sheets, mixing their wine and breaking their bread. She led them out into the middle of the room, one on each side of her, and made them caper on the parquet floor; she played with them, and if they became vexed she would slap them down with the flat of her hand. At a single caress they flocked around her, like two famished dogs; and at a gesture of impatience they would double up, cringing like repentant animals. They would rub against her, in quest of morsels; they both had a wooden bowl, and into these, with joyful howlings, from time to time they would plunge their two red muzzles.

The two bonces no longer agitated the little woman as they had before, and no longer fascinated her, like two scarlet wolf-masks superimposed on familiar faces. She loved them equally in her child-like, pouting way. She would say: 'My dolls are asleep; my little men are taking a walk.' She was bewildered when someone came from the hospital to enquire which of the two she was going to keep. The question was absurd, it was like demanding she cut her husband in two. Often she would punish them, the way children do when their dolls have been naughty. She would say to one: 'Look, my little lad, your brother's been bad, he's naughty as a monkey—and so I've turned his face to the wall, and I shan't turn him back until he's said sorry.' And then, with a little laugh, she would turn the poor, penitent body back again, and kiss its hands. Sometimes she would even kiss their dreadful stitches, and then privately wipe her mouth afterwards, pursing her lips. Then straightaway she would almost split herself laughing.

Imperceptibly, however, she got more used to one of them, because he was the gentler of the two. Quite unconsciously, since she had long given up any hope of recognition. She preferred him, like a favourite pet that one likes to caress the most. She spoiled him more and kissed him more tenderly. And by degrees the other *Sans-Gueule* grew sad, for he sensed about him less and less of her feminine presence. He would frequently remain curled up on his bed, his head hidden under his arm, like a wounded bird. He refused to smoke, while the other, knowing nothing of his grief, went on exhaling streams of grey smoke through every vent in his purple face, to the accompaniment of little squawks.

So the little woman started to tend to her sad husband, without really understanding his sadness. His head in her bosom would shake with deep sobs that came from his chest; and a kind of harsh groaning would shake his torso. This poor occluded heart was prey to a terrible jealousy, an animal jealousy borne of feelings mingled with memories, it may be, of a former life. She sang him lullabies, as if he were a child, and calmed him by laying her cool hands upon his burning head. When she realized he was very ill, big tears would fall from her laughing eyes onto his poor mute face.

And soon she was prey to a poignant anguish, for she thought she recognized gestures he had made in an earlier illness. Certain movements seemed familiar from before; and the way he held his emaciated hands reminded her of hands that had been dear to her, and which had brushed her sheets, before the great abyss had opened up in her life.

And the wail coming from the poor abandoned one pierced her heart; and in a breathless uncertainty, she once more scrutinized the faceless heads. They were no longer just two purple dolls—one was a stranger—and the other was part of her own self. When the one who was ailing died, all her grief returned.

She now truly believed that she had lost her husband; and she ran, full of hate, towards the other *Sans-Gueule*, and then stopped short, seized by her childlike pity, in front of the wretched red mannikin who was smoking away joyously, uttering his little cries.

52 and 53 Orfila

To one side of a wide road planted uniformly with trees, whose close-cropped foliage made each of them resemble a sugarloaf on a frail stem, was a flat, yellowish wall, with two identical wings at either end. The paint on the entrance gate was dreary; it led into a sandy oblong courtyard which separated parallel buildings with their tall glazed doors; the two-storeyed constructions had low roofs from which grey-slated bell turrets rose at regular intervals. Seemingly endless grey cloisters led off from the corners of the yard; and a series of little garden beds, round, square, triangular, and lozenge-shaped, in which the flinty earth could be seen between the thin grass, varied, along

with the benches, the melancholy stretch of enclosed ground with a
few traces of pale green.

Amongst this geometrically arranged vegetation, descending the
steps, under the glazed doors, around the single pool of dusty water,
emerging from the dull mouths of old stone which stretched away on
every side, groups of almost immobile human beings moved haltingly
forward, heads shaking and knees trembling; old men and old women,
some of whom, to judge from their ceaselessly nodding heads, seemed
to be saying *yes, yes,* while others, their heads wagging from left to
right, said *no, no*; ancient affirmatives and negatives stubbornly on
the move, but feebly and without variation.

The men wore hats that had lost any pretence of shape, the crown
either knocked in or knocked out. But several wore them ambitiously
at a rakish angle. The women let their thin white hair flow loose
under dirty bonnets; but some of them wore curled wigs, which
looked startlingly black above their parchment faces. Crossing each
other in the garden area, some old beaux would bow with a flourish,
while some of the old women clucked and simpered behind their
glasses. And they would gather in groups, to read the local newspapers and offer each other a hand; while the more addled among
them stared in dismay at the wily little smiles which they could no
longer understand.

The hospital where they lodged admitted them from the age of
sixty upwards, for a thousand francs or so a month and a little extra
for the meat dish. The rich had their own room, which was given a
number, off a corridor. No one was possessed of a name anymore.
You were Voltaire 63 or Arago 119. All distinguishing signs, that had
served in society over a lifetime, were left at the admissions desk; this
animated cemetery was more anonymous than the ones that hold
the dead.

It was a regimented society, with its own rules and conventions.
The owners of the private rooms off the corridors, having the wherewithal to lose at the gaming table and offer to pleasant members of the
opposite sex delicate morsels from the canteen, despised the wretched
denizens of the common wards, where one had no escape from prying
eyes, either to wash or to hide one's bald head.

Entitled to twice-weekly medication, they would lay siege to the
in-house nurses beforehand, for a glimpse of the register. They
would come with torn old bits of paper on which they had written

their order, as if on a trip to the grocer's; and they took pleasure in imitating a cough, which they forced from their rasping lungs, in exaggerating the pain in their twisted limbs, in feigning insomnia, in complaining of imaginary ills. At the ward round they outdid each other with their complaints, so they could hold aloft in triumph their chits for the bath, their phials of camphor, their flasks of glucose. They would place them on their bedside table, and gaze at them one by one, as if they were healing works of art or provisions they had laid in at a bargain price; but their greatest joy was to possess more than anyone else—since for them these objects were their last vestiges of property.

Orfila ward was inhabited by two old women who were too poor to rent a private room. Two rows of beds, of dubious whiteness, stood opposite each other, and lying on the folded sheets was a double bank of female busts, wrapped in camisoles. No. 53 would get up, still having some use of her legs, despite rheumatism of the left knee and partial paralysis of the left arm, which was folded over her waist. She was respected, because she was said to be in receipt of a little money from some distant relatives. But this she preferred to save and use as she liked, rather than pay the administration in exchange for a room of her own. In the bed directly opposite, no. 52 would vex her by flaunting her greater mobility; she had the use of both arms and only a touch of gout in one of her toes. But due to a weakened muscle, her lower right eyelid drooped, showing the bloodshot underside of the eye.

These two women were rivals, not only in body but in matters of the heart as well. As far as human passions were concerned, nothing had diminished in these old men and women. There existed make-believe *ménages à deux* or *à trois* in the rooms; there were violent exhibitions of jealousy; warring parties flung snuff-boxes and crutches at each other in the corridors. At night, ragged shadows waited at doors, armed with a menacing bolster, night-bonnet pulled down to the chin. There were bandy-legged pursuits, sufferers from coxalgia going headlong, jealous spats between old women chattering as they washed their linen: one would sing the praises of her man, who was decorated and well turned-out; the other vaunted hers, who still had the use of all his members.

So it was that sometimes bony fists would make contact with bony cheekbones; hair was pulled out, leaving the pointed or pitted skull

even balder. Spectacles were smashed over black tobacco noses; sharp old elbows would appear in symmetry, hands placed on hips. And frightful querulous oaths would ring out all day long.

War broke out between 52 and 53 over a pipe made of red barley-sugar. There was an old military-looking gent—almost certainly a former concierge—who paid regular visits to 53 Orfila, supposedly his cousin. The words 'my cousin', sounding incessantly in the tooth-less mouths of both parties, rang like an echo in the ears of the nurses, who in consequence lowered their guard. But 52 had taken a fancy to her neighbour's man. She puckered her mouth, rolled her eyes, brushed him with her camisole when he passed, with a little stammer. The others heartily detested her, because she could move about so much. Thick, rheumy laughter provoked in others nervous coughs of exhaustion. Flattered, the old man gave up his games of bowls and cards to spend the afternoon flirting. No. 53 straightened his tie, administered his eyedrops, and gave him some precious electrical pills which she kept in a little box hidden under her pillow.

But she couldn't help gazing jealously at 52's night-table. No. 52 consulted regularly with the doctors, and returned with numerous bottles that she would smugly put on display. The day when the old man gallantly produced from his checked hankie the red pipe, no. 53 squirmed with joy, pumped up her pillow and, leaning on it, pipe beween her teeth, stared out her rival.

She waved the pipe around like a child, sucked on it, and looked at the end she had sucked; she made bawdy innuendos that were not quite picked up, but not quite lost either.

In any case, from that time on 52 disappeared at the same time every morning. No one knew where she went. For several days she seemed distressed. And then she got happier and happier. Eventually, returning one morning from her mysterious walkabout, she thumbed her nose magnificently at 53's red pipe, and parting two fingers, she made the sign of a pair of horns over her forehead. Then she touched her right arm with a kind of mocking despair, as if pitying 53 for not being able to do as much.

This was the breaking-point. A plot was hatched in the ward against the brazen hussy. People affected to spit when she passed, and touched their eyes, simulating nausea. They whispered among them-selves, and cut 52 out from everything. A rustle of paper and the scratching of pens could be heard in the evening.

And yet the old man, feigning innocence, would still come to see his 'cousin'.

No. 53 showed no signs of irritation. But she was less effusive, and asked her cousin, pointedly, what he did with his mornings. The old man rubbed his hands and lied through his teeth.

The day came when the head doctor came round, causing a stir of excitement. He stopped in front of no. 52 and said aloud to the nurses: 'This one will change wards.' Astonished, 52 asked: 'But why, doctor?' The doctor replied, as he continued on his round: 'Your companions will inform you.'

No sooner had he left the ward than the concert began. Breathless whistles and catcalls came from everywhere, followed by raucous coughing. Some of the old women drooled with pleasure. Others beat their sheets in a paroxysm of laughter. And no. 53, who had raised herself right up, waved her pipe about and screamed: 'Why, my lambkin? Because we have petitioned against you. The whole ward. Your bloodied eye is just too *disgusting*. It puts us off our food.'

And in a raucous, rasping, husky chorus the whole ward of invalids cried out: 'Yes, yes, your eye is *disgusting*!'

Stupefied, 52 lay back on her pillow. To her left, a woman whose eye-muscles were paralysed, wagged her head from side to side and up and down, observing her discomfort beadily, like a parrot. To her right was an old woman with the shakes, whose jaws clacked frenetically, open and shut. Her face was smooth and mask-like; unceasingly, with her fingers she rolled imaginary cigarettes on her coverlet.

Lucretius, Poet

LUCRETIUS was born into a grand family that had long since withdrawn from public life. His early days were lived in the shadow of the black porch fronting a tall house built on a mountainside. The atrium was severe and the slaves silent. Since his childhood he had been nourished with a contempt for politics and men. The noble Memmius, who was the same age, suffered the games that Lucretius imposed on him when they played in the forest. The two of them marvelled at the deeply wrinkled bark of old trees, and at leaves quivering in the sun

like a green veil streaked with light. They mused on the striped backs of the wild piglets which snuffled the earth. They passed through swarming streams of bees and moving columns of ants on the march. One day they broke through from a thicket into a clearing completely surrounded by cork-oaks, which were growing in a circle so densely packed together it seemed like a well sunk into the blue sky. The place was infinitely restful. As though they were on a clear, wide road that led to the rarefied air of the divine. Lucretius was touched there by the blessing of calm spaces.

Accompanied by Memmius, he left the serene temple of the forest to study eloquence at Rome. The aged gentleman who ruled over the tall house found him a tutor to teach him Greek, and enjoined him not to return until he had learned the art of despising the world and all its ways. Lucretius never saw him again. He died alone, railing against the tumult of society. When Lucretius returned, he brought with him into the tall empty house, under the severe atrium among the silent slaves, an African woman who was beautiful, barbarian, and perverse. Memmius had returned to the paternal home. Lucretius had witnessed bloody factions, feuding parties, and political corruption. He was in love.

At first his life was an enchantment. Against the wall-tapestries the African female pressed her tangled mass of hair. Her languid body married with its full length the contour of every couch. She held mixing-bowls full of foaming wine, with her arms encrusted in translucent emeralds. She had a strange way of lifting one finger and shaking her head. Her smiles had their deep source in the rivers of Africa. Instead of spinning, she would shred the wool patiently into tiny flecks that floated round about her.

Lucretius wanted nothing more ardently than to melt into that beautiful body. He squeezed her metallic hands and placed his lips against her dark, scarlet mouth. The words of love were exchanged and sighed out; they made them laugh and became worn out. The pair of them brushed against the supple and opaque veil that separates lovers. Their desire grew ever fiercer and sought to become the other. It reached an inflamed extremity that is released over the flesh rather than deep in the entrails. The African withdrew into her remote heart. Lucretius grew desperate at being unable to consummate his love. The woman grew haughty, grim and silent, like the atrium and the slaves. He wandered into the library.

It was there that he unfolded the scroll on which a scribe had copied out the treatise of Epicurus.

No sooner had he done so than he understood the huge variety of things in this world, and the futility of trying to turn them into ideas. The universe seemed to him similar to the little flecks of wool the African scattered through his halls. The bees in their clusters and the ants in their columns and the leaves in their moving tissue were like groups and sub-groups of atoms. And within his own body he felt an invisible mutinous people, eager to fly apart. The gaze seemed to him to be more subtly embodied rays, and the image of the beautiful barbarian was now a pleasant and colourful mosaic; he felt the end of this infinity of movement to be sad and vain.

He viewed the bloodied factions of Rome, with their armed and insulting partisans and claimants, as analogous to the swirling of troops of atoms dyed with the same blood, fighting for some obscure supremacy. And he understood that the dissolution that comes with death was nothing other than the releasing of this turbulent mass that rushes on to a thousand further futile movements.

So when Lucretius had received instruction from the scroll of papyrus, on which the Greek words were interwoven with each other like the atoms of the world, he went out into the forest through the black porch of the tall ancestral house. He saw the stripy backs of the piglets, with their snouts still snuffling at the ground. Next, slashing through the thicket, he was once more in the middle of the serene temple in the forest, and his eyes plunged into the blue well of the sky. And it was there that he placed his repose.

From there he contemplated the teeming immensity of the universe; all the stones, all the plants, all the trees, all the animals, and every single man, in all his colour, with all his passions and his instruments, and the history of the most diverse things, and their birth, their diseases, and their death. And as part of all-encompassing and necessary death, he perceived the individual death of his African bride. And he wept.

He knew that tears spring from a special movement of little glands underneath the eyelids, and that they are caused by a procession of atoms arriving from the heart, and that the heart in turn has been struck by a succession of coloured images emanating from the surface of the body of the beloved woman. He knew that love was caused by

nothing more than the swelling of atoms which desire to join with other atoms. He knew that grief at the death of a loved one is the worst of all earthly illusions, because the dead person has ceased to be unhappy and to suffer, while he who is left to mourn does no more than afflict himself with his own miseries and dream darkly of his own death. He knew that there remained of us no simulacrum to shed tears for our own corpse laid out at our feet. And yet, for all his close knowledge of grief, and love and death—that they are but vain images when contemplated from the calm space where he would seal himself off—he continued nevertheless to weep, and to desire love and to fear death.

Which is why, on returning to the tall and gloomy ancestral house, he went up to the beautiful African, who was brewing something up in a metal pot on the fire. For she too had been thinking, and her thoughts had joined the deep source of her smile. Lucretius looked at the boiling liquid on the brazier. He lightened bit by bit and became like a green turbulent sky. And the beautiful African shook her head and lifted her finger. Then Lucretius drank off the potion. No sooner had he done so than he lost his reason, and he forgot the Greek words on the scroll of papyrus. And for the first time, because he was mad, he knew love. And in the night, having been poisoned, he knew death.

Paolo Uccello, Painter

His real name was Paolo di Dono; but the Florentines called him Uccelli, or Paul of the Birds, because of the numberless painted birds and beasts that filled his house; for he was too poor to feed animals or procure those he did not know. It was even said of him that at Padua, commissioned to paint the four elements, he painted a chameleon as the attribute of the air. But since he had never seen one, he represented the creature as a large-bellied camel with a gaping mouth. (Now, as Vasari* explains, the chameleon is in fact small, dry, and lizard-like, not a great gangling beast like the camel.) The truth was that Uccello cared nothing for the reality of things, but only for their multiplicity and the infinite lines and angles that form them; so he painted blue fields, red cities, knights in black armour on ebony horses with mouths aflame, and spears bristling skywards in every

direction like rays of light. And he used to draw in *mazocchi*, which are those wooden circles covered with cloth and placed on the head, so that the folds of the cloth hang down and frame the face. Uccello made them pointed, square, multifaceted, pyramid, or cone- shaped, in strict accordance with the dictates of perspective, so much so that he found an entire world of permutations in the folds of the *mazoc-chio.* The sculptor Donatello would say to him: 'Ah, Paolo, you are neglecting substance for shadow!'

But the Bird went on with his painstaking work, and he assembled his circles and he calculated his angles and he examined every crea- ture in all of its aspects. He sought help with Euclidian* problems from his friend the mathematician Giovanni Manetti.* Then he would shut himself away and cover his parchments and boards with the trajectories of curves. He devoted himself to the study of archi- tecture, aided by Filippo Brunelleschi: but he had no intention of applying his knowledge to building. He limited himself to examining the network of lines, from base to cornice, the intersections of right- angles, how fan-vaulting converged at the keystone, and the fore- shortening of ceiling beams that seemed to join together at the far end of long galleries. He made drawings of every creature in all its movements, and of the human figure in its every attitude, intent on reducing them to their simplest lines.

Next, like the alchemist who pores over alloys of metal and organs and who observes their fusion in the furnace to extract gold, Uccello poured every form into the crucible of forms. He gathered them in, combined them, and melted them down, with the aim of obtaining their transmutation into the source-form from which all the others derived. It is for this reason that Paolo Uccello lived like an alchemist in the depths of his little house. He believed that he could transform all lines into a single ideal perspective. He sought to conceive of the created universe as it might be seen by the eye of God, who sees all forms issuing from a single complex centre. Around him lived Ghiberti, della Robbia, Brunelleschi, Donatello—each of them the proud master of his art; and they mocked Uccello for his obsession with perspective, and for his poor house with its cobwebs and empty larder. But Uccello was prouder still. With every fresh combination of lines, he hoped to have discovered the secret of creating. His aim lay not in imitating the thing, but in developing the sovereign poten- tial to extrapolate all things, and the strange series of folded hoods

was more of a revelation to him than the magnificent marble figures sculpted by the great Donatello.

So lived the Bird, and his thoughtful head was shrouded in his cloak; he noticed nothing of what he ate or drank, but lived exactly like a hermit. So it was that one day, in an open field, near a circle of old stones half-hidden by the grass, he noticed a laughing girl, who was wearing a garland on her head. She had on a delicate long dress, drawn in at the waist by a pale ribbon; her movements were as supple as the curves she was tracing. Her name was Selvaggia,* and she smiled at Uccello. He remarked the movement of her smile. And when she looked at him, he saw the little lines of her lashes, and the circles of her pupils, and the curve of her eyelids, and the subtle folds of her hair, and in his mind's eye he tilted the garland on her head into a multitude of positions. But Selvaggia knew nothing of all this, for she was only thirteen years old. She took Uccello by the hand, and loved him. She was the daughter of a Florentine dyer, and her mother was dead. Another woman had come to live in the house, and she had beaten Selvaggia. Uccello brought her home with him.

Selvaggia would spend the whole day squatting in front of the wall on which Uccello drew his universal forms. She never understood why he preferred his curves and right-angles, to the tender face lifted towards his own. In the evening, when Brunelleschi or Manetti came by to study with him, she would go to sleep at the foot of the inter-secting angles, after midnight, in the shadowy circle cast by the lamp. In the morning, she would wake before Uccello, and it would be a delight, because she would be surrounded by the colourfully painted beasts and birds. Uccello drew her lips, her eyes, her hair, her hands, and he captured her body in every attitude; but he never once did her portrait, unlike the other painters when they loved a woman. Because the Bird did not know the joy of depicting one individual: he never stayed put. He wanted to soar, in full flight, over everything. And all Selvaggia's forms and attitudes were thrown into the crucible of forms, along with the movements of animals, the outlines of plants and stones, the rays of the light, and the wave-patterns made by ter-restrial vapours, and by the waves of the sea. Uccello did not think of Selvaggia, but remained eternally bent over his crucible of forms.

But there was nothing whatever to eat in the house of Uccello. Selvaggia dared not say anything to Donatello or the others. She said nothing, and died. Uccello drew her body as it stiffened, and her thin

little hands joined together, and the shape of her poor eyes, now closed. He did not know that she was dead, any more than he had known she was alive. But he added these new forms to all the others he had assembled.

The Bird grew old, and no one could understand his paintings. There was nothing but an entanglement of curves. There was nothing of the earth—no plants, no animals, no men. For many long years he worked on his supreme masterpiece, which he showed to no one. It was to be the fruit of all his researches, and in his view it was the very image of them. It represented Doubting Thomas, putting his fingers into the wound of Christ. Uccello completed the painting in his eightieth year. He had Donatello come, and he piously unveiled his painting. Donatello exclaimed: 'O Paolo, cover your painting up again!' The Bird enquired of the great sculptor what he meant: but Donatello would say nothing more. And so Uccello knew he had accomplished a miracle. But all Donatello had seen was a chaos of lines.

Some years later Uccello was found dead on his pallet. His face was radiant with wrinkles. His open eyes were fixed upon the mystery revealed. Tightly clasped in his hand was a little parchment in the form of a circle, covered with intersecting lines, which went from the centre to the circumference and from the circumference back to the centre.

PIERRE LOUŸS

A Case Without Precedent

THE library belonging to Monsieur le Président Barbeville of the bench was his haven of delight. He called it: my bachelor's den.

Every morning, while still in his dressing-gown, he would ascend. Having abandoned his chambers, where he had nothing to do since his retirement from the bench, Monsieur le Président Barbeville, still spry, would climb a little spiral staircase made of stone which led up to the top floor, and he would never open the door without a smile of pleasure.

His treasured books were lit up by a vast glow of greenery. One could see, through the small panes of a large Louis XIV window, the trembling of fresh new leaves. Two chestnuts, whose tops stood taller than the roof of the old red town-house, created a barrier of foliage the sun could not penetrate. But they cast upon the floor a light and moving shadow which imparted an almost pastoral air to the hermit's cell.

Enthroned in a large armchair-cum-desk, based on a model belonging to the Duc d'Aumale, the excellent Monsieur Barbeville would place his spittoon to the left, his cigarette-holder to the right, and his book directly before him.

He had a passion for books. It was almost the only passion that the law courts afforded him, though he was still entirely capable of enjoying many others, and even, at remote intervals, did so. But experiences of that kind gradually became, if not exactly difficult, then increasingly imprudent; and to reassure his doctor, these days he would more often open an old book than a young blouse.

*   *   *   *   *   *   *   *   *   *

One morning, as he was reaching the end of a curious pamphlet he had acquired the day before, his doctor paid him a friendly visit.

'My dear fellow, what excellent timing,' said the old man with warmth. 'I have a question for you, and top marks to you if you reply

correctly. I've found a point of precedence which would have stumped me, had I not just read about it.'

'Oh, I give up already!'

'Wait. It concerns marriage, and even though it turns on a point of law, it also concerns medicine, as you shall understand in a moment. I have never seen or read anything quite so extraordinary. For fifty-two years I have subscribed to the *Gazette des tribunaux* and to the supplements to *Dalloz;** I myself have heard thousands of cases; I have been regaled with the strangest judicial cases of our time; but nothing quite like this. You find me dumbfounded.'

Monsieur le Président Barbeville settled more deeply into his arm-chair, thrust his hands into the pockets of his dressing-gown, and slowly formulated the following question, articulating each term with clarity and precision:

'How can an ordinary marriage agreement, made with the full consent of both parties, involve, by immediate and ineluctable necessity, on the part of one of the parties and with the other acting as accomplice, the crimes of kidnap, false imprisonment, procuring, exhibitionism, multiple rape, incest, adultery, and polygamy?'

Stunned at first by the list, the doctor then burst out laughing.

'Take note,' went on Barbeville, 'take note of what I said: by imme-diate and ineluctable necessity. These facts are neither successive in time nor due to the initiative of one of the spouses. At the very instant the legal consummation of the marriage takes place, *all these crimes are perpetrated at once!* and neither of the spouses can prevent this being the case, unless they renounce their union.'

The judge's friend pondered for a while, and then asked:

'Is it a fairy-tale?'

'Not at all. Nothing could be more authentic. The case is possible, probable, and true. I shall go further: if the case is to my knowledge unique, there must obviously have been precedents in the past, and it will come up again in the future, I have not a moment's doubt. The girl's situation is not, in fact, unique, and nothing is the fault of the fiancé: any man in his place would have undergone the same ordeals.'

'So tell me. I'm completely at a loss.'

Monsieur Barbeville began thus:

'You'll grasp the thing immediately. An Italian, living in Paris, gave birth one day to conjoined twins. The birth was secret, and the midwife didn't think of informing the Academy of Science.

The child (one or two baby girls, depending on whether you examined her from the top or from the bottom) had two heads, four arms, two chests, a shared pelvis, and only two legs. Such cases are not unheard-of, I believe?'

'No. Especially among stillbirths... Go on. Now I'm with you.'

'But have any been known to survive?'

'Several.'

'They must have been, dare I say, solidly constructed monsters. Give me an example.'

'Ritta-Cristina, two little girls, born in Sardinia around 1830. They were very like the description you have just given; two chests but one pelvis. Their parents brought them to Paris, to show them off at the fair, but the authorities considered such an exhibition to be offensive to public morals and proscribed it. Without other resources, the poor family had to leave the children in a fireless room, and they died of bronchitis.'

'Was there an autopsy?'

'Yes.'

'Did they have separate nervous systems?'

'Entirely, except for the lower abdomen, where sensations were transmitted to both brains at once.'

'Excellent! You'll see how your example backs up what I'm about to tell you.'

The old judge inserted a long cigarette into his meerschaum holder, and warmed to his theme:

'The two little girls born to this Italian were registered under the names of Maria-Maddalena. They survived. Their mother never showed them off, but she cared for them very tenderly. They grew normally, and attained the age of puberty. At sixteen years of age they had turned into two very pretty teenagers, despite their beauties being so strangely conjoined. If the siren's tail didn't prevent her from seducing men, we shouldn't be surprised that Maria-Maddalena could stir the heart of a lover.

'In fact, both girls fell in love; but only Maddalena was loved. A young man fell for her; but since he was full of respect for the other, the sisters thought they shared a common love, and they responded together with all the fire of the first flush of youth. Alas, this illusion could not last. The young man felt he must put an end to it. One day a letter arrived, written in his hand, addressed to

'Mlle Maddalena'. As you can imagine, this awoke in the neighbouring breast a thousand serpents, and when the request for marriage
was officially made, Maddalena said *yes*, and Maria said *no*.

'They implored, they entreatied, but all in vain. The mother took
sides with the lovers, and tried to persuade the refractory girl, but she
too met with failure...'

'It's absolutely hilarious!' exclaimed the doctor, shaking with
mirth.

'Tragic, my dear chap! This has all the makings of an unimaginable drama. To be the enemy sister, the rival in love; to be half-joined
to the one you abhor, and condemned by nature to see all the caresses
lavished on the other; what am I saying, not just to see, but to feel
them as well! And then to carry the fruit of a lover doubly detested!
Dante invented nothing like this; it surpasses in horror anything
devised in the annals of Chinese torture.

'So—to go on with the story—the Italian, who was set upon
marrying one of her daughters, despite the other's opposition, sought
out the local mayor and asked him if he would consent to celebrate
the marriage under such conditions. The mayor hesitated, saying
that the question was of unprecedented complexity; he felt he had no
authority to judge; his humdrum tasks hardly qualified him to resolve
a case involving such legal niceties. In the end he asked the concerned
parties to send him two lawyers, who would argue the pros and cons.'

'Did the hearing take place?'

'Yes. But in private, obviously, in the mayor's office, with no one
else present except the deputies and the clerk.

'Maddalena's lawyer was the first to plead. The exordium was
ironic, the presentation of the facts facetious. He started his argument in the same tone. In turn, he invoked article 1645 ("the obliga-
tion to render up with the thing, its accessories"), or article 569, even
more abusively applied. Then, setting these jokes aside, he laid the
dilemma out before them: either Maria-Maddalena consisted of two
distinct and different women, or she was one woman. If the first case
were true, her sister's consent was clearly not necessary. If the second
were true, then the case was even clearer. This was the thesis he
adopted, and developed. No one had ever considered, in reality or in
the imagination of the poets, that multiple limbs implied multiple
individuals. A calf with six legs was still a single calf. Argus's hundred eyes* do not belong to a hundred people. Janus* had two faces

but they belonged to one and the same god. Cerberus* takes a singular, despite having three heads. Why should Maria-Maddalena, who is physically indivisible, be made up of two individuals, when the very meaning of individual, etymologically defined, means that which is indivisible?'

The doctor laughed, 'I like his argument!'

'Furthermore,' the lawyer went on, 'even admitting the existence of two minds, in this case psychology is nothing to the purpose, it is marriage we are discussing. And marriage has a very precise end in view, which no one can dispute. Now, Maria-Maddalena may have come into the world with a double brain, she is perfectly single from the nuptial point of view. Of the two women you can discern down to the waist, thereafter the single organ makes a single spouse.'

'Clearly.'

'The lawyer representing the other sister replied that he would not get waylaid, like his fanciful colleague, in mythological digression, but would rather plead for common sense. The very fact that Maria and Maddalena have gone to law against each other proves, he said, that they are two people. "Maria refuses to get married. If Monsieur X marries her sister, my client will be the victim of kidnap: this, aggravated by the fact she is a minor, constitutes the first crime. Once kidnapped, she will be held against her will in the marital home of the petitioners: false imprisonment—the second crime. Once there, our falsely imprisoned minor will be forced to be present during all the intimate caresses exchanged between the spouses: indecency and exhibitionism, the third crime. By force she will be brought to bed next to a man, with Maddalena as his willing, and interested, accomplice: procuration and enslavement, fourth crime. Despite her resistance, her virginity will be taken at the same time as her sister's, because her physical constitution demands that it be so: rape, crime number five. The guilty party will be her brother-in-law: incest, crime number six, not recognized in law, but I retain it as an aggravating circumstance. Finally, the man is married: adultery, crime number seven. Is that it? No, there is more: the marriage of one requires the marriage of the other twin, since the two of them are indivisible, as my colleague has just proved with his luminous powers of deduction. You will be forced therefore to write out two marriage certificates, but with one and the same husband named on them both. By saving him from adultery, you inculpate him with bigamy,

incriminating yourself as a party to the fact. You'll both end up in the labour camp!"'

'Was the verdict postponed for a week?'

'No! The mayor protested there and then that he had never had the slightest intention of giving his consent, and the marriage never took place.'

'The Lord be praised!' said the doctor gaily.

EXPLANATORY NOTES

BARBEY D'AUREVILLY

Don Juan's Crowning Love-Affair

First published in *Les Diaboliques* (Paris: Éditions Dentu, 1874) (the edition was partially seized by order of the public prosecutor); a second edition (Paris: Lemerre) appeared in 1882.

3 *Maison-d'Or*: or more formally *Maison-Dorée*. A fashionable Parisian restaurant from 1840 until the end of the Second Empire, it was situated on the Boulevard des Italiens, at the corner of the rue Lafitte.

D'Arnaud de Brescia: (*c*.1090–1155), Italian reformer who preached in favour of a return to the Early Church. His teachings were judged heretical, and he was excommunicated, and then executed.

4 *The mille è tre*: (Italian) one thousand and three, the number of Don Juan's conquests according to Leporello, in Mozart's opera *Don Giovanni* (Act I, scene 2).

the victim's ball: allusion to the balls that were instituted after 9 Thermidor (the date of Robespierre's overthrow and end of the Revolutionary reign of terror). Entry was restricted to relations of the guillotined.

Orgon . . . Tartuffe: in Molière's *Tartuffe* (I. 3) Orgon cannot conceal his real interest in the object of his question, just as the Marquise is keen to hear about Ravila.

Jules-Amédée-Hector de Ravila de Ravilès: Barbey uses his own Christian names. In French, 'Ravila de Ravilès' is a play on words—literally 'ravish her/ravish them'.

5 *Faubourg Saint-Germain*: the area in the seventh *arrondissement* of Paris, around the rue Vaneau, which was the heart of aristocratic society.

Mesmer chain: Franz Anton Mesmer (1733–1815), German doctor who claimed to have discovered 'animal magnetism', a fluid he prescribed, and which he claimed to be universally remedial. Patients sat round a basin of 'magnetized' water and held thumbs, a procedure said to favour the circulation of the 'fluid'. In Paris, Mesmer had a passionate coterie following on the eve of the Revolution.

The witty Prince de Ligne: Charles-Joseph, Prince de Ligne (1735–1814), French military commander. He frequented the cultivated elites of Europe, and was the author of *Mélanges militaires, littéraires, sentimentaires*. Alcibiades was the famously dissolute Athenian politician and friend of Socrates.

5 *Comte d'Orsay*: Alfred d'Orsay (1801–52), a celebrated dandy, conversationalist, and art-lover—described by Barbey in his study of dandyism, *Du Dandysme et de George Brummell* (1845).

6 *Commendatore*: in Mozart's opera, the marble figure of the Commander, the figure of death, who comes for the impenitent Don Giovanni during his final dinner.

   The Amphitryons: the reference is to Molière's play. Amphitryon is the Theban general impersonated by Zeus in order to sleep with his wife, and his name is synonymous with the figure of the generous 'host'.

   Sardanapalus: legendary king of Assyria, known for his dissolute life. He committed suicide by throwing himself onto a huge pyre in the courtyard of his palace, onto which he had flung all his goods and chattels, including wives and concubines.

7 *Byron*: Barbey was a lifelong admirer of George Gordon, Lord Byron (1788–1824), the dashing, dandified, aristocratic Romantic poet.

8 *Regency period*: Barbey refers here to the *Régence* of Philippe d'Orléans, at the beginning of the eighteenth century, reputed for its dissolute *mores*.

9 *Melusina the sea-nymph*: a figure from medieval legend. Because of her sin, Melusina was condemned to become half-woman, half-serpent every Saturday night.

10 *Café Anglais*: a fashionable restaurant for the rich and the *jeunesse dorée*, situated on the Boulevard des Italiens.

   Jagellons: celebrated Polish dynasty founded by Ladislas Jagellon (1348–1434). The Czartorysky family descended directly from the Jagellons.

11 *wild oats*: the original French, 'j'avais fini mes caravanes', is piquant, and hard to translate without explanation. The expression was used by aspiring Knights of Malta, who had to participate in a fixed number of campaigns against the infidel before they qualified to join the Order.

13 *en ferronnière*: after Leonardo da Vinci's portrait *La Belle Ferronière*; the hair worn with a chain or a band around it, attached to which is a jewel that rests against the centre of the forehead.

   Borgia comes before Machiavelli: Barbey refers to the Florentine prince Cesare Borgia (1457–1507) famous for his debauched lifestyle, as a guide to the arts of love, much as Machiavelli (1469–1527) was a guide to politics.

14 *three tails*: the horse-tails hung from a Turkish pasha's lance designating order of rank, three tails showing the highest-ranking officer.

15 *"little mask"*: the expression *petite masque* was a familiar one to designate a cheeky or a mischievous child.

17 *dos-à-dos*: the love-seat, sometimes known in French as a *boudeuse*, or 'sulker', designed with the two seats placed back-to-back.

VILLIERS DE L'ISLE-ADAM

The three stories here were collected in *Contes cruels* (Paris: Calmann-Lévy, 1883).

The Presentiment

[title]: the French title is 'L'Intersigne'—a word belonging to Breton folklore, and thus especially attractive to Villiers. It refers to an obscure sign or an augury, which announces a death. To the word 'signe' is added some kind of mysterious exchange or intervention, appropriate to this classic example of *le fantastique* in literature, relating events that cannot be rationally explained away.

[epigraph]: 'Consider, O Man, what you were before birth, and what you will be until your end. For sure there was a time when you existed not. Then, constituted of vile matter, you were nourished in your mother's womb by her menstrual blood, clothed in membranous matter. Next, enveloped in a vile garment you came among us—in that tunic, that adornment! And you have forgotten from where you came. Man is nothing but a rank sperm, a sack of excrement, food for worms. Knowledge, wisdom, reason, without God, pass by like clouds.

'After man, comes the worm; after the worm, horror and putrefaction. In such wise man changes into what is not man.

'Why do you adorn yourself, why do you fatten your flesh, when, in a few days, the worm will try your sepulchre? Why not adorn your soul, which must come before God and the Angels in heaven?'

From the *Meditations* of St Bernard of Clairvaux (1090–1153), founder of the Cistercian Order.

22 *Autumn solstice*: there is no such thing, of course.

23 *Avicenna's cassia brew*: Avicenna (980–1037), the great Arab doctor and philosopher.

Robert d'Arbrissel: (*c.*1045–1116), an itinerant preacher who founded the Abbey of Fontevrault. He was famous for the extreme severity of his ascetic practices.

at the very instant: the first use of phrases in italics, that recur and carry a mysterious charge in the story.

27 *Joseph de Maistre*: (comte), 1753–1821, politician, philosopher, and writer, opposed to the French Revolution (he fled to Lausanne in 1793). De Maistre reiterated his monarchist and papist beliefs in *Considérations sur la France* (1796).

28 *death-watch beetle*: in French, *horloge-de-mort* ('clock of death'); the name is clearly freighted with meaning here.

35 *Rabelais's "good companion"*: in *Gargantua et Pantagruel* by François Rabelais (1494–1553) 'le bon compagnon' is an epithet used at one point of the libertine, cunning knave, and coward Panurge.

The Desire To Be a Man

This story is a reflection on the actor and his shifting roles, and on personal identity, born of Villiers's close knowledge of the Parisian theatre, and his abiding ambition to write successfully for the stage.

36 *Bourse*: the Paris stock-exchange, situated in the second *arrondissement*.

the curfew: Villiers sets this story very precisely in the days following the Commune (1871), when the curfew was still in force.

37 *the Caudine Forks*: the mountain pass in southern Italy in which the Samnites trapped the Roman army in the Second Samnite War (326–304 BCE). The Samnites then humiliated the Romans by forcing them to pass, man by man, under the yoke—this time made of Roman spears, since the greatest humiliation for a Roman soldier was to lose his spear. Villiers uses the expression in its familiar sense, meaning anything that someone is forced to do unwillingly.

Boulevard du Crime: now the Boulevard du Temple. At the time, the centre of Paris theatreland; it was in theatres along this street that cloak-and-dagger melodrama was performed, hence the list of Renaissance Italian clans that follows.

Esprit Chaudval, born Lepeinteur, known as Monunteuil: the elaborate triptych of names serves to underline the old actor's essential lack of any stable identity.

38 *Frédérick Lemaître*: birth-name Antoine Louis Prosper Lemaître (1800–76), French actor and playwright, one of the most famous players on the Boulevard du Crime.

Thalia . . . Melpomene: the classical Muses of Comedy and Tragedy.

Ellevious and the Laruettes . . . Dugazons: characters from the Opéra-Comique of the period.

40 *Erostratus*: an Ephesian who, with the purpose of winning for himself immortal fame, set fire to the great temple of Artemis in Ephesus in 356 BCE.

41 *my crime will be disinterested*: Chaudval's 'disinterested' but murderous intention here resembles the crime of Deshoulières in Jean Richepin's eponymous story (see below); Chaudval, like Deshoulières, would be a 'dandy of the unpredictable'.

Corneille: Pierre Corneille (1606–84), the great French playwright, slightly senior to Racine. Corneille's greatest play was the tragedy *Le Cid* (1636).

42 *Rostopschin*: Count Feodor Rostopschin (1760–1826) was appointed Governor of Moscow under Tsar Alexander I, during the Napoleonic Wars. He was credited (by the French) with the burning of Moscow in 1812.

43 *the Stylite*: St Simeon Stylites (390–459), Christian ascetic from near Aleppo in Syria, who lived unprotected from the elements on top of a tall column. His name is now synonymous with extreme ascetic practice.

44 *Orestes*: in Greek mythology, son of Agamemnon and Clytemnestra. He murdered his mother to avenge the death of his father. He appears in several plays, and Euripides named one of his tragedies after him.

Sentimentalism

[title]: 'The sentimental habit of mind; the disposition to attribute undue importance to sentimental considerations, or to be governed by sentiment in opposition to reason; the tendency to excessive, indulgence in or insincere display of sentiment' (*OED*). The French title is 'Sentimentalisme', a word that does not exist as such in the relevant edition of the *Littré* dictionary (1878). I follow Pierre Reboul in considering that Villiers uses the word—in the light of what follows, referring to those people who gush about their feelings—pejoratively. See Villiers de l'Isle-Adam, *Contes Cruels*, ed. Pierre Reboul (Paris: Gallimard, Folio, 1983), 395.

46 *of being insensitive*: Maximilien here aspires to the condition of Baudelaire's ideal dandy: 'But a dandy can never be someone vulgar', and 'The beauty of the dandy's character consists in the coldness of his demeanour, and his unshakable resolution, not to give way to emotion...' (see Baudelaire's essay 'Le Dandy', in *Oeuvres complètes*, vol. 2 ed. Claude Pichois (Paris: Gallimard, Pléiade, 2011), 709–12).

CATULLE MENDÈS

What the Shadow Demands

This story was collected in the volume *Rue des Filles-Dieu, 5* ou *L'Héautonpératéromène* (Paris: Charpentier et Fasquelle, 1895).

52 *the prison of La Roquette*: La Grande Roquette, opened in 1851, was the central prison in Paris at the time, at the entrance to which, in the street and in view of the public, a special base was constructed for the guillotine.

59 *wiping it off the map*: Mendès must be referring to the cataclysmic eruption of Krakatoa in 1883, in the vicinity of Java and other islands, that caused tsunamis with innumerable casualties in their wake. News of this catastrophe caused a stir in Europe and North America.

62 *the universal law would no longer be transgressed*: it is here that the story shows most clearly its appurtenance to the genre of *littérature fantastique*, defined as an occurrence that cannot be explained rationally erupting within a framework obedient to the laws of nature.

LÉON BLOY

These three stories were collected in *Histoires désobligeantes* (Paris: Dentu, 1894).

A Dentist Terribly Punished

68 *an uncanny resemblance to the man Gerbillon had murdered*: the idea that a child might bear a resemblance not to the biological father but to the object of the mother's obsessions is to be found in Goethe's *Elective Affinities*, and also in Barbey d'Aurevilly's *Ce qui ne meurt pas*: 'Allan's mother, who was English, had apparently spent the full nine months of her pregnancy staring at a portrait of Lord Byron... and it was his countenance... that she had given to her son.'

The Last Bake

Charles V: the Holy Roman Emperor and ruler of Spain Charles V (1500–58), who voluntarily abdicated in 1556, living in monastic seclusion until his death.

69 *the divine Bourget*: Paul Bourget (1852–1935), the most fashionable novelist of the period. Catholic, traditionalist, and didactic in tendency. Opposed to Naturalism, he set out to write the 'moral anatomy' of his age. But he came to be seen by his peers as the portraitist, and the flatterer, of the rich—hence Bloy's mockery.

invention of the Crematorium: Bloy visited the crematorium at Père Lachaise cemetery, and he wrote about the experience in his Journal on 3 April 1893: 'One day I shall undoubtedly write about this infamy, which calls down upon itself all the furies of God.'

70 *Benjamin Franklin's expression*: i.e. 'Time is money.' The saying was first promulgated by Franklin (1706–90), one of the founding fathers of America, in his *Advice to a Young Tradesman, Written by an Old One* (1748).

71 *the 'Columbarium'*: a place where cinerary urns are kept and commemorated, usually by small inscribed plaques. The Père Lachaise cemetery in Paris has a fine example.

The Lucky Sixpence

Bloy draws on folk-tale tradition for the horrible dénouement of this story, whose sources are legion. One notorious example, drawn from classical sources, is Shakespeare's *Titus Andronicus*.

75 *half-remembered melodrama*: Bloy may be remembering the famous 'mourning dinner' held by Des Esseintes in Paris, in the first chapter of *A Rebours*, in which the entire decor was done out in black.

OCTAVE MIRBEAU

'On a Cure', 'The Bath', and 'The Little Summer House' formed part of the volume *Les Vingt et Un Jours d'un neurasthénique* (Paris: Fasquelle, 1901); 'The First Emotion' was collected in *La Pipe de cidre* (Paris: Flammarion, 1919).

On a Cure

76 *Ariège*: one of the southernmost *départements* of France, bordering the Pyrenees.

78 *The future!... Progress!...*: the narrator tells us that early on, as a young man, Fresselou had 'tasted the poison of metaphysics'. His *contemptus mundi* here bears the imprint of Schopenhauer's pessimism, but seemingly without the philosopher's belief in the consolatory powers of art.

The Bath

80 *Woman is a marvellous animal*: a commonplace of the time. In his essay on 'La Femme' included in *Le Peintre de la vie moderne*, Baudelaire quotes approvingly Joseph de Maistre's view of woman as *un bel animal* (see Baudelaire, *Oeuvres complètes*, vol. 2, 713).

81 *sphingids*: the family of lepidoptera known as the hawk moths or sphinx moths, after the shape of their caterpillars.

The First Emotion

83 *at the Ministry of Education*: Mirbeau himself, like Huysmans and Bloy, had first-hand experience of the humiliation and boredom experienced by the *petit employé*, or office clerk.

Petit Journal: a hugely popular daily newspaper which ran from 1863 to 1944. At its height, in the 1890s, the paper had a circulation of 1 million.

84 *the Eiffel Tower*: Gustave Eiffel's famous iron structure was erected between 1887 and 1889, in time for the *Exposition universelle* of the same year.

The Little Summer-House

87 *Panama Syndicates*: in 1892 close to a billion francs were lost in the scandal surrounding the bankruptcy of the Panama Canal Company, the stricken speculative enterprise founded by Ferdinand de Lesseps. Members of the government took bribes to keep quiet about the situation, which led to the greatest financial scandal of the Third Republic.

some Reinach to hand, or some Yves Guyot: Joseph Reinach (1856–1921) was a French politician implicated in the Panama scandal; later he became the fiercest champion of Alfred Dreyfus. Yves Guyot (1843–1928) was a politician and economist, and a defender of free trade. Presumably Mirbeau's allusions to these men is ironical, given the fate of the Panama Canal Company.

88 *Orléanist Monarchy*: the period of constitutional monarchy that began with the July Revolution of 1830, and enthroned Louis-Philippe, of the Orléans branch of the House of Bourbon, as king. He was known as the 'Bourgeois King'.

88 *Fragonard*: Jean-Honoré Fragonard (1732–1806), French painter of the rococo style, famous for his elegant genre scenes portraying a hedonistic society; his subjects are often erotically charged, as in the famous painting *The Swing*.

91 *on all of this!*: the frenetic rehearsal of the narrator's fears in the preceding section recalls some of Poe's similarly distraught narrators.

JEAN RICHEPIN

'Constant Guignard' and 'Deshoulières' were collected in *Les Morts bizarres* (Paris: Decaux, 1876), 'Pft! Pft!' in *Cauchemars* (Paris: Charpentier et Fasquelle, 1892).

Constant Guignard

[title]: the name in French contains word-play. *La guigne* means to be dogged by bad luck. Add to this his first name, and it is clear the protagonist's endless misfortune seems to be predestined.

93 *Cayenne*: the notorious penal colony off the coast of French Guiana, otherwise known as Devil's Island. It was in operation from 1859 until it was finally closed in 1953.

the military substitute: in the days of obligatory military service, a man's turn to serve was sometimes decided by a lottery system. He could, though, pay for a substitute to take his place.

95 *Papavoine*: Louis-Auguste Papavoine (1783–1825) was executed for stabbing to death two children in the Bois de Vincennes, without apparent motive.

the asylum at Charenton: the celebrated lunatic asylum near Paris, that once housed the Marquis de Sade, was founded by the Frères de la Charité in 1645, and was noted for its humane treatment of inmates.

Place de la Roquette: located in Paris, where public executions by guillotine were carried out (see note to p. 52).

Deshoulières

96 *a veritable Proteus* : Richepin pushes to the point of absurdity Baudelaire's insistence that the dandy should discipline his life as if it were lived continuously in front of a mirror. Proteus, a sea-god in Greek mythology, was famous for changing his form.

97 *his deplorable homonym*: Richepin is presumably referring to the prolific and mediocre poetess Antoinette du Ligier de la Garde Deshoulières (1638–94), who rose to prominence in the literary circles around Louis XIV.

99 *Tertullian . . . De cultu foeminarum*: Tertullian (*c*.160–225), a Father of the Church, sometimes credited as the founder of western theology. His *De cultu foeminarum* ('On Female Fashion') is a tract counselling Christian women to dress modestly and without ornament.

the Widow: i.e. *La Veuve*, historical French *argot* for the Guillotine, as in 'my father married the Widow' (Victor Hugo, *The Last Day of a Condemned Man*).

100 *He was . . . page-boy style*: the last two lines are elliptical: 'Il avait trouvé l'*imprévu* de la guillotine. Il s'était fait couper la tête *aux enfants d'Edouard*.' The phrase *aux enfants d'Edouard* refers to the sons of Edward IV of England, the 'Princes in the Tower', who were later portrayed with the famous 'page-boy' haircut.

Pft! Pft!

[title]: I have retained the original French title; its meaningless yet suggestive syllables work equally well in English.

GUY DE MAUPASSANT

'At the Death-Bed' was first published under the pseudonym Maufrigneuse in the review *Gil Blas*, 30 January 1883, and collected in Guy de Maupassant, *Oeuvres complètes*, vol 28, *Oeuvres posthumes* (Paris: L. Conard, 1908–10); 'A Walk' in *Yvette* (Paris: Victor Havard, 1885); 'The Tresses' in *Toine* (Paris: Marpon et Flammarion, 1884); 'Night' in *Clair de lune* (Paris: Ollendorff, 1888).

At the Death-Bed

105 '*Rolla*' : the long poem by Alfred de Musset (1810–57) recounting events in the life of the famous rake Jacques Rolla, and showing up the life of prostitutes and the poor. In this poem of 1833 Musset seems to deplore the libertinism ushered in by *philosophes* like Voltaire, which in turn casts an oblique light on the greater debunking of romantic love carried out by Schopenhauer.

106 *vestiges of his thought*: Maupassant is surely giving his own estimate of Schopenhauer's devastating influence, and he himself underwent it. But there is an element of mockery in the black humour of this tale, directed at those for whom the philosopher had become the object of a cult.

A Walk

109 *the model employee that he was*: compare Mirbeau's treatment of the same theme, in 'The First Emotion', above.

111 *Quand le bois reverdit*: roughly translatable as: *When the woods are green again | My lover says to me | Come and take the air, my love | Under the greenwood tree.*

The Tresses

116 *the flâneur*: literally, the 'stroller' or the 'saunterer'. In nineteenth-century Paris the type took on an exemplary literary pedigree, thanks largely to the thought and work of Charles Baudelaire, where the *flâneur* becomes emblematic of a certain type of modern, urban experience.

118 *Dictes-moy où . . . d'antan?*: two stanzas from the 'Ballade des Dames du temps jadis' (the 'Ballad for Ladies of Times Past'), part of François Villon's poem *Le Testament*:

> Now tell me where has Flora gone,
> The lovely Roman, her country's where?
> Archipiades, Thaïs that shone,
> Her cousin once removed? And fair
> Echo speaking across the air
> Of pools and meadows where sounds go,
> Her beauty more than human share:
> Where is the drift of last year's snow?
> (...)
> Where's queen Blanche, like lily, swan –
> With siren voice she'd sing an air?
> Big-footed Bertha, Beatrice gone;
> Alice, and Arembourg, Maine's heir;
> Lorraine's good Joan, in Rouen square
> Burnt by the English. Where d'they go,
> O Queen and Virgin, tell me where,
> Where is the drift of last year's snow?

From François Villon, *Poems*, trans. Peter Dale (London: Anvil, 2001), 75.

120 *Sergeant Bertrand*: François Bertrand disinterred corpses to assuage his sexual appetites; after a much-publicized trial he was sentenced in 1849, and since then his name has been associated with necrophilia.

122 *Les Halles*: at this period the great central wholesale market of the city, celebrated by Zola as 'the belly of Paris'. The market was demolished in 1971, replaced by the Forum des Halles, a modern shopping precinct.

GUSTAVE GEFFROY

The Statue

This story was collected in *Le Coeur et l'esprit* (Paris: Charpentier, 1894).

126 *the Parc Monceau*: the luxurious quarter of Paris in the seventeenth *arrondissement* that developed throughout the nineteenth century. It was home to many art-collectors, among them the Rothschild, Cernuschi, and Ephrussi families.

Villa Médicis: the splendid Villa in Rome, on the Pincio, just above the Spanish Steps. It was purchased by Napoleon for the French state in 1801. To this day the Médicis receives artists-in-residence, winners of the 'prix de Rome', for periods of up to three years.

128 *drawn direct from nature*: it is impossible not to think that Geffroy had in mind Auguste Rodin (1840–1917) as part of the inspiration behind this

story, and perhaps it was his works that so troubled the sculptor here. Rodin was celebrated for his exact anatomical imitation of nature, both in his sculpture and his drawings.

JEAN LORRAIN

'The Man Who Loved Consumptives' was collected in *Sonyeuse. Soirs de Province. Soirs de Paris* (Paris: Charpentier, 1891). 'An Unidentified Crime', 'The Student's Tale', and 'The Man with the Bracelet' were collected in *Histoires de masques* (Paris: Ollendorff, 1900).

An Unsolved Crime

130 *Mardi Gras*: Lorrain is referring here to the 'Carnaval de Paris', a huge and joyous ceremony, held around Shrove Tuesday, involving masks and disguise, whose origins date back to the Middle Ages. In the 1890s it reached something of a climax, with the invention of confetti and the paper streamer. The Carnival fell out of the popular calendar in the 1950s, and despite various efforts to do so, has never been successfully revived.

nervous troubles: Lorrain was a self-confessed ether addict, so much of this description can be taken as autobiographical.

The Man with the Bracelet

139 *Voici le soir charmant, ami du criminel*: the first line of Baudelaire's poem 'Le Crépuscule du soir' ('Evening Twilight') from *Les Fleurs du mal*. 'Here is the delightful evening, the criminal's friend' (trans. Francis Scarfe).

pognon . . . rousse: French criminal slang or *argot*. Equivalents in English might be 'dough' (as in money) and 'the cops'.

140 *smiling head of Scylla*: in the original Greek legend, the sea-monster Scylla was supposed to have had six heads, and a ring of barking dogs around her belly. Along with the whirlpool Charybdis, she guarded the Straits of Messina, and devoured the sailors who escaped the whirlpool.

Banville . . . 'You Will Return': Théodore de Banville (1823–91), poet and prose-writer, admired by Baudelaire. The story referred to here by Lorrain has never been identified.

Je vois un port rempli . . . vague marine: from Baudelaire's 'Parfum exotique' in *Les Fleurs du mal*. 'I see a port all filled with sails and masts that ache still from the briny wave' (trans. Francis Scarfe).

141 *Hôtel Pimodan*: formerly the Hôtel de Lauzun on the Île Saint Louis. Baron Jérôme Pichon acquired it in 1842, and welcomed poets and artists as lodgers (including Gautier and Baudelaire). The famous 'club des haschichins', described by Baudelaire in *Les Paradis artificiels* (1860), was founded in 1845 by the painter Émile Brissard.

142 *Ah! malheur à celui . . . gauche!*: lines taken from Musset's poem 'La Coupe et les lèvres' ('The Cup and the Lips', 1832). Literally: 'Woe to him who lets debauchery | Plant herself like a nail in his left breast.'

Canler's Memoirs: Louis Canler (1797–1865) was head of La Sûreté (the Criminal Investigation Department). His *Memoirs* were published in 1862.

Wagram dance-hall: the celebrated *Bal Wagram*, built in 1812. It became a *café-concert* and its large ballroom was often used for political meetings.

The Man Who Loved Consumptives

143 *Legendre's Play*: actually Shakespeare's *Much Ado About Nothing*, in the translation by Louis Legendre, whose 'adaptations' of Shakespeare were in vogue among theatregoers in the 1880s.

144 *Garde ta fille, elle est trop chère!*: 'Keep your daughter, she is too expensive!' The expression does not occur in the original. Legendre must be adapting Claudio's lines, 'There Leonato, take her back again, | Give not this rotten Orange to your friend' (IV. i).

Roybet . . . Ziem . . . Porel: Ferdinand Roybet (1840–1920), fashionable society painter of the period, specializing in portraiture and depicting theatrical costume; Félix Ziem (1821–1911), watercolourist and traveller, famous for his paintings of Venice and the East; Paul Porel (1843–1917), actor and man of the theatre. He became Director of the Théâtre de l'Odéon where the performance of Shakespeare's *Much Ado* in Legendre's adaptation, described by Lorrain here, was staged in 1886.

145 *The Saint-Ouen horror crime*: a woman under the name of Valentine Dolbeau was found strangled on a deserted road near Saint-Ouen. The culprits were identified, a woman and her two lovers. The former, whose real name was Pauline Siller, had adopted the name Valentine Dolbeau, until the real Valentine Dolbeau became a danger, and so they did away with her. Account taken from *Le Progrès illustré*, 27 Nov. 1892.

GEORGES RODENBACH

The Time

First collected in *LeRouet des brumes: contes posthumes* (Paris: Ollendorf, 1901).

151 *without an idée fixe*: compare Van Hulst's obsession with collecting time-pieces with a similar fixation, differently placed, in Maupassant's 'The Tresses' above.

152 *rue de L'Âne-aveugle*: 'Blind Donkey Street'. Rodenbach evidently relishes the picturesque street-names of Bruges, which add to the element of fairy-tale in the story.

153 *Godelieve*: by choosing this name Rodenbach further charges his story with medieval legend. Born near Bruges, St Godelieve (*c*.1049–70), patroness of unhappy spouses, especially of women abused by their

husbands, was a beautiful girl who desired to become a nun. Feeling obliged to marry, for the sake of her parents, she suffered torments at the hands of her spouse, one Bertolf, who in the end had her strangled and thrown into a well. He consequently repented and entered a monastery near Rome. Godelève was known to be highly gifted with needle and thread, a trait Rodenbach retains in his story, along with her saintly, ascetic appearance and her apparently 'immortal longings'.

155 *Memling Madonna*: Hans Memling (*c.*1430–94), German-born painter who moved to Flanders. He is thought to have resided in Bruges in 1473.

REMY DE GOURMONT

All four stories were collected in *Histoires magiques et autres récits* (Paris: Mercure de France, 1894).

Danaette

[title]: Gourmont's allusion here is clearly to the Danae of Greek mythology, a princess of Argos, who was impregnated by Zeus when he visited her in the form of a shower of gold.

The Faun

162 *Arlette . . . Robert le Diable*: the mother and father of William the Conqueror, also known as William the Bastard, since Robert le Magnifique (called Le Diable) kept Arlette as his concubine and never married her.

163 *with a pointed beard*: the appearance and behaviour of Gourmont's faun here resembles the satyr of Félicien Rops, in his etching 'Satyriasis'.

Don Juan's Secret

[epigraph]: 'such things are vain dreams'; the expression is also to be found in Lucretius' *De Rerum Natura*.

On the Threshold

168 *the gallows name*: *fourches patibulaires* was the name given to the gibbets that were once a familiar sight in the French countryside.

171 *German metaphysicals*: among them, most probably, Schopenhauer, who proposed a neo-Buddhist form of detachment in the face of absurdity and desire.

JULES LAFORGUE

Perseus and Andromeda

The story was collected in the posthumous publication of Laforgue's *Moralités légendaires* (Paris: Éditions de la *Revue Indépendante*, 1887).

[title]: in Greek mythology, Andromeda was chained to a rock to assuage the fury of Poseidon, aroused by the hubris of Andromeda's mother Cassiopeia. The sea-monster Cetus kept guard over her. Returning from slaying the Gorgon Medusa, Perseus slew Cetus and rescued Andromeda, and then married her. Andromeda was placed among the constellations, alongside Perseus and Cassiopeia.

173 *ineffable fit of the sulks*: the monotonous island is really a physical analogy for Schopenhauer's absurd universe. Laforgue was a devoted student of Schopenhauer's philosophy.

174 *how bored I am!*: Andromeda's bored, disenchanted, and yet histrionic tone here is typical of Laforgue's persona in many of the *Moralités légendaires* and the poems that make up *Les Complaintes*. It is an ironic variant of Baudelairean *spleen*.

175 *daughter of the king of Ethiopia*: Andromeda was a princess of Ethiopia, her mother, Cassiopeia, was queen.

Catoblepas: 'In ancient authors, some African animal, perhaps a species of buffalo, or the gnu, a species of antelope' (*Oxford Latin Dictionary*). 'Now made the name of a genus including the Gnu' (*OED*).

176 *Pyramus and Thisbe*: the Babylonian tale of star-crossed lovers, as told in Ovid's *Metamorphoses* and retold in Shakespeare's *A Midsummer Night's Dream*.

Spinoza: Baruch Spinoza (1632–77), Dutch philosopher, renowned for his concept of the indivisible substance of Being, known as pantheism, and frequently viewed as a type of atheism. He made his living as a lens-grinder.

180 *The Truth About Everything*: the Monster's philosophy lesson that Andromeda has absorbed like a kind of bedtime story is steeped in Schopenhauer and in the jargon of Edvard von Hartmann (1842–1906), whose *Philosophy of the Unconscious* (1869) was one of the first works to posit the existence of an impersonal, psychic unconscious that creates and drives the world.

185 *Bellerophon . . . Chimaera*: ancient Homeric legend. Bellerophon, the son of Glaucus and grandson of Sisyphus, was set tasks intended to kill him, such as slaying the Chimaera, a fire-breathing monster, 'lion in front, serpent behind, goat in the middle'.

186 *Garden of the Hesperides*: the garden at the world's end in the far west, which contained a tree of golden apples, guarded by the Hesperides, the 'daughters of the evening', with the help of a dragon.

Pillars of Hercules: the two mountains on either side of the western entrance to the Mediterranean.

189 *Cadmus*: in Greek mythology, the son of King Agenor, brother of Europa, and founder of Thebes.

Phrixus and his sister Helle: children of Athamas, victims of their stepmother Ino's jealousy. About to be sacrificed, they escaped on the back of a ram sent by Hermes or Zeus. Helle fell off into the sea, thereafter called the Hellespont. Phrixus reached Colchis on the Black Sea and sacrificed the ram to Zeus. Its fleece was later captured by Jason and the Argonauts.

190 *Eteocles and Polynices, and pious Antigone*: warring Theban brothers, and Antigone, their sister, whose loyalty to family over *raison d'état* is the subject of the tragedy by Sophocles.

Monsieur Amyot de l'Épinal: the abrupt change of scene at the end of Laforgue's retelling of the legend is enigmatic. The little dialogue between Monsieur Amyot de l'Épinal (whose name Laforgue may have chosen as a kind of ironic conflation of the French Renaissance translator of Plutarch, Jacques Amyot, and the 'Images d'Épinal', or popular prints of religious and fairy-tale subjects) and the Princess of U... E... serves to heighten further the urbanity of tone used throughout the tale, and to foreground its existence as pastiche. Laforgue may have borrowed the setting from *Nuits espagnoles* (1854), a collection of stories by Méry (Eugène Didier), in which a group of socialites gather one night in a castle on the heights of Granada, tell stories, and apostrophize the constellations.

191 *Lohengrin and Parsifal*: heroes of the Grail Quest in the Germanic tradition, and of Wagnerian opera.

MARCEL SCHWOB

'The Brothel' was collected in Marcel Schwob, *Oeuvres*, ed. Sylvain Goudemare (Paris: Phébus *libretto*, 2002). 'The *Sans-Gueule*' was collected in *Coeur double* (Paris: Ollendorff, 1891); '52 and 53 Orfila' in *Le Roi au masque d'or*; 'Lucretius, Poet' and 'Paolo Uccello, Painter' in *Vies imaginaires* (Paris: Charpentier-Fasquelle, 1896).

The Brothel

192 *'May The Lord Have Mercy Upon Us'*: inscription seen on doors during times of the Black Death, along with the sign of the Cross.

Morgiana ... brigand: Schwob is alluding to an episode in *Ali Baba and the Forty Thieves*, collected in the *Thousand and One Nights*.

The Sans-Gueule

[title]: literally, 'the faceless ones'. I have retained the French, partly because there is no English equivalent as piquant, and also because Schwob's story so hauntingly prefigures the *gueules-cassées*—the name given to soldiers whose faces were horribly disfigured in the First World War. Schwob may be thinking of an episode from the Franco-Prussian War of 1870.

Lucretius, Poet

Schwob's account of the life of the Roman poet and philosopher Lucretius (Titus Lucretius Carus, *c*.99–55 BCE) depends heavily on the very few sources available, which are in any case probably corrupt (notably the story, told by St Jerome, that the poet died after quaffing down a love potion). Certainly Lucretius addressed his great poem, the *De rerum natura* (*On the Nature of Things*), to his friend Gaius Memmius, ostensibly to assuage the latter's fear of death by denying the afterlife, and belittling the role of the supernatural in human affairs. The poem is based on the beliefs of the Greek philosopher Epicurus (341–270 BCE), a materialist who considered the universe to be an infinite and eternal dance of atoms that cluster together and then break apart. There is no afterlife, and the aim of this life is to attain a state of *ataraxia*, or stress-free tranquillity.

Paolo Uccello, Painter

205 *Vasari*: Giorgio Vasari (1511–74), Tuscan painter and architect, whose celebrated biographies of the Renaissance artists, *Lives of the Painters, Sculptors, and Architects* (1550), supplies the inspiration and some of the incidental detail for Schwob's account of Uccello (1397–1475). The painters, sculptors, and architects of the *quattrocento* that Schwob introduces into his text—Ghiberti, della Robbia, Brunelleschi, Donatello—were all contemporaries of Uccello's, whose lives Vasari also describes in his book.

206 *Giovanni Manetti*: presumably Schwob means Antonio Manetto (1423–97), a Florentine mathematician who, according to Vasari, taught Uccello geometry and the principles of perspective. He also wrote a biography of Brunelleschi.

207 *Selvaggia*: Vasari notes merely that Uccello had a wife, who commented on her husband's obsession with perspective. He would spend all night trying to find the vanishing-point, and when his wife called him to come to bed he would reply that perspective was a lovely thing. He also left a daughter, Antonia, who had some knowledge of drawing, and became a Carmelite nun. The details concerning Selvaggia therefore seem to be Schwob's invention.

PIERRE LOUŸS

A Case Without Precedent

Collected in *Archipel* (Paris: Charpentier-Fasquelle, 1906).

210 *Gazette des tribunaux . . . Dalloz*: French legal publications. *La Gazette des tribunaux* was founded in 1777, and taken over by *La Gazette du palais* in 1935. Dalloz, a legal publishing firm, founded by Désiré Dalloz in 1845, exists to this day.

212 *Argus's hundred eyes*: in classical mythology, Argus is the Latinized form of the Greek Argos 'Panoptes', the all-seeing. He was a giant, and guardian of the heifer-nymph Io.

Janus: the two-faced Roman god of beginnings and transitions; he looks two ways, into the past and the future.

213 *Cerberus*: the three-headed dog of classical mythology, that guards the entrance to the underworld.

American Literature

British and Irish Literature

Children's Literature

Classics and Ancient Literature

Colonial Literature

Eastern Literature

European Literature

Gothic Literature

History

Medieval Literature

Oxford English Drama

Poetry

Philosophy

Politics

Religion

The Oxford Shakespeare

A complete list of Oxford World's Classics, including Authors in Context, Oxford English Drama, and the Oxford Shakespeare, is available in the UK from the Marketing Services Department, Oxford University Press, Great Clarendon Street, Oxford OX2 6DP, or visit the website at www.oup.com/uk/worldsclassics.

In the USA, visit www.oup.com/us/owc for a complete title list.

Oxford World's Classics are available from all good bookshops. In case of difficulty, customers in the UK should contact Oxford University Press Bookshop, 116 High Street, Oxford OX1 4BR.

GUY DE MAUPASSANT   **A Day in the Country and Other Stories**
A Life
Bel-Ami
Mademoiselle Fifi and Other Stories
Pierre et Jean

PROSPER MÉRIMÉE   **Carmen and Other Stories**

MOLIÈRE   **Don Juan and Other Plays**
**The Misanthrope, Tartuffe, and Other
Plays**

BLAISE PASCAL   **Pensées and Other Writings**

ABBÉ PRÉVOST   **Manon Lescaut**

JEAN RACINE   **Britannicus, Phaedra,** and **Athaliah**

ARTHUR RIMBAUD   **Collected Poems**

EDMOND ROSTAND   **Cyrano de Bergerac**

MÁRQUIS DE SADE   **The Crimes of Love**
**The Misfortunes of Virtue and Other Early
Tales**

GEORGE SAND   **Indiana**

MME DE STAËL   **Corinne**

STENDHAL   **The Red and the Black**
The Charterhouse of Parma

PAUL VERLAINE   **Selected Poems**

JULES VERNE   **Around the World in Eighty Days**
Captain Hatteras
Journey to the Centre of the Earth
Twenty Thousand Leagues under the Seas

VOLTAIRE   **Candide and Other Stories**
Letters concerning the English Nation

ÉMILE ZOLA   L'Assommoir
The Attack on the Mill
La Bête humaine
La Débâcle
Germinal
The Kill
The Ladies' Paradise
The Masterpiece
Nana
Pot Luck
Thérèse Raquin

	Eirik the Red and Other Icelandic Sagas
	The Kalevala
	The Poetic Edda
LUDOVICO ARIOSTO	Orlando Furioso
GIOVANNI BOCCACCIO	The Decameron
GEORG BÜCHNER	Danton's Death, Leonce and Lena, and Woyzeck
LUIS VAZ DE CAMÕES	The Lusiads
MIGUEL DE CERVANTES	Don Quixote
	Exemplary Stories
CARLO COLLODI	The Adventures of Pinocchio
DANTE ALIGHIERI	The Divine Comedy
	Vita Nuova
LOPE DE VEGA	Three Major Plays
J. W. VON GOETHE	Elective Affinities
	Erotic Poems
	Faust: Part One and Part Two
	The Flight to Italy
JACOB and WILHELM GRIMM	Selected Tales
E. T. A. HOFFMANN	The Golden Pot and Other Tales
HENRIK IBSEN	An Enemy of the People, The Wild Duck, Rosmersholm
	Four Major Plays
	Peer Gynt
LEONARDO DA VINCI	Selections from the Notebooks
FEDERICO GARCIA LORCA	Four Major Plays
MICHELANGELO BUONARROTI	Life, Letters, and Poetry

OXFORD WORLD'S CLASSICS

*For over 100 years Oxford World's Classics have brought
readers closer to the world's great literature. Now with over 700
titles—from the 4,000-year-old myths of Mesopotamia to the
twentieth century's greatest novels—the series makes available
lesser-known as well as celebrated writing.*

*The pocket-sized hardbacks of the early years contained
introductions by Virginia Woolf, T. S. Eliot, Graham Greene,
and other literary figures which enriched the experience of reading.
Today the series is recognized for its fine scholarship and
reliability in texts that span world literature, drama and poetry,
religion, philosophy, and politics. Each edition includes perceptive
commentary and essential background information to meet the
changing needs of readers.*

FRENCH DEC

French Decadent Tales contains thirty-six stories from fourteen authors, spanning the period from the mid-1870s to the beginning of the twentieth-century. While 'Decadence' was a European-wide movement, its epicentre was Paris, the cultural capital of the *fin de siècle*, glittering and fascinating, sordid and corrupt. The vast majority of the stories here take place in this modern laboratory of the human spirit, their heroes or anti-heroes caught in a time of bewildering transition. Richly varied though they are, these writers are united in their hatred of an age of rampant commercialism and vulgarity. Self-styled 'aristocrats of the spirit', influenced by the dandyism of Charles Baudelaire, they sought to escape from an optimism they deemed ungrounded and philistine. In their writings they explored extreme sensation and moral trangression; drugs, spiritualism and the occult, and every variety of erotic experience. Another efficient remedy was the philosophical pessimism of Schopenhauer: men such as Guy de Maupassant, Octave Mirbeau, and Jules Laforgue were steeped in his thought. The writings of Freud, on hysteria and fetishism, are also prefigured in some of the stories here. In an age when the spread of mass newspapers and journals created a voracious appetite for 'copy', the *fin de siècle* seethed with literary experiment. Describing Remy de Gourmont's stories as 'little tops' revolving violently and erratically before returning to inertia, Marcel Schwob speaks for the art of the short story in general, which reaches a type of perfection in this period: brief, incisive, trenchantly ironic, and often cruel.

STEPHEN ROMER is a specialist of French and British modernism. He lives in the Loire Valley, where he is Maître de Conférences at Tours University. He has translated widely from the French and has edited, amongst others, *20th Century French Poems* (Faber, 2002). He has published four collections of poetry, the most recent of which, *Yellow Studio* (Carcanet/Oxford Poets, 2008), was shortlisted for the T. S. Eliot Prize.